POWERS OF DARKNESS

POWERS
OF DARKNESS

Mary Napier

THE BODLEY HEAD
LONDON

A CIP catalogue record for this book is
available from the British Library

ISBN 0–370–31372–0

Printed and bound in
Great Britain for
The Bodley Head Ltd
20 Vauxhall Bridge Road
London SW1V 2SA
by Mackays of Chatham PLC
Typeset in Monotype (hot metal) Plantin by
Gloucester Typesetting Services

First published 1990

I

THE body of a man lay as flat as a mat in the middle of the main street of Hamada, the only port and second city of the Manangan Republic. The African sun scooped pools of darkness into his upturned face, slicked yellowish sheen over emaciated skin. Heat shimmered in the dusty air and the body was already beginning to stink. Squatting around the corpse a group of women moaned and swayed, chanting praises of the dead man in husky, exhausted voices. They would be accursed if they buried him unsung, yet before the first mourning dirge was finished their breath began to whistle in their half-starved lungs.

Crouched alongside them a small naked child clasped his knees and frowned at the weeping women. When one of them motioned to him he shuffled closer and kissed the dead man reluctantly on the forehead. 'Farewell,' he whispered, speaking clearly in spite of his weakness, as became the only remaining male in his family. Briefly, his poignant courage redoubled the women's sobs.

On either side of the body, the child and the crouching women, people passed indifferently about their business, death too ordinary to attract more than a glance. The life of man was a fistful of sand which began seeping through his fingers as soon as he picked it up; so hurry, hurry past commonplace mortality before you, too, vanished into the dust.

Jean Gregory hurried past with the rest, her eyes averted. When she first came to Hamada three weeks before she had made the mistake of intruding on private grief, hoping to help, and had nearly been lynched without understanding why. If Pierre Morlaix of the UN mission had not been waiting for her in the jeep, at the very least she would have been badly beaten or, worse still, been rescued by a drunken, undisciplined patrol of General Forla's troops; Forla the Magnificent, the All-Wise, Supreme Being, dictator of Mananga.

'God Almighty,' Jean said, deep in her throat, and it was a prayer. 'I'll go crazy if I'm stuck here much longer.'

'We all went crazy months ago. Surely you noticed?' Her

companion, Lewis Anderson, answered easily. He was tall and fairhaired, with thick shoulders and a tanned, sensual face; he walked as only Americans can walk, a lithe, deceptive saunter.

'No, I didn't notice,' Jean answered.

'No?' he teased.

'No. You've accepted it, that's all.'

'Like I said. No one could get crazier than the day they accept Hamada as normal.'

'Oh, but you can. You can see it for the corrupt obscenity it is and personally murder that fat disgusting slob, General Forla, while he giggles among his henchmen on a beach.'

'Jean —' Anderson said in alarm. 'Jesus, keep your voice down.'

She shrugged. 'I'm beginning not to care.'

When they reached the end of the street there was a stretch of waste ground before a high barbed-wire fence which separated them from the port, where concrete berths, rusting cranes and railway tracks edged a deepwater bay, ultramarine under a pale parched sky. Knots of people stared wistfully through the wire at grain and milk powder being carried off a ship in single sacks: the dockside crane had ceased to work and General Forla forbade foreign ships to cheat his subjects of a wage by using their own derricks. On that far side of the wire there were warehouses with flapping corrugated roofs, piled cargoes fouled by vermin disintegrating in sun and wind, and a block-and-asbestos office building with the blue UN flag drooping limply above it; all reached through a high double gate guarded by soldiers in dirty uniforms drinking beer. Several trucks were drawn up in line by the gate, their drivers gossiping in the shade and sharing the soldiers' beer.

'Our new trucks,' said Anderson tersely.

'Which General Forla's Minister of the Interior has said were most regrettably stolen by brigands.'

'Yeah, they've sure been stolen, anyway. Thank God Pierre's waiting for us like I told him. Keep close, look at the ground and for Christ's sake don't answer anyone back.' Beyond that guarded gate Jean could see a blue and white UN jeep drawn up and waiting, Pierre Morlaix waving her an encouraging kiss. Passing the harbour wire was always an intimidating experience.

'Your papers?' One of the guards spat on the ground without moving from his slouch beside some sandbags.

Anderson handed over a wad half an inch thick, splodged with

6

official stamps running in the heat. 'General Forla ordered us to visit his Minister of Transport at Hamada railroad station, to discuss when we might move some freight up country.'

The guard's eyes fastened greedily on Jean. 'Shit like you get their throat cut for disrespect to our great ruler.' He jumped to his feet, unslinging his automatic rifle; from slouch to threat between one breath and the next. 'Show respect! Show respect to the All Highest!'

Anderson hesitated only fractionally and then bowed, his hand like steel on Jean's arm compelling her to do the same, not that she needed any persuasion. 'I would never wish to show anything but the deepest respect towards the All Highest.'

'Yeah, yeah,' said the soldier and fired his weapon from the hip, sending a stream of bullets twanging along the barbed-wire fence, scattering the scarecrow crowds.

'We were summoned by the All Highest's personal order to go to the railroad station, now he orders us back behind wire again.' Anderson spoke slowly, carefully, knees instinctively bent as if in the hope of ducking bullets if they came. Not a word, not a breath out of place to soldiers already high on alcohol vaporised by the sun.

A sergeant swaggered over, a curved knife stuck in his belt. Small, expressionless, hungry for trouble but not quite daring to provoke it when faced by all those official stamps on papers bearing General Forla's signature. But before Anderson could react his hand had reached out to jerk the American's sunglasses off his face and put them on his own. The guards laughed and clapped, the sergeant smirked, Jean watched out of the corners of lowered eyes, torn between terror and rage. Keep your eyes down, Lewis Anderson had said, and he had been here two years instead of her three weeks, and usually got on well with Mananga's impossible officials. Keep your eyes down and pray they will not decide that today it might be safe to arrest a foreigner, perhaps hide her in their guardroom for casual rape, or kill both of them for the simple pleasure of it. There was only the most vestigial uncertainty to stop them: the protected status which the UN, and Anderson in particular, had so far enjoyed.

'The All Highest's orders.' Anderson pointed to the papers and bowed again.

'Yeah, yeah,' repeated the soldier.

'Quiet, fat ass,' shouted the sergeant, and swung his gun so the soldier fell. 'United Nations good, eh?'

'The All Highest says, United Nations very good,' Anderson agreed emphatically.

'Okay, you can march.' The sergeant swung back the gate. 'You want a beer?'

'Sure, thank you.'

Grinning, the man finished the can he held, tipping his head back, licking the last drop, then suddenly flung it with all his strength straight in Anderson's face, the range three feet.

His laughter followed them through the gate and into the jeep, Pierre Morlaix letting in the gear the moment Jean helped Anderson into the back. The can had struck him just below the eye, the force of it almost blinding him with tears, blood flowing from an inch-long cut.

'*Mon Dieu*,' said Morlaix. 'I thought they were going to have you then. I really thought they were going to.'

Anderson fumbled for a handkerchief, shoved it against his cheek. It wasn't the blow which was so shocking but the sheer contemptuous venom of such a gesture, face to face.

Morlaix slewed in his seat, and from reaction shouted as if they were on the far side of a street instead of in the back seat of his jeep. 'You were so lucky, Jean, they picked on Lewis. Why did they, I'd like to know? *Dieu*, a woman at their mercy and today they didn't care. But you'll have to leave. We'll all have to leave soon. It's getting worse every day.'

The jeep's tyre stuck in one of the narrow gauge railway tracks which wandered across the quay and skidded, so he had to turn back to his driving.

'I don't know why they didn't either,' Jean said flatly. 'I'll look at your eye when Pierre stops driving like a lunatic, Lewis.'

'It's okay. An empty beer can isn't much of a missile.' Anderson squeezed her hand reassuringly, but each felt the other tremble.

Pierre left them at the entry to the block where the UN mission lived, worked and sweltered under its asbestos roof, and went round to chain up the jeep. Not that a chain would prevent it from being stolen if someone with General Forla's backing happened to fancy it, but the jeep was their last vehicle and worth the gesture of a chain.

'I'll look at your eye,' Jean repeated. 'There'll be infection on a beer can, the same as everywhere else around here. So don't try to be a hero and then use up some of the few drugs we have.'

He shrugged and sat while Jean took out antiseptic, a gauze pad and tape from a sealed pack. The cut might be small, but here even a graze threatened blood poisoning or worse. 'Aren't we lucky a nurse dropped in unexpectedly,' he said, his hand on her waist.

'Even more lucky I don't let you get infected, just to give myself something to do,' she retorted.

Jean Gregory's feelings had always lain close to the surface and, in spite of a disciplined effort in recent years, kept striking through any attempt at disguise. Lewis Anderson grinned, moved his hand from her waist to her back; three weeks was a long time and he wasn't usually so patient, but then Pierre wanted her too and while the three of them were confined in this one small place most of his usual approaches had failed to pay off. Nor did his taste normally incline towards determined and capable women, although he wouldn't have complained about any female who dropped off a ship to share his temporary exile on Hamada Quay. But Jean's mixture of cool professionalism and hot temper, the contradiction between her strong body and transparent emotions happened to attract him. She also had the kind of thick hair which easily becomes a jaunty crest and in her case only just missed being red, the lightly freckled skin and dark eyes which often go with it. A pleasant-looking woman and no more, perhaps twenty-seven or -eight years old. Only the expressiveness of her face lifted her out of the ordinary and that could only belong to rather a nice person, Lewis uncharacteristically decided. At the moment she was intent, brown eyes only inches from his, and something beyond just wanting briefly stirred in him. 'You ought to get out when the *Saqqara* sails,' he said abruptly, and jerked his head at the ship unloading at the dockside.

'Keep still, will you?' Jean pinched his chin, tipped back his head to press on surgical tape. 'Thanks very much, but I don't fancy the *Saqqara* or her crew any better than Hamada, and anyway, I came here to do a job.'

'Sure, and in three weeks of waiting you haven't reached nearer to doing it than Hamada Quay, holed in behind barbed wire. I guess you'd be more valuable back in England. There must be hospitals there which could use a goddamn stubborn nurse on their roster.'

9

Jean laughed into Anderson's one open blue eye and flicked the gauze pad with her finger. 'You'll do. I spent the last seven years of my life in British hospitals and now I've volunteered to come to Mananga. I'm not scuttling home the first time things don't happen to work out. People wouldn't be starving here if things did go right very often. That clinic I've been sent to reach in the hills, needs a nurse pretty badly. And all the more because I'm three weeks late getting there.'

'You're going to be the hell of a lot more than three weeks late, when nothing even begins to look like moving. Look, you were sent in by ship because your organisation thought the railroad was working. As it was until the day before you landed. But now it isn't, because General Forla has decided to take a vacation on Hamada beach and while he's here he uses it as his private supply line, tells his thugs to throw everyone else off.'

'He won't be here for ever. I'm surprised, really, he's stayed so long in a hole like Hamada, aren't you?'

'*Non*, I am not surprised,' Pierre exclaimed from the doorway. 'I have visited Mananga City and it is terrible in the heat. There are also guerrillas who cut off water and electricity whenever the army is too drunk to chase them any more.'

'I've been telling Jean she has to be aboard the *Saqqara* when it leaves.' Anderson opened the icebox. 'Shit, the power is off again.'

'We all ought to go,' said Pierre.

'Then why don't you?' demanded Jean.

He shrugged. 'I'm paid by the UN and they have not ordered me to leave.'

'Wouldn't the UN accept the judgement of their officers in the field if they reported it was pointless and too dangerous to stay?'

The two men exchanged glances, and it was Lewis Anderson who answered. 'We're as safe as anyone is in a place like this. Forla's quite smart enough not to kill UN personnel except by accident. You're different, for Christ's sake. You aren't even UN but some Medicaid outfit no one ever heard of; they must be mad to send you here when even the Red Cross pulled out last week. You're also a woman, and don't start mouthing bullshit about it not making any difference. Being a woman makes the hell of a difference in Mananga, and three weeks is long enough for you to learn I'm right.'

'Yes, I have,' Jean answered quietly. 'And the Red Cross hadn't pulled out when I left London. But I'm a nurse, maybe the only replacement nurse with any chance at all of reaching those sick people in the hills. I can't just turn around and go, when the railway may be open again tomorrow or next week.'

'What makes you think the railroad is so safe?' demanded Anderson angrily. The gauze pad on his cheek twitched, his mouth tightening with temper.

For a moment they stood facing each other, tall sunbleached man and slight woman, unreasonable rage easily set loose by futility confined within baking hot walls; by drunken menace and barbed wire which cut them off from the work they had come to do.

Then Pierre Morlaix, practical Frenchman, broke into a quarrel they had nearly had a dozen times these past stifling days and nights. 'Let's eat, if you can face monkey meat again. I found cans of vegetables and made some bread. It has a strange taste of *je ne sais quoi* — but you English say a change is as good as a feast, Jean. It is not true, but change maybe is better than nothing in Hamada.'

Jean smiled back at him. 'The first cabaret show takes the floor at nine.'

Anderson muttered something under his breath and went through into the tiny office, slamming the door behind him.

'Lewis has been here two years, me only six months, and all that time affairs have become more difficult.' Pierre began opening a can of corned beef, liquefied by heat, which made up most of their stores.

Jean nodded. After less than three weeks in such conditions she felt ready to scream at the first sharp word. All the same, bickering among themselves made everything worse. 'Do you think I shall be able to get up to Kosti soon?'

'*Non.*' He shook his head vigorously.

'No, not soon, or no not ever?'

He shrugged, expressive Gallic commentary on the whole state of Mananga. Pierre was short and dark and hairy, wore incredibly short shorts and usually contrived to provide a little comfort out of the most unpromising circumstances. 'Me, I think that anyone who says he can guess at what may happen here tomorrow is a fool. I began my service with the UN in Mananga — oh, six years ago — before Forla came to power and it was beautiful. Not organised, but joyful. The people welcomed you to their hearth. Now, after quite a short time of Forla it is ruined, and, in my experience, another of the same kind usually takes a Forla's place. In such a country anything can happen.'

Anderson came back from the office. 'I thought I heard shooting.'

The three of them stood still, listening, but heard only some distant, tinny shouting. 'Maybe Forla decided to declare another national holiday,' said Pierre.

'Yeah, maybe. The telephone's working again, which is a good sign. First time in a week.'

Jean went outside, longing for air, a walk, a few moments' solitude, anything away from living in intolerably close quarters with two only moderately congenial men. But the heat defeated her: heat slamming off concrete, sticking her shirt to her back, even the breeze was like the draught from a furnace which only served to cake dust up her nostrils. Pray God it would be cooler in the hills. As the sun dropped lower a sliver of shade grew around the building and she leaned against a wall, staring out to sea. How marvellous it would be to dive down and down into that sparkling water, to soak sweat and frustration away. But the harbour was filthy, the long golden beach only a couple of miles to the west temporarily occupied by General Forla, his women, assorted henchmen and bodyguards. For her, even trying to go there was out of the question. Jean sighed, and then immediately pulled herself up for defeatism. When she volunteered to join an overseas medical team she had accepted the likelihood of danger, but never imagined that all she would achieve was to become a nuisance: an anxiety for Pierre and Lewis, who, as male UN officers, were apparently safe; a source of friction between two bored and frustrated men.

She turned her head, her eyes narrowed against the glare. On a clear evening she could just glimpse the Kosti Hills, swaying like plumes above a mirage. Somewhere in the safer distances up there a medical clinic was functioning, apparently unmolested by General Forla, if only she could reach it. She couldn't turn back, not yet, however dangerous Hamada appeared. This temporary check must disappear soon: Forla return to Mananga City and the railway reopen, or his venal, profiteering ministers give back some of the UN's lost trucks. She smiled to herself, pushed her hair back from her damp forehead and felt her heart slow to its normal beat. How absurdly close she had been to quarrelling, bursting into tears even, and all because intractable circumstances could not instantly be bent to suit her convenience.

Lewis came out to stand beside her. 'Those trucks we saw are coming in through the wire.'

They watched silently while a convoy of vehicles drove past in a whirl of dust and drew up by a warehouse further down the dock. Activity hummed momentarily while doors were opened, tailgates dropped, canvas rolled up. 'They're taking our food!' Jean exclaimed indignantly.

'They've been taking it for days. This just happens to be the first time they haven't cared who saw. Before, they came at night or raided the stacks piled on the dock.'

'Aren't you going to —'

'No, I am not going to waste my breath protesting and get beaten up! If Forla himself hadn't said it was okay they wouldn't have come when we could see, and if Forla says it's okay then sure as hell no one will listen to me. Besides, we've got tons of stuff rotting here which can't be shifted while the railroad stays closed. Better if it is sold off at a profit someplace, and sweetens a few officials.'

'They are not only taking food,' said Pierre, coming to stand beside them.

'It's food,' said Lewis sharply.

'*Non*, those stacks there were in our consignment, but not on our manifest. I checked, but preferred not to look inside. I think perhaps they are arms.'

'Arms!' exclaimed Jean. 'That whole shipment came in for UN distribution.'

'Then someone tampered with it.' Pierre looked philosophic.

'Has anyone ever tried asking General Forla?' asked Jean after a pause. 'I mean, just telling him how his pals have stolen trucks given to help his people, and now they're stealing the food as well?'

Lewis laughed. 'Nope. They surely have not.'

'But shouldn't someone? You did say he wouldn't harm UN officials. You're too useful, I suppose, bringing in hard currency goods he can maybe trade for profit.'

'No, they damned well shouldn't. I've seen the bastard several times and managed to do some business with him. In fact I've been thinking I might take the jeep and go see him on the beach, but you don't get a guy like Forla to listen unless there's something in it for him. Goddammit, he expects his sidekicks to steal our trucks, he'd be suspicious if they didn't.'

13

Jean was silent. Lewis had been out here more than two years, Pierre said. Of course he had to know best, but just to stand and watch while their grain was stolen and cargoes tampered with, seemed wicked. Abruptly, their three heads snapped to the right as a burst of automatic fire ripped a hole in the drowsy twilight, followed by an explosion. A small yellow cloud of smoke drifted above to roofs of Hamada.

'I thought I heard shots earlier,' observed Lewis.

But nothing followed that short, sharp outbreak. The convoy of trucks left, tooting their klaxons triumphantly, piled high with crates and sacks. After that, people slowly drifted back to the far side of the wire and, as if to prove that Lewis was right when he said that to do business in Forla's Mananga there always had to be loot for the General first, once the evening cooled some soldiers lifted the entry barrier to allow a shuffling queue to enter. By then Lewis and Pierre had piled up an orderly line of sacks so that they could cope with the numbers, and began ladling grain and milk powder into outstretched hands and bowls. Jean had set up a small medical point, as she had done each of the nights since she arrived, crude white light flaring, dust blowing, the conditions about as unfavourable as could be imagined. Yet the guards on the wire always refused to let anyone in to collect rations before dark, sometimes refused to let anyone in at all, and had demanded a permit before she could set up a clinic in the town — a permit no one possessed the authority to issue. Since she was only waiting from day to day for the means to leave Hamada, rather than antagonise everyone by attempting to argue, she simply treated whoever happened to be allowed on the quayside to collect emergency food.

Tonight, it quickly became apparent, she wouldn't be able to treat anyone.

Bewildered, she watched as people she recognised as grateful patients from previous evenings bolted back towards the wire the moment she approached them, sometimes even sacrificing their chance to receive some precious food. A child whose inflamed eyes showed signs of healing; a woman whose jaw had been dripping pus from an infected tooth only two nights before and who would be in agony again without another injection; a pitiful feverish baby carried by a mother whose beseeching eyes belied her refusal of help.

'Come,' Jean touched her arm, a gesture which transcended language barriers, although after a crash course in London and some tuition here from Pierre, she could make herself understood. 'I will not hurt your baby. Keep hold of him, if you wish.'

The woman hesitated, but then violently broke loose, the child's head rolling helplessly. Her mouth screeching like a crazy bird, her finger thrusting curses into Jean's face.

Such intensity of hate was quite horrifying, and Jean had to force herself to answer quietly, steadily, as if this was no different from a rough Saturday night on a London casualty ward. It was scarily different, though, and the dry shake in her throat emphasised that difference. 'I can help your son if you will let me. Otherwise he may die.'

The woman screeched again, threw a corner of her skirt over the child's swollen face as if against the evil eye and vanished into the crowd, spreading panic where she passed. A great many people in the same instant decided to grab what food they could and run instead of waiting patiently in line, noise changing to a more rhythmic beat as feet joined voices in proclaiming menace. Jean could hear Lewis yelling above the din; he spoke fluent Manangan and his burnished tall fairness usually marked him out for respect. The crowd hesitated, while their movements became more flurried than before, as if only the lack of a leader prevented the next nightmare stage of violence.

'*Allez*,' said Pierre easily, and hefted another sack of grain. 'Who still wants *la grande cuisine à la Hamada*?'

No one understood, but flippancy helped to carry the moment of panic past, when any more shouts for order might have shattered it into fragments. The dazzle of danger faded into mournful exhaustion as quickly as it came, which could as swiftly blaze up again.

Jean joined Pierre and Lewis ladling grain, milk, a handful of salt and sugar, into an endless succession of bowls. No point even thinking about trying to treat anyone tonight. And because their lives perhaps depended on keeping calm, they had never felt so close to each other; they joked and laughed among themselves until the people around them began to smile again, and soldiers came as they always did to drive the crowd back through the wire with blows and kicks.

'Jesus, what was all that about? I thought we were dead.' Lewis flopped on an unopened sack and lit a cigarette as the soliders' shouts faded into the distance.

Pierre shrugged. 'They're on edge. About the shooting we heard probably, and took it out on the first soft target. If nothing else happens they will have calmed down tomorrow.'

'Jean, you're getting out on the *Saqqara*, and that's an order.' Lewis's cigarette flared as he sucked on dry tobacco.

'You're not my boss, and I've said already I fancy the *Saqqara* rather less than staying in Hamada.' She felt exaggerated relief that they had successfully outfaced danger, but was also filled with foreboding for the future. A crowd like that would remember the smell of fear on strangers.

'She is right. I do not like the *Saqqara* either for a woman alone,' observed Pierre, beginning to add up quantities of food in a register.

I don't know why they bother to keep records, then stand and watch their supplies being stolen, Jean thought, irritated. 'How much were you able to distribute where it's really needed, before Forla came down to Hamada?'

'About three-quarters of the total,' Lewis answered.

'But now the trucks are lost and the railway closed.'

'I radioed what had happened a week ago. The UN takes its time, but if I'm not able to lean hard enough on Forla, eventually they'll find somebody who can. He needs loans, gold-plated beds, God knows what. I'll go tomorrow and grovel to the bastard, see what I can do, then radio again if the answer still looks like zero.'

As he spoke the lights went out; in the town, along the waterfront, everywhere. 'Better than usual,' remarked Pierre.

'At least the icebox will have had time to chill,' Lewis agreed. Usually the electricity failed soon after dusk. 'Jean, listen to me. You have to go. Try again in a month or so if things settle down.'

'It's too late,' she answered. 'Look.'

As their eyes grew accustomed to darkness they could see that, while they had been arguing, the *Saqqara* had cleared her hoists and gangplanks, discreetly paid off the many officials empowered to stamp papers and take armed guards ashore, and had cast off from the quay.

'Her skipper was friendly with the *chef du port*, I expect they ran some racket together. I wonder what warning he gave that they should slip away so silently?' said Pierre sombrely.

'A warning? You think there was some warning?'

'Of course. Don't you? Only fear for their skins could make such a bad crew do anything well, and this time we did not even hear them curse.'

None of them spoke again until they reached the illusory safety of the UN block, its tiny rooms and kitchen feeling desolate in the dark, everything dripping with humidity. Lewis lit a lamp and went to fetch beer from the icebox; the one point in their favour was that they were surrounded by stores, even if most of them were basic and unappetising.

'If Forla won't see me tomorrow, then I'll warn base we might have to pull out in a hurry.' Lewis came back holding cans of beer.

'They'd send a ship?'

'If there's real trouble, why not? We're sure as hell not going to get out by air.' The only airport was near Mananga City, four hundred miles from where they stood, up a railway which no longer ran; five hundred at least by dirt-surfaced and guerrilla-threatened roads in trucks they didn't have. It helped to think about the US, French and Royal Navies not too far over the horizon. It would be an international incident all the same, and a dangerous risk of many other lives if a ship should have to come in without permission, past shore batteries of rusting missiles unreliably manned by trigger-happy troops.

They slept intermittently, each covertly braced for a quick getaway. Jean felt very cowardly, lying dressed and straining her ears for the slightest sound, but as the moon rose she realised the others had done the same. Not that there were many precautions they could take, caught as they were between the sea and General Forla on his beach, his marauding troops and a terrorised population.

But, lying and thinking her own uncertain thoughts, Jean was glad she had taken such precautions as she could.

2

J EAN's camp bed had been set up in a narrow passage between
their mess room and the tiny office, the only available concession
to privacy. No concession at all, when she could hear Pierre and
Lewis tossing and muttering through an open doorway. What had
really happened last night in the warehouse? She still wasn't sure.
Not sure either if mere cussedness had so far kept her here, or was
it the difficulty of escape or, just possibly, excitement? There were
several different reasons why she had jumped at this chance to
come to Mananga, and perhaps the most important had been her
own need to break away from past intolerable constraints.

Before leaving London Jean had been carefully briefed about
conditions in Mananga, her resolution, health and competence
examined, a great many innoculations shot into her bloodstream.
Yet she realised now that no briefing could begin to prepare anyone fresh out of the West for the reality of a state so completely
stripped of rules. Even Hitler had imposed brutality within a
framework of everyday laws and industrious public services; in
Mananga there was only violence within the void of a tyrant's will.
Yesterday, when she and Lewis had been summoned to meet the
Minister of Transport at the railway station he had ranted at them
one moment, the next fawned like a beaten dog, terrified that some
chance shift of policy should trap him unaware. In the streets such
traffic as existed drove how it pleased, while troops and police
added to the chaos. According to Lewis the situation had deteriorated sharply over the last few weeks, and Jean believed him. The
doctor briefing her in London had mentioned trouble for foreigners only as a distant possibility; but then he had spent his time
in the hills and returned to England over two months previously.

'Once you reach the hills the climate is quite good,' he had said,
as if that was the worst hazard she was likely to face. 'It's cool at
night and Forla's men are too lazy to leave the few roads and single
railway. Behave sensibly, and you should be able to get on with
your work unmolested. Forla owes too much money for guns and

wants more guns tomorrow, to start looking for trouble by locking up a Western nurse.'

Well, maybe, Jean thought wryly. Tonight it looked as if by closing the railway, Forla the All Highest had found a way to profess innocence to the West while making sure that UN supplies found their way into his personal market economy.

She dozed uneasily towards dawn and woke to hear Pierre clattering pots in the kitchen. *La belle France*, she thought drowsily. Without Pierre we would never believe it possible that flour, bottled water and bully beef could be made even half-way palatable. With Pierre, breakfast was pâté, hot crisp discs of bread, and a liquid it was possible to imagine might be coffee.

Outside everything was quiet, almost eerily so after the night before.

'You and I had a rendezvous this morning with the *chef du port*, if you remember,' Pierre said to Lewis over coffee.

Lewis went over to look out of the window. 'Appointments don't mean anything in this place. They're a way of getting rid of you.'

'He's the most helpful official around, and said he might find a truck we could use.'

'He's a corrupt bastard like the rest, except he spits behind your back instead of in your eye.'

'*Certainement*, he is corrupt. What other way is there of doing business in Mananga? So, we just might be able to pay for what we want and he be trustworthy enough to deliver it. We can't grill inside this office for ever, Lewis, waiting for things to settle, because perhaps they never will. We have to get food moving again before it rots, and if not by rail then the *chef du port's* truck could be the only hope we have.'

'One truck!' Lewis rocked on his heels. 'Are you crazy? What use is one truck in thousands of square miles of hills?'

'It's a start. It's what we're here for.'

'We're not here to antagonise Forla by shipping single trucks of flour. Jesus, it could take a month just to reach the hills if the road is cut, a truck could get stolen at the first crossroads for all we know. Our job is to ship large consignments regularly, and that means the railroad and Forla's co-operation. Which is what I mean to try and get. You waste time on a punk harbour-master if you like, but for God's sake don't stir up any trouble. I wouldn't want

Forla to start getting excited while I happen to be hanging around His Majesty's bloodstained presence.'

'*Alors, bonne chance, mon ami.*' Pierre sounded unconvinced, but admiring. Even for a UN officer, going voluntarily to visit General Forla could be regarded as foolhardy to the point of madness.

They saw Lewis off in the jeep soon afterwards. 'How about a kiss for that luck of Pierre's?' he demanded, looking at Jean.

She kissed him gladly. 'Oh God, take care. Are you sure —'

'I'll be okay, you'll see.' His hands hard on her body, the kiss turned into a deep swift raid on her senses. Then he was gone, cornering in a shower of grit, pulling up with a squeal of brakes by the guarded gate. To their surprise, once the soldiers heard where he intended to go, their mood of surly obstruction instantly changed. They became almost alarmingly helpful if the truth was to be told. Jean and Pierre's last sight of the jeep showed a pair of armed escorts perched up behind, shouting and firing shots in the air to clear the road ahead, a road which, like most others in Hamada, was already so lacking in traffic that shots made only the rats scuttle for cover.

After Lewis had gone their tiny concrete block seemed empty, time lagging past, the day the hottest yet. 'If he is not back by the time of tonight's radio schedule, I shall at once report him missing,' Pierre said, while that breathless sun seemed poised directly overhead. They were both lying on their beds, nearly naked, pouring sweat, Jean conscious that she ought not to be naked, alone with Pierre, who wanted her quite as badly as Lewis did. But today surely it must be too hot for caution and their wait too anxious, Pierre anyway less forthright about his wants than Lewis.

'Yes,' she said, and looked at her watch. Three-thirty. Lewis had been gone since ten that morning. 'Don't you think you should call up now?'

'I'll wait until the schedule.' He was staring at her. 'Jean, *chérie* —'

'No,' she said hurriedly, and grabbed at a shirt. 'I just happened to be stuck here three weeks too long. We don't mean a thing to each other, really.'

'We could give each other a little happiness, which I think is what matters. If you weren't stiff like a — a —'

'Hamada bread roll?' Jean said, and laughed. 'I suppose I am. I don't mean to be. But just me with two of you, here, perhaps it's as well.'

He sat up, put those hairy legs over the edge of the bed. 'Is it Lewis?'

'No,' she said, annoyed. 'It's me. I don't see why I have to let one of you — or is it both? — have sex with me, just because you happen to be around.'

'It is easy to see you are English,' he said, and then grinned. '*Je m'excuse, mademoiselle.*'

She laughed, and for several reasons had never been more delighted suddenly to hear the jeep skidding to a stop outside. Both of them shot off their beds, and fell over each other in a scramble to reach the door. Lewis looked them over critically. 'Had a nice afternoon?'

'No,' said Pierre frankly. 'You look pleased with yourself, I think.'

'Good,' said Lewis softly, staring at Jean with a half-smile on his lips. 'I'm glad to hear it, because I haven't either. But it's okay, I think. That supreme and almighty being, His Excellency General Forla, shone the greasy light of his countenance on me and said he was finding the beach a little hot. He intends to return soon to his bright pink palace in Mananga City in order to wrestle, night and day, with the problems of ruling an ungrateful people. After he has gone, he thinks there may be space for our food on the railroad again.'

'Do you believe him?' asked Pierre.

Lewis climbed down out of the jeep, and stretched. 'God knows. I had a swim with the bastard anyway, so the trip was worth it for that alone.'

'*You swam with him?*'

'It was hot, like the man said. He spends the day screwing women in the shallows, says it's the only place he can do it. A hundred and ten in the shade, he could have a point.' Lewis laughed, stretched again, and something about his contentment made Jean wonder whether the easiest way to get favours out of a dictator could be to join in his pleasures, and she wasn't only thinking about swimming. Well, it wasn't any of her business what Lewis did.

Pierre was staring at him too, but with uncomplicated envy, though whether this was over women, or the bravado which enabled Lewis Anderson to charm even a tyrant, Jean couldn't tell.

Lewis had lunched with Forla, so he sat and watched Jean and

21

Pierre eat a snack they hadn't fancied in the heat while alarmed about his safety. An unexpectedly awkward meal, the rivalry between Pierre and Lewis having been stoked in several unexpected ways by the events of the day. Lewis reacted from strain with over-confidence towards a still highly uncertain future; while Pierre's envy and resentment changed to satisfaction as he realised that Jean was conscientiously trying not to feel shocked by Lewis frolicking with General Forla as a means of doing business. She might have disliked it less if his reason for going had been simple pleasure. As perhaps it could have been? No, she thought. That would imply a degree of familiarity between utterly dissimilar men which the circumstances refuted.

But, so far as their immediate circumstances were concerned, nothing apparently was changed, a fact which Pierre did not fail to point out. For whatever reason, very few faces pressed against the wire. There was no traffic; no ships in port; even no shooting, when they had grown used to casual shots punctuating the day. There was only the sun at blowtorch heat and three dissimilar people forced into voluntary, tedious, confinement. It might have been easier if they had been imprisoned by force; then they would have combined against their captors, clutched at their common interest instead of irritably rubbing against rivalry and prejudice. As the searing sun finally dropped towards the horizon, Jean left the two men to snap and snarl between themselves and when she came back from a mercifully solitary stroll was relieved to discover Lewis sitting alone, his good humour restored by a chance to relax. Since Jean considered some relaxation necessary too, when none of them knew how much longer they would be isolated on Hamada Quay, it was a while before either of them noticed that Pierre had vanished.

'He deserves to get beaten up for being such a fool,' Lewis exclaimed angrily. 'Going to Forla made sense and one day should help to get us the use of the railroad again. But if I've learned anything out of living in godforsaken assholes like this, it's that when the gooks get jumpy they're best left to cool off alone, and he ought to have learned it, too. He's been in the field eight years, for Christ's sake, even if not in Mananga.'

'Where do you think he's gone?'

'How should I know? To teach some monkey how to broil rat's liver maybe, just to show me — you, I guess,' he grinned suddenly,

'—that if I can go to Forla's beach then he's got the guts to do some other goddamn useless thing.'

'You don't like it out here, do you? I mean, no one could like having to crawl to Forla. Nor this heat and streets full of soldiers, but it seems to me you've lost respect for what we're trying to do. Yes, you'll risk your life seeing Forla because that's your job, but you call the people gooks and despise instead of pity them.'

'No, I don't pity them and nor will you if you've any sense. They smell pity a mile upwind and hate you all the more. I guess I first came to Africa a repentant capitalist, now I keep remembering all those Americans paying good dollars to send their grain so it can rot on Hamada dock. This country could feed its own people most years, even occasionally export a surplus if they'd let us show them how. The Israelis make dry hills give crops and American farmers could do the same here, if they were let alone to get on with it. Sure, I'm tired of being robbed by Forla's sidekicks, of sending free US food upcountry to be burned by guerrillas, or maybe looted by Forla's army, and so will you be if you stick around long enough to see what goes on.' Lewis kept his back to her, as if he needed privacy to tear honesty from its hiding place.

'If I do, then I hope I shall have the sense to leave,' Jean said, after a pause. 'You have stayed, and if you stay then I think—'

Lewis turned. 'Yes, please do tell me what prim Nurse Gregory thinks. Three weeks in the Republic of Mananga but I'm sure you'll have some goddamn futile platitude on offer.'

'All right,' Jean said evenly. 'I dislike Hamada and what I've heard of General Forla. But then I don't like the word gook either, nor the thinking which makes a Westerner use it. I came here to do a job the same as you did, and respecting the people you come among happens to be part of it.'

They stared at each other across the table, filled with antagonism: a tall angry man, his face long and flat-planed, fair skin burned to the colour and texture of reddish earth; a woman whose soft breasts and arms and hips showed even under practical clothes, a frame which looked so slight, but was in fact capable and sturdy, her eyes not soft at all but sharply aware under tilted lids. 'Sorry if I was rude,' she said, not sounding sorry at all.

'Say what the hell you like, there's nothing else to do.'

'Then I'd have to say we can't afford to quarrel, even if we enjoy it,' she answered candidly.

He grinned reluctantly. 'Okay, we don't quarrel. So, what else is new? Pierre still isn't back.'

'And I wonder why there's no one coming for a handout of food tonight.'

Lewis glanced outside. 'The guard never lets them in before dusk.'

'I know, but the people always hanging around the wire have gone. I looked out of the back window.'

Even so, they decided to walk across to the warehouse as usual, Lewis hefting out sacks while Jean set up her tiny clinic. Better to do as they had always done than face the accusation they had refused to help Forla's people. 'See what I mean?' said Lewis tightly, after two hours' waiting in which no one came. 'Who's really to blame if Manangans starve, the wicked West or their own stupidity, when someone must have ordered them not to come?'

Jean didn't answer, then sniffed the air as they walked back to their concrete hutch. 'I smell cooking, Pierre must be back.' She broke into a run, hugged him unselfconsciously where he stood stirring onions in a pan, the differences of the afternoon forgotten. 'You wretch, we were so worried about you! Where on earth have you been for so long?'

He kissed her joyfully on the lips, relishing an opportunity. '*Voilà, chérie.* I ask myself again, why do we not do this often?'

Jean shook him, laughing. 'Because I never kissed a fat hairy Frenchman before, that's why.'

'Now is that kind? Hairy, yes, and French, but fat? *Mon Dieu,* who is fat in Hamada?' He kissed her again, lingeringly, until Jean drew back, sensing Lewis glowering behind her back. She had been so relieved to see Pierre safely back she had hugged him without thinking, but jealousy was the most destructive of all emotions to add to an already explosive mix.

'Where the hell have you been?' Lewis snapped.

'Swimming,' answered Pierre carelessly. 'The same as you did earlier. And buying onions. I decided, quite suddenly you understand, that I could not eat another mouthful of canned meat without onions.'

Lewis looked thunderstruck. 'You went to Forla, too?'

'Me? No. I swam in the harbour, which is dirty but cleaner than Forla, I think.'

'I longed to swim yesterday but couldn't face neat sewage,' Jean said witsfully.

'Close your eyes as well as your mouth, *chérie*. At the far end of the mole it is not too bad and also I could see round to the beach. Everyone seemed to be running about very fast and jeeps were driving up and down the dunes. When Forla told you he might soon go back to his palace, he didn't say immediately, did he, Lewis?'

'No.' Lewis's eyebrows snapped together in a frown.

'The *chef du port*, Monsieur Albedo, says there is trouble in Mananga City.'

'There's always trouble somewhere in Mananga.'

'Big trouble. Maybe Forla has been forced to pull out faster than he expected.'

'What did Albedo think about the railroad?'

Pierre stirred the pan thoughtfully. 'Monsieur Albedo did not know what would happen, but he thought that Forla was not too interested in allowing us to ship food where it might be used by rebels. He confirmed that he could get us a truck if it is safe to drive the streets again after Forla goes. For a price, of course.' He looked at Jean. 'His grandson is ill in the town. If you can cure him, we can have the truck.'

'Yeah?' drawled Lewis. 'We've only his word he knows where to find a truck, and if he does he'll very likely lose it when Forla's troops pull out. Jean risks her life to treat some kid, that doesn't mean there's a truck. It means Albedo wants some treatment free. Tell him to bring his grandson here.'

'I did. He says he is too sick. Delirious. They could not smuggle him past the gate.'

'Of course I'd go anyway if I could.' Jean felt nervous just saying it.

'I told you, it's a trick. And one truck's no good anyway,' said Lewis angrily.

'If the railroad should open again for food we shall need a truck to carry if from here to the station,' Pierre answered. 'You forget that since Forla came to Hamada we've lost every vehicle we had except the jeep.'

They kept arguing through a meal only marginally improved by onions, Pierre remaining in favour of risking something to get a truck, Lewis definitely against, Jean firm that now she had a willing patient she must reach him if she could.

'I wouldn't have mentioned it if the *chef* hadn't been confident he could take you through the wire,' Pierre said apologetically. 'He ought to know a safe way if anyone does, and with a friendly guide even Hamada should be all right.'

Mr Albedo arrived very late; a cheerful, dark, smooth-faced man, hugging an extravagantly gold-leafed cap into his stomach. 'Good-day, good-day,' he bowed and wiped his face on a handkerchief stamped with a portrait of General Forla. 'Mama Doctor?'

'Yes,' said Jean, avoiding Lewis's derisive look. In a country where most local doctors had fled or been murdered, it wasn't worth explaining she was only a nurse.

'You come? I take scrummy care.'

She nodded, smiling. 'Is your grandson very sick?'

He spread his hands. 'Jolly bad sick. The dickens of a sick, I think.'

'A fever? Sick in his stomach? What should I take?' The only way not to laugh at his ancient rusted English was to stick with essentials.

He tapped his groin. 'He shot.'

'Shot! How old is he?'

Again the spread hands. 'Six, seven years. You come quick. Four days pass.'

'He was shot four days ago? Why didn't someone bring him before? Four days —' she hesitated. She was not a surgeon, and even if she had been, a child shot four days ago in this climate was almost certainly beyond help. 'Of course I'll come, but he must ... you know it is probably too late?' She hastily repacked her medical satchel, having expected fever rather than injury, and turned to follow him.

'No, no,' exclaimed Albedo when Lewis and Pierre would have followed too. 'I look after Mama Doctor. Crikey, do not worry.'

Pierre answered in Manangan, speaking too fast for Jean to understand, and a heated argument followed.

'For heaven's sake,' she said at last. 'Don't let's waste any more time. I'm sure Mr Albedo will look after me, and two must slip into the shadows easier than four.'

Albedo nodded vehemently. 'It very bad if jolly great crowd come. Cowardy-custard soldiers shoot easy in the dark.'

'I bet they do,' said Lewis grimly. 'Jean, you can't go into Hamada alone.'

'I won't be alone. I'll be with Mr Albedo.' He nodded again, fairly dancing with impatience. 'Lewis, listen. I must at least try to help this child, and who could be more trustworthy than his grandfather to take me? I may have to stay if there's any hope of saving him, don't worry if I only send a message back.' She felt keyed up rather than afraid. After three wasted weeks, following more weeks of preparation before, she was quite simply pleased to use her skills at last. Except this child must be dying. Must be; and then eccentric Mr Albedo might turn against her.

'Lewis, I think Albedo really is okay,' Pierre said.

'Let's go,' Jean turned to Albedo, slinging her satchel over her shoulder, while Lewis still hesitated; part of her wanted him to come, no matter what, the other saner part agreed with Albedo that the fewer people trying to move around the streets of Hamada after curfew, the better.

Outside, a blast of wind whirled dust in their faces but helped to cover any small sounds they made crossing the open quayside to reach the wire, blew between the warehouses as they waited interminably for reasons Jean couldn't grasp, pounced on them as they moved at last, this time parallel with the wire which took them further from the guarded gate. Here the quay ended in abandoned gun-emplacements and more coils of wire, left in careless tangles as a snare for swimmers. Certainly it would be possible on this dark night to swim far enough out to outflank those trailing ends of barb, but hampered by medical kit and clothes, the prospect was as unenticing as the foul water itself.

As if sensing her hesitation, Albedo reached to grasp her hand. 'Do not worry, all is tickety-boo,' he whispered.

Before the night is over, I just have to discover where he learnt his English, Jean decided.

The quayside was everywhere littered with rusted cable, mouldering flour, old crates; it was impossible not to make some sound as he guided her through the maze, all the while keeping close to the wire. 'No soldiers,' he exclaimed at last, and gestured. 'They guzzle and swig out of wind. You wait. Do not worry.'

By now her eyes were accustomed to the darkness; the blackest dark out to sea, where one of the torrential Manangan storms must be brewing, a lighter darkness through the wire; fortunately the electricity still seemed to be off. An occasional dim glow from a paraffin lamp or cooking fire showed where the town began, but

27

little else. With luck, most inhabitants of Hamada as well as the guards would be huddled away from the wind.

'Mama Doctor!' hissed Albedo.

Jean picked her way through debris to where she saw him beckon, jumped nervously as something clanked softly overhead. 'What's that?'

'Jiminy, it our safe way.' He bent over something, grunting with effort.

Very slowly, a shape moved against the sky. A crane, Jean realised after a moment, its rusted arm cranked by hand on recently greased ratchets.

Jean put down her medical satchel and added her weight to the handle too; never in her remotest imaginings had she expected to cross the wire by crane. This was clearly what Albedo meant to do. As harbour-master, he had probably considered many means of moving both men and goods illegally, and a usable crane had a great deal to recommend it.

'I go. You come.' Albedo picked up her satchel.

'I'll take it.' Jean had visions of her precious drugs and syringes being dropped from a height.

'No, no. You use both hands, just the ticket, I hope.' He scrambled up the crane with surprising agility, considering he was wearing a suit and cap and carrying her bag. Jean followed more slowly, groping for footholds. A steel hawser ran vertically to her right, the crane a maze of diagonal struts, roughened by rust. If there were rungs to climb, then she didn't find them, and had to haul herself up bodily from one crosspiece to the next until her head bumped against Albedo's feet.

'Here is,' he whispered. 'Here is. Watch.'

Jean only wished it wasn't so dark. Albedo must be showing her how to reach the crane's outflung arm and then scramble along it above the wire, but all she could see was the shuffle of movement as he vanished. Cautiously she followed. An uneasy, awkward climb this, with metal slanting treacherously around her. Then she touched a ledge; no, wider than that, a platform, probably for maintenance of the hoist. At the junction of vertical body and horizontal jib, a small fenced platform ran completely around the structure. A comfort just to know it was there, and exactly what she needed.

Immediately, however, it was a barrier, because to reach it she had to climb out where it projected and then over its protective railing, while a forty-foot drop yawned behind her back. If there was some easier way then she missed it. One slip and her least injury would be broken legs. She waited until her breathing eased and then reached up to grip that railed edge; perhaps only imagination suggested that it started to bend from the moment she began walking her feet up those infernal sloping struts. She felt an enormous temptation to hurry but forced herself into care, rust a rough ally for the holds she needed. She moved one foot at a time until she was crouched with her chin level with that platform, hands spread wide, trying to summon the courage to abandon caution and bring one leg up and over that rail, and so roll into safety. Spreadeagled and alone, for the first time that night Jean felt completely terrified. Her face pressed against steel, a hot wind snatching at her back; God, she had not come to Mananga to climb cranes in the dark. Then she was angry; angry with herself, with imbecile General Forla and absurd Mr Albedo, who between them conspired to put her in this ridiculous situation. Anger was the best antidote of all to fear, but also the precursor of reckless lunacy. Without thinking any more about it, she shifted her hands as if the space behind her back did not exist, hauled up and fairly flung her leg over that rail, the weight of her body transferred in a single triumphant movement. Quite suddenly, the railing which she had felt quiver before, bent sharply under the strain she had put on it. The smooth steel platform swung up and into her face, leaving one leg kicking wildly into space, the other leg and hand crackling from the strain of holding on to the remaining secure stretch of rail. There was only one thing left to do, and she fairly drove herself upward, snatching at the platform and struts unseen in the dark. Then she was up and over, lying on the narrow platform with her breath gulping in great sobbing whines.

She could have lain there for ever, blissful in release from strain. But there was no sign of Albedo and the thought of trying to find her own way along a crane jib in the dark, barbed wire beneath it if she fell, soon brought her to her feet. Maybe she was just tired, but the shock of feeling that rail bend had banished both anger and fear as if nothing worse could happen now, her mind determinedly blank to what else might easily happen.

The jib stretched out in front of her, a latticed rectangle with cables running parallel below. Because it was horizontal it actually appeared much less perilous than the climb upward in the dark, although she cursed Albedo for not waiting to demonstrate the safest way. This crane was probably in regular use for smuggling goods off the quay, there must be an easy way. If those cables were braked, then she could shuffle along them, holding on to the jib as she went. If they weren't, then her weight might be enough to shift them on the drum. But surely she was lighter than a damned great shank of cable and a hook for grappling freight? Tentatively, she tested the cable with one foot. It felt as solid as a bar, the safest way over the void that anyone could wish.

She forced herself to continue, moving slowly and deliberately, lowering her weight inch by inch, arms and hands hooked into the struts of the jib ready to take the strain. The cable held. No sag at all, although such mathematics as she possessed suggested that the leverage her weight exerted would increase the further along the jib she went. But what the hell, this was easy and risk the name of the game tonight. Shuffling sideways like a sailor along a yardarm, with as many handholds as she wanted for balance and support, Jean never saw the barbed-wire fence pass below. She only knew she must be beyond it when the swinging end of cable appeared out of the dark.

Albedo was waiting for her there, white teeth flashing a welcome. 'Jolly good show, Mama Doctor. Now is easy-peasy.'

He had a rope ladder hung from the hook and, as he said, climbing down was easy, if alarming. The ladder whipped about like a striking snake until he anchored the end, and then Jean slipped down the remaining rungs without difficulty.

The dusty space where they stood was deserted and Jean watched as Albedo used a long wooden pole to unhook the ladder and hide it under a heap of rubble, the pole shoved afterwards into coils of barbed wire so that it looked like another support. A pity, she thought, that the Manangans did not use the same ingenuity to run their country as was put into outwitting some small part of its chaos; in spite of those terrifying moments when she tried to reach the platform, their whole passage across the wire could not have taken five minutes.

'Come,' Albedo said softly, and together they crossed the open ground which separated the town from the port area. Here and there lay the skeletons of old vehicles, occasionally some heaps of concentrated stench Jean preferred not to wonder about. But at least there did not seem to be any soldiers, and only the occasional other figure, warily keeping at a distance. In this town everyone was afraid; at the mercy of racketeers and an army intent on loot. General Forla himself was only a scant few miles away, an unbridled pasha in his tents, and reputed to enjoy no diversion so much as an agreeably drawn-out murder.

The outskirts of Hamada were made up of unsurfaced streets pitted with scummy ponds, the few two-storey buildings decaying fast, the rest little more than shacks. Jean lost her bearings almost at once, since Albedo made it clear they had to take a circuitous route to avoid manned checkpoints, 'chickenpoints', as he called them. Once they had to climb hurriedly over a fence, another time some soldiers were enjoying target practice down the length of a wider street they had to cross; it took twenty minutes of impatient waiting before they apparently exhausted their ammunition and Albedo and Jean were able to slip across unobserved. By then the wind was roaring and banging more fiercely than ever among corrugated iron roofs, raindrops like warm blood smacking into the dirt.

'Good,' whispered Albedo succinctly. 'We middle town now. Good, very good if soldiers funk out of wet.'

In her few previous expeditions into Hamada, Jean had been fascinated by the way all the buildings were decorated. Large pictures of Forla the All Wise were pasted to most flat surfaces, his blunt jaw and false smile shredding in sun and wind. Most of the shops were little better than booths, but nearly all were brilliantly daubed with paint and often a picture showing whatever was sold inside: a vermilion bull charged out above a butcher's stall; a ten-foot fish curled around a deserted slab. The only trouble was, in Forla's Mananga meat and fish had practically vanished along with everything else. Such trade as there was took place covertly and mostly by barter, in the hope of avoiding confiscation by hungry troops.

A flash of lightning followed by an enormous crack of thunder lit up the one main street as they reached it, the storm disembowelled by heat the moment it moved in off the sea. Jean was drowned, deafened, disorientated by the power of the rain which followed, Albedo's hand on her arm urging her to greater speed as torrents of water began almost instantly to scour down the alleys of this, the old colonial section of town between the railway station and the main square.

31

Then he hauled her inside a doorway and they stood, instinctively shaking off wetness like dogs, in a narrow lamp-lit room. 'Crikey, Mama Doctor, I am sorry. But you have rain sometimes in England too, I think.' Albedo looked even wetter than Jean felt, cap and smart shoes shapeless, dye from his jacket smeared across his shirt.

Jean thought of gentle Gloucestershire rain and laughed, delighted to have reached here safely. Only then did a different worry resurface, about the miracle Albedo and his family expected her to perform with a child shot four days previously.

Albedo's daughter was narrowly boned and gracefully slim, as unlike his cheerful roundness as it was possible to be. 'Her mother a hill lady,' Albedo whispered proudly, and pinched her arm as if to make sure Jean noticed the finer points of breeding.

'The child? How is the child?' Jean demanded anxiously, and fumbled for translation among her few words of Manangan.

The woman instantly burst into explanations, but her gesture was unmistakable: arms raised limply, fingers curved inward like a ballet dancer holding on to life, before opening with infinite sadness to relinquish it. The child was dead.

They took Jean upstairs to see him; he had died only shortly before and would be buried in the dawn. A tiny wasted skeleton, a bullet hole in his thigh the size of a fist; poisoned and drained of blood, God knew how he could have lived four days with such injuries, and why he should have lived at all only to die in torment. As Jean stood looking down at him it was the ancient powers of evil inhabiting this land which seemed to hover in reeking darkness above the bed, insatiable for blood, thriving on hate and fear.

3

AFTER such a tragic anticlimax to all their efforts, at first Albedo and Jean could not summon the will to set out on their return journey. Yet there was a need for haste. Dawn was still several hours away, but prowling uniformed gangs would return on the streets once the storm rumbled away down the coast.

Albedo's daughter waited on them, bringing a liquid in tiny cups which was unlike anything Jean had ever tasted, and pancakes to dip in a pot of thin broth kept simmering on the hearth. Albedo apologised for such poor fare, but Jean had an uncomfortable feeling they were eating the family's last reserves. Three other children peered from a corner, large-eyed and puff-bellied, but it was clear that every convention of hospitality would be offended if she refused to eat. She ate as little as possible, however, and shared her pancake with the smallest child. Albedo jerked his head, apparently feeling that some explanation was necessary. 'Her man in the hills.'

As a guerrilla or a fugitive? Jean wondered. Probably it made little difference, and equally probably he would never be back. 'This child's foot is swollen. Would your daughter like me to look at it?'

'Yes,' Albedo said, without consulting her. He had felt diminished since his feat in conjuring a mama doctor out of the storm had not received the reward it deserved and cheered up at once. When the child howled and clung to its mother, he simply picked her up by the ankles and held her upside-down by the lamp. The foot was cut as if someone had probed there with a blunt edge, the sole shiny with pressure, and since there was no point in arguing with Albedo's methods Jean worked as quickly as possible, disinfecting, swabbing, injecting. As the child's sobs began to strangle for lack of air, she delicately tweezered out a long rough splinter which was followed by a gout of blood and pus, and hastily slapped on sterile gauze. 'Keep it covered and clean,' she said haltingly to the mother and held up three fingers. 'In three days she should be well.' She felt ridiculously pleased that their journey was not wasted after all. Without help, even so slight an injury as a splinter could kill an undernourished child.

She was not to escape so lightly, however. Albedo was so delighted by his protégée's success that he could not resist whispering about her triumph to his daughter's neighbours: the first Jean knew of her fame was a woman knocking at the door as she prepared to leave, a child in her arms. Others followed, slipping in as rumour spread that a miraculous mama doc had arrived in the street: a boy flaming with scabies; a man blinded after being beaten up; an old woman whose toes had been eaten by rats while she sat paralysed.

Even Albedo became alarmed as the commotion spread, while

33

Jean desperately tried to sort out those few she might be able to help from the many for whose terrible needs she possessed neither the most basic drugs nor the skill to alleviate their agony. She had brought drips and rehydration packs, benzyl which might relieve the scabies, as many medicines and antibiotics as she could pack in, but these wretched, desperate people clung to her as their hope of a miracle, when, without facilities, surgical training or X-rays she could not begin to treat more than a handful. She learnt quickly that for some the ceremony of treatment was a comfort; ointment, a pill, clean bandaging. Infected cuts and children wasted by diarrhoea she could positively help, with Albedo repeating her instructions and waving his fists in a mime the women would more easily remember. The rest ... with the rest she was soon in danger of inviting anger as those hopes of a miracle disappeared.

Suddenly someone screeched above the babble and there was a scramble for the door; the child Jean was treating was snatched off her lap, the old woman with rat-gnawed feet humped out on an even older man's back.

'Soldiers!' hissed Albedo, and extinguished the lamp. They stood, Albedo, his daughter, Jean, and an apparently healthy young man who had remained behind, tense in the glow from the hearth while a jeep drove fast down the alley outside, men shouting as they passed. It pulled up maybe thirty yards from where they stood, was followed by other, heavier vehicles, a great many voices yelling above the roar of engines.

'What's happening?' Jean breathed, and could just see Albedo shake his head. He did not know either, this was quite different from the usual drunken search or casually fired weapons. There seemed to be engines all around them, a convoy in the main street a couple of blocks away as well as these closer engines shaking fragile walls; Jean hadn't realised there were so many vehicles in Hamada.

'General Forla go to Mananga City,' said the young man softly from the corner, speaking stilted English. 'It is dangered by guerrilla while he with women on Hamada beach.'

Albedo drew in his breath. 'How do you know?'

'I know. We laugh and watch beach like ant hill.'

'I am harbour-chief! If General Forla call and I jolly well not there, he kill everyone in port,' cried Albedo, alarmed.

34

'They won't kill you, if you're not there,' the young man answered indifferently, in Manangan.

'But my clerks! My Dick and Harrys! I must go at once!'

This time when the other answered, it was to say something very low and deadly which Jean gathered meant that he would stop Albedo by force if he meant to help Forla, his reason, she was sure, that Albedo might try to save his clerks by betraying this stranger in their midst. Because he *was* a stranger, his build different from the coastal people of Hamada and his skin lighter, his manner supercilious towards creatures he clearly regarded as inferior.

Outside the noise was becoming worse, exhaust fumes stifling in air which, after the storm, was already humid enough to condense like tears on their skin, and shooting soon followed to increase the confusion. The Manangan army was hung about with expensive weaponry, frequently carried with safety catches off; guns were fired by accident all the time, as much for pleasure as in anger. In anger as well of course, but the worst gun battles often flared when everyone had been loosing off merrily and some unfortunate unit got caught in crossfire by mistake. Through the single window Jean could see gun flashes streaming into the sky, and heard a sharp hard cracking not too far away as some heavier weapon joined the celebration.

It tailed away at last, until only the sound of troops shouting among themselves was left, the rattle of spent cartridges falling on roofs and in the streets, screamed orders too and then engines racing off to join others in the main part of town. Jean drew the first breath she remembered taking since the firing began; flimsy hut walls were no protection from high velocity bullets.

'We go at once,' said Albedo, tugging at her arm.

The young man dragged himself out of his elegant slouch against the wall and sauntered over to the door. 'I bring someone and you take him where he want to go.'

'No!' Albedo was almost weeping. 'I not want big rumpus. Quiet, quiet, Mama Doc and I like snakes in the grass.'

'Steve quieter than you, fat boy.' He snapped his fingers contemptuously under Albedo's nose. 'You wait and I fetch.'

'Steve?' asked Jean. Any moment there would be a fight here as well.

But the young man had already gone, vanished like a wraith into the dangerous street.

35

'Oh blimey, Mama Doc,' wailed Albedo. 'We fixed bad now.'

'Let's go, then, before he gets back,' said Jean. But that, it became clear, Albedo was unwilling to do, muttering darkly about the revenge of bad blokes once they were angered.

There was still a great deal of noise all around but no longer directly in the street outside, as if General Forla was in fact gathering his men to pull out. If so, they would naturally concentrate around the main square and railway station just beyond. The sudden silence was uncanny until the young man reappeared in the entry, another figure behind him. 'This Steve. You keep him safe. Steve, I wait each night for you.'

'Okay, and thanks, Mezak.' The voice answered in Manangan but, astonishingly, sounded unmistakably American. When the speaker came into the glow of the hearth Jean could just make out narrow, almost academic features and pale eyes above several days' growth of beard. 'Mr Albedo? Mezak says you are kind enough to take me to the UN office on the dock.'

Albedo threw up his hands in a gesture of despair, but seemed to have decided that taking this new stranger was a lesser risk than wasting more time arguing, or the likelihood of a knife in his belly if he disobeyed disdainful Mezak.

'Hallo there,' said Jean.

The American, Steve, swung round. 'Good God. When Mezak said there was a mama doc he crossed his fingers and spat, so I imagined a Macbeth witch broiling toads. What the hell is a female Britisher doing holed up in Hamada?'

'We go!' Albedo smacked his fist into his palm. 'Everything phut if we not go at once!'

Jean agreed with him, her watch showing three in the morning, activity in the town increasing all the time. They had to be back over the harbour wire before the first streaks of dawn silhouetted them climbing that damned crane, an exchange of pleasantries far less important than staying alive. She slung her satchel across her back, little more than instruments now left inside, whispered thanks and sorrow to Albedo's daughter and followed Albedo out of the doorway.

'Here, Steve,' Mezak said. 'Take my gun.'

The American shook his head. 'No, thanks.'

'You take,' Mezak insisted, and thrust what looked like an old army revolver at him. 'It bring you luck. You say no, I come too.'

'You're needed here.'

'Then you take,' Mezak said unanswerably.

Steve smiled, and put it in his pocket. 'You win. I'll make sure to bring it back safely.'

And as they stood accustoming their eyes to the darkness Jean saw Mezak also touch Albedo on the arm and flick his fingers meaningly across his throat. It was difficult to imagine what this Steve must be like if an ice-cold blackguard like Mezak parted with a cherished weapon, and made threats to preserve his life.

It was a huge relief to be outside again, no matter what the danger. Heat, pain and the stink of injuries inside a confined space had given Jean a grating ache between her eyes, the experiences of this night ramming home just how little she could do to help the sick in conditions of discontinuity, threat and dirt. She had to reach that clinic in the hills, where she could work apparently without too much disturbance and as one of a team, however small. Now there was this Steve, another complication in a situation already worsened by jarring personalities.

But first their journey back to the wire needed every scrap of concentration; there was traffic roaming, horns blaring, headlights blazing away to their right, and random vehicles careering through the sidestreets. It was nerve-racking to slip from one shadow to the next when, at any moment, a truck might burst out of nowhere without a second's warning. Then there was that single wider street they had to cross, where soldiers had been enjoying target practice on their way out. Now it was bustling, a woman's voice screaming in the distance, a squad of soldiers tinkering with a stalled truck in the gutter.

Jean could see Albedo wringing his hands with anxiety as half an hour passed, and still there wasn't any chance to cross.

'Can't we outflank ... go round?' Steve murmured.

'No! One way riffraff camp, other way main square. Soon we have to go back, I think.'

Perhaps another ten minutes dragged past, then, as Jean was again wearily shifting weight from one leg to the other, klaxons suddenly began blipping in rhythm and a convoy of vehicles swept into view, scattering everything in their path. Soldiers dived out of the way or leapt in their vehicles to join the cacophony as trucks crammed with men tore past like devils, an automatic rattle of shots streaking over roofs on either side of the street. In the middle

37

of the column was an enormous black American saloon with its windows sealed shut and clearly weighed down by armourplate, a gold and purple flag the size of a bedsheet flapping above its roof. No need to be told that this must be General Forla, on his way to embark with his troops on a return to his capital. The uproar was indescribable, and worsened when two armoured personnel carriers locked tracks and crunched a truck, by which time the rest of the column had swept out of sight, sucking nearly everyone along in its wake. A single figure lay flattened in the mud where he had been thrown out of the crunched truck and run over in the mêlée.

'Quick!' said Steve, while Jean and Albedo still stood dazed, and they crossed the road at a run, reaching shadows again just as another truck turned the corner, bathing the roadway in light. After that, little more than sensible caution was needed to bring them to the further edge of town, from where they could see the wire barrier between them and the port outlined against the sky. Only that stretch of open ground and the wire to cross before they reached the fragile safety of the UN office.

Only. Before Jean set out, she had thought of the port's wire fence as the major barrier to be passed.

They had crossed the waste ground and Albedo was scuffling in sand to uncover the cached rope ladder when steps suddenly crunched towards them and a voice shouted. Shots instantly flashed out of the dark, whining into wire, punching grit with an unmistakable smacking thud. Albedo was thrown backwards feet above head, while Jean and Steve, who had been standing a little to one side, dived instinctively for cover behind a pile of oil drums. In the silence following the shots the soldier exclaimed aloud, then came forward at a run, pumping more bullets into Albedo's slack body. Probably he had seen only a single figure by the wire, but his boot caught in the rope rungs of the half-uncovered ladder and he swung round, gun lifting to fire again; then he staggered back with his arms outflung to lie without stirring across Albedo's legs, the crack of a single shot deafening in Jean's ear.

It had all been so quick she had not had time to feel afraid, and could not imagine now that Albedo might be dead, his body almost blown apart by bullets; her only coherent thought was that she would never discover where he had learned his English.

'A few more shots tonight may not be noticed,' Steve said quietly. 'Wait here, and I'll have a look around.'

Jean waited, still feeling nothing while he vanished and re-turned, dragged Albedo and then his killer to the sea wall, where it was easy to tip them into those coils of wire she had seen on the way out, slopping lazily in the tide. Death was so commonplace in Hamada that no one might ever bother to drag two more bodies out of so inconvenient a place. Only when Steve came back for the last time did Jean's unnatural apathy dissolve and in its place a deep shivering begin. Perhaps the worst part of this horrific night was her unsought companion's calm, apparently as impervious to re-morse as he had seemed to danger. Now, she saw him consider her unsafe state and decide with academic detachment how best to deal with it. No wonder Mezak liked a man as cold-blooded as himself.

'How do we get over this wire?' he asked. He spoke in a flat tone, no inflection to his voice. For God's sake, this unemotional bastard had just killed a man. The only completely unsurprising thing was that chilly Steve, Mezak's pal, happened to be an excellent marks-man with a borrowed gun.

Jean bit her lips, trying to stop that weakening tremble, the consequence being that it spread from her lips to her jaw. Albedo died trying to get us back over that wire, she thought fiercely. 'There's a pole. The ladder goes on the hook of that crane you can see.'

At first she couldn't find the pole, her fingers trembling too. Subconsciously perhaps she did not want to find it, the thought of climbing up and then along that exposed crane jib while her bones shook in her flesh was quite terrifying. But she found it at last and felt steadied by this trifling success, the next step was to concen-trate on showing how the ladder could be lifted up and hooked. Not far behind them the town still erupted with noise, here ... here, there was still only the two of them, and blood scuffled out of sight in dry earth.

'Okay,' Steve said, when he had mastered the knack of notching the ladder home. 'You first, but wait at the end of the jib until I come.'

Jean was so infuriated by his assumption that only minutes after witnessing the first murders of her life she could climb and wait and lead the way over wire and down jibs in the dark, that she brushed past him without speaking. She climbed like an auto-maton until she reached the hook, stepped unhesitatingly to the cable, and stood gratefully feeling a post-storm wind brush strongly over her face. Above the sea the sky was turning the palest of pale greens, time ebbing swiftly now and taking their frail margin of safety with it. A creaking struggle to her left suggested that Steve was having some difficulty in climbing an unanchored ladder and then pulling it up behind him. Good, she thought with unreasonable satisfaction.

The sideways shuffle along the cables was as easy as before, simplicity itself to discover a way down from the platform once she could explore it from above. Two slotted handholds were bolted to an edge she hadn't previously seen, and her sense of relief was so great that she climbed over the edge as if scrambling down crane struts was routine. Only as she was about to lower herself again, from slotted handholds to sloping steel supports, did reaction strike again, like the undertow from a deep black tide which would drown her if she moved.

Steve squatted on the platform beside her face. 'You think you're the only one who's got the shakes?' He touched her face with his hands. They were icy-cold and twitching. 'It doesn't alter the fact we have to get into cover before anyone else happens past and spots us against the sky. So hurry it up, will you, please.'

Infuriated again, Jean was aware of being manipulated. Only clinical judgement could at such a perilous moment have measured the precise mix of compulsion and understanding which might get her moving again; but, jerkily, first one hand and then the other detached itself from those secure handholds and gripped hated, sloping struts. Her feet slithered across wet metal, her heart pounding as often there seemed no grip at all, the slope very steep, crosspieces and bolts too far apart. She could scarcely believe she'd made it when the ground jolted solidly against her groping feet, extraordinarily difficult to remember that they must be just as cautious on a quayside which, after so many perils, seemed deceptively like home. Then it was only that last stretch to reach the UN building, the door swinging inward as she reached it.

'Thank God,' said Lewis, and held her tightly.

4

'WHY does anyone behave the way they do in this crazy country? Forla may have simply decided to pitch camp in the freight yard instead of on the beach, for all we know,' Lewis said angrily.

'He could have done. I don't think he has.' Stephen Retz had washed, shaved and changed into some of Pierre's spare clothes by the time Jean woke up again; the effect was to make him look even more exacting than the night before, and very much less suited to squalid camping conditions on Hamada Quay. Through her training and also by personal inclination Jean was sensitive to physical characteristics, and now she could study him in daylight she was struck both by their visitor's edgy movements and by that intellectual face. Today, incongruously, he was also wearing glasses of a very American rimless pattern which to her suggested nothing so much as a professor of philosophy: introspective, clever, watchful. Not at all like her expectation of someone who last night had killed a man and thrown two bodies in the sea.

'Why are you sure Forla has returned with his troops to Mananga City, Monsieur Retz?' Pierre asked. He was intrigued by this unexpected newcomer, too, Jean could tell.

'Because he should have returned there a month ago. Dictators are interested in keeping power above everything else, and unless this one fights for his capital soon, he'll lose it.'

'You a guerrilla or something?' Lewis demanded.

'No, although last night I may have seemed like one.'

'Today you're sure as hell acting like one. Pierre and me, we're UN officers, we can't go hijacking trucks or shooting our way out of trouble. Jesus, those Geneva stiffs would be the first to make sure we were tried for murder, and if you fancy a Manangan gaol then I certainly do not.'

They were sitting over one of Pierre's better breakfasts, the sun scorching down outside. In spite of all the disturbances of the night Hamada now sweltered in silence beyond the wire; even the guard at the gate had disappeared out of sight and Pierre said that so far he had seen only half a dozen people moving circumspectly in the distance. As for Jean, she had woken late and still felt strung up and unreal, this peaceful day a mockery of terror and sorrow in the night.

Nevertheless, she, Pierre and Lewis had all been dumbfounded when their visitor, who introduced himself as Stephen Retz, suggested quite calmly over coffee that with Forla gone they should move without delay to take over the railway station and start shipping food.

'What makes you think you could take over a whole railway and then run it, anyway?' Jean asked. 'Forla's bound to have left some troops behind.' So far she had hardly spoken, afraid that speaking might cut loose emotions only with difficulty held in check. Like tears for Albedo, for instance.

'Of course. But they're a bunch of gangsters rather than an army and Forla will have taken his best men with him to Mananga City, who probably would put up a fight. Make a surprise attack at night on a base garrison like this, and most will take off in whatever transport they can move.'

'You plan to defeat Forla's army singlehanded?' Pierre demanded caustically.

'You're crazy,' Lewis added. 'Cooked by the sun. Of course we couldn't help if that's what you're thinking. My God, we might as well tear up the UN charter and shoot the Secretary General. Okay, a single company of US Marines could probably take over most of Mananga, but there's only three of us, and we sure as hell aren't marines. We haven't a hope of stampeding even blind drunk troops and this is the country's only port. There'll be a couple of thousand men left lying someplace around the town. Or were you thinking of doubling your force by asking Jean to help?'

'I don't suppose you're the sort who expects women to help, are you, Mr Retz?' Jean turned to Lewis, 'Surely you can see he isn't alone?' She felt impatient with the lot of them for refusing to grasp the essentials of the situation, and most especially with Stephen Retz for thinking UN officers might start mounting military attacks. She, on the other hand, was not UN and wanted very much to reach the hills.

Stephen looked at her thoughtfully; behind those glasses his eyes were masked and almost colourless. 'I admit that Mezak gives

42

the impression of having a great many bloodthirsty followers not too far out of reach.'

He didn't deny it, Jean thought. But if he has any sense at all, he'll realise that Mezak's bandits ravening around Hamada will be quite as bad as Forla's outfit. 'You imagine you might be able to control them?'

Those eyes narrowed, as if unexpectedly aware of another detached and critical judgement. 'No. But Mezak might, if I cut him a deal he can believe in.'

'Then what?' demanded Lewis. 'Okay, you take Hamada with a bunch of bandits. I don't think you can, but suppose you do. What next?'

'We get the railroad working. There's only one locomotive because Forla used the rest, but there'll be some flatbeds and wagons in the sidings they couldn't make roll in a hurry. I'd be surprised if we couldn't couple up a train inside twenty-four hours. Then we load up food and medicines and steam to Kosti, half-way between here and Mananga City, where I've fixed for some trucks to be waiting. It's around a hundred miles from there into the high hills, where we should be out of Forla's reach for a while. Maybe it is only a single trainload, but even that much could mean life rather than death for a great many people.'

There was a long silence while Lewis and Pierre looked at each other and Stephen Retz looked at his own fingers as if he wanted to stop their irritable tapping at the table edge, and couldn't. As for Jean, she watched all three of them, her own mind already made up.

'We got to discuss this,' Lewis said at last and jerked his head at Pierre. Together they went into the office and shut the door behind them.

'They won't do it,' Jean said. 'They can't. You have to see they can't. If you should be able to take the town for however short a time, they might help to ship some food. But that's all. They can't possibly prejudice UN operations all over the world because someone they never met before decides to hijack a railway for the day.'

'Two days. One to fix and load a tow of wagons, repair the locomotive and get up steam. Then it's the hell of a climb up to Kosti pulling freight.'

'Two days,' she agreed, smiling. 'How long have you been planning this?'

'Four or five weeks, maybe. Ever since I realised there wouldn't be any supplies coming into the hills before winter.'

She frowned. 'The railway's only been closed three weeks.'

'Who says? It's months since most shipments out of here reached where they were meant to reach.'

She stared at him, mind spinning. 'That can't be true.'

'It's true.'

'But ... if it is, where has all the food gone? Lewis told me that until Forla closed the line they cleared several trains a week out of here.'

Stephen took off his glasses and put them in his pocket as if clearing decks for action, revealing those eyes as seawash grey. He was older than the rest of them, maybe nearly forty, and controlling himself with more effort than she had realised, those drumming fingers betraying uncertainties his words denied. High lined forehead, long thin nose, thin straight mouth as tense as a spring. 'I wasn't certain until I reached here whether the UN set-up in Hamada was plain stupid or in on the racket; now I'm guessing it was neither. They took the easy way out, that's all. Shipped the goods, reported all was well and took care not to know that most of their freight went straight into Forla's private stockpile. Like they said, they didn't fancy the inside of a Manangan prison.'

'Nor would I.'

'No, but neither would I like to starve in the Kosti Hills while Forla peddled my supplies in exchange for guns and women.'

'You know the hills well? Is the clinic in the Kosti Valley still all right?' Jean demanded eagerly. 'They would never have sent me out from England if they hadn't thought it was functioning without too much trouble.'

'It's open. Two Austrian doctors—monks—and an elderly nun run it, but they're out of drugs and diesel for the generator. Hand bellows and a few sniffs of smuggled anaesthetic when they operate.'

'Six crates of medical stores came in on the same ship as me.'

'Good, we'll take those and some diesel as first priority. Trains usually only stop at Kosti so the locomotive can take on water, but a mule track runs from there right over the highest range of hills and into the valley beyond—that's where your clinic is. I've reconnoitred it and I think we can get trucks through that way, although it won't be easy. Forla will never hear until afterwards how food reached where it ought to be.'

'I don't get it,' Jean said slowly. 'You're here ... you have to have been in Mananga to find out what happened to several months of UN supplies mysteriously missing up a single track railway. You know what has come in, you say, so you must be official. But here you are in Hamada, planning to run off Forla's army. Last night you ... also killed a man.' Her voice altered abruptly as bloody memory came flooding back.

'We would both be dead if I hadn't.'

'So what's the difference, him or us?' she asked tightly.

'Why, none,' he answered at once. 'Which could be why I didn't want to carry Mezak's gun.'

Jean was still trying to work out what he meant when Pierre and Lewis came back into the room.

'We talked it over,' Lewis said curtly. 'If Forla's men should happen to get chased out, we'll help you get food out of here. But you have to make it look as if we were unwilling — we'll talk about how to fix that, and fix it good. Jesus, we have to work here after you've pulled out and away. One other condition: you sign for everything you take.'

'Why?'

'Why do you think? It's UN food and I'm responsible for it.'

'You don't know me, and any name I chose to scribble quite likely wouldn't mean a thing. Especially when there's tons of food rotting here no one will ever account for.'

'He is right,' Pierre said. 'I told you it is better not to put anything on paper, Lewis, in case Forla finds it.'

'That's the deal,' said Lewis angrily.

Stephen Retz's fingers were tapping, tapping now. 'The UN is a bureaucratic outfit, right? They check paper and signatures even if Forla probably wouldn't. To them, you and me signing documents at the very least means you've got something to explain. Maybe you want to explain. Maybe the UN is getting restless over food wasting at Hamada, and this would help to show how you jumped at any deal which gave a chance of breaking the log jam. Get credit for initiative, even though I wouldn't say you jumped, precisely. Or do you see it differently?'

'I see we're UN officers caught where whatever we do is wrong.'

Those fingers suddenly stopped their tapping and Retz's hand clenched tight instead. Then he squeezed a small sour smile. 'Should I tell you something? One of my ancestors was a brigand who got himself pardoned by the King of France because he handed over everything he'd looted through a long and evil life, in exchange for a fat gold pension. Choosing the right moment to start a little virtuous reinsurance is an old trick and a good one, especially if you're a crook.'

'The Cardinal de Retz! I remember learning about him at school,' exclaimed Pierre. 'How interesting to meet one of his descendants.'

'Through the bastard line, of course.' Words unimportant as those inquisitorial eyes lifted suddenly and fairly skewered into Lewis.

Jean watched too, her heart heavy. I'm too soft, she thought. Lewis deserves a crocodile like Retz on his tail and here I am, feeling sorry for him.

For an instant Lewis looked as if he couldn't believe what he heard, then his skin darkened and his head nodded as if an un-spoken question was answered. 'You take that back.'

Stephen lifted his eyebrows. 'How can I? Old de Retz has been dead these three hundred years.'

'You meant me, you bastard.'

'I can't imagine why you should think so.'

Neither could Pierre, looking from one to the other in bewilder-ment; neither would Jean have known what either was talking about, but for the past few minutes ... when Stephen had said that Lewis and Pierre perhaps might only have taken the easy way out. She now realised that he hadn't meant it; had tested her perhaps. As he was now testing a different possibility, and guilt had instantly seen an insult where it most definitely was intended, while inno-cence had not. Lewis, who said it was only worth shipping food in bulk up a railway which happened also to have its terminus in Mananga City, while Pierre considered a single truckload worth trying when people were starving in the hills. Lewis who had seized a chance to gain approval from his UN masters, who were perhaps becoming suspicious.

'You got a gun, you think you can say what you like.' Lewis still did not seem to realise his mistake, as if bluster wasn't the worst mistake of all.

'No. You are the one saying everything I came here to dis-cover.'

'Lewis —' Pierre hesitated, then fell silent again, as if for the

46

first time he, too, began to look into the past and see a different pattern emerging.

All four of them were silent, staring at each other, then Stephen stood up. 'Well, I guess that's as far as we need to go. I am meeting Mezak again after dark, and if we do succeed in running off Forla's men I'd be grateful for any help you care to give afterward at the railroad station.' He went outside.

'For Christ's sake! You heard him, Pierre. When we get back to the States you can be my witness and I'll sue the bastard for slander, take every last dollar off him,' Lewis exclaimed.

'*Oui*, I shall be a witness, I expect. More's the pity,' Pierre went to stand with his back to the window, his face hidden in sun dazzle. 'Oh, Lewis, *mon ami*, why did you lie to me?'

'What do you mean? When did I tell anything but the goddamn truth about this stinking country?' He was beside himself with fury and staring at Jean as if she and not Retz was his accuser.

'I'm not sure, but sometime, somewhere, I think you began to lie a little. Then a little bit more.'

Jean slipped out; how intolerable to listen to denials, recriminations, enmity, between two men who had been friends. Even worse to know, intuitively, that Lewis wasn't so much furious at being caught, when quite probably he did not regard himself as having done anything wrong, as dangerously enraged by being humiliated in front of her.

Outside she found Stephen sitting in a minute slice of shade, his back against the wall. His head turned. 'Sorry about that.'

'Sorry for pretending you thought they might both be innocent? Or did you think I was in the racket too?'

'You couldn't have been. I would have heard if you'd been here while the railroad was still open. You'd be surprised how quickly gossip flies up the line.'

She was disconcerted to discover that he had, in fact, considered her as possibly guilty, the idea only rejected on purely practical grounds. 'How nice to be able to gossip in all those native dialects, as well as planning coups before breakfast.'

He smiled, but abstractedly, very little of his attention to spare for her. 'Mezak's a useful fellow to know.'

'What are you going to do now?'

'About Lewis Anderson? Nothing, here. I came to confirm a hunch that someone official had to be in on a racket which involves most of the UN supplies to Mananga, and then to make sure he wouldn't be around to foul things up again when the railroad is eventually reopened. Probably he'll just get fired. Gathering evidence for a criminal prosecution from the crooks who call themselves Forla's government won't be easy and isn't my business anyway.'

'Don't you think you should talk to Lewis again? Just to condemn him without trying to understand what things have been like here ... I'm not sure it does anyone any good.'

He did not answer, might almost not have heard her.

You really are a bastard, Jean thought. But vicious enmity between men who should have faced their common danger — tried to achieve their common purpose — together, still seemed quite absurd to her. 'Sitting on our hands behind this wire in the heat sends all of us a little crazy after a while, and Lewis has been in Mananga for over two years. Of course he's had to cut a few corners to get things done. Like you. For heaven's sake, you're planning to steal a whole railway! You don't really think you might get away with it, do you?'

He looked at stacked crates, crumbling sacks and empty berths along the quay. 'It's worth a try. The State Department suggested I look around after our ambassador reported he wasn't happy about rumours of aid being siphoned off by Forla. Most of the freight shipped in here is paid for in one way or another by the US taxpayer.' He paused. 'It was only after I spent a while in the hills that worrying about the taxpayer began to seem less important. I got angry, I guess. You hear a kid scream because there's no anaesthetic when he needs an operation, and then you discover there's crates of the stuff sitting on Hamada dock or in Forla's private warehouse. You just want to ship it up, to hell with protocol. Maybe I've spent too much of my life defending dollar signs, but it began to seem that simple in the hills.'

'If you do take a locomotive up the line, I'm coming too.'

'Okay.'

She failed to hide astonishment, having expected argument. For all she knew, Retz might be red hot with women, but he surely hadn't given the impression he'd welcome one underfoot. 'Thanks.'

'It's two hundred miles up that railroad to Kosti, most of it through unsettled country, and then there's that mule track I told you about which trucks have never driven before. You'll still be safer coming than staying here after we leave. It's suited Forla so

48

far to keep his troops the far side of a few strands of wire, because he was making good money out of the UN operation here. He'll be back down that railroad like Attila the Hun once his racket is bust wide open. Those crates of medicines you brought in alone are worth more than gold, sold off as aphrodisiacs. Food is vital to keep farmers on their land instead of dying in refugee camps, but canisters of oxygen, drums of diesel for the operating theatre generator, the drugs you brought, are desperately needed too. Without them, that clinic you hope to reach will soon be forced to close.'

'That's what I came out here to do,' Jean said with satisfaction. 'I can't fight Forla and I'm wasting my time doling out pills and starting treatments I can't finish, like last night. I'll only be really useful in a place where people can bring their sick and wait without fear, perhaps for weeks, while they're properly treated.'

'Probably we're both wasting our time, only it takes a while to realise it. But at least in the hills the climate's better,' he answered, and sounded as if he mocked himself as much as her.

5

THOSE were nearly the last words Jean exchanged with Stephen Retz before he went back over the wire the following night, and they left a disagreeable echo in her mind. It was as if he could only accept compassion by deriding its purpose, and afterwards she remembered that day as one of the most unpleasant in her life. Far from trying to discuss anything with Lewis, for most of it Retz simply vanished, as if to make it entirely clear that so far as he was concerned, once his hunch on corruption was confirmed he saw no point in wasting effort over reasons or excuses. Human beings were as easy to click shut as files in a cabinet. This was far from the case, however. Pierre and Lewis continued to wrangle throughout the baking hot afternoon, self justification and accusations becoming wilder, until they eventually detonated aggression which, in air saturated by heat, temporarily exhausted both men without either being able to feel the victor.

Jean lay on her bed listening to them, longing for electricity to turn the fan, and roused briefly when Retz reappeared at dusk. 'I'm going now. You should be able to hear if our attack is successful, but don't move from here until either Mezak or I come for you.'

'*Bonne chance, monsieur.* We shall pray for your success,' Pierre said, which probably meant he remained unconvinced by Lewis's arguments of innocence. 'There is food prepared if you would like it.'

Lewis laughed. 'Oh, sure, I'll be praying too.'

Stephen did not answer, ate swiftly and in silence, nodding his thanks to Pierre. Jean followed him to the door and when they were outside, said bluntly, 'Have you thought he might try to warn someone?'

'Of an attack? No. With Forla and his ministers gone, he must know he'd more likely be beaten up than listened to if he tried to approach some gun-happy junior officer on the streets.' He lifted a hand in farewell and slipped out silently into the dark.

As soon as Retz had gone the atmosphere subtly eased, as if without his presence Lewis was freed again from the prison of guilt. He and Pierre needed to get on together amicably and, anyway, there was no other company except themselves.

The night passed quietly although the sound of occasional shooting could still be heard from the town, but that had become normal; complete silence would have made them uneasy. Next day there were even people back by the wire, begging for food, the guards firing occasionally to scatter them. Then they would wait at a distance, patiently hunkered in the sun, still hoping to be let in at dusk. Other troops roamed aimlessly, shouting among themselves and staring menacingly through the wire, but trucks were scarce, armoured vehicles had vanished. They had all gone with Forla, Jean supposed.

'Those troops are beginning to realise there's nothing left in Hamada worth robbing except our stores on the dock,' Pierre said grimly.

'You think they might break in?' Jean tried not to sound nervous, but only a fool wouldn't feel alarmed. Yesterday, danger had been close enough to touch, today it was poised to spring.

'It must have been General Forla himself who kept them out of here for so long, and then only because we were his *réserve*.'

'You see?' burst out Lewis. 'Are you just beginning to see how you have to play along with whoever happens to rule this fucking country or get chopped? Forla's a bastard and a killer, but the only guy whose orders mean a thing. This whole place is a protection racket, you pay or you're rubbed out. Well, I paid and you tell me where in the Third World a percentage isn't creamed off aid by the rulers of countries we're trying to help, before anyone can begin to operate. Then come the other percentages: to truck drivers; customs officials; you name it. Everyone knows it happens but, oh no, we mustn't tell in case the West stops giving.'

'There is a difference between paying a percentage to operate and the whole operation vanishing in percentages,' Pierre said.

'Care to tell me where you'd stop? The first ten per cent to Forla? Everyone has to pay that. The next ten per cent to his Minister of Transport and the ten after that to sweeten a few brigands into not burning our trucks? In the States you pay for shipping goods and here the payment happens to be in bribes. Then maybe you get called to go in front of Almighty Forla personally, who tells you he wants twenty per cent instead of ten, thirty maybe, and there's guys fidgeting behind your back. So you think, hell, I didn't come out here to die when all that would mean is Forla gets the lot. Dictators get chopped sooner or later, it's worth hanging in there and hope things will get better. Hanging in there is all we've been doing these last few months and you know it.'

'Yes, that is true,' agreed Pierre.

'Okay then, so we survive to start over, maybe with Forla, maybe with some other assassin lucky enough to cut his throat. Provided that lunatic Retz doesn't kill us in the backlash after he fails to take Hamada. Now you tell me where I might have stopped. How you would have kept things moving without getting killed or run out of a country even the Red Cross quit in disgust.'

'I think—' Pierre stopped, then went on more slowly. 'I can't judge you, Lewis. Of course it is difficult to stop anything once it begins to roll.'

'Jean?' Lewis was smiling for the first time since he had been trapped into guilt the day before.

'Don't ask me.' She wasn't about to stir that particular brew again, especially while they were forced to live on top of each other. 'I'm frightened just looking at armed drunks through the wire.'

'Jesus,' he said with satisfaction. 'Once you start facing a few questions out there in the shit, it sure gets easier to pass the buck.'

There the matter was allowed to rest, on something approaching level terms, a common front reformed against an increasingly threatening outside world of which Stephen Retz had tacitly become a part.

The drifting groups of men increased in size during the day, and became more active as the sun dropped towards the horizon. Occasionally an NCO would send men slouching off about some duty, otherwise such little discipline as had previously existed among the men guarding their gate seemed progressively to disintegrate.

'They'll break in tonight,' Pierre said tersely. 'No one wants to be seen making the first move, but once it's dark, they will come.'

Lewis was staring out of the window, staying back out of sight. 'I don't think so, unless there are rumours we don't know about, that Forla isn't doing too good up in Mananga City. We're his, aren't we? Scum like those guards won't dare to tread on their Almighty Ruler's toes so long as he's likely to be back.'

'They will come. I can feel it,' said Pierre positively. 'Let's get on the radio and report the situation. Jean—'

'They'll see us if we try to leave this building while it's still light,' she said. For a hundred yards around their UN office the quay was clear of obstruction and the sight of three foreigners scuttling to take cover could be the spark which ignited determination to storm the wire. In any case there weren't many hiding places along the dock. They might dodge among piled sacks or hide in a crate for a while, but wholesale looting would soon discover them. 'If they do decide to break in, our best chance of getting out must be to climb that crane again. Providing they wait until after dark,' she added.

'That is a good idea.' Pierre snapped his fingers. 'Maybe we could find Monsieur Retz and go with him to the hills.'

'Oh, he'll be too busy deciding how to storm the railroad to bother about UN wimps.' Out of the three of them only Lewis seemed excited rather than afraid. The prospect of something happening after weeks of inactivity, then more frustration over Jean, immediately sent most of his systems into overdrive. Perhaps also, because he alone had met Forla the Almighty face to face, he found it particularly difficult to believe that his army, rabble though they were, would dare to violate one of the dictator's own possessions.

As for Jean, once she realised the extent of Lewis's confidence, perversely she began again to think that his dealings with Forla must have been more than the reluctant by-product of intolerable pressures. Maybe it had started out that way, but surely only a strong and mutual advantage could induce Lewis to remain so optimistic in such upromising circumstances.

She grimaced to herself. Unpromising must be the understatement of all time.

'Lewis can do what he likes, but you and I are getting out of here as soon as it is dark enough to move,' Pierre said, busying himself over the cooker.

'Anything is better than waiting in a trap,' she agreed, and packed a rucksack with essentials and iron rations, added her emergency medical gear and a flask of bottled water. Outside the shouting had increased in volume and she had a hunch that once she left this office she would never be back. Then she lay down on her bed again, trying to relax. Heaven knew what strains the night ahead might hold. Outside, shouts had become a continuous threatening rumble: an even bet whether darkness or an invasion by drunken soldiers would come first. Already aimless prowling had changed to a rhythm, laced boots and bare feet stamping in the dust until a cloud of filth seemed to hang in the breathless air. In the distance a single streak of smoke rose above the roofs of Hamada, as if an exceptionally rapacious robber had found one last thing to destroy.

In a land where the sun dropped over the horizon as if on strings, that evening a maddening half-light seemed to linger for ever. By then Lewis had agreed to leave with Jean and Pierre — for her sake, or so he claimed. He still maintained that Forla's orders would protect them, but was beginning to speculate that the uprising in Mananga City might have been more serious than he thought, the dictator perhaps threatened for the first time in three years of brutal rule.

Suddenly everything flickered. As if in hallucination, long dead fans and the icebox whirred, lights glowed. Then another, longer, flash was followed by a dull, flat boom away in Hamada, and the power failed again, exaggerating the darkness. '*Viens!*' urged Pierre, and opened the back door. 'Let us go while they do not look.'

They ran together to the quay edge, where crates and sacks lay jumbled together, and as they reached it noise broke out behind.

Howling, whistling, wailing, rejoicing noise, darkness hiding both the savage joy of those who broke through the wire and the agony of others trampled underfoot or impaled on barbs in the scramble.

Lewis gripped Jean's hand, hard. 'You were right.'

What the hell does being right matter, she thought, and followed the two men along the dock edge, picking their way past uncoiled hawsers and heaving piles of rotting rubbish. The grace to admit a wrong opinion made no difference, except she liked Lewis better. But wrong or right they couldn't have left before, were probably only postponing the inevitable by leaving now, because with the mob already broken in, there was no chance they could reach the crane. Unless Retz could indeed strike successfully and fast at the town, and then come with whatever men he had to their rescue, they were trapped. A stretch of wire nearly fifty yards long had been flung flat, a great many writhing bodies bearing witness to the mindless force which had driven a human wedge through viciously coiled strands and then trampled over its own shock troops.

Jean could feel her heart pounding, a cringing pain in her knees as they crouched and weaved behind such cover as existed, crawling down the rough outer face of the quay when Lewis discovered some broken concrete at the water's edge. There they could huddle while above their heads the jubilant noise continued: once, there was a great crash and several crates hurtled past to splash in the water, followed by screams and laughter, otherwise the atmosphere suggested nothing so much as a street carnival.

'Get ready to slip into the sea and keep only your face above water,' whispered Pierre, his arm hugging Jean close.

'They'll be sleeping this off by morning, maybe I'll be able to go find an officer,' Lewis said softly. 'Unless he has fallen from power, Forla will have left a governor somewhere in town. It's still hang in there until we get a break.'

They crouched on that fallen concrete, lapped by the sea and with the quay edge behind their backs, for what seemed an endless space of time. Gradually, gradually, the noise along the dock lessened, until only scuffling steps, low voices, an occasional cry were left. 'If they have gulped down raw flour and milk powder on empty stomachs they'll be feeling pretty sick,' Jean breathed.

Cautiously Lewis straightened, pulled himself up the wall a

handhold at a time, until his eyes were level with the quay; from her cramped crouch Jean saw him grin at what he saw. He came back down with a rush, that wall was nearly sheer. 'There surely are some bellyaches up there.'

'Can we get past?'

He shook his head, frowning. 'I don't think so. Too many scavengers picking over the remains. We might be able to swim round the point while everyone is minding their own business.'

Swimming through scummy water to unknown landing points was an unattractive prospect, it also meant abandoning their packs; Jean did not even bother mentioning she was only a holiday swimmer when the other risks were so great. Fear for her life might improve indifferent breaststroke, and if it didn't — well, anything was better than waiting for daylight to discover them.

It was as they stood to strip that disaster happened, impossible to know exactly how. But without warning someone leapt from the quay on to Lewis's shoulders, yelling in triumph, and more followed, sending Pierre staggering backwards so that he and several attackers fell struggling in the sea. All around her, Jean heard curses and the grunting barks of extreme exertion, saw a figure kneeling on the quay edge pull a stubby gun off his shoulder. When he fired, the shots were ear-splitting shocks, beyond mere noise. Explosive smoke hung in the heavy air as, deafened, she scrabbled for a foothold and then reached up to seize a handful of dirty uniform and heaved. No time, no thought beyond the most basic of reactions: terror; violence; self-preservation. The soldier threw his weight backwards and her fingernails tore, all of them fighting now with maniacal desperation as more figures piled out of the darkness, so many they began to attack each other. Hands, feet, jarring bone everywhere, shoving, punching, kicking above and below the quay and into the water. Not all the advantage was with their attackers as Lewis briefly tore loose from the mêlée to deliver a savage kick at a soldier Jean tried to hold and who was about to thrust her bodily back up the wall. He lost his balance and with a yell of terror dropped both his gun and his grip on her, in an attempt to save himself from falling into the sea. Lewis scooped up the gun as it fell and immediately starting firing, shots scything indiscriminately into the dark. More yells and screams, more hysterical fighting between acrid bodies possessed by devils. Then a tremendous blow reached out of the dark and Jean felt herself falling, falling, until she distinctly heard her own head burst on concrete. Her only remaining instinct was an overwhelming terror of falling unconscious into water.

Darkness. Complete and dreadful darkness. There were sounds and voices and Jean felt she ought to move, but could not remember why. And moving brought darkness rushing back inside her skull. Much later, she distinctly heard a voice say: 'Leave her, she'll be all right.' Retz's voice. She knew it was him because he didn't sound as if he cared much whether she was all right or not. And because she felt indignant at being left alone to die the blackness ebbed a little, allowing pain to seep in around its edges; then she wanted to hug that blackness tight, oblivion her only friend. Soon, pain was everywhere, but sharpest between her eyes, so that, wincing, she tried to duck aside. Pain like a sledgehammer when she moved and the blackness swinging now, an iron ball on a chain.

6

WHEN Jean next opened her eyes the pain had drawn back to the base of her skull, ready to drill through her brain at the first incautious move. She lay still, being very, very cautious; also puzzling over a low evening sun, the stain of it on the ceiling above her head. What she remembered last was a starlit night. It must have been some time later when a shape moved at the frayed edge of her vision and she focused on an ear outlined against the glowing reflection of her lost day.

'How are you?'

'All right.'

'So I see,' said Stephen Retz.

'Lewis?'

'Okay.'

'Pierre?'

'Dead, I'm afraid.' No attempt from him at softening unpleasant facts.

She closed her eyes. Easy-going Pierre, who could have enjoyed the most agreeable of circumstances in his native wine-growing

Beaune, but chose instead to try to help others in places like Hamada. She slept a little, stirring often, and this time her darkness gibbered horrible dreams.

Metal clinking against metal brought her awake again, to find that the pain had become a sulky, manageable ache.

'I've brought you some tea,' Lewis said.

She wanted to laugh, her breath catching on a sob instead: watch it, Jean. Don't get in the way with tears. 'Thanks for the thought. Of course a Britisher in a crisis has to have tea.'

'It tastes disgusting but maybe that's just tea.' He bent to kiss her. 'Me, I'd like to celebrate you're okay again, but Retz said, No alcohol.'

The tea was indeed strange-tasting but blisteringly hot and full of sugar; she hated sweet tea but gulped it thirstily, feeling energy pump back into her bones. No alcohol, no. Not for concussion; she fingered her head gingerly, locating the worst of the ache behind her left ear. A pad of gauze neatly taped on there, a fine sight she must look, with bloodshot eyes most likely and a bald patch cut out of her hair. But how welcome was life when Pierre ... She turned over restlessly, still feeling very weak but knowing she could not afford the luxury of grief.

When she woke again she felt quite different; limp at the edges still but hugely hungry and impatient over lying useless for another single moment. She felt better still after washing in tepid water; almost normal once she discovered some crumpled but fresh clothes to wear. She was back again in their office building, which she had never expected to re-enter; yet what she saw was utterly unfamiliar: glass and metal scrunched underfoot; the radio was trampled nearly flat; the bed where she had been lying the only remaining furniture, and that had been salvaged out of bits and pieces. Doors and windows had been splintered, there was even a three-foot hole through one wall which looked as if a mad giant had punched it with his fist. No cooker, no pans were left, only a few biscuits wrapped in a piece of paper on the floor. Jean hoped they were left for her and ate them ravenously, a measure of her recovery that they only increased her appetite. Her thoughts swerved abruptly: Pierre would have made something palatable to eat out of trampled scraps, and if necessary have cooked it in an oil drum.

Now it was up to her.

Cautiously, she went outside and trudged through hammer-strokes of sun dizzily searching for food in a chaos so unimaginable she accepted it without thought. Spilled mounds of flour flopped with squalling gulls, sugar melted in the heat, powdered milk was a black absorbent pudding where diesel fuel had spilled into it. Splintered crates lay everywhere, also bodies buzzing with flies. Better not to look at those, except perhaps she ought, in case one still lived.

No. There must have been some injured, but either Retz's hillmen or the abused people of Hamada had neatly eviscerated every one of those she saw in uniform, and had carried off those they knew.

'Hey!' Lewis emerged from the wreck of a warehouse. 'You're supposed to stay in bed.'

'I'm better now, and trying to find something to cook.'

'We've shifted most of what could be salvaged up to the railroad station. That maniac Retz is still set on hauling freight up to the hills, although the guy in the telegraph shack says that far from being toppled, Forla is stronger than before.'

Jean digested this, her mind still sluggish. 'What happened? The last thing I remember is Pierre falling into the sea, and people fighting all over us.'

'I pulled him out after it finished, but some bastard had knifed him and he died.' He saw the look on Jean's face and added. 'In New York or Paris maybe he could have been saved, but he was way past anything a nurse could do. Hell, it wasn't your fault you were unconscious.'

'I never do seem to be around when I might be useful,' she said bitterly. 'Has anyone salvaged our gear from down by the water? One day that medical kit of mine will come in handy.'

'It's in the office. You remember that soldier with the gun?' She nodded. 'Well, without you I wouldn't have been able to take it off him and we'd both be dead.' He held her, kissed her, this time welcoming her back to warmth in a singularly arid world. 'Am I glad to see you alive! When we scraped you off the concrete I thought at first you were dead, too.'

Jean laughed, and needed to hold her head. 'I felt it for a while.'

He kissed her again, but more gently, and walked with her into some shade. 'That surely was one hell of a weapon I managed to grab. A high velocity spray-gun which cleared away the mob like flushing a drain. Then afterwards I didn't know what the hell to do. I got Pierre out of the sea but he was dying, you were alive but snuckered. Sure, I could kill anyone who looked over that edge of quay, but all they had to do was wait and we'd shrivel when the sun came up. Then some flashes and explosions went off the far side of town and some time later Retz came in with his hillmen. I guess he had an easier job than he expected, with nearly everyone down on the dock, either groaning with bellyache or trying to figure out how to kill us.'

'They ran?'

'Most armies caught like that would run, and Mananga's ran best of all. You see, Retz had fixed up some rockets out of tubes and home-made explosive. They weren't too lethal but they spat so many sparks they looked like everyone's least favourite avenging spirit. There were guys praying and jumping into the sea, one bunch stripped off and started howling at the moon. You never saw such a sight, I laughed until I got a cramp. I hate that supercilious bastard Retz, but those rockets were something else again.'

'I wish I'd seen it.' Jean couldn't remember full-hearted laughter since she had arrived in Hamada.

'It also made my memory click. In the States, Retz Corporation is big in agricultural marketing, fertiliser, things like that. And terrorists long ago discovered you can make explosive out of fertiliser. He's one of those corporation Retzes all right, I guess they learn to fry up chemicals while in diapers.'

Jean shrugged. In Hamada, it didn't seem to matter who Stephen Retz's relatives might be. 'Where is he now?'

'At the railroad station. I told you, he's still got this crazy idea of running a freight train up the line, though the latest rumour says Forla survived a coup and is stronger than ever. That railroad has to be a trap, and there'll be troops back here inside a few hours. Retz has two dozen men at most.'

A truck driving fast across the open ground between Hamada and the dock slowed to turn through the now gateless entry and came towards them, its wheels churning up dust from burst flour sacks. Stephen Retz climbed down from the cab. 'Glad to see you're back on your feet. How's the head?'

'Fragile. How's yours?'

The frown between the pale eyes eased. He did indeed look utterly exhausted; a slight, gaunt figure smothered in dirt. 'The same. We're pulling out in an hour provided the locomotive boiler

59

doesn't burst, so if you could collect anything you want to take —'

As Jean went to fetch her pack she caught a glimpse of herself in a broken mirror. Startled, she paused and looked more carefully. She had thought Retz looked awful after two days and nights of firing rockets, repairing and loading trains, but she looked worse: bruised, with overbright eyes, scuffed hair, drained face and tightly tucked-in mouth. Well, I could try to change the mouth, she thought wryly, and smiled mockingly at her image. In the mirror a grotesque smirked back and she turned away, the only certainty that she wouldn't see herself again for a while, and a good job too.

Hamada Town was quiet as they drove through, the only vehicle in the streets. There were people standing around, a few stalls open and children playing without fear, the adults looking glum and apprehensive in spite of plentiful looted food from the dock.

'Poor devils, they know Forla's men will soon be back,' Stephen said.

'You should have thought of that before you took the town,' Lewis snapped.

'What difference would it make? Everything troops can wreck is wrecked already, lives used as target practice until two days ago and again tomorrow.'

'The difference is, they've had two days' respite,' Jean said. Even two days' respite from terror would make its return more unbearable.

'Yes, I'm afraid that's so,' Stephen answered after a pause, and none of them spoke again until they reached the railway station.

As they drew up at the square brown station building, Mezak walked catlike out of shadow. 'Welcome to free Mananga.'

'Thank you. I was sorry not to see your brave attack, since it was so successful,' Jean answered politely.

'We attack every day soon,' he answered, but she was glad to see that her compliment had pleased him.

The station building was empty, a hiss of steam out in the sun beyond it. 'If I lived here, I'd be yelling for a passage out of town,' Jean said, surprised by this emptiness, to Lewis. Stephen had already hurried ahead with Mezak.

'Out of town to where? There's only salt pans along the coast, Forla's riding high in Mananga City, and up in the hills Mezak's cousins would cut the throats of coast people who set up camp. Outsiders are potential land-grabbers, or, even worse, government

60

spies. Retz may talk about taking food to the hills; what he's really done is drop Hamada deeper in the shit.'

When they reached the locomotive it didn't inspire much confidence, in fact it looked as if it should have been shovelled into a scrapyard years before. Steam leaked from a great many valves, and tandem tenders were stacked with as much wood as coal. Lewis laughed at Jean's expression. 'It's British, did you know? So I guess you won't dare tell me it's about to fall apart.'

They climbed up to the footplate and he showed her a brass plate: *No. 246711 Swindon Engine Works 1936.*

'Swindon!' she exclaimed. 'That's only twenty miles from my home.'

'Nineteen thirty-six,' said Lewis derisively. 'You see how many freight wagons Retz has coupled on behind? This rust-bucket will explode the first slope we reach.'

'I bet you it doesn't,' she said instantly. 'My grandfather built engines at Swindon, come to think of it he could have worked on this. Only the best workmanship survives out here fifty-four years, of course it'll take us wherever we want to go.'

'It took half a day to shift it out of the locomotive shed. Ten dollars it never reaches Kosti, okay? I'd make it more except I hate to take the money.'

But in Jean's eyes No. 246711 had been instantly changed from an unreliable heap of metal into a valued ally; she chuckled to herself, recognising this feeling as absurd, but undeniably it was there. 'Are you leaving Hamada with us, too?'

'I have to, now,' he answered curtly, clearly detesting being beholden to Retz even for a ride. But any foreigner found in Hamada would be butchered by Forla's returning, vengeful, troops, their distant chief's protection would mean nothing in such bloody chaos. Yet something in Lewis' attitude made Jean wonder what else he might have in mind: he detested Retz and regarded this trip as suicidal, the attack on Hamada as self-indulgent madness. Yet he did not give the impression of a man expecting to be led into disaster within a few hours, rather of having quite different plans of his own. Jean left him contemptuously examining broken dials in the locomotive cab and swung herself down on the track again — no platforms here. Thirteen assorted wagons and flats were coupled behind the two tenders, all well loaded, and Mezak was strolling proprietorially towards her, two similarly light-boned followers at his heels. He inclined his head as he passed, the expressions of the others did not change: they were hill people closed within their own tight world again, where women did not count.

She walked slowly along the length of the train, noticing hastily patched sacks and makeshift lashings, then back again through crushing heat towards where the locomotive was almost lost to sight under clouds of steam. An ancient passenger carriage with slatted seats was hitched nearest to the tenders, Stephen standing on its step and speaking to Mezak, now squeezed inside between piled crates.

'You've got the crates of medical supplies!' Jean exclaimed when she saw them. 'When I couldn't see them anywhere on the quay I thought they must have been smashed up and looted.'

Stephen turned. 'They didn't get time to break open too many sealed containers. We may have to drop off some wagons if the boiler can't build up enough pressure to pull them all up the gradient to Kosti, so I put these where they ought to be safest.'

She laughed. 'I've bet Lewis ten dollars a Swindon-built loco-motive will take us anywhere we want to go, but he doesn't believe me.'

He grinned, taken by surprise. 'A few more pounds of steam and we'll set out to prove it.' He dropped on the track beside her, slamming the door on Mezak.

'About Lewis,' she said abruptly. 'It isn't my business, but I'm not sure he plans to come all the way to the hills.'

'Well, that's okay, because I don't want him in the hills. I reckoned I couldn't leave him behind to be murdered, but it sure would make life easier if I did.'

'Of course you couldn't leave him, but—'

'I'll show you.' He scratched some lines on cinders underfoot. 'The track runs more or less straight through desert until it reaches the foothills and then begins a long dogleg to gain height. The last stretch into Kosti is pretty steep, and that is where we shall be most vulnerable, crawling up switchback bends. My guess is that Anderson plans to hike to the frontier; from the outer edge of that dogleg it's only a hundred miles away, and he'd be able to carry enough food and water to reach it if he walked by the stars at night. I expect he'll ask you to join him, but a hundred miles is a long way in this climate. I wouldn't think you could carry enough

enough water, and still march as fast as you'll need to. Reaching that frontier on foot will anyway be a race between dehydration and heat exhaustion.'

With that warning Jean had to be satisfied, especially when, so far, Lewis has simply appeared pleased to discover that Stephen might possibly be related to some rich Retzes in the United States.

For heaven's sake, she liked Lewis and he liked — perhaps more than liked — her. Only instinct nagged that there might be more than resentment on his mind. Stephen knew too much. In Hamada it perhaps made sense to compromise with a dictator, pay bribes in order to operate at all, but once Stephen reported to his superiors that a UN officer had misappropriated considerable quantities of stores and faked records to hide what he was doing, then Lewis would be lucky only to be fired, and he must realise it. He might talk about damages for slander, but what he really wanted was revenge for being made to look criminal in front of a woman he desired, to discredit Retz and make his testimony valueless. An inevitable, human reaction, which Retz's own harshness had to some extent provoked. What Jean could not help seeing now was that once Pierre had been killed the most effective revenge of all for Lewis was to prevent Retz from ever leaving Mananga; admiring his rockets made no difference to that stark fact. Liking Lewis made no difference to Jean's wry self-knowledge that what she really enjoyed about him was his easy recklessness.

It was still difficult not to believe herself the victim of hysterical imaginings, brought on by fright and concussion. Even more humiliating if those doubts about Lewis were fuelled by puritanical distrust of her own emotions, so recently released from their prison in the past. As a consequence of these reflections, when she rejoined Lewis on the footplate she responded to him more warmly than she intended, and watched laughing while he stoked up steam. Together, they studied such dials as appeared to work and invented rude rhymes about the corned beef pancake she cooked on a shovel in the firebox.

'Surely there must be a driver and mate somewhere?' she said. Her mouth, quite literally, had watered while the cab filled with cooking smells, now her stomach protested queasily over such heavy fare.

'Plenty of them, but they're all too scared to break cover.'

You couldn't be surprised by that, Jean reflected. Anyone who came with them must vanish into the hills afterwards or be killed on his return, and railway employees would be local Hamada men with families to worry about.

Retz and Lewis were tripping over each other, both of them stoking now, their sweat sizzling on red hot surfaces each time the firebox door swung open, the excitement of departure beginning to grip them all. 'God knows what the valves are set for, we could wait all day trying to reach a pressure the designers may have wanted fifty years ago,' Stephen said at last. 'Jean, will you start her off? Lewis and I have to stoke until we get the hang of how to make her run.' He showed her a brass wheel and long notched lever. 'That lever is the main regulator, all you have to do is slam it over when I say. Then wind open the valve.'

Jean nodded, although the idea seemed truly monstrous that she should drive an engine of such size and weight, which once released would immediately romp away down the line beyond control. Come on, Grandad, she thought, and grasped that brass lever he might have fitted into place, we'll get out of here together. She smiled at the filthy, gasping men. 'Sorry I haven't brought champagne for the ceremony.'

'Iced water would be my choice,' Stephen observed, and joined Lewis again by the firebox. He looked even more exhausted than before, and shovelled with jerky, awkward swipes, whereas Lewis had almost instantly mastered the knack of how to throw fuel economically into the heart of the fire.

Jean's own sweat was beginning to chill as she watched the pressure needle creep slowly up its dial. Then, without warning, the main valve blew off with a roar, rocketing steam into the air. Gauges began to fall back and without waiting for Stephen's shout Jean slammed over the regulator and furiously began winding at the brass wheel. She glimpsed Lewis straining to ease off rusty brakes, but otherwise nothing happened. No forward movement at all, nothing.

She had been braced for a lurch, expected this damned great heap of iron to take charge of them all, and wondered panic-stricken what they had done wrong. Then, slowly, the pistons began to turn, the noise of escaping steam changed pitch, wheels jolted into motion: metal shrieked on metal and all Mezak's hillmen screamed at once in their wagon as steam fought the inertia of God knew how many sluggish tons. When it began to win, that same dead weight kicked all the way up the couplings from behind.

'Close her down a bit,' Stephen said, quite quietly, by her side. A fearful impression of speed swooping out of nowhere now. Scrub, buff-coloured earth, station buildings tearing past, all three of them grinning with relief when winding down that valve slowed their pace to a manageable crawl. And, as soon as they were moving, Jean admitted to herself that several times she had not expected to leave Hamada alive. At least if she died now it wouldn't be hunted like a rat through rotting sacks of flour.

At first their train gasped jerkily past tin and concrete warehouses, huts, rusting machinery, squalor relieved only by a few bright colours. Whooping children ran alongside, adults watched from their doorways and probably thought about Forla's returning troops. But, quite quickly, the town was left behind and the track ran between dry denuded hillocks shimmering into white haze where unseen salt pans stretched along the coast. After several miles of experimentation, gradually they worked up speed again, Jean leaning professionally over the cabside trying to spot possible obstructions and revelling in slipstream breeze, however hot and gritty.

'You okay?' Lewis came over and put his arm around her shoulders.

Jean patted the steel bulkhead. 'Wonderful. I told you Swindon engineering would see us out.'

'The bet was all the way to Kosti.' His long hard body was tight against hers from knee to breast; or maybe hers was tight against his, triumph an instinctive catalyst of the senses. But when she looked up at him, smiling, his eyes were fixed where Stephen was still stoking, willing him to turn and observe one hell of a guy called Anderson grab a woman in his first spare moment after hijacking a train.

Disconcerted, annoyed with both herself and him, Jean drew back. 'Pressure falls pretty fast if only one of you stokes.'

'We have to spell each other sometime, I guess.' He leaned out beside her. 'Jesus, you could almost imagine this wind is cool.'

'All right, you keep watch and I'll help stoke,' she said, irritated, and pushed away from him with such determination he was taken by surprise.

Stephen turned as she picked up the other shovel. 'There's

some timber to feed in. Tonight you can take a turn at keeping the firebox warm.'

'Tonight?' She began throwing jagged blocks which looked as if they had come from a dismantled building into the fire. Trees had vanished from the Manangan plain long ago.

'I wouldn't be able to stay on my feet until we reach Kosti, and we need to take on water before beginning to climb. There's no road near the only water tower on this stretch of track, it ought to be safe to stay a few hours.'

Clang ... shovel ... clang ... rake out ... clang. Throw in wood. As an art, synchronised stoking wasn't easily learned, the hungry heart of a firebox radiated molten heat each time its door was swung open, dull enervating heat while it was shut, and Stephen Retz was too tired to learn. He also looked a man more used to planning tasks for others to execute than physically labouring at them himself. Swindon Engine Works had also designed their locomotive boilers for high grade coking coal, not wood and dust swept off a dock; the result, a great deal of effort for a pressure barely adequate to keep them moving.

'Look!' shouted Lewis, the interruption so dizzily welcome that at first Jean only gulped air in relief. When she looked over the side of the cab she saw he was pointing at unexpected flashes of sun half-way up a distant slope. It took several seconds to grasp that those flashes must be windscreens ... a whole column of windscreens bumping down the miniature cliff which here divided the plain from the salt pans. 'Forla's troops on their way back to enjoy themselves in Hamada,' Lewis said grimly.

Stephen nodded, his face unreadable, his eyes narrowed against the evening glare.

'But your conscience won't so much as twitch now you see them on their way?'

He didn't answer.

'What do you think they'll make of a train going up the Man-anga City track?'

'Maybe nothing, yet. These are the sweepings of one of the world's worst armies, and Forla doesn't encourage independent thought. If they hear eventually that freight has been shipped to the hills instead of into Forla's market they'll radio the information on.'

'And you still say we hole up tonight? You must be crazy. We have to use the time we've got to get clear before someone sends troops to intercept us.'

'I agree. Unfortunately, I can't last to Kosti without some sleep. Anyway, our fuel needs shifting forward in the tender and we have to pick up water. I guess we just have to chance those extra hours we need or risk fouling things up because I can't think straight.' He rubbed a hand absently across the sunken bones of his face, his eyes still on those distant windscreens.

'I suppose no one else's brain is worth a shit,' Lewis exclaimed angrily.

'If you really wanted to get this load up to Kosti, then yours would be as good or better than mine. But if I have to watch you as well as learn how to nurse a freight train up all those gradients I need the use of my senses.'

'Mezak's gooks can shift the fuel. They can stoke, too, goddammit. Why should we sweat while they put their feet up? If they did some work for a change we could be out of that siding inside an hour,' said Lewis stubbornly.

'They'll shift it if I ask and show them how, but they can't stoke. They'd be like puppies underfoot when all their lives have been spent in a valley where even trucks are pretty rare.'

'Any fool can swing a shovel.'

'Sure, but this is too unfamiliar in a hurry. They'd be as likely to worship a fire which is a thousand times hotter than anything they've ever seen, and think it sacrilege to stoke it.' He wiped his face again, savagely, as if to force those senses of his to stay where they belonged, and went back to the firebox, where the pressure gauge was already dropping fast.

Jean went back to watching while Lewis helped to shovel again, watched him increase the pace and repeatedly force the older man to miss his aim, and send a shovelful of coal skittering across the floor. But the gauge swung sharply upwards and without being asked Jean wound the brass wheel fully open again; so far as she was concerned the sooner they reached this siding where they could rest, the better.

By then they had left all traces of salt behind and the plain beyond was slowly becoming rockier, the hills Jean had seen as a hazy outline slowly hardening against the evening sky. They steamed across several unsafe-looking bridges above dry gullies, even passed the occasional desiccated tree, as if Mananga had once known more reliable rains, but no other sign of life at all. No trails made by animals or humans, no birds, only an occasional whirling dust-devil in the distance.

Soon Jean was praying for that infernal siding to come in sight before the light faded completely: at this speed they must have eaten up a hundred miles by now, surely. Twice she suggested taking over stoking from Stephen, during this last stretch they ought to be able to manage on less pressure after all, but he refused. 'Once I sleep I shan't even kick awake for a while. It shouldn't be too far now.'

She opened her mouth to argue, intercepted a look from Lewis which was a mixture of jealousy and suspicion, and shut it again. One thing they most certainly could not afford was a brawl which Lewis inevitably would win.

A fierce red sky was flaring in the west before she decided finally that what she saw wasn't another skeleton tree. 'I think we're there.'

Lewis came over. 'Yeah, that must be it.' He pulled back the regulator, hauled on the brakes, but without any particular effect, and Jean couldn't help thinking about crawling up gradients to-morrow when, if their brakes failed to work, their only anchor would be their locomotive's ability to keep slowly puffing upward; but she was too tired really to care. A day which had begun with tenuous recovery from semi-concussion was ending with the return of a splitting headache which would soon tip her senses, too, into oblivion.

They overshot the water tower by a quarter of a mile, which meant they had to learn how to shunt back, followed by a weary search for the key which allowed Lewis to slam over the points into the siding. When they came to rest at last, Jean leaned over the side of the cab feeling dizziness reach out of heat which settled everywhere like wool the moment their forward motion ceased. I ought to cook, she thought vaguely. While the firebox isn't needed I could use it to cook something really edible.

She ought to, but she couldn't. She climbed down a step at a time and stood staring around her, physically unable to do another thing. Stephen stumbled past to open up Mezak's wagon, revealing a huddle of misery inside. Excited, shouting hillmen at the beginning of the journey had become a collection of sick and frightened ghosts; the swaying of the wagon worse than a big dipper to men used mostly to travelling on foot. Only Mezak emerged with his dignity intact: grey-faced and unsteady, but poised to kill anyone who dared to sympathise.

Already Lewis had climbed the stilts beside the siding on which rested a flat metal tank, and was learning how to pump up water from some unseen source, as if to prove how little time they needed to waste here. Well, let him get on with it, Jean thought vaguely. She needed a rest. Stephen Retz needed rest. Now Mezak's men looked as if they might die if they were kept away from fresh air and stillness a single moment longer.

All she hoped was that Lewis didn't drive the train away during the night.

7

JEAN woke to discover it was still dark, and lay staring at struts against the sky. A crane over wire, she thought, confused, before realising she was lying under a water tower somewhere in the Republic of Mananga. A slice of sky and a couple of bright stars peered back at her from between tank and struts, and the gentle sigh of steam could be heard close at hand. She stretched cautiously, relieved that her body felt as if it belonged to her again, her headache caged into the far recesses of her brain; her most immediate thought that she must look even worse than yesterday, when she had been shocked by that glimpse of herself in the mirror. If that tower still held some water then she couldn't have woken in a better place.

She felt around until she found some rungs, climbed up and reached inside the tank, delighted when the tips of her fingers touched water. Lewis must have pumped up more than the boiler could accept; and how impossible in ordinary life to imagine the sheer sensuous pleasure of stripping off filthy clothes and soaking in eighteen inches of gritty water, of rinsing hair and clothes while remembering to avoid more than minimal sounds. A solitary naked woman here would belong to the man who found her, and yet she never remembered a risk more infinitely worth while.

The element of danger, the vast strange starlit night and cooler temperature all increased her sense of unreality. Here predators prowled and the world returned to its primitive menace and enchantments; by the time she dressed again in sodden clothes, Jean could almost have imagined that the locomotive lazily leaking steam was some prehistoric monster basking in a swamp.

At the foot of the tower she encountered Lewis, his eyes flicking instantly to her wet clothes, his expression changing as he realised that he had missed her bathing by perhaps a couple of minutes.

'Hallo,' she said, and smiled at that expression.

'And hi to you. Do you often walk around dripping wet?'

'I'll dry by the firebox. It must be my turn to keep up steam and I thought I'd cook a meal while I can.'

'That's my Jean,' he said, and laughed.

Her whole body tried to jackknife as he kissed her, but he was too strong. Lewis had remembered both her wiry strength and how instinctively she had responded to him the day before, and wasn't taking any chances. He reckoned she was willing and best not given time to think about anything besides their mutual need. His mouth was hungrily on hers, his hands offering caresses as well as uncompromising strength.

But those hands and mouth were suddenly snatched away so fast she nearly fell, Lewis swearing and half swung round by shock.

'Steve tell to watch you, big bastard,' Mezak said pleasantly, and eased his knife a fraction deeper into Lewis's back.

Lewis sucked in his breath but did not dare turn further. 'Take it out or I'll kill you.'

Mezak snapped his fingers at Jean. 'Go, woman.'

Jean went, the primitive command welcome in a primitive situation, and more shaken than she cared to admit, which, she told herself firmly, was absurd. She liked Lewis. And why kid herself any longer? She had come to Mananga because it represented a personal breakout from a long and irksome prison. She was used to looking after herself; you needed to be, in inner city hospitals. Then she shrugged; fear wasn't something you could rationalise, nor the death of liking between one moment and the next.

Suddenly it became naggingly unpleasant to search for food through loaded wagons in the dark, to step over sleeping men and hear sand rustle as one after another they stood up to watch her. Well, if Mezak was prepared to knife Lewis because Stephen Retz asked him to, he would certainly knife any of his own followers who stepped out of line, she reflected, annoyed by her own cowardice. Which, when she faced it squarely, was what alarmed her most, the prospect of being fought over by hostile, temperamentally intolerant men, her only value as a trophy for the winner.

She found some agreeably different food, though; a large rusted tin of potatoes, six smaller ones of pease pudding and two of Scottish haggis, together with an untouched crate of tinned jam roll. Jean found herself imagining some phantom British presence abandoning its more inedible rations in the heat of Hamada, there to gain such a nauseating reputation that the remnants remained immune to theft for years.

But anything which wasn't corned beef or flour was welcome. She heaved a selection of tins on to the footplate and, when she climbed up herself, found Lewis morosely feeding the firebox. It was an awkward meeting, made easier by the difficulties of trying to heat a meal on a shovel thrust into glowing embers.

'Do you suppose Mezak and his men will prepare their own food?' Jean asked, into the silence. If the relatively sophisticated inhabitants of Hamada had shunned jam roll and haggis, then she couldn't imagine Mezak touching them.

'The bastards can starve for all I care,' he answered, scowling. 'Christ, how much longer are we going to sit on our butts wasting time and fuel?'

Jean was beginning to feel on edge herself. After all, they had only escaped from Hamada half a day ahead of Forla's reoccupying troops, who were bound to hear that a loaded train had gone up the line, and decide eventually that this was worth reporting. When she climbed down again to fetch a can of water she was glad to see two camp fires lit, with men starting to gather around them, the scent of cooking sharp on the night air.

'It looks as if we might soon be off,' she said, returning to the footplate. By then she had decided that Retz had probably set Mezak to watch Lewis to make sure he didn't steal the train, and felt in consequence rather more cheerful about it.

Lewis stared at the mess she was mixing on the shovel. 'Jesus, are you sure we won't all die of food poisoning, or do you Brits always live on stuff that looks like pus and shit?'

'Always,' Jean said, firmly. 'That's why we have such good complexions.'

71

The fire was dulling rapidly while she needed the door open, yet it was fiercely hot trying to stir stew on a shovel. Those cans were old, and she didn't fancy eating the contents without some pretty thorough cooking.

'Hurry it up, will you? The gauge is practically back on the floor,' said Lewis irritably.

'It's nearly done. Don't you think someone ought to go and rouse Stephen?'

'If I knew where the bastard was I'd have kicked his ass a couple of hours ago, but he's taken the goddamn points key and vanished into the bush, leaving us as sitting ducks until he decides to crawl out of a hole someplace.'

So Stephen had not relied only on Mezak to make sure their train did not vanish in the night, and they were stuck until he reappeared. Since Mananga was as renowned for banditry and guerrillas as for misgovernment, Lewis might be justified in considering this a fairly selfish solution to one man's need for undisturbed rest.

'I expect Mezak knows where he is,' she said aloud.

'If he does, he isn't telling.' With sudden frustration Lewis slammed the flat of a shovel against the side of the cab, the sound like a mighty gong in the stillness, bringing figures around their camp fires leaping to their feet in alarm. 'Jean—'

'Yes?' Carefully, she withdrew stew from the firebox. 'It may look disgusting but it doesn't smell too bad. Should I go and ask Mezak if he'll please wake Stephen, do you think?'

Lewis's expression softened and he gripped her shoulder, hard. 'Jean ... I'm sorry if I startled you back there. But we've been around each other quite a while and I hoped you felt good about it too. I didn't expect you to get upset, when my guess is we both want the same thing, and fast.'

She started to laugh. 'Of course, why should I get upset? If we did happen to want the same thing. Fast, of course.'

But, abruptly, he was infuriated by laughter. 'You're behaving like some silly small-town virgin, and you know it. You come to Mananga where people are wiped in the dust if their dictator sneezes, and unless you snatch some pleasure fast then tomorrow you could be wiped out too. We'd have a good time together if you would only relax and let me try — and not only here. I swear I can get you out of this mess, if not one way then another, and after-

72

wards we'll fly someplace like California for a while, where all we have to think about is ourselves.'

Jean stared across the narrow cab at him, and discovered she was actually tempted for a moment. Food for the starving in Mananga, the clinic where she could help lessen a few of its many miseries, of no account beside the hunger of her senses. On his own terms, Lewis would be a sensuously satisfying companion; together, they most probably would have fun and no hard feelings when they parted. Then she shrugged and carefully put down the shovel full of stew which she was holding. 'I'll go and see if Mezak is willing to roust Stephen out.'

She did not need to go far; already dawn was close and she was able to see two figures talking earnestly by the water tower. She waited, knowing Mezak's disdain for women, until he left to start herding his men back on board a train they now regarded with understandable loathing.

'We began to wonder if you'd got lost,' she said then to Stephen.

'If I have to sleep while Anderson is around, I prefer to do it out of sight.' He sounded quite different, vigorous and alert, and had also bathed in the tank.

They began raising steam soon after, and if neither Stephen nor Lewis precisely complimented Jean on her cooking — and it did taste very strange — they all felt immensely better for a satisfying meal at last.

The dawn was spectacular even by Manangan standards, gold and violet streaked with electric green. 'Storm season coming up,' observed Lewis.

Their train eased back on the main track as the sun flashed above the horizon, the morning feeling wonderfully cool as their speed increased. No one spoke of the day to come, when stoking through noontime heat up steepening inclines would be a labour straight out of hell itself.

Indeed, Stephen and Lewis seldom spoke at all while spelling each other at the firebox, this stage of their journey almost ludicrously humdrum.

'Has Mananga any air force?' Jean asked suddenly, some time later.

'A few old British and Russian fighters, and a squadron of heli-copters,' Stephen answered. 'They're always short of spares and the pilots moonlight on their own account as well as Forla's, smuggling all over the place. One or two helicopters are usually available for duty if anyone wants them badly enough.'

'Then won't they come looking for us as soon as the alarm goes out?'

'I'm hoping no one will give one train among the half-dozen or so Forla has run this past week too much thought for quite a while. Manangan bureaucracy takes one hell of a time to react.'

'We'd have to be pretty lucky for it not to react all the way up the Kosti, don't you think?'

'That wouldn't be luck, it would be a fucking miracle,' Lewis interjected. Like Jean, he was looking up at the sky, alarmed by a threat neither had previously considered.

'I don't think so, no.' Stephen was maddeningly offhand. 'But even if it should ... well, I flew in one of their helicopters and I've never been so frightened in my life. Provided we reach the higher hills I don't think they have too many pilots capable of hovering accurately enough in the kind of downdraughts this heat produces to do much damage with cannon or machine-guns. They don't have any gunships.'

Jean looked at him speculatively. If Stephen Retz had been frightened in Mananga's helicopters then they must be lethal, she thought. But often after that she found herself looking into the dazzle away to the south, the direction from which any aircraft would come and with very little warning.

All morning they clacked uneventfully across a plain dotted with little prickly trees. The steam gauge remained steady, the sky empty; there were no more crumbling bridges. Jean almost began to feel bored, as if a change from tedium might be pleasant rather than a split-second plunge back into danger.

It was as they began on the sharp curve back towards the hills, which had drawn noticeably closer behind shifting layers of dust, that Lewis drew Jean aside and said, low-voiced, 'I aim to quit this teakettle maybe another half-hour up the line and if you've changed your mind I'd—what I mean is, I'd be very happy if you would come along. I reckon we could reach the frontier in three or four nights. Sure, it's a tough hike, but a darn sight safer than heaving chunks of timber while waiting to be bombed. Of course that crazy sonofabitch knew that if the Manangan air force fly all over the place smuggling, they can reach a railroad when it suits them.

Sometime today they'll be here, and if they don't hit us or the track they'll come again until they do.'

'One man can't stoke alone when the gradients begin,' Jean said flatly. 'If we both leave, then somewhere this train has to stall. You know the brakes won't hold such a load, so it will start slipping back. The passengers might jump clear, but all the food and medicines would be lost.'

'There's Mezak and his gooks. Like I said, let them stoke.'

'Stephen didn't think they could, and Mezak seems willing to do most things for him.' She watched, quite detached from temptation now, as his face tightened at this allusion to Mezak coolly inserting a knife in his back.

'Then he'd better tell them that if they want to live, they stop behaving like prima donnas,' he snapped. 'Christ, it's not my fault if Retz chose to take out a train with only monkeys as hired help. The bastard deserves to jump off a cliff when it stalls someplace on a gradient.'

He knows, Jean thought with a pang. He knows exactly what must happen if we both pull out.

'We're losing steam.' Stephen's voice prevented the need for a reply and she wondered how much he had overheard as anger sharpened their voices.

'It's hot for a guy your age to keep stoking long. Here, watch me lift that goddamn gauge.' Lewis began slinging in fuel with conscious, graceful power.

The steam gauge hesitated and then continued its drop towards the etched danger line.

'There's water leaking out somewhere.' Stephen pointed to a brass arrow levered directly from the boiler. It, too, had dropped quite sharply.

'There's your answer, then. How far to the next water tower?'

'Kosti.'

'You'll never get this heap up there with a leak in its boiler.' Lewis straightened and grinned at Jean. 'Pay your ten dollar bet and hike to the frontier, or wait like a decoy duck for Forla's air force to arrive. There aren't too many downdraughts to spoil their aim around here.'

Stephen stared at that water dial and then back at the pressure gauge, frowning. He looked better than the day before, but already worn down by the effort of feeding that voracious boiler in punishing heat, his body little more than skin and sinew beside brawny, triumphant Lewis. Whether he liked it or not, he had to accept insult or lose a fight his adversary would enjoy; on the other hand, those calculating eyes and tightset mouth suggested a man only a fool would provoke. 'If we are losing water, and that dial says we are, I'd expect pressure to rise for a while, not fall,' he said at last, and went over to jerk the regulator back out of its notch.

'Hey!' shouted Lewis. 'We need to use the steam we have, not waste it.'

But the locomotive wheels were already slowing their beat, coupled wagons shuddering and clinking as traction was lost.

Stephen squatted in front of the firebox to peer inside, his sweat instantly beaded scarlet. He grunted and drew back. 'Yes. Look. There's a plug leaking in there, you can see it hissing.'

Lewis hesitated and then stooped too, all three of them studying what looked like a large, shaped bolt which was hissing water where no water should go, the fire dulling and steaming where it reached. 'I suppose it's hardly ever been maintained,' Jean said defensively; ludicrous that her first reaction should be to feel responsible for an engine which might, or might not, have been manufactured by her grandfather, when this surely spelled disaster for them all.

'As any fool would have known.' Lewis reached for the regulator. 'So let's use what steam we have while it lasts. I measured the closest point to the frontier, and it's near where the hills begin. If we can save an extra night's hike by reaching there under power, it'll make the hell of a difference.'

'Stay away from those controls.' Stephen picked up one of the bars used for raking the fire. 'The longer we leave that leak the more water we lose, as well as pressure. Those plugs are there for a purpose, draining down to clean the boiler tubes maybe. If one leaks, then it can be driven tight again.'

'Oh sure,' said Lewis sarcastically. 'Wait the rest of the day for the firebox to cool and there won't be any water left at all. Or pressure. Not to mention Forla's air force bombing us to hell and back, stopped in the middle of an empty plain. Get out of my way, will you? Because if you won't stoke then I can manage alone until we reach where we need to go.'

'No,' said Stephen again. Slowly the train was sidling to a halt. 'Jean, get Mezak here, will you?'

'You keep him out of this. Sure, he can hold a knife in my back.

It doesn't alter the fact we start hiking now, or else use what's left of our steam to get us closer to the frontier.'

'Get Mezak, Jean,' Stephen repeated, and shifted his grip on the firebar, adding to Lewis, 'I'll break your arm if you touch anything. You won't reach anywhere trailing broken bones in the heat.'

Jean dropped down on the ground. Precious time was being wasted in useless argument, although this time she agreed with Lewis. If they did have to walk to the frontier after all, it made sense to use whatever steam was left to cover as much ground as possible. But Retz was so obsessed by reaching Kosti, he seemed incapable of seeing that a scheme which had looked pretty doomed from the outset finally lay in ruins.

Mezak came willingly as far as the ground below the cab, but showed no inclination to climb up. 'What you want, Steve?'

As an answer, Lewis was shoved out on the step at the point of Stephen's firebar. 'Keep him safe until I say, will you?'

'I keep.' Mezak hauled Lewis unceremoniously to the ground, grinning. 'Stand still, big bastard.'

Stephen looked down from the cab. 'Don't rely on Mezak not to knife you just because I asked him to keep you safe. You do anything stupid, like swatting at a fly when he tells you to stay still, and you could lose a hand.'

Lewis stood up slowly, stared first at Mezak and then up at Stephen. 'You fucking maniac. I might have known you would hide behind someone else's knife. You realise an aircraft could come out of the sun any moment, while we're stalled here squabbling?'

'Yes,' said Stephen curtly. 'Jean, have you got bandages and dressings in that medical grip of yours?'

She nodded, beginning to wonder whether Lewis was right to call this apparently rational man a maniac.

'Break them out, will you? And fetch another can of water.'

She hesitated, then brought her satchel from where she had wedged it out of the way, and climbed down again to fetch the water. When she returned Stephen was poking at ash and dulling flames in the firebox; he looked collected enough and intent on what he was doing.

He stood up when he heard her, picked his and Lewis's shirts out of the corner where they had been flung while they stoked. 'Make these good and wet but go easy with that water.'

She dribbled water on the shirts, and couldn't resist pressing her face in dampness for an instant, filthy as they were. 'If I promise not to say you must be crazy, will you please tell me what you're doing?'

Swiftly, he was wrapping the wet shirts around his neck and across his back. 'Now use some of your bandages to tie pads of whatever you can find across my arms. I'm going to try and drive that plug back in.'

'*You're what?* You can't! It'll take hours for the firebox to cool enough for you to be safe inside!'

'I don't think so, if I'm quick.'

'You'll kill yourself,' she stammered. 'Your lungs will burn out and then you'll fall into that fire. Believe me, I know what that sort of heat can do. I've seen enough ruined bodies after they've been cut out of burning cars.'

He took the wad of bandaging from her and began winding it up his arm in precise quick flicks, anchoring the shirt up to his neck before beginning to fumble left-handed with his other arm. 'It's the only way not to lose all our pressure and most of our water. I've raked the fire right back, it's lucky the leak is near the door.'

Reluctantly, Jean took over swathing his right arm; he was going in anyway and showed no sign of listening to anyone besides himself, so she might as well make sure that unskilful bandaging did not leave a single gap of skin. 'Here,' she stripped off her own shirt, wrapped it around his hands where he gripped a firebar, poured more water all over him without caring about waste. 'Please ... I never helped kill a man before.'

'My life is my own,' he answered, and as he turned the glow of fire turned his eyes to charred, black pits. He hesitated just for an instant, then took a deep breath before lifting a pad of gauze over his mouth and nose, and ducked down through the narrow fire-door. Only so slight a man could have avoided touching searing metal. Jean glimpsed the steam gauge still showing nearly two hundred pounds of pressure and fell on her knees beside that door, where solid heat was thrown in her face, even from a raked back and dulling fire. Stephen was bent nearly double in that blisteringly confined space, very delicately tapping at the leaking plug. Once ... twice ... then a harder, driven blow.

Steam rising from his body, wrappings singeing while she

78

watched, and then he was back at the entry, fumbling to step high enough to avoid touching hot metal coaming, but sufficiently unsteady to brush equally hot steel sides when he tried. Stripped of her shirt, Jean reached bare arms into furnace heat, gripped crinkle-dry cloth and hauled, so that they both sprawled together on the cool metal floor.

Jean rolled instantly free, grabbed the can of water and poured it over Stephen's face and chest, over her own stinging arms. As the steam cleared his eyes opened on the glimmer of a smile. 'I remember asking you to go easy on the water.'

'Can you breathe all right?'

Still lying flat, his chest lifted and fell. 'Sure. It was quicker than it seemed.' His hand lifted and touched her arm. 'You're the one who is burned, not me.'

She had only felt the sting of heat before, now, as shock receded, her upper arm began to flare. 'The modern treatment for burns is gallons of cold running water. I've got a spray which will help.'

'Cover it in this climate,' he said roughly, and came to his knees, then to his feet again. Holding the side of the cab, he stooped to look inside the firebox.

'Is it all right?'

'I think ... yes, probably.' He fumbled in her pack, pulled out a spare shirt and tore off one sleeve to make it fit more easily over her scorched arm, 'Put this on and I'll call Anderson back up to start stoking again.' His lips just touched her cheek, more in courtesy than tenderness. 'Thank you.'

He didn't sound particularly grateful for being helped, Jean thought. The wrappings on his back and arms were crisped by heat, his forehead, nose and neck were scorched, but he seemed to have taken astonishingly little harm. Looking back at what had seemed an endless time while she watched him char, Jean decided he must have been inside that firebox less than thirty seconds. In. Three strokes with a bar. Out. Precise, disciplined movements in a situation where every instinct shrieked in panic.

As for herself, she sprayed her arm, went to sit out of the way in the tender and closed her eyes while the pain gradually subsided. She, too, had been quick enough only to scorch, but the moment she sat, shock made her drowsy. Or was it God knew how many disturbed nights, the atmosphere of hate and menace? Her headache, too, had begun again to niggle at the back of her skull.

79

She roused to yet more quarrelling voices; how intensely she had begun to long for peace! Unimaginable, now, that she should have come to Mananga looking for excitement after all those years of tedium and denial.

Very distinctly, she heard Lewis say, 'Get out from behind Mezak's knife and I'll kill you.'

He would, she thought. After today I really think he would, and she struggled closer to awareness.

Not long after that she felt the welcome clack of rails as, steam restored, the train pulled away again, a faint, enormously welcome breeze finally rousing her completely.

Stephen came over to where she was finishing bandaging her arm. The skin was red and shiny but not broken. 'Can I help?'

'It's fixed.'

'Sure?'

She nodded. 'How about you?'

'I could use some spray on a few blisters.'

She handed it over, sensing that he preferred to tend himself. 'Is Mezak still watching Lewis?'

In the shifting light of sun, smoke and fire, she wasn't sure whether he smiled or not. 'Mezak doesn't care for the footplate of a locomotive.'

'I heard Lewis say he'd kill you, and don't pretend he didn't mean it.'

'I won't. He also wants to reach the frontier and even a fight he won wouldn't improve his chances. I'm watching my back, don't worry.'

They hit the first gradient not long afterwards, their speed slowing until they seemed to crawl through blazing noonday heat. The cab became an inferno, Stephen and Lewis stoking in alternate fast bursts, Jean taking spells of flinging in timber and raking fuel forward in the tender. They were all filthy and exhausted when Lewis, after resting briefly, stretched and began washing in the drain of water still left in the can. 'I'm leaving now,' he said to Jean. 'Sure you won't change your mind?' He no longer expected her to, she could see, and this was another rancorous grudge against Stephen Retz rather than herself.

'Quite sure.'

'It only needs one bomb on the track to stop you. And the deeper you go into the hills from here, the further you are from the frontier. When you have to bale out, they'll also know exactly where to look.'

Jean shook her head without answering.

'Once I've gone, don't rely on Retz to see you safe. All he thinks about are his own crazy schemes.'

Unexpectedly, she smiled. 'I came here intending to look after myself, although I admit Mananga's different to anything I expected.'

'I bet.' He drained the last drops of water into his mouth and then, in the same movement, whirled around, stiff-armed, with the can still in his hand. A skull-crushing blow, delivered without any warning at all where Stephen was shovelling coal dust off the floor.

Jean's shout of warning and the clang of metal were instantaneous as Stephen flung up the shovel to protect his head; though he must have been watching Lewis out of the corner of his eye, a lightning-swift recoil was the only possible defence.

The two men stood facing each other across the smoke-filled cab, each breathing with the quick hard strokes of fury, existence narrowed to eye and arm and makeshift weapon. The light was deceptive, the space confined, rust-edged metal a cruel weapon at such close quarters. In another violent movement, Lewis threw the can he still held straight at Stephen's face and, as he ducked, grabbed a firebar from where it was clipped against a bulkhead.

A single mistake and the price most probably would be death, if not instantly then from infection later, in these conditions. Both men were now moving cautiously, as if those first savage blows had cauterised Lewis's rage and left him coolly ready to take advantage of any opening his enemy might offer. Because, while Stephen possessed the natural fast reactions of an intelligent man, he lacked almost everything else he needed to defend himself against a toughly muscled enemy possessed by bitter hatred.

Jean's thoughts were frozen by her eyes as she watched them, a mortal quarrel the very worst thing to happen when they should have been concentrating every fibre on taking food to the starving and outwitting Forla. That it had happened was somehow symptomatic of everything which had been wrong with this journey from the beginning. Yet all she could do was stand aside, wrung with futile rage. If she moved now, then the distraction of movement alone could kill one man or the other. Lewis, particularly, would consider that he had given her every chance to step back from madness, and his rankling sense of jealousy alone might make him try to use her if he could.

She saw Stephen whip taut as he again used his shovel, this time to block a driving blow from Lewis's firebar, metal screeching on metal, breathing raucous in the smoke, concentration a weird, almost visible thing. Slowly but inexorably the edge of Stephen's shovel was being forced up and to one side, a fraction at a time. Sweat was pouring off both faces, into their eyes, gathering on jaw and collarbone. Soon Stephen would have to give way completely, that firebar rasp past his guard to plunge into flesh beyond.

Jean had just decided that she could not wait another second before risking a move when there was another slithering whine, Stephen's last despairing move still so fast it nearly deceived the eye. Nearly, but not quite. Instead of waiting to have his guard forced aside, he had disengaged with such suddenness that Lewis stumbled almost to his knees. But somehow he recovered, and pivoted to deliver a killing, final blow. As he did so Stephen struck downwards, brutally hard and directly at his feet. He leapt aside with a yell, and since he was wearing boots was less hurt than he ought to have been.

Both men fell back a pace, watching each other through eyes stripped naked by fear and fury, throat muscles knotting as lungs gasped for air. Then Lewis's teeth showed in a smile and he went straight back into the attack, the bar in his hand thrust into Stephen's face and, as he jumped aside, a single smooth movement drove it underarm instead, directly into his enemy's unguarded stomach.

And found it guarded. Already off balance as he avoided the strike at his head, Stephen took the fractional chance remaining and dropped his shovel, freeing his hands for a snatch at that driven bar, somehow to grab and deflect it from his stomach, but at the cost of seeing it waver up towards his ribs ... his neck ... both men with their hands locked on that bar, Lewis's superior strength jerking the point inch by inch towards Stephen's throat.

Stephen's eyes were blank above ashen bones as he arched back and further back to keep that point from the soft tissues of his neck. Lewis was relaxing and straddling his feet wider to gain the leverage he needed, swinging Stephen around bodily like a gaffed fish when he saw Jean try to reach the shovel Stephen had dropped, the effort bringing dark blood into his face, the smile back on his lips.

She dodged and stumbled into a steel bulkhead, the shovel kicked out of reach. Instead, she grabbed a chunk of wood from the tender and hurled it into Lewis's face; when he jerked aside with a curse the movement enabled Stephen to thrust the bar point sideways, past his throat and over his shoulder, to strike a spark where it hit metal. Then, freed from that instant threat of death, he dropped his grip on the bar and fell on one knee, perhaps the only movement he remained capable of making, seized one of Lewis's ankles with both hands and jerked. Even then Lewis was able to use his weight savagely and by intent, twisting so as to drop heavily across Stephen instead of on to the steel floor, slamming the breath out of him; grunting with satisfaction as his knee drove deep below softly yielding ribs.

He had won.

'I told you to keep out of my way,' he said, and settled with delicate pleasure to the task of forcing back Stephen Retz's head until the neckbones snapped.

Jean hit him with the water can while his absorption was complete, the force of it sending him sprawling but without taking his senses, since the can was empty. And in that moment she knew that their best hope of safety lay in hitting him again and again until his skull crumpled. He and Stephen had fought for a variety of reasons, most of which she thought absurd; what he would regard as her defection made him the implacable enemy of them both.

But though the thought came it was discarded, leaving her scarcely aware it had been there. As he climbed to his feet again she hit him once more, clinically hard with the edge of the can deliberately used. She might not want to kill him, but felt no pity either. He fell back, moaning, this time out of action for the time she needed to try to revive Stephen. There was no water in the cab, so she used the stinging freshness of spirit from her medical kit instead. And nearly unconscious though he was, above all from Lewis's knee driven brutally against collapsing lungs, he, too, understood the need for urgency. As soon as his eyes opened Jean saw them shift, harden and focus where Lewis stirred again already: retching drily in fumes from the firebox and a hand pressed where the can edge had cut his scalp. Two minutes more of safety, definitely not more than three, she thought, and turned back to Stephen.

Mercifully, where he lay the air was clearer, though it was difficult all the same to pick out husky words from greedily gulping lungs. 'Take off the regulator. Brake.'

As soon as we stop I'll get Mezak, she thought. But no; she would never persuade him to climb up where a monster brewed its magical fires. The brakes were steam driven, leaking, almost useless, and even here only just managed to prevent them from slipping back. Jean was astonished to discover that during the few minutes of the fight they had at last reached the hills after so long journeying across featureless plain.

Both Lewis and Stephen were standing again when she turned, a hand each on the cabside for support, Lewis still shaking his head as if trying to clear it. Concussion and double vision, she thought, pleased. That ought to give us time to kick him out.

Stephen seemed to have the same idea, moved very awkwardly into the tender and came back with Mezak's revolver which he had used in Hamada. He must have cached it where Lewis couldn't find it, but where he hadn't been able to reach it in an emergency, either. 'Get down out of here,' he said thickly.

'I'm sick,' Lewis mumbled.

'Lie up tonight and you'll be all right,' Jean said brusquely. 'If you stand back I'll make up a pack for you to take.'

'Yeah, it took two to beat me and cowards prefer to leave their victims for the vultures to pick clean.' He had stopped holding his head and begun calculating some fresh possibilities.

'Christ,' said Stephen wearily. 'Get out, will you, while we're still laughing at the movie. You don't want to come to Kosti, you were about to light out on your own before. So climb down off this cab and start hiking.'

Lewis made a sudden wordless sound, but climbed down to stand beside the track looking up. 'I'd like to say you only saved that neck of yours until next time we meet, but I guess it's a waste of breath. Forla will do the job for me.'

He glanced up at the cloudless blue sky, and laughed.

8

'No,' said Jean furiously. 'You're bloody well going to rest whether you like it or not. I want to reach those hills alive, not get bombed or flayed alive by Forla because you're too tired to think. I told you, I was brought up on a farm. I can stoke a boiler if I have to, so long as nothing else seems to be happening. The only pity is I shall need you to tell Mezak what to do, otherwise I'd say at the moment we'd get through almost anything better if you slept right through it.'

'Thank you,' said Stephen icily.

'You know what I mean, and don't bother to explain that fighting a man twice your weight and ten years younger with a shovel is your scene because I shouldn't believe you.' She felt uptight and didn't see why she should mince words with an awkward bastard who imagined the world stopped spinning without his hand on its axis. And instead of listening to the few hoarse words which were all he could piece together, she began energetically shovelling fuel. When she turned she saw he was stiffly raking coal and wood where she could reach it; the first tender was nearly empty and using the second involved flinging down and forward what they needed.

It was filthy work and by the time he finished, argument was finished too. He collapsed across her pack and his, legs and arms sprawling as he fell. Thank heaven for that, she thought sourly; damned arrogant men, as vain and tiresome as brawling kids. She chuckled to herself; she would need Stephen Retz around and making sense if a single tube in that locomotive boiler malfunctioned. For the moment, however, she enjoyed being on her own. Forla, possible bombs and stoking a locomotive were simplicity itself compared to enduring the strain of two deeply antagonistic personalities who saw every circumstance as fresh cause for offence.

As the next hour passed without incident beyond the firebox's insatiable greed, her spirits rose still further. There were no aircraft in the unconcealing sky; no sign of guerrillas in the hills now closed in around them, nor of Stephen waking from his sleep. He would feel like he had tangled with a mincer when he woke, but his cure should be helped along by no longer needing to watch his back.

Strange that she should have felt Lewis's pull of physical attraction so strongly, yet be so relieved that he was gone. Stranger still that she had lived three weeks alongside him and not perceived any unusual dangers in his personality. Or had those dangers been spawned by Mananga, and was this same distortion in Stephen Retz as well, as he obsessively drove a trainload of food up railway track, into lorries, over mule trails to reach a valley he had only recently seen?

She straightened her back, wincing. No point wondering so far as Lewis Anderson was concerned, since she was unlikely ever to see him again. As for Stephen, by accident her future had become bound up with this man she did not know, and there was nothing she could do about it. In Hamada, two men rather than one had offered her a choice, here most likely there was none.

Meanwhile there were other matters to worry about. For instance, this locomotive was crawling slower and slower up a gradient which had become alarmingly steep. The track seemed rougher, too, some of the jolts almost bad enough to derail a wheel. Anxiously she looked at levers, dials and valve controls, wondering what the hell beyond mere shovelling she could do to encourage greater speed, but only her own ignorance stared back at her. By then she was incapable of stoking any faster, reeling with fatigue and desiccated by heat. When she tried, she felt her senses begin to slip, pain in her shoulders and raw hands all that prevented her from blacking out completely.

'My wits — or some of them — are back.' Dimly she recognised Stephen's newly unfamiliar croak. 'Your turn to enjoy the hardest floor I ever lay on.'

Jean never remembered answering, her voice, too, lost at the far end of that filament of pain. Nor did she sleep this time, but sat with her head on her knees drifting uncomfortably towards full consciousness again, aware that the clack of rails was slowing even further, the pall of smoke and dust quite awful once there was no slipstream to blow it clear of the cab.

'Are we going to make it?' Her voice was back where she could use it.

'There's less than a hundred yards to go before we're on the level again for a while. Yes, I hope so.'

Clack ... clack.

Clack ... steel screeching on steel as the wheels began to slip. If they began to slide backwards ... Jean stared at the brake handle, visualising all those leaking steam pipes and inadequate couplings under two tenders and a string of heavily laden freight wagons. Come on, you damned great heap of Swindon machinery; if only we knew how to fire you properly you could make it. All of a sudden she was filled by a fierce affection for wheezing, leaking, willing old 246711. But they didn't know how to stoke or control her properly, and so they were going to stop and begin to slip back without brakes to hold them, less than fifty yards from the summit of this climb.

Then, with a final gusty sigh they heaved past a crumbling wooden marker and began picking up speed again.

'We'll have to uncouple a wagon before we try the pull up to Kosti,' Stephen said, and gingerly applied the brake.

It felt enormously strange to leave the cramped and noisy cab, climb down on unfamiliar earth and walk through singing silence back along the length of the train. The air felt cool after the crushing heat of the plains and wind gusted out of higher hills all around. Scarlet-podded bushes grew here and there, and high on a distant ridge Jean could see a row of trees. 'This is much better than Hamada,' she said buoyantly. 'I don't think I'm a tropical person, really.'

'Perhaps it's that farm where you grew up.' Stephen was definitely more human now Lewis had gone.

'If you were honest you'd admit you damned well had to rest,' she said indignantly.

'Oh, sure. And you that driving a combine on some British farm doesn't compare to stoking locomotives in the heat.' They reached the last wagon and he crouched to strike up the coupling and disconnect it from the rest. He hesitated, then walked back to the next wagon, and began disconnecting that.

'Do we have to leave two behind?'

'I'm careful by nature, I guess. When I loaded up it seemed worth taking as much as we could, at least as far as the foothills. But the fuel's so poor even eleven flats are quite a load up that last slope to Kosti. Maybe someone can shunt back to pick them up later.'

Mezak stuck his head out as they walked back to the cab. 'Airplanes, Steve.'

'Where?' Panic instantly came racing back, and they strained their ears, squinting into the sun.

He flipped a hand. 'Kosti, I think.'

All Jean could hear was wind humming strongly off the hills and a nearer hiss of steam.

Stephen climbed up on Mezak's wagon and stood with him on the roof, listening. 'I'm not sure. Perhaps it could be aircraft.'

'I hear,' said Mezak haughtily.

'Look!' called Jean. 'Is that the way to Kosti?' She pointed over to the left where, beyond a distant ridge of hills, it was just possible to imagine thin smoke drifting into cloudless blue.

'No,' said Stephen slowly. 'Kosti must be nearly dead ahead. Now I wonder what —'

'That the way to our valley,' announced Mezak. 'Airplanes bomb King's Highway I think.'

'Let's get going,' said Stephen, climbing down. 'God knows why they've decided to bomb a goat track, but —'

'King's Highway,' interrupted Mezak, bristling.

'Sure, and your king did a fine job of engineering, until Forla and a few rulers before him let it disintegrate. I'd still like to know why Forla sent aircraft there.'

Mezak nodded graciously, acknowledging a compliment on behalf of dead kings. 'Forla like bombing anything.'

'I bet he does,' Stephen said to Jean as they slowly drew away from the two stranded wagons. 'What bothers me is that there's something between Kosti Town and the hills which he thought worth bombing.'

Now their locomotive was pulling two fewer wagons its speed increased at once, even though the way became increasingly tortuous as the track gained height. Bright yellow scrub appeared and mingled with the red-podded bushes, hills shaded pale mauve against the sky; steep, rocky and beautiful. 'The rains failed last season and I'm told they weren't much the year before,' Stephen shouted above the roar of the engine. 'The railroad goes through Kosti Town, but most of the crops are grown in a valley beyond that line of hills, where the climate is quite temperate, provided it rains in March and June each year.'

'And now it's February.'

'That was what riled me up, seeing farmers forced to eat their seed grain while food rotted on Hamada Quay and Forla used the little foreign exchange Mananga has to buy luxuries and guns. They're frugal peasants in that valley, they don't need much to get them through until a new crop ripens. But without food coming in now, the grain all Mananga needs will be eaten instead of sown. Then everyone starves next year.'

Jean stared at him, wondering. Though she did not doubt what he said was true, and on his own Stephen Retz was less intimidating than she expected, there remained something almost theatrical behind this blind determination to bring a single trainload of food where it belonged, no matter what the odds.

Soon afterwards they hit the last long incline before Kosti, but without the same anxiety that they might not make it to the top. Speed dropped and dropped again, smoke snaked back in greasy coils to blot out the view, but the click of wheels, though slow, remained confident until the summit was reached and smoke blew aside again to reveal the first habitations they had seen since Hamada.

At first these were only a few huts fluttering with washing, then they passed a water tower and some dilapidated sheds, before beginning to catch glimpses of ochre buildings in the distance. A swarm of children waved from a wall, more skipped and tumbled alongside the track as they ground to an untidy halt and shouted in amazement when a woman waved back to them. Jean felt totally elated but also strangely bewildered by an arrival which thrust real people, real smells and shapes back into her consciousness after a journey in which only their own tiny and discordant world had any meaning.

As they stopped a naked small boy stuck out his tongue at her and, laughing, she put her thumbs in her ears and waggled her fingers at him like another disrespectful urchin; taken by surprise, he laughed too, tripped and somersaulted in the dust.

By the time she looked away, Mezak was strutting past, chest thrown out and followed by sick-looking followers fingering guns.

'I hope you know how to make Mezak behave again, once he's enjoyed his Roman triumph,' she said to Stephen.

'I doubt it, but he's from the hills and regards Kosti half-breeds as scum. The trouble will come if we happen on to different sides for some reason, when I guess we just have to try and hide the fact as best we can. Right now I'm worrying about not seeing any of the trucks I fixed would meet us here.'

Jean looked down at the chaos beside the line and decided she would have been astonished if anything fixed at least three weeks before had actually been ready and waiting. 'Perhaps they're on their way.'

'The King's Highway,' said Stephen suddenly. 'Those aircraft must have been bombing trucks coming down from Mezak's valley. Stay here, will you? Women are safe around here when there aren't soldiers in town, but pretty easily despised if they act out of place.' He slid down on the track and pushed over to where Mezak was standing in respectful space, staring distantly down his nose.

Jean watched them begin to argue, but without real interest. What she wanted was a bath, some food, and a bed. Without ever thinking about it, she had also expected Kosti to be friendly, and already she sensed an undercurrent of hostility. They had succeeded against stacked odds in bringing a load of food close to where it was desperately needed, but already fists were being shaken and only the children shouted with real pleasure, as they would whenever a locomotive stopped to take on water.

Perhaps half an hour passed before Stephen came back through the crowd and beckoned for her to come down. 'You are a welcome guest in the house of Mezak's aunt's cousin, which sounds reasonably safe. They take family loyalty seriously hereabouts.'

'There's bad news, isn't there?'

He looked annoyingly non-committal. 'Maybe.'

'It's my skin as well as yours!' she said, exasperated. 'I'd like to know if Mezak's aunt's cousin is likely to turn nasty in the night, after we've brought in food I thought they would be more than a little pleased to see.'

He rubbed at his face, stubble rasping, almost too tired to explain anything at all. 'There's been a crop here. Not much, but they aren't starving. Bringing food in hits everyone who has hoarded a sack of grain to sell and could halve their prices overnight. In seasons when your crops are small, you need those higher prices to survive. But for those with nothing to eat, up in Mezak's valley for instance, those same high prices clean out a lifetime's saving and then their lives. Now, perhaps because Forla has bombed the mule track I planned to use, the Kosti grain merchants

90

are almost sure we can't shift what we've brought up where it's most needed. Once they're convinced of it, someone more unscrupulous than the rest could decide to steal the lot, and if we made a fuss maybe cut our throats as well. Or the equivalent. So, until I check what happened and how much can be salvaged, we're confident, okay?'

'Oh,' said Jean blankly. A little colour grew under the dirt on her cheeks and vanished again, leaving her paler than before. 'I'm confident as hell, waiting for a knife in my equivalent.'

Stephen laughed, taken by surprise. He looked around at the crowd, now goggling at them instead of Mezak, and laughed again, exhaustion making laughter choke in his throat. 'Now I know I'm a long way for Seattle.'

Jean wondered whether she was being particularly stupid not to understand what he meant. 'I don't think I ever saw you laugh before. Or are we laughing to deceive the locals with that confidence of ours?'

He grasped her hand and together they began shouldering their way through the crowd. 'I laughed, thou laughest, we both deceive, you are yourself. New verb.'

9

KOSTI was a town full of gossip and contradiction; at once hospitable and hostile, overshadowed by the threat of Forla and yet without a uniformed soldier in sight, which somehow was disquieting rather than reassuring. A town of undernourished people briskly trading minute quantities of goods to emaciated families come down from the hills with the last of their possessions to offer in exchange. The first casualty of want is pity for the greater misfortunes of begging strangers underfoot.

Jean was welcomed into one of the ochre two-storied houses which formed a single, wider street to one side of the central square; her hostess, Missa Felima, squealed with concern at her bedraggled appearance and sent her daughters scurrying for hot water, crocks of soap and gorgeous loofahs plaited out of twigs. Felima, her husband, was more guarded, quarrelled with Stephen at the edge of Jean's hearing and, after he had left, commanded his sons to guard the entry against all comers, possibly including Jean herself, should she decide to leave without permission. At least that was what she gathered, her rudimentary grasp of the language further confused by unfamiliar accents, and the timber gate was closed while she luxuriated in her impossible dream of a real hot bath, poured by giggling servants into a storage bucket.

By then she was simply watching what happened as a spectator might, without any feeling of involvement; when she woke next day it was different. For a start she must have slept from early evening to the following noon, and the result was magical. Clean, rested and freed from the burden of oppressive heat for the first time since leaving England, she stared at the room in which she lay with buoyant curiosity. It had a low roof and limewashed walls pierced by a single window through which she could see a chink of blue. She was covered by a bright woven rug but felt only pleasantly warm; either the thick walls screened out midday heat or Kosti's climate was exactly to her liking.

She leapt out of bed, threw open sun-cracked shutters and gazed out eagerly, but the view was something of a disappointment. Her room looked over a minute courtyard, probably most inhabited rooms faced away from uproar in the streets. There was no one in sight although voices chattered somewhere she couldn't see; the same red-podded bushes which grew on the hillsides here cascaded down one wall, and a large pot steamed gently on some embers. A plank table and nondescript piles of goods nearly filled the remaining space, and while she watched a naked child wandered into and out of sight.

Her rucksack and medical satchel lay in one corner of the room, her recollection of how they had reached there distinctly hazy. Dressing in clean if crumpled clothes was another enjoyment to be savoured. She felt stiff and her scorched arm was mildly uncomfortable, but nothing to worry about. The best medicine of all was this sense of ease after strain, the fresher air, a new and confident belief that the real Mananga, from which she had so far felt excluded, welcomed her to itself at last.

Her joyful mood received its first jolt when she met Missa Felima in the courtyard and discovered that her smile had been replaced by grudging surliness. Where, the night before, gestures and Jean's scrappy Manangan had been understood, today incomprehension flourished. Her thanks were brushed aside and requests for information met by blank stares.

'Stephen? Steve?' she asked, after she had eaten a bowl of gritty porridge washed down by a strange but agreeable drink which might be distantly related to mint tea.

Missa Felima shook her head, lips pursed.

'Is he coming here?' Jean was beginning to feel both puzzled and alarmed, isolated too, when she had not the slightest idea where Stephen might be nor when — if, even — she might expect him back.

The other woman shrugged, then frowned as if to demonstrate that no communication was intended, picked up Jean's plate and walked away out of sight into back-quarters where, quite clearly, it would be discourteous of a guest to follow.

One of Felima's sons stared at her suspiciously from where he lounged by the gate; a hawk wheeled overhead against a bright, cloudless sky; sounds from the street blew softly on the wind. Otherwise nothing. This house which last night had bustled with sons, daughters, servants and various sizes of children was now apparently void of life, and she was as much on the outside of Mananga again as if she had steamed past in a train.

Actually, Jean would have enjoyed sitting peacefully in the sun for a while, had the atmosphere not been so unnatural. That sense of abandonment increased like steam in the boiler of her brain, searching for weakness through which to explode.

It's reaction, she told herself firmly. Surely a nurse ought to understand what delayed shock can do. Certainly the violent days she had lived through continued erratically to jar at her emotions, even while she forced herself to look as if she hadn't a worry in the world. But the remedy she needed was not to sit around, but to start tackling some problems of the present. Another good reason for moving was that she was beginning to itch, as if a great many household bugs were passing on the word about a rapturously different flavour of the month.

Through half-closed eyes Jean studied the boy by the gate. One of her more distinct memories of the previous evening was Felima ordering that gate to be guarded, which at the time she had hazily attributed to some convention about women walking unescorted in the streets of Kosti. Now, she no longer believed this to be the reason, while also feeling sure that that boy would prevent her

93

from leaving. But why? And where *had* Stephen vanished to this time, damn him? She had seen no troops on the streets yesterday, but this was still Forla's Mananga. Because they had journeyed safely from Hamada did not mean they were out of his reach in Kosti. The opposite, in fact. If Forla had indeed emerged triumphant from an attempted coup, then once he was securely back in power he would be even more violent than before, and move to crush the slightest opposition.

This hostile atmosphere and her own virtual imprisonment, might mean his troops were already gathering to re-enter the town.

Casually, Jean stood up and smiled at the boy at the gate, who continued to pick his teeth, unconcerned. Better not try to pass that gate and be refused, but instead play out the charade of a guest protected from harm. She sauntered around the tiny courtyard sniffing at flowers, touching carved wood, pretending not to notice when the boy shifted position to keep her in view.

Eventually, as if she had become bored, she climbed back up the stairway to her room, but then went on down the passage, cautiously investigating the upper part of the house. Voices gossiped behind one door, a child whined while someone scolded in another. No point risking justified hostility by going in, when, so far as she could see, each room on this floor was identical to her own. At the corner of the passage, which ran round two sides of the building, an agreeable breeze drifted through an open trapdoor; hoping fervently that she would not discover more of the family up there waiting to exclaim over her lack of manners, Jean climbed up until her eyes were level with the roof.

This was empty except for a few racks of drought-shrivelled vegetables, the space much smaller than she expected; a minute rectangle between the front of the courtyard and the street. From here it was possible to see that the house, which looked quite spacious from below, tailed away behind the courtyard into a jumble of sheds and barns. Plenty of room there for children and servants to be sent out of earshot while she was left to stew alone. Jean climbed up the remaining few steps, crawled past wobbling racks to make sure she stayed out of sight, and peered over the edge of the roof into the street beyond. Narrow and dusty, it was more like a tunnel than a street; there were people talking in groups, boys scurrying, women trudging under burdens, old men sitting gloomily on doorsteps. Staring down at that scene, Jean had an uncomfortable feeling that if she understood anything at all about this country then she might have been able to guess a little of what was happening from the feel of Kosti's streets. As it was, she could sense tension here, too, but without a shred of evidence to support her instinct.

Beyond some roofs she could glimpse a market square, in the distance a straggle of buildings surrounding the railway. A spectacular backdrop of high hills framed parched brown growth crisscrossed by irrigation channels which reached to the edges of the town, as if in a good year quite a lot of cultivation went on here. There were also the deeply eroded banks of an almost dry river, and a few windswept trees. If only all softness had not been destroyed by privation, and if only she had been able to wander wherever she wanted, then probably there would have been a great deal she liked about Kosti.

Once it became dark she might be able to climb down from here and escape into those streets, but in daylight someone would see her the moment she lifted her eyes higher than the parapet. And, if she did escape this way, she needed to decide first where she could go; how to begin trying to find Stephen, because nowhere in this town could a single foreign female hide out for more than a few hours.

High on the flank of a hill a small cloud of dust was moving. Jean watched it idly at first and then with growing uneasiness. No one in the street could see that advancing line, which, she now decided, must be several vehicles travelling fast. Although if Kosti expected General Forla's troops to descend on them at any moment surely someone would be watching?

She found herself cursing Stephen for having left her like unwanted baggage in a house which had become a trap, cursing him steadily, fluently, silently, with words picked up from years of work on accident wards and in Gloucestershire fields, which previously she had scorned to use. Then she pulled herself up sharp. Mezak had vouched for this house, which must have made it appear safe in a country where the tie of blood was strong, she so exhausted that without rest she could not last much longer. Stephen had also been on a plateau of exhaustion where any apparently easy answer to a problem must have seemed a godsend.

But it felt easier to panic here than in Hamada, where the sea had offered an illusion of rescue ships and NATO navies sailing into the harbour in a crisis. Around Kosti there was nowhere left to run, in bare, dry countryside threatened by famine. Jean did not even know in what direction the clinic lay which she wanted so much to reach.

Several minutes passed while that menacing line of dust drew closer, until it blew across a whole hillside in a monstrous storm of threat, and still no one else seemed to see it. Or if they did, to feel any worry. Jean bit her lip, not knowing whether to shout a warning or stay silent; perhaps she had begun to see risk where none existed, and those trucks were a routine convoy.

At that moment, and cutting through town hubbub instantly, a shot was fired somewhere beyond the market square. This was followed by a visible wave of crisis, as if a dozing watchman had suddenly woken up, and looked, unable to believe his eyes.

Everyone scattered at once in the street below, and a great commotion broke out in the courtyard behind her.

'Missa, come!' A hand jerked at Jean's ankle so that she nearly leapt over the balustrade in fright.

A good-looking girl with a baby on her hip was at the trapdoor entry, beckoning, a finger to her lips.

'I was just looking.' Absurdly, Jean felt like a guest caught out searching her host's cupboards.

The girl laughed silently. 'Sh-shh. You come with me now.'

There didn't seem anything to do except sheepishly to follow her down the ladder, the baby's face bobbing and smiling just in front as if in reassurance. Once they reached the passage again, the girl glided ahead and disappeared down the stairs, a flip of the palm as they passed Jean's bedroom door indicating that she should return inside.

The willing prisoner, Jean thought ruefully. If only I understood what is going on maybe I would feel braver; ironic to remember that she had felt light-heartedly happy less than two hours before. Now this recurring nightmare of total insecurity made her as meanly self-centred as most other inhabitants of Mananga.

Very faintly, and then with increasing vigour, the whole house was beginning to shake. 'Not an earthquake as well!' she said aloud. So many calamities at once had become almost impossible to take seriously: she heard herself giggle and felt a little courage return. More yells, indignant now, floated up from the courtyard, the shudder becoming a roar of engines as the column of vehicles

Jean had seen swept into the narrow streets of Kosti, noise bouncing off crumbling plaster, exhaust smoke shimmering in the sun.

Those trucks were also stopping, dust falling from the dry ceiling as they stopped directly outside, followed within seconds by the sound of heavy blows on the locked gate. Keeping the wall at her back, Jean moved across to the window and looked cautiously into the courtyard, only to encounter a furious stare from her host of the night before. He was standing, straddle-legged and shouting, holding what looked like a World War Two tommy-gun. At his shout his sons came running, and stood in an uneasy wedge at his back fingering an assortment of weapons, mostly home-made. Jean could only be glad that thanks to a more merciful female dependent, she hadn't been caught on the roof by anyone so clearly longing to purge his rage on easy victims.

The naked fury of that look made her recoil, but not far enough to lose sight of the courtyard. Her life was on the skids as much or more than everyone else's from those fists beating on the gate; even inexplicable, bitter enmity was insufficient to overcome her need to see what was happening.

Below, Felima was now cursing whoever was demanding entry, and followed up curses with a burst of fire from his gun. Plaster, bits of stone, red pods like blood hurtled everywhere, turning cries of support from his sons and servants into howls of fright.

He made a derisive gesture, almost as if regretting he hadn't hit anyone, and strode over to shout some query through the gate, perhaps realising that he couldn't afford too many ricochets in a courtyard stuffed with his own dependents.

Stephen replied. Jean didn't hear what he said, but recognised his voice instantly and only just stifled a shout of relief. Stephen. So it was his trucks she had seen driving down the hillside! She had wondered whether it could be, but the sense of threat had been too great to believe it. Meanwhile, Felima was still belligerently waving his tommy-gun in the courtyard and refusing to open the gate.

I don't understand any of this, Jean thought, but maybe I don't have to, when all I want is to get out of here. Carefully, she moved across the room, picked up her satchel and rucksack and softly opened the door. A couple of children too young to worry about the uproar were playing in the passage, everyone else was probably glued to that scene in the courtyard. One of the children started to wail at the sight of a stranger and Jean went up the ladder like a Gloucestershire gipsy into a horse market. Five medium-sized trucks were drawn up along the narrow length of street outside, the engines booming, their fumes as poisonous as marsh gas in the confined space. She couldn't see Stephen, presumably out of sight in the arched entry immediately below; the soft truck tops just out of her reach. Jean wriggled back hastily to the vegetable racks, unable any longer to hear the altercation between Stephen and Felima, but another burst of fire emphasised growing acrimony. Hastily, she selected a large, partly dried gourd and dropped it over the parapet, so that it burst with a satisfying splatter on the cobbles below.

Stephen stepped back into sight, head up, no greeting, but instantly weighing possibilities. He might at least smile, Jean thought. But already he was shouting through the closed gate again to keep the gathering in the courtyard quiet, before reappearing to sprint round to the nearest truck. Jean put one leg over the parapet, felt it crumble, and waited impatiently while he reversed, scraping metal against the side of the house by coming as close to the wall as he could. More furious shouts echoed up behind her as the Felima family not unnaturally assumed that these intruders were about to assault their home, and the tommy-gun fired again, this time straight through brittle gate timbers to rip the canvas truck cover and thud into the houses opposite. The truck in front of Stephen's took off in a rasp of gears, those blocked in behind began to blare their horns, making confusion worse. Jean grabbed her rucksack and came off her parapet in a shower of dried mud and plaster, bounced on canvas and very nearly rolled off again into the road. Skinning her fingers and an elbow on the way, she scrabbled to hold on to an already moving truck, hit something hard and wriggled over the sharp edge of an open door, feeling Stephen reach up to steady her while steering the truck one-handed.

'Good girl,' he said, and this time he did smile.

'Now would you mind just telling me what the hell is going on?' she said indignantly.

He laughed, and the truck hit an edge of wall with a hollow clang.

She grinned, feeling enormously better once that feeling of

isolation vanished. 'Perhaps you just enjoy being shot at with a tommy-gun.'

'Not particularly, no. I'm sorry if you thought I'd taken off, but these are the only trucks left after Forla's air raid on Mezak's King's Highway. So called. It took most of the night to get these running, since I'm not a great mechanic and Mezak's too proud to touch a spanner. What we have to do now is load up and get out of here, and fast.'

'But why should everyone be so hostile?' Jean demanded. 'We came here at some risk to ourselves, hoping to help. Or have I got everything wrong?'

'Nothing in Mananga is that simple. Mezak tells me now that Kosti men run to Forla like rats after meat, although he never let on before that there might be a snag. You remember I said last night that Kosti might see food for the hills as something which pushed their prices down? Well, Mezak's aunt's cousin's husband, Felima, has some hoarded grain he means to sell to the high valley farmers, once prices climb another few hundred per cent. Of course they won't be able to pay, and handful by handful will be forced to pledge next year's crop. They've some irrigation here, and the grain dealers of Kosti are optimistic another few months of drought might even make them rich. The only split has to be with Forla. He keeps his troops out of here in return for free grain to feed his army. It wasn't such a good deal when Kosti had to starve to save that grain, but worth it when the only alternative was pillage, Hamada-style. Once they start getting their claws into the high valley farms where the best crops are grown, the picture changes. Maybe you can't blame them. When life is a matter of kill or be killed, everyone becomes a savage.'

'In that case, I suppose we can't blame Mezak either for not explaining all that until after we'd brought some food for his valley,' said Jean thoughtfully.

'It would have helped if he'd offered a few hints before we made several avoidable mistakes. For instance, I wouldn't have accepted a night's lodging for you with one of Kosti's grain hoarders, even if he was Mezak's blood brother. I'm also beginning to wonder what other surprises he's kept back until it suits him to explain some more.'

'Don't you think Mezak must already be in debt to the Felima family? If he saw a chance of writing off some obligation on his land, then a woman probably equals a wheelbarrow-load of dung. Or less.' Jean now felt some sympathy for Missa Felima, if not her husband, whose welcome had turned to resentment when she learned that a temporary guest might become repayment on a loan, perhaps remain for ever as a hated rival. Then she thought of dirty, squat Felima, and shivered.

Stephen put his hand on her shoulder, tentatively, as if unsure of her reaction, and for the first time she glimpsed the maniacal speed of last night's work, the frantic scramble to get himself and five trucks back to Kosti once Mezak casually began to hint at a quite unsuspected situation there.

But almost instantly his full attention was wrenched back to the road, as their trucks swept together into the station yard. Jean had not realised until then that the vehicle directly ahead had men in it, but as it stopped a dozen or more dropped over the tailgate and started running. There were some scattered shots, but apparently in greeting rather than anger, because triumphant shouts quickly followed. 'We left behind everyone except Mezak and me to guard the train,' explained Stephen. 'Otherwise our freight would have vanished while we went to fetch the trucks. But I guess Kosti thought that all they had to do was wait. We would have had to leave it behind anyway once we realised the King's Pass was blocked.'

'They're certainly making up for a quiet night,' Jean said resignedly, as a fusillade of jubilant shots whipped over the station roof. Really, she was getting quite accustomed to guns being fired for fun.

Eventually Mezak swaggered out of the main station entrance and came over to where they waited beside the truck. He met Jean's eye without embarrassment. 'The greedy fucks feasted all night, but other wagons okay.'

'My God,' said Stephen. 'Don't tell me twelve men ate their way through a whole wagonload in a single night.'

'Brave men eat more,' answered Mezak loftily.

'Then let's get loaded up, shall we? Before the Kosti merchants decide that food isn't going to fall into their barns after all, and come to fetch it.'

'Not everyone feeling good, Steve.'

'If they ate all night after more than a year of starvation rations, I guess they wouldn't. We still need to load up and get out while we can.'

'Kosti men come secretly with poison, I think. We not move today.'

Stephen's eyes narrowed. 'They find something to drink?'

Mezak hummed a little tune.

'For God's sake get your drivers out of there before they start on whatever it was the others found. Mezak ... get back in there quickly, please.' He sounded calm, but Jean saw his face tighten and sensed urgency. Before he had always been careful to treat Mezak as a valued superior.

And Mezak frowned at once, offended. 'Drivers my best men.'

He went back inside the station all the same and Stephen followed, which Jean thought might be tactless. She stayed where she was, leaning against the truck and enjoying sunshine which no longer burned where it touched. Mezak would be infuriated by any woman who saw his power humiliated, the question of whether she could ease the agony of his men, who had drunk some nameless filth, was quite academic until he gave her permission to try. Jean still felt an outsider to the real life of Mananga, but she was beginning to learn how Mezak's mind worked. Meanwhile, a few minutes' respite from crisis wouldn't be unwelcome.

Stephen came back looking exasperated. 'They found a drum of brake fluid.'

'Will you ask Mezak if he'll let me see what I can do to help them? It won't be much in these conditions, I'm afraid.'

'If you can fix a few drips, fine, but we haven't time for much more. Otherwise Kosti will be barricaded up so tight, we'll never get through. They have to take their chance in the back of our trucks all the way to the King's Pass and their valley beyond. We've only four drivers, too, because the fifth started gulping brake fluid before Mezak got back to stop him, so we have to leave one truck behind anyway, which is goddamn waste. It's going to be a tough journey for critically sick drunks.'

'I can drive a truck,' Jean said. 'At least, I've driven tractors and loaders not much smaller than these at home on our farm. Combines too.'

'How much smaller?'

'Smaller.' She wasn't getting drawn into details. They needed that fifth truck to help take every sack of grain and drum of diesel they could, not leave them behind for the Kosti merchants to hoard. 'The gears may be different but if you would show me how they work, I ought to manage all right.'

'Didn't you hear me say we've been left alone here because Felima and his pals know we can only reach the hills by driving back through Kosti? They'll be blocking the streets, laughing about how we're saving them the trouble of loading all those sacks. And if we should manage to break through, that track up to Mezak's valley is lethal. Jeeps occasionally go that way, but recently it's only been used by mules. That's why I thought no one would guess we could bring food up through Kosti, instead of transshipping in Mananga City. Now the pass at the top's been bombed and I'm not sure how we're going to make it.'

Jean could feel fright reaching all the way to her heart. 'What else do you suggest we do? Go with a truck short, when even with five we shall have to leave several wagons full of stores behind? Like drums of diesel for the clinic generator, so more kids will scream through operations without an anaesthetic?'

Some of Mezak's men who had begun to load the first truck stopped work again to listen uneasily to their quarrelling voices. Stephen Retz represented the brainpower behind this lunatic expedition; Mezak was brave and skilful but, left to himself, would never have conceived a scheme which stole supplies from under Forla's nose and brought them all this way in a stolen train. If Stephen began to show doubt now, these hillmen's pride in their achievement would swiftly disintegrate, particularly now they understood how many difficulties still lay between them and ultimate success. As Stephen very well knew, and he turned at once to reassure them.

While his attention was diverted, Jean ran back to the last truck. It started easily, the controls much as she expected even though there were more gears and chipped-paint knobs than she had ever used. She revved the engine gently, just enough not to stall it, and moved off as though the truck slid through butter, then drove across jolting ruts towards the railway line, praying that reverse was where it ought to be.

The gear went into place with a grating, metallic clunk, but the truck reversed neatly enough. Lucky it wasn't articulated, she had never mastered the art of reversing trailers without a great deal of trial and error. She switched off and jumped down, pleased to see the tailgate was precisely lined up with the door of a loaded freight wagon.

'You goddamn crazy maniac,' said Stephen coldly. 'You missed running over a drunk by six inches.'

Jean whipped round, horrified, and for the first time saw a huddle of limbs by the track. She dropped on her knees beside scarcely breathing bones. 'I suppose rusty water out of the locomotive boiler would be better than nothing if I could get a tube inside them,' she said anxiously. In her satchel she possessed a single length of tubing between as many as twenty paralytic hillmen.

'I wouldn't think it'd make much difference.' He sounded resigned rather than harsh.

'You'll let me drive the truck?'

Unexpectedly, he laughed. 'Yep. If you're sure you can manage it. We do need that fifth load badly, and you, I hope, are on your way to spend a wet season in a clinic out of Forla's reach. I prefer not to watch you starve, when I happen to like the way you are.'

And so, while Mezak yelled imprecations at his remaining supporters in the background, Stephen drilled gear discipline into her as if she was a trainee he had never seen before, his voice levelly insistent to ensure she would remember what he said as she tired, sharply snapped if she fumbled even for an instant. So different from his softer words only minutes before, a man of so many facets that she began to feel dazed rather than comforted by his presence.

Soon, they must leave such safety as these exposed and dangerous sidings offered and hazard the passage through Kosti, itself only the perilous beginning of their next journey.

'How long?' she asked, and her lips felt stiff.

'Since the people of Kosti realised what we mean to do? An hour perhaps. Too long, anyway.'

While they sweated to load trucks and she learnt how to drive hideously unfamiliar machinery, Felima and his fellow dealers would have been blocking the streets of Kosti against them. And when the loading was finished, there were still moaning bodies to wedge wherever they might escape being crushed, while Jean managed somehow to rig up makeshift drips for those men who might survive the journey, and ransacked her satchel for painkilling injections if dulling agony was the best she could hope for. The trucks were piled so high that the sick had to take their chance, since Mezak assured her they would be thrown out with the garbage if left behind. Mezak himself had recovered every scrap of his usual assurance, bawling at his men as if they were an army and ordering more freight to be piled in whenever Stephen's back was turned. Sensibly enough, he also lashed filled sacks to the trucks' radiators and bonnets as shields, and distributed Jean's precious crates of medical supplies through all five trucks in case any were lost. A huge quantity of goods would have to be left behind, split sacks and rifled wagons revealing the haste with which everything had had to be done.

Jean settled herself inside the second truck while Stephen held some last-minute discussion with Mezak, her hands gripped so tightly on the wheel that her knuckles hurt. Offering to drive an unfamiliar vehicle up a mule track to a shattered pass was one thing, to use it like a tank to burst out through a hostile town was another altogether. When Stephen came over his expression was all shadow and sharp, sweat-streaked bone, and, somewhere beyond her most immediate terrors, she began for the first time to wonder what, exactly, might be waiting for her if they should, through several miracles, find safety for a wet season in the hills.

'Listen, Jean,' he said quietly. She had already discovered that Stephen Retz was always quiet when things were worst. 'Listen and don't forget. I'm going first, then you, then Raffel and Alinza. Mezak is afterguard. Follow me exactly, very close. Don't worry about anything except staying close. I'd like to be going last in case something goes wrong, but they know we're coming and breaking through isn't going to be easy. Once we do get through, I'll stop and wave the rest of you past. Raffel and Alinza know the track up to the pass and you can guess how Mezak handles a truck.' His expression relaxed for an instant. 'All three of them drive like they were on a circuit, so let them go past and after a while the only thing you'll see will be their dust. Don't try to keep up. Take it slowly even if we're pursued. That track is lethal and not designed for trucks. Okay?'

'I follow Mezak and the rest once we get through Kosti,' Jean repeated obediently.

'I shall be ahead until we're through, then right behind you. Don't look round or worry about me once you've pulled past.' He reached up and prised her hand off the wheel, while all the time those light eyes of his smiled into hers, as if he tried to hypnotise her into confidence. 'We have to play this by ear, so just keep close. Afterwards, take it slow. Real, real slow, right down through the gear shift. I'll block the track if necessary to make sure you have the time you need.'

Jean nodded, wanted to say something, swallowed, and nodded again. 'We haven't left anyone behind?'

'Mezak checked, and he wouldn't leave a follower.' He ran over to his own truck and, deliberately, Jean forced herself to use these last seconds somehow to settle into a kind of calm. Her mind was filled by a jumble of impressions rather than thought: of purple thunderheads building above the corrugated station roof and Mezak climbing like an athlete into his truck, hand pointing as if it held a cutlass at the charge; of their faithful locomotive standing cold and forgotten; of flour dust spilled on the road, the shimmer of exhaust as Stephen's truck started up ahead.

All five trucks swung in convoy out of the station yard and on to the road leading back to Kosti. The town was out of view beyond a low curved hill, the roadside completely empty. No curious faces, no children running to beg, no carts or ancient jeeps scurrying for pickings from abandoned freight. If they hadn't known there was danger ahead, this unnaturally empty road would have proclaimed it.

A sick boy called Saul had been jammed on top of some sacks beside her. He wasn't as comatose as the rest and she smelt terror on him, too; there was no way either of them could escape it. She turned and smiled at him, jerked her head as if trying to pretend fear must wait outside, and tremulously he smiled back. In such great stress she had forgotten the few Manangan words she knew and he was nearly too sick to speak, yet when they smiled fear was somehow forced outside, where it would wait and watch, and come again very soon. In fact, now they had started, Jean needed to concentrate so hard on following Stephen closely as he increased speed that, briefly, she almost forgot fear.

Not far into Kosti now and, as if in answer to her thought, Stephen's brake lights flashed, dulled again, came on brightly. He would not stop for anything short of a road block, but his towering load of diesel, sugar and flour blinded her to what lay ahead. Jean bit her lip, muscles jumping in her arms; not to know what the hold-up was immediately brought fear flooding back.

Stephen's truck continued to roll slowly forward, as if he was taking vital seconds to add up risk, then it picked up speed again. God, he was increasing speed again. In her relief, Jean let in the clutch with too much of a jerk and the engine stalled.

The sudden silence was appalling, and while she was stopped from ahead came a crash and shriek of metal. Sweating, fumbling, still not able to see what was happening, Jean ground savagely at the starter while for a heart-stopping moment the engine refused to fire; when it did, there was an angry screech as she trod on the throttle, unable to do anything smoothly any more.

She knew she was grasping the wheel like a lunatic, terrified of getting everything wrong a second time, drew her foot back so slowly her knee went into spasm and the engine nearly died again. Frantically, she revved up and fairly threw that infernal truck forward, only to see why Stephen had hesitated. A jumble of farm machinery had been hauled across the road where it passed between deep ditches, as if the inhabitants of a close-by shack had attempted a private hijack of their own. His truck had easily flattened rusted iron and carts, the only danger that there might be hidden guns waiting to open fire. But these were peasants who dreamt of wrecking a single truck to snatch provisions for themselves; Jean saw desperate, aghast faces as she roared past, looking at the ruin of their few possessions for no gain, and she yelled at them to run to the station while they could. Probably they could not hear her, but she hoped they might realise that while the merchants of Kosti were occupied with bigger game, the freight yard was wide open.

How many people have we damaged, how many helped by this mad determination to do something, anything, rather than be beaten? she wondered fleetingly, and could remember only damage. In the end, would Lewis be proved right, and all their efforts only make everything worse? Too late, now, to think of that.

Kosti next, less than a mile ahead.

Jean kept trying to convince herself that she had mastered the art of driving a truck not much larger than a combine, but without success. She also needed to stay tense, when this was the kind of risk which only the super-charged reactions of utter terror might help her to survive.

As they drove into the outskirts of town she could see people in sidestreets and on roofs, some of them shouting like children at a circus. The irony of it all was that nearly everyone would probably be in debt to that same ring of dealers, would hate and fear their power quite as much as the country farmers did. Yet it never occurred to anyone to make common cause with strangers. All they wanted was to enjoy a once-in-a-lifetime chance of grandstand seats in a shoot-out, and maybe a quick grab at some loot for themselves afterwards.

Unexpectedly, Stephen turned sharply left at the first corner, and then again, so they were almost back into the country. Jean couldn't understand what he planned, when he had already explained that there was no way of outflanking Kosti. The town had grown here because it commanded the only bridge across the river, and all around it lay deep irrigation ditches waiting for the winter rains which, even though dry at present, would swallow up a truck.

Jean's palms slipped on the flat-angled steering wheel as she dragged at it to make sharp, jinking turns, finding distance and clearances enormously difficult to judge when perched so high above the road. The scene was like a barnyard when the fox has broken in as Stephen swung into alleys so narrow that his truck crunched baked mud walls on either side: a frantic flutter of protest and leaping for endangered lives. No one had imagined they might try to come through these back slums, when the only way out of town remained that bridge beyond the square. Stephen's klaxon blaring now, all their klaxons blaring as madness deepened its hold, a rattle of shots ricocheting down a street to their right as someone, who perhaps was manning a road block they had avoided, opened fire. Chipped tiles showered on Jean's truck roof, and there was a hollow booming clang as she hit stone steps where a whole section of mud-walling shuddered into dust as Stephen thrust his truck between them. More destruction, she thought dizzily. Now they were caught in a cross-hatch of tiny streets and their speed dropped to a walking pace as first one wall and then another had to be nudged aside.

They turned right and back towards the centre of town at last, but into a tiny rutted cemetery; Jean nearly hit the cab roof when Stephen accelerated across even so minute an open space, snapping off missionary crosses and Manangan carvings as he went. More shots to their right, as if everyone who had waited for them there was pelting back to new positions; the bridge must now be very close.

Jean stamped on the brakes as Stephen's lights glowed danger red again, and wrenched at the wheel as he turned. Instantly a whole magazine of fire came ripping down the length of a street towards them, hurling fragments from split crates on his load into the air and thudding into sacks. A scream echoed faintly from one of the following trucks, Jean and Saul crouched as if thin steel bodywork could give them protection against bullets; at least the weaponry of Kosti was old, most of it apparently aimed too high. There was a shocking, evil yowl in her ears as a bullet tumbled end over end after hitting a strut, then they were back in the temporary safety of another alley, the promise of dangerous sunlight dead ahead. They were very close to the northern edge of Kosti, only some high crenellated walls topped by pepperpot-style watchtowers between them and the river, the parallel track ahead the only remaining way they could reach the bridge.

Stephen pulled aside, stuck his head out to shout above the roar of engines as the other trucks lined up too: all apparently without crippling damage. 'Engage your auxiliary gearbox! Tell Mezak to pass it on!'

Jean waved a hand in acknowledgement and yelled across to Mezak, who came scorching over. Whatever his faults he was quicksilver fast in a crisis. 'Steve bloody good!' he shouted, his face set in a fierce victorious grin, and ran without argument to pass on the message to the other drivers.

If Jean had wondered before why Mezak should approve of anyone so unlike himself as Stephen Retz, she now knew the answer: sheer brass nerve. She couldn't imagine what he intended next but here they were, two-thirds of the way through barricaded Kosti and lined up for a breakout. Her own confidence was beginning to glow again in response to success, luminous and strong. Where she had been wrung out by fear and doubt now she was all sparks and fire because they had nearly made it, with only some damfool bridge still holding them up, but a bridge which was certain to be narrow, and where there had been plenty of time to construct a solid barrier.

Nerve-sharp and riding a high of excitement, Jean struck back the red knobbed lever which engaged the second gearbox as Stephen had shown her, while he waited perhaps another thirty seconds to make sure everyone had the message. Then he launched his truck like a missile, not down the track to the bridge as Jean expected, but straight at the wall ahead. Plaster and brick disintegrated, but this time the masonry was thick enough for the truck to hesitate, one wheel spinning off the ground, before it heaved forward again. Jean followed blindly; too late, too late for doubt, although she heard scandalised yells from people who must have run after them through the streets, a screech from Saul beside her. The wheels of her truck leapt on stubbed edges as plaster, brick and stone exploded across the bonnet and then they were through and into kaleidoscopic glimpses of baked grass spaces, more fortifications, some splendid ornamental timbering. This fort looked older than any colonial past, a priceless survival from Mananga's own inheritance and criminal for them to damage it. In such surroundings trucks were dinosaurs let loose, smashing all they touched.

Jean wasn't quick enough to follow exactly behind Stephen as he spun his wheel to hit the next wall squarely; hit it instead at an angle and this time debris flew up in her face to smash the windscreen. For an instant she was blinded as shatterproof glass turned opaque, before most of it fell in sugary pieces all over her and Saul. A whole section of wall had collapsed under that ferocious double impact and for a flash of time she was driving alongside Stephen across a parade ground. He threw up a hand in mock greeting and Jean laughed back in the madness of it all, how insignificant was destruction in the intensity of action. Then they needed to stamp on everything to avoid a tree and he skidded in front again to absorb the next impact, this time of the fort's outer wall. He hit it sideways in the now-familiar blast of mudbrick and rubble, slewed again and plunged out of sight.

Jean couldn't believe it. One moment Stephen's Chevrolet truck had been right in front of her and the next it vanished. Then momentum carried her, too, through that gap and she saw immediately beyond it a steep bank leading down to the river, in times as dry as these a sluggish trickle in which Kosti washed its clothes, drank and watered its few beasts. Here a sandbank had been used by generations of women for beating clothes and gossip, the steep riverbank worn into a rough slope by countless feet, although at that particular moment they, like everyone else, must have been panting behind them through Kosti's streets. Stephen's truck swept down that incline and along the sandbank like a charging bull to hit the river at forty miles an hour. Water seethed like steam in the sunlit air, the truck slewing on slime but carried forward by sheer speed until, crabwise, it hit trampled ground on the opposite bank, straightened with a jerk, and began to haul up a much steeper slope to safety.

Now it was her turn. Stephen had had the advantage of coming like a projectile out of the fort, Jean needed to accelerate all the way down that slope, realising that only speed could take her through; realising, too, that Mezak and the other drivers had not been able to see Stephen and how this must be done. Only here had the bank been sufficiently worn down for such an attempt to be possible, but even so there was no margin for error. Jean's teeth snapped on her lip, filling her mouth with blood, as they hit that sandbank and ploughed into water beyond, which soaked her instantly through the broken windscreen. The steering wheel vibrated like a mad thing as she struggled to keep the truck going fast across that narrow, firmer, bank of sand, the engine whined in too low a gear for speed, tyres spun on ooze the instant they reached water, a jerk like a hangman's noose as the bonnet unexpectedly reared up in front of her staring eyes. Already they were out and clawing at that further bank, as steep as hell so the truck felt as if it would flip on its back at any moment. Dimly Jean was aware of the bridge away to her right, of distant shouts and scattered shots, everything overlapping as her Chevrolet threshed sideways before wearily hauling up to hard ground again at the top of the bank.

'Go on!' yelled Stephen, and punched the air. 'Go on! Don't wait!'

Already Raffel was down in that sticky, churned up river bottom, more shots skipping dangerously across the water. Jean did as Stephen wanted, since this wasn't a time for argument, but hauled aside as bone-dry fields stretched ahead, the road to the hills on a bank beyond. First Raffel and then Alinza went past in a cloud of dust, their faces split in enormous grins. Mezak was a good leader all right, and had waited to bring up the rear. An agonising pause followed while uproar grew at the bridge, perhaps quarter of a mile away, before Mezak's truck came roaring up, dripping mud as if he had only just managed to pull clear. He flipped a hand to her as he passed, in grudging accolade.

Jean craned her neck out of the cab window, but couldn't see Stephen anywhere. His truck had taken the brunt of most impacts in that crazy drive through Kosti, it could easily be too damaged to continue. Or he could have been killed while waiting for four other trucks to pass. She was reversing to go back when he appeared at last, flashing his lights impatiently for her to get going, a strange screech in his engine which hadn't been there before.

But he was out. They were all miraculously out of Kosti, nearly unharmed, and must now drive helter-skelter for the hills, hoping they could get over the King's Pass where, so Stephen had said, the grain dealers of Kosti would not follow them nor, with luck, Forla either.

Jean kept glancing in her mirror but it was difficult to see much, because now they were driving faster her eyes watered fiercely in the blast of air coming through the windscreen. Fortunately Mezak and the other two had already vanished ahead as Stephen had predicted; she could not possibly have driven in their dust. Beside her, Saul had revived slightly and was giggling with relief, but she kept worrying about that screech in Stephen's truck, about pursuit as well.

Ten minutes must have passed since they had regained the road out of Kosti, and Jean began to count. If there wasn't any pursuit inside a half an hour then she hoped it meant that no one had recovered fast enough from surprise to follow them. There must be some fierce recriminations going on among the dealers of Kosti, which might hamstring action long enough to give them a winning lead. Fifteen minutes. Twenty. Twenty-two.

Saul had been leaning out of his side of the cab, but turned to say something Jean couldn't catch. 'Steve?' she shouted back; from the sound of it, his engine might seize up at any time.

Saul shook his head and waved his hands as if he held a gun, pulled an imaginary trigger, looked sick again. The merchants of Kosti had decided on pursuit.

10

THE first rattle of automatic fire came a few minutes later. No nonsense about tommy-guns, someone back there possessed a modern, high velocity weapon. The road had already deteriorated into a pitted yellow ruin, twin tyre-tracks deeply gashed along its length so that Jean's truck swayed, lurched and pounded unmercifully. It would have been easier to drive across the baked pastures, but irrigation channels as far as the eye could see made that impossible. The light was becoming strange as well, as thunderheads to the west sucked brightness from a pewter-coloured sky, which at any other time would have been a matter for rejoicing, since life itself depended on good rains this year.

After perhaps an hour of trying to maintain as high a speed as possible on surfaces which varied from awful to appalling, the road at last began to twist on itself, curling between dry gullies, the bends coming closer together and with less warning. Take it slowly, Stephen had said, and her speed was dropping remorselessly. Yet they could not afford to waste a single yard of their lead; Jean listened tensely to occasional shots from behind, which also helped her not to think about how narrow the track had become, understanding now why Stephen insisted she should pass him once they were out of Kosti. At least their pursuers would have to stop and wait for their aim to settle on such rough surfaces as these, if more than a freak shot was to strike home.

Then, without warning, she reached the first hairpin bend. It might have made a good breathing space for mules, but surely was impossible for trucks. Yet there was no sign of Raffel, Alinza, or Mezak; if they could drive laden vehicles up there, then she could too. She also had to drive it quickly, that was the snag, or the load her truck was carrying would stall them and force her to reverse, which was unthinkable. Their pursuers would also reach Stephen — by now they must already be very close.

The hairpin wound between rock on one side and a steep drop on the other, the road rising in between. Jean stopped and engaged the auxiliary gearbox again, wiped her hands on her knees, started to wipe them again and swore at herself. She had to go now ... now, before her nerve was gone.

The engine roared and shook as she revved it too fast for such a low ratio, the outer tyre so close to that drop she felt it slither on loose shale. She could not hurry, had to take it at a crawling pace with her headlights switched on in the gathering gloom. Her teeth clenched so hard together her jaw began to ache. This truck was a massive and dangerous beast, and pursuers with guns something she could not think about now.

Jean gave the engine every ounce of the power Detroit had built into it, the road steepest just at the worst part of the hairpin. She squeezed as tight as she dared into jagged cliff, wheels churning on the very edge of the chasm to her right, the bonnet like an out-thrust stubborn jowl before her eyes as the truck refused to obey the wheel crammed frantically over in her hands. Saul moaned, she shouted, noise bounced off rock as dust whirled in through the broken windscreen, enveloping everything except that one narrow trail they had to take, or die. Headlights predatory in dimness, the truck a self-willed animal taking them to disaster. Tight, tight, tighter into rock, an echoing clang from scraped steel which sent her heart thudding against her ribs as a spark flicked up and past her eyes. Then they were round, the gradient flattening and the engine shireking from surplus horsepower.

Up through the gears and then down again, fast, as the next bend came.

Then the next. The Kosti Hills were only some seven thousand feet high, but crumbling, slanted strata made them a formidable barrier on this northern slope. No wonder Stephen said that once they reached the hill country they should be safe for a while, particularly in the wet. As Jean drove higher she glimpsed him several times, apparently safe and toiling up behind her. One of Mezak's men was clinging perilously to piled freight in the back of his truck and, as she watched, he hacked with an axe at a drum of diesel and heaved it over the tailgate. It burst in a spray all over the road, and he followed it with a couple of sacks of flour which also split. There wasn't any sign of pursuit, so perhaps Stephen had left some drums on that first appalling bend as well, where oil and flour would have to be scraped up with a shovel before anyone could pass; no question of surviving even a shallow skid on such a track as this.

Feeling encouraged, Jean turned back to her own driving. After those unnerving hairpins, the way levelled out to swing over a ridge, then dipped again to cross a rock plateau, the going much easier for several miles, especially now she felt there was time not to take unnecessary risks. But her eyes burned from dust blown through the windscreen, her back ached and her arms trembled from the strain of heaving at heavy machinery. Time to think was not a particularly good idea, either, while Mezak's valley still seemed impossibly far away.

High against the evening sky she could just see a notch she thought might be the pass where they would cross this range of hills and begin descending again, where the road, such as it was, had been bombed. A long way below it were some pinpricks of light she supposed must be Mezak and the others; a long, long way below. When she saw how far even they still had to go, she wished for a moment that she, too, had drunk brake fluid and could rest comatose between disasters.

Another sharp corner was coming up, steeply downwards this time with a boulder sticking through the track surface. No point any longer even pretending this was a road. As she swung to take that corner one wheel was forced up the boulder edge, the cab canting so steeply she found herself looking straight down to a gully a long way below. A breath-stopping lurch turned her senses into glass and instinctively she tried to steer higher up the slope, but all the time that wheel was climbing higher up the protruding boulder, and steering higher only slanted the truck more. Jean could not drag her eyes away from that space directly below where she was sitting, from grit showering down as their outer wheels scraped the very edge of the abyss, and found herself clinging to the steering wheel as if somehow it could save her.

Saul roused as he had at every crisis and screamed; Jean's mouth was too dry for that.

Slowly, slowly, they were tipping over and there was nothing she could do to prevent it, the truck leaning out and downward until they fell, somersaulting as they went.

'Jump!' she croaked to Saul, but he was too weak to jump and on her side there was only space.

Despairingly she stabbed at the throttle, felt a responding roar of power and a lurch as something bit on shifting surfaces she couldn't see. There was a dreadful howl and spatter of stones before rock and dry earth swam sickeningly into sight again, where only space had been. They were back on the track with another hairpin showing ahead.

Very gradually the ache in Jean's arms ebbed and she became aware that she had switched off the engine, Saul huddled beside her with his head in his arms like a foetus in the womb. She shook her head, trying to clear the waves of vertigo. It was no good stopping now, when what she must somehow do was tackle the next hairpin.

But she was terrified of that engine, did not want ever to switch it on again. She could not, dared not. She closed her eyes and breathed cool air pouring through the windscreen, nerving herself to turn it on.

Saul plucked her arm, gabbling something through lips still

loose with fear, stabbing a finger back the way she had come; Jean's mind so stagnant that for a moment a quite different horror swept over her. Stephen had been caught. Because, as soon as she listened, there was his klaxon blaring not far below. She wrenched open the door, the ground so far out of reach it took an enormous effort to climb down; when she did, her legs bent under her.

But Stephen was still safe, that was the immediate, immense relief. His truck was stopped on the bend directly below and the moment he saw her he lifted his arms, hands clenched together above his head as if to indicate she should wait, then ran with a couple of other figures round to the front of his truck. Now she was standing to listen: somewhere lower again she could hear more engines, shouts, the racket of an occasional shot, too far away to be an immediate danger, but close, too close, for any of them to feel safe.

Jean couldn't see what Stephen was doing, and whatever had finally gone wrong with his truck they certainly couldn't waste time on it. Then she heard a crunch and saw its silhouette change shape, lurching as a foundered elephant might, down on its knees. Soon Stephen and the others came toiling up towards her, making the best pace they could while carrying three sick men between them.

Jean started to go and meet them, but hesitantly because her legs still felt as if they had been kicked; then she and Stephen were holding each other wordlessly while breath heaved in his lungs after that wickedly steep climb, both of them far beyond the place where each fresh effort became a little death.

Then he said, 'Jean?' his voice shaken by gasps, his hands locked on hers, imprisoning them both, shock springing its own particular trap they had previously avoided. He did not kiss her, instead laid his cheek for an instant against hers before adding, 'My dear. Climb back inside that cab and we'll get the hell out of here.'

Jean was never able to remember much about the next part of their drive, except that it was a fearful struggle to fit everyone inside her truck. Probably she dozed for a while because when she finally roused Stephen was driving and Saul lay coiled like a snake between her feet. Wind beat against the sides of the truck and a full moon soared among a myriad of stars, everything below part dim, part silver. Hills heaped up colourless, the spaces between them huddled into shadow, the track trying to shine and make their passage easier.

Slowly Jean struggled back to full awareness, horribly stiff, her eyes on the loveliness of a peaceful earth, the wind in steep valleys and sweet green grass in Gloucestershire fields, the laughter by a fire on winter evenings. People said that your life reeled past when you were dying, but on the edge of death she had known only terror; now the moon brought memories of a gentler landscape and helped to set fear aside.

For nightmares to feed on later, perhaps.

Jean looked across at Stephen and needed to swallow tightness before she spoke. Even then she only managed trite banality. 'If I'm tired, you must be worn out. For heaven's sake, let me drive again for a while!'

'Talk to me and I guess I'll stay awake,' he said, and smiled. 'It isn't far to the top and we should find the others waiting for us there. I haven't seen any wrecked trucks on the way and if they've reached as far as this they ought to be all right. We'll take turns to watch and sleep until dawn, no one would make it past bombed rock shelves in the dark.'

'We aren't being chased any longer?' She discovered a quite extraordinary relief in talking and the more ordinary the words the better, as if these past hours had anaesthetised emotion.

'No. Those bends slicked with flour and oil would stop a mule in the dark and they won't shift my truck in a hurry.'

'What did you do?'

'To the truck? I took the front wheels off and released the hydraulic jack. It should have bent the axle. You probably heard there were some bearings about to go up in flames, I couldn't coax it any further. At least it's blocked the track until someone summons the courage to ask Forla if he'll lend them a tank to shove it aside.' His fingers briefly touched hers. 'I wanted to ditch it before, but I couldn't make you hear my klaxon. I don't think I could have lasted much longer, watching you drive with one wheel over a precipice.'

'Two wheels,' said Jean feelingly.

His mouth tightened, although she had meant it as a joke. The kind of joke that gets pasted over a few dark places in the mind. 'I must have been crazy to let you try it.'

Jean turned to study a face which a week before she had not

116

known and now was part of her life, whatever happened. He was wearing those damned deceptive spectacles again, his expression hidden behind reflections from the dashlights. They also helped a little to shield his eyes from the wind and dust. 'You let me try because we needed that extra load of stores. You knew then that even if we got through, we might have to use a truck to block the track.'

Words. Flat and useless, but this was not the moment for anything beyond the commonplaces which would help to keep exhausted senses functioning; this last stretch to the highest point of track so tortuously difficult that even bright moonlight made driving it in the dark insane. But, as Jean soon discovered, neither her mind nor her emotions reacted well to the idea that grinding up a hillside was all that mattered. Their focus dizzily shifted until she was conscious of each breath Stephen drew, the tremor of his muscles as he fought recalcitrant metal up that last slope to the pass, the shape of his hands and the tilt of his head.

Yet she did not know this man and he did not know her.

They found the others where the track widened just below the pass, and Mezak came over with his hands held wide in greeting. 'Good, very good, Steve! Was good fun, I think!'

'You could call it that.' Stephen heaved on the brakes and climbed down, creakingly stiff.

'You lose a truck?'

'It wasn't the same since it hit the fort wall. We may be able to salvage some of its load after the pursuit goes home. The track is blocked behind it for a while.'

Mezak looked thoughtful. 'We try if rains not come.'

Stephen and Mezak stood talking for quite a while, those among his men capable of it crowding around and chattering excitedly among themselves. Jean just looked at the starlit sky, from which yesterday's thunderheads had vanished, and stretched gratefully. No good thinking she could join in a council of war in the Kosti Hills, and it would only complicate things if she tried. Actually, she would have enjoyed to unwind as the men were doing, by re-telling hair's breadth escapes and cracking lousy jokes, slapping each other's backs. Because she couldn't, she began again to remember the colossal trail of damage left behind them: a smashed historic fort and battered walls in the mean streets of Kosti, the bullets meant for them which might have hit a child. These were tragedies which would loom larger in scores of lives than high politics. And all they had to show for their efforts — for men dead from drinking brake fluid and the vengeance of Forla's soldiers in Hamada too — was four trucks of food and stores. A whole train-load might have seemed worth some human suffering, but where in the scale could you set a mere four trucks?

One thing was certain, for Stephen's sake, and now for hers as well: they needed to get these last four through.

After a while Jean climbed back in the cab hoping to get out of the wind, but the broken windscreen meant it wasn't much warmer than the hillside, the transition from heat to chilliness astonishingly sudden. Then Stephen came back, looking bleakly angry.

'What's the matter?' she asked.

'I'm not sure, but Mezak's got plans of his own all of a sudden. He wanted to start off again at once and when I said no, he prac-tically bit chunks out of the rocks.'

'Why should he be in a hurry, when driving down in the dark could lose another truck? You've been away from here — what? — three weeks down to Hamada and back? One more night can't make any difference.'

'God knows, but it sure is making some difference to him, so maybe he's about to spring some other piece of vital information he forgot to mention before. Let's get some sleep, anyway, because my guess is tomorrow will be as full of shit as today.'

They slept huddled together for warmth, Stephen's arms around her. He was instantly and unromantically unconscious, and when Jean drowsily worked it out she decided this must be his first rest in more than forty strain-filled hours. She could not see his face but before her senses, too, swooped into sleep, she was aware of contentment in this, the most unsafe resting place of her life.

II

THE next dawn broke with the eastern sky full of jagged clouds, which made Mezak sniff the air and say the rains were coming. Apart from that one remark his manner was stiffly unforgiving after his quarrel with Stephen the night before, their relationship changed for the worse because he had been forced to acknowledge, on the threshold of his own country, that he needed a foreigner's help to take heavily laden trucks across the shattered approaches to the King's Pass. Mezak relied on charisma and courage to inspire his followers, had warmed to Stephen Retz because any leader enjoys relaxing sometimes with an intriguingly different mind. Now he had lost face and would not be content until he felt his authority restored.

He even formally demanded his revolver back, previously lent to Stephen as a proud gesture of friendship.

They ate mush and beans together around a makeshift fire but scattered in silence back to their trucks, almost as if yesterday had been a defeat, and Saul preferred to cling wretchedly to the back of Alinza's truck rather than share a cab with persons he now perceived as his leader's enemies.

'Do you think Mezak might recover his temper as quickly as he lost it?' Jean asked. She was fairly sure herself that he wouldn't, but realised that she knew very little about Mananga's hill people.

'No.' Stephen was frowning, their truck jolting forward a yard at a time across shifting shale. 'Not until he's trodden on my tail a few times, that is.'

It was disconcerting to observe how quickly they could be put on one side as irrelevant, once that was the way Mezak wanted it. They stopped and started on shelving rock all morning, while everyone's patience deteriorated. There were bomb craters to be filled and burned-out vehicles which must be winched aside, several bodies which needed burial under cairns of stone. Fortunately the craters were shallow, in most cases flakes of rock had simply been blown off the surface, but any labour was made worse because they were all tired and irritable, suffering from reaction after several days of extraordinary exertions.

Jean watched Stephen consciously try to step aside from leadership in a situation which might have been designed for his particular brand of skills, how he kicked a stone or sketched a gesture to suggest a way forward rather than advocate it directly, but all for little gain. He was technically trained in a way Mezak could not be, his insight into what might be possible absolutely vital. Nor was his forceful intellect easily disguised; trucks working their way past obstruction in the Kosti hills a problem he expected to solve like any other. The void left by his withdrawal was as obvious as his presence had been before. This Mezak understood, and resented it all the more.

Actually, in daylight parts of their passage were not too difficult, providing everyone took the most finicking care. It was awareness that Stephen had been right which was the irritant: this quite definitely was not a route which could have been safely tackled by reckless, over-exhilarated drivers in the dark.

'What is Mezak's position in this valley?' Jean asked, while she and Stephen worked a little apart. Always, now, they were a little apart from the rest.

'In the old days he would have been the headman. In a democracy the mayor, even the local senator. His family are the largest landowners and did a deal with guerrillas some time back to leave them alone in exchange for food. That's the trouble with the valley. It could be rich, if only everyone in it didn't have to pay protection money several times over to both sides in every quarrel. Pay the guerrillas, pay Forla, pay his blackmailing officials, the Kosti grain dealers. Between them, in the end, they'll squeeze out life itself. Now I'm beginning to wonder whether Mezak hasn't decided that one friend is worth a host of enemies.'

'The guerrillas,' Jean said flatly. 'You think Forla bombed that pass because he heard Mezak's valley had thrown in with the guerrillas.'

Stephen turned to look at her, pale eyes meeting brown and at the back of them a smile she couldn't misunderstand. After a moment both looked away, which left Jean to face the fact that anything she thought she knew about her own emotions was out of date, a discovery even more disturbing than her contentment of the night before. 'I think so, yes, although I hoped you didn't,' he said eventually. 'You should be safe up at the clinic, but I'm worried about you anywhere guerrillas can call the shots. That clinic's been there fifty years or more, undisturbed, but you never know how guerrillas might jump next. I only wish there was somewhere safer for you to go.'

'Thanks.' She was coldly, furiously angry that he should think her own safety was all she cared about. 'You must remember to tell me about valley funeral rites as well. I should hate to muck up my chances of survival by doing the wrong thing after they push you over a cliff.'

'My dear,' he said, eyes fixed on the ground, 'You know I only brought you here because there wasn't anywhere else away from Forla. Speaking for myself there could have been other reasons, but I am the wrong man for you and this is the wrong place. Now it's more dangerous than I thought and I'm the bastard who made enemies out of Mezak and Lewis Anderson, who otherwise might have helped you.'

He was different from how he had been yesterday; and changed again from how he was during their journey on the locomotive, Jean thought, studying him covertly. Today is strictly no-emotion day, except for tension he could not entirely hide, and that look which meant there was one of his reactions she hadn't misunderstood.

Beyond the pass the ground fell away in a series of precipitous rock steps and in places the track was hardly marked at all. Beyond, Jean saw for the first time the great Kosti Valley: stretching as far as sight could reach and covered like a jigsaw with irregular enclosures which reached into every pocket of soil. 'It's beautiful,' she said.

Stephen nodded. 'What men do down there is the trouble.'

It took them most of the day to reach the valley floor, quite often forced to beckon each other down places Jean never imagined a truck could go. Stephen said a fine-weather road had been built some years before out of the far end of the valley so that its crops could be trucked direct to Mananga City; since it was also convenient for sending in the occasional punitive expedition, such direct communications was far from being desirable once General Forla came to power. However, after it was bulldozed through this old King's Highway had fallen into disuse, although the grain merchants of Kosti drove along it occasionally by jeep to collect their debts.

They finally reached the first parched enclosure on the valley floor as the last of the daylight faded, and everyone cheered, comradeship momentarily restored. Then the rest raced together with klaxons blaring along a narrow lane while Stephen climbed down to pour some diesel in his tank. 'This is where we peel off for the clinic, while it looks like Mezak has forgotten us until the morning.'

'Perhaps by then he won't worry about us at all.'

He grunted, whether from disbelief or stiffness as he climbed back into the cab, Jean couldn't tell. Both of them were feeling unbelievably dirty, tired and bedraggled; and thoughts of hot water, a place at last in which to feel settled and begin her work were flying like optimistic banners in her mind.

Now they had reached it, the valley became a trapping maze of thrifty cultivation, where unnumbered generations had laboured to gather rocks into walls and free good soil for crops. The only plan to its twisted trails was the warp of land, the weft of work. A few emaciated people shouted as they passed, most simply stared at crates and sacks as if they couldn't understand the hope these represented.

'The clinic is on a spur where it won't take up useful soil, and in good seasons the fathers used to grow tomatoes, squash and potatoes, so they told me. After three dry years they switched to corn and last year even that failed,' Stephen said.

'Did you live up at the clinic?'

'I visited sometimes. Mostly I've been on the move.'

'I'm sorry, but I just can't see the fit,' she said frankly. 'You and this place, I mean, now I've watched you for a week. I simply don't believe you've spent your life hiking in the hills or humping sacks of flour.'

He grinned unexpectedly. 'What, then?'

What, indeed? She shifted in her seat and looked at him consideringly, aware that she had wanted to look at him again for some time, if only the emotional temperature had not plummeted so swiftly back to zero that even snatched looks seemed an intrusion. And Stephen Retz had a disagreeable knack of making the most innocent intruder feel like a burglar caught red-handed. 'You said you came to look for disappearing US aid,' she said eventually, 'but I'd be surprised if you were a policeman or military. Or an official. Unless America grows quite different bureaucrats to us, you chance your luck too much. You're not a journalist, either.

The ones I met scavenging around casualty wards were the dregs, but I can't see you wasting time digging around in other people's lives. You may happen to look like a professor —'

'That's because I haven't often been able to shave,' he said caustically.

Secretly, she was amused to see that this was the suggestion he disliked. 'Well, you don't strike me as an academic. You fix things and move on, just observing what happened wouldn't interest you at all.' She laughed. 'Oh, I don't know! There's so much a fixer could do: engineer, property tycoon, oil exploration. I'd guess something like that.'

'Jesus,' said Stephen Retz. 'You an astrologer as well in your spare time?'

'You mean I reached pretty close?'

'A chemical engineer, originally.'

'Those rockets you made at Hamada,' she exclaimed, remembering. 'Lewis mentioned a Retz Corporation and seemed pleased you might be worth good money. To claim damages from if he got fired,' she added, when he looked puzzled.

'Conspiring with Forla must have rotted his brain. If he tried that on, I'd tie him up so tight with lawyers he'd lose everything he stole in costs.' He braked, took off his glasses, wiped them and his eyes, and put them on again. That broken windscreen had been more than just a nuisance as the day wore on. 'There aren't any lights on at the clinic.'

'Where is it?'

'You see those higher enclosures? About two fingers left.'

'I see something,' Jean said after a moment. It was very nearly dark, but she thought she glimpsed walls against rougher background. 'You mentioned the fathers were short of diesel; perhaps they're hoarding any they have left for emergencies.'

'They always kept a wick burning by the door in case someone wanted help. They also knew we hoped to bring some diesel in. I think we'll hide the truck and play it safe until we're sure everything up there is okay.'

He had half expected something to be wrong, Jean realised, wondering whether, because he feared trouble, he was looking where none existed.

They left the truck behind some walls where it might escape notice until daylight, the occasional smell of smoke betraying the presence of human habitations scattered along the valley floor. As they set out to walk the mile or so up to the mission clinic, a single flicker of lightning lit the hills high above their heads and in the distance they heard a rejoicing shout. Everywhere, people would be straining their eyes and praying, begging a variety of gods that this season the rains would not again rumble around the hills and vanish, leaving them irrevocably to starve.

They followed a footpath directly up the lower slopes of the valley, walking as cautiously as they could, their legs feeling very strange after so long cramped inside a cab. Jean couldn't really contrive much sense of danger here in this peaceful-seeming valley they had struggled so hard to reach, and thought instead how pleasant it was to be walking in warm evening air, freed at last from the antagonisms of the day. After all, she had come to Mananga to be a nurse, not to drive trucks or crunch other people's homes; had been surrounded ever since she arrived by people who needed her skills desperately, yet so far had scarcely helped anyone. Even today, when she could have broken into one of the crates to find more tubing and medicines to ease men retching up their stomach linings, Mezak had curtly brushed her aside, and refused to consider unloading a single truck.

Now she was only a few hundred yards from the clinic she had crossed half the world to reach, where experience and joint effort could accomplish something of worth at last.

Stephen slowed and put back a hand to check her. 'I smell smoke.'

She could smell it too, as she had from cooking fires while they walked up the valley side. She also thought she saw a patch of something smouldering in blackness.

'Wait here,' breathed Stephen.

She shook her head. 'No.'

They couldn't argue in case there really was danger waiting close, and went forward more slowly still. Nothing stirred; only, in spite of their care, undergrowth crackling underfoot. Stephen stopped, both of them stopped, straining their ears into the wind. No question now, this silence had to be the silence of desolation. Jean could sense Stephen hesitate between the need to discover what had happened and caution because she was with him, and went forward herself a step at a time. There could be burned or dying people praying for help in a ruined clinic, although if it had indeed burned down you would expect to find people from the valley crowded around.

She exclaimed aloud as she tripped over a body; a child, arms outspread, already cold.

When they reached further up the slope they found little flames here and there still flickering, piles of debris which glowed when you kicked them, metal just warm to the touch, including a generator blistered by the fiercer heat of burning fuel. This fire had happened many hours ago. If it had more than smouldered through the day they must have seen smoke on their journey down from the pass. On a charred verandah lay a dead goat, near a vanished door two incinerated bodies looked as if they had prayed together as they died. Jean did not need to be told that these must be the two Austrian medical monks; their tiny wards wrecked but empty except for an elderly woman who still wore a white nun's robe. She, too, was dead.

'Come,' said Stephen urgently, and pulled Jean up from where she knelt beside the nun. 'They would understand why we can't wait to bury them.'

Jean nodded, unable to speak. Impossible to say whether the doctors were dead before they burned, but the nun quite definitely had been shot. The absence of dead patients in the wards, too, suggested they had been allowed to leave before the clinic was set ablaze. The child was perhaps a victim of confusion.

As they picked their way back down the hill, Jean felt numbed by what had happened, her earlier anticipation turned to ash with the clinic. Enormous hostile spaces hissed in dark wind, mocking at eager hope; the stars which had seemed so beautiful became spiteful, cold and terrible. The Austrian brothers and the nursing nun were strangers to her, but they had not been strangers in the Kosti Valley, to whose people their lives had been devoted. There they had violently died, and though Jean was trained to accept injury and death, part of herself seemed to be murdered with this whole tragic land, where life had become so brutally hard that only the lust to kill seemed to survive.

Near where they had left the truck they saw a crumbling barn and went inside. It was completely empty, as if anything which might be of use to man or beast had been used up long before, but they needed to decide urgently what to do and, mistakenly perhaps, a barn seemed better than an open hillside in the wind.

'Either we decide to take the truck, or we don't,' Stephen said at once. 'It's as basic as that. If we do, then we have to drive, tonight, as fast as we can for the road to Mananga City and hope to God it's passable. We know the track back over the pass to Kosti is blocked and we'd only be thrown in gaol if we went there, anyway. On the other hand, Mananga City means General Forla and his troops. It's anyone's guess how much he's heard about us, personally, being concerned in an attack on Hamada and hijacking a train.'

Jean had sat and put her face down on her knees as soon as they reached the shelter of some walls. A week ago, when she had stood beside the body of a shot child in Hamada, she had felt the powers of evil beside her in the dark; now they were there again, devouring everything they touched. An enormous effort was needed to think of life instead of death. She lifted her head. 'He bombed the pass, didn't he? That probably means he's heard this valley has joined the guerrillas. To me, that's what burning a mission clinic confirms. Forla may think the train is them as well, and never hear of us at all.'

'So, we just tell everyone that we drove out of here because we didn't want to get mixed up in rebellion against Mananga's great and glorious leader, that unsuspicious guy everyone loves so much,' said Stephen drily. 'The other choice is not to take the truck, skim off as many supplies as we can carry and start hiking for the frontier. Say a hundred and fifty miles up the valley and then over the hills again.'

'Are you sure we can't stay?' said Jean slowly. 'Mezak came with you to Hamada and he's been a good ally, until today. All right, you quarrelled, but there's no doubt now he's the boss again and people get over sulks all the time. He can't have been mixed up in burning the clinic. Those ashes are nearly cold, he has to have been with us when it happened.'

'Sure, but he knew, though, didn't he?'

'He couldn't have.'

'The trucks came from here to rendezvous with us. Their drivers will have told him the guerrillas had arrived and what they planned. He would never have let us peel off on our own tonight unless he knew there was no place for us to go. I was as surprised as hell when he drove off and left us alone.'

' "Unless he knew there wasn't anywhere we could go," ' repeated Jean, and felt the skin prickle along her spine. 'If you're right it won't make any difference what we decide, because he'll be waiting.'

'Then we have to stay a jump ahead. Get out tonight while they're still celebrating.' His face was as unreadable as a hatchet in faint starlight.

They both heard the sound at the same moment, a click of stone on stone. 'You come out of there,' called Mezak. 'I your friend, Steve. You come out and we talk.'

They hadn't any choice, not the ghost of a chance, although Jean saw Stephen look swiftly around as if assessing hopeless odds; hiding in this barn revealed as a disastrous mistake. But even if they could escape this particular trap, the supplies in their truck would be under guard, would have been watched from the moment they left to walk up to the clinic, so it had never mattered what they did. Without food and water they could never reach the distant frontiers of this drought-stricken land.

Once outside they were quickly surrounded by figures only part-seen in the darkness, led down the hillside and then by winding lanes along the valley. At some point on the march their truck passed them in a flurry of dust, Mezak waving from behind the wheel. If his anger of the previous day was satisfied, he at least could perhaps be regarded as not unfriendly. Or so Jean tried to tell herself, by now too weary even to dread what might be waiting for them when this journey ended. The walk seemed endless, on rough trails through the dark and into swirling wind.

Their captors talked low-voiced along themselves, the clatter of weapons unmistakable all around. No one hustled or tried to rough them up, and when Stephen tripped the man at his side prevented him from falling, and made what sounded like a joke because everyone laughed, laughter from which Jean took such comfort as she could, which wasn't very much. When they reached a straggle of houses at last, Mezak reappeared holding Jean's rucksack and satchel in his hand, a conscientious host welcoming his guests. Their escort stopped talking and Jean sensed other watching eyes, a crowd of people standing unseen in the dark.

'Here,' said Mezak, and threw open the door of a hut. 'I send food. This better than hillside.'

He left without waiting for an answer, shutting the door behind him.

A tiny wick spluttered on a plank table, illuminating plastered walls, rugs thrown in a corner, a bowl and a jug of water. 'This is their guest hut. I stayed here before we went down to Hamada.' Stephen unzipped a grip standing in the corner. 'Clean clothes, thank God.'

Jean stood looking at bare walls, that heap of rugs, embers in the hearth. 'It doesn't look as if they plan to kill us.'

'No.' His tone sounded as if he meant, Not yet. He picked up the bowl and placed it on some embers in the hearth. 'Let's make the best of what we've got. As Mezak said, it could be better than a hillside.'

His voice was flat, his manner detached. Different again, Jean thought despairingly, when at this moment what she craved more than anything was a little human warmth. It could also be very wearing, living with a man who was never the same from one moment to the next. The odd thing was that, temperamentally, Stephen Retz did not strike her as in the least capricious.

If in Hamada she had been infuriated to discover that, a woman between two men, she immediately became a prize to be won rather than a person, here everything was different. As guests of Mezak for God knew how long or for what purposes, she was certainly going to live with Stephen in every sense of the word, whether she wanted to or not, and she happened to want to very much. I am the wrong man for you, he had said; but that was his judgement, not hers. Even without Mezak it probably would not have kept them apart for very much longer. With Mezak and his secret plans ... she smiled ruefully to herself: danger, that enemy of thought, father and flatterer of desire, soon forced its own imperatives.

As for herself, she had reached the state of mind which lived only for the moment. A hut, water, food and Stephen Retz, not necessarily in that order, temporarily fulfilled most of her wants. They would just have to take it on from there.

She remained cheerful while they took it in turns to wash in tiny amounts of water, ate mush and beans dumped on the table by a handsome, deadpan youth, and drank the same strange brown brew she had tasted in Kosti. They didn't talk much, though, Stephen chewing inattentively and answering anything she said at random, until gradually Jean's mood flattened into introspective exhaustion again. Hideous charred wraiths seemed to lurk in dark hut corners, weeping not over death but for the absence of their

God after a lifetime of dedication. Warm, clean and fed, but bereft of comfort, Jean propped her head on her hands in the hope she would think more clearly and was almost instantly asleep.

When she woke it was daylight again and she lay trying to remember what had happened. They must be in Mezak's village, whether as guests or prisoners was anyone's guess. The clinic was burned ... no, today she would refuse to remember that. She herself felt rested but tightly strung, and when she sat up at once saw Stephen lying by the hearth. In early sunlight striking through the window he looked old, cold and worn. Jean stood up to bundle together some of the rugs in which she lay, but when she turned, he was awake.

'You gave me all the rugs,' she said. 'And the bed.'

He scrubbed at his face, characteristically annoyed at being caught off guard. 'If you call it a bed. Brushwood isn't much softer than the floor.'

'But warmer.'

'It'll be hot in a hut once the sun comes up, if they keep us here all day.' He stood stiffly and went over to open the door. A boy on guard outside jumped to his feet and lifted what looked like an old British army rifle and pointed it, shaking his head. 'For Christ's sake, I'm not going far.' Stephen shoved the muzzle aside, hard, filled with reckless, early morning anger. 'You'll blow off your hand if you try to fire guns full of rust. Fetch Mezak, will you?' he added in Manangan.

The boy yelled and tried to jerk the muzzle free; Jean heard the trigger click, but either through rust or forgetfulness over a safety catch it didn't fire. People came running, stood staring in a circle while the boy shouted about what had happened; when he finished, everyone's attention shifted at once from him to Stephen and Jean, standing together in the hut entrance. No one spoke, and Jean thought she had never seen countenances so void of animation.

Only Mezak was smiling as he pushed through to reach them. 'Good morning, Steve. You want to come out? Good, you come. You, too.' He snapped his fingers at Jean before swaggering away again, very conscious of the impression he had made.

A shy girl was pushed forward who bowed to Jean, palms upward in a gesture of greeting, then beckoned for her to follow.

'It's okay, I think,' said Stephen.

Jean, still a dogged believer in the power of simple goodwill no matter what else happened, agreed. The more people here they could smile at and exchange halting words with, the better their chances of survival, provided she kept the wraiths of those Austrian brothers shut away out of sight, who had worked here for years and still had died when the guerrillas came.

Half an hour later she felt quite optimistic again. The girl, called Turka, took her to her own hut, went into peals of laughter at Jean's attempts at conversation, although they ended by understanding each other quite well, and offered her one of the local twig loofahs with which to scour her body in the absence of water to waste on washing. From there they went to the women's latrine, which, from smug comments, Jean gathered was infinitely preferable to the men's.

When they met again at their hut, Stephen had shaved and looked more himself, less like bones flung out to dry. 'There's quite a camp out beyond the village,' he said at once.

'Guerrillas?'

'I should think so. I asked Mezak but he wouldn't say.'

'More surprises,' Jean said resignedly. 'And more mush and beans for breakfast.'

He grinned. 'You wait until you've lived three months mostly on flour and water paste.'

'Three months? That's how long since you flew into Mananga from America?'

'More or less, it's easy to lose count around here.' He stood up restlessly. Two guards were now on the door, both carrying weapons more modern than a rifle; it looked as if they would be confined to this hut at least for today. 'You wouldn't believe it, but five hundred years ago this place was a city. There's ruins larger than Boston at the time of the Tea Party. The old Manangan kings ruled from here and made their slaves dig contour channels to catch the rains and prevent erosion. I've seen covered cisterns a hundred feet long which would have seen a big population through a drought. Except nowadays they leak.'

'Did you come to see if you could restore the system?' Jean asked curiously. She still couldn't work it out; Stephen was far too quickly exasperated by inefficiency to be accustomed to roughing it in the wilds. He had also trained as a chemical engineer, not in hydraulics.

'I came to track down fraud, like I said, but travelling around while trying to discover what had happened to more than a year's worth of supplies, I spent time looking at old water channels too. Until Mezak and I got talking about how we could maybe ship food up here from Hamada, and the rest you know.'

'Except there now seems quite a lot neither of us know.'

'Oh, I think we can figure out most of it once it's too late,' he said sharply. 'In Mananga there are only gangsters and victims. Forla and anti-Forla, trampling everyone else underfoot. In the end Forla and the Kosti merchants between them squeezed Mezak and his valley so hard they decided to take sides before they starved, and I didn't realise fast enough that when you become anti-Forla you have to become a gangster, too. That food we freighted from Hamada will feed guerrillas and not the valley farmers, so maybe it's just as well we brought less than we hoped. Now, everyone here who can becomes a guerrilla, because all the rest will certainly starve.'

'The clinic ... Catholic brothers would have treated even guerrillas if they were hurt. There wasn't any need to kill them.'

'Guerrillas march light and don't expect their wounded to survive. A clinic would only interest them as the random factor in a very simple equation. Forla and anti-Forla, victim and murderer; those brothers meant more than that to this valley. I met them and I'm ashamed to admit I found them too innocent, almost ... well, made juvenile by isolation, if I'm honest. But they were good men and the valley is full of juvenile innocents who could relate to simple goodness. I can see why they had to die once guerrillas decided to use the valley's last hope of food to help them win a campaign against Forla. The brothers wouldn't have liked that and they'd have said so.'

Jean's eyes locked with his and this time neither looked away. What Stephen said made sense, the only reason they weren't dead, too, that they weren't seen as a threat, as principled Christian brothers had been. Quite possibly Mezak also had a purpose for them, death held over while they might be useful. Very distantly, a rumble of thunder sounded in the wind as if to emphasise the storm building all around, and in reply the same cries of welcome from the streets outside. But no rain. No rain again, only a few clouds drifting beyond the hills and heat during the day which was worse than tending a locomotive firebox. Then the thunderheads drained away again, accompanied by wails of desolation like those which must have greeted an onset of plague and the wind became cold instead of blisteringly hot.

The sulky, good-looking youth brought them food again at dusk and it was obvious he had eaten some of it on the way; difficult to blame him if he had. Both Stephen and Jean were hungry, restless and tense, neither used to idleness. Their physical proximity was a quite different strain and in unexpected ways, when heat, under-nourishment and close surveillance made a natural release of desire impossible, which itself became intensified by restraint.

Sometime during the afternoon, as the long hot ominous hours of confinement seemed to last for ever, Jean began to tell Stephen about herself and why she had come to Mananga, only to find him a predictably skilled interrogator who accepted very little at face value. 'We have a farm,' she said, in answer to a question. 'And it was beginning not to make sense that we should be told to cut back on production while half the world was short of food. All of a sudden there were grants to turn our fields into camp sites, people suggesting we ought to sell our dairy herd. If Dad and my brother had wanted to manage tourists they wouldn't have spent their lives in love with a pattern of fields. Since I came here it all looks crazier than ever, but I haven't found too many answers either, if giving grain to the starving means handing it over for racketeers to sell, guerrillas to steal. Even in Kosti they saw free grain as something which spoiled their prices. But there must be better places than Mananga where it's different.'

'I sure as hell hope so,' said Stephen. 'You, though. You didn't down tools and come here because of campers on your farm.'

'I'm a nurse. I'm needed here.'

'Sure. And in all those hospitals in England. So, why Mananga? Someone must have warned you what it could be like.'

'Not really. The clinic was safe, they said. It had been here a long time and never had any trouble. Forla was tough on his people but never worried foreigners, he needed them too much.'

'I guess most foreigners take care not to tangle with him, except maybe at a conference somewhere safe like Geneva. You still haven't answered, why Mananga.'

'I didn't see the fit with you, either, remember? If it's so damn hot we can only sit around examining our consciences then it's your turn next. I think you guessed already, I didn't come to tend the Third World's bleeding heart.' She paused. 'I thought I did.

It helps to imagine that was the reason, but when you're really frightened and too exhausted for pretence, you start looking at a few lies and not believing them any longer. I came because I'd spent nearly six years in a trap. I got engaged to the boy next door, never looked at anyone else, really, and he had a motor-cycle accident three weeks later. He took those six years to die. Right from the beginning I knew he would probably die, certainly never be a man again, but it didn't seem decent not to pretend I was waiting, to promise that of course I would. So I did, and the worst thing was to discover that by the end all I really wanted was for him to hurry up and die. That side of yourself takes some facing, and after it was finished, when I decided to light out and start making up for all the living I hadn't done, I suppose I needed to choose somewhere I felt good about. So I came to Mananga, and if anyone tried to warn me then I didn't want to listen.'

'Me, too,' he said, and hesitated, an inappropriate look of concentration on his face, as if he was considering a problem from an angle he hadn't seen before. 'Anderson mentioned the Retz Corporation. My father founded it and I spent fifteen years working to build it into an outfit I was proud of, then the next two defending it from predators who decided it was worth taking over. At the finish I was richer than my broker and my lawyer, but not much. I'd lost the Retz and my wife had gotten tired of me thinking more about it than her. We didn't have kids who might have helped.'

I expect she also liked the thought of all those takeover dollars just waiting to be divided, Jean thought but did not say.

'I needed to start over and couldn't find the guts,' he added, and sounded as if it was a relief to explain. 'I wasn't used to bumming around golf courses. My brother works in the State Department and he remarked that several consignments of Retz fertiliser had been lost in Mananga, along with nearly everything else we sent, why didn't I take a look. I was drinking too much and I guess he knew there wouldn't be too much Scotch out here for me to start seeing those red snakes crawl up the wall.' There was something in his tone which told Jean how close he had come to seeing those red snakes; even in Mananga a rotgut spirit was distilled from grain desperately needed for food and available for dollars.

'Searching a conscience isn't something anyone wants to do too often,' Jean said, and hoped he understood she did not mean to poke about where she wasn't wanted.

133

Those telltale fingers started drumming before his hands lifted off the table out of sight. 'It seemed a way out. Quit everything for a while and at least Mananga doesn't attract tourists. That was the way I saw it. Then, when the going got rougher, I felt ashamed to quit again. I'm more used to boardrooms and chemical plants than Mezak on an adrenalin high, but once I realised the people in this valley could feed half Mananga if only they got a straight deal, I began thinking how to reach that food rotting on the quay at Hamada. I wanted to prove something to myself, I guess. What I actually did, of course, was bring you and a load of freight all the way to a new guerrilla base, encouraged them to come here, too, and burn out those brothers in the clinic.'

'We all have to accept we influence people just by existing,' Jean said slowly. 'I have learned that, at least. It isn't your fault guerrillas came to the Kosti Valley and if you're right, then Mezak is making the best of a situation he didn't foresee, either.'

'Good intentions in heavy hobnailed boots.' His tone was bitter.

'They're better than most other intentions I've seen so far in Mananga. Forla and anti-Forla: until that changes everything else is irrelevant, including us.'

'Go home, Yankee,' he said with a glimmer of a smile.

'Go somewhere else for a while, if we ever get out of here,' she answered feelingly. 'I suppose I might persuade the guerrillas to let me work here while those six crates of medical supplies last out, but they're as likely as Forla to call antibiotics aphrodisiacs and trade them for guns. Unless that's me swinging from innocence to cynicism too fast.'

By then dusk had come at last and, freed from their guards' curiosity, he did not answer but instead came over and held her as if danger did not exist, their stillness slowly filling with what both had wanted since ... perhaps from the first moment they met in a Hamada backstreet. His mouth was seeking hers and the sharp angles of his body were under her hands. Distantly, Jean tried to remember that this was this and nothing more, that he had warned her he was the wrong man for a woman whose only experience was of watching in faithful anguish and frustration while a loved friend paid, nerve by painful nerve, for a wet-night skid at a hundred miles an hour. That she had also known she must be wrong for a sophisticated man at home in America's West Coast business and social world, she tried to remember but soon forgot. Forgot every-

134

thing except that here and now he wasn't wrong for her. Then forgot that too, taken unaware by the urgency of a man who had been many months alone; her own urgency too, so long and ruthlessly stamped out of sight. Yet even in urgency the shadow of tenderness remained, of care and skill when, startled, he realised the completeness of what she had told him and that this really was the first time for her. And then, when she ceased to forget, it was joyful splendour she remembered first.

Stephen slept much longer than she did, lying quite still as if it was a long time since he had known peace. Whereas for Jean, a new happiness existed in lying drowsily awake. She also decided it seemed distinctly odd to realise how little she still knew about Stephen Retz when he could so effortlessly make her body sing. But already it seemed less important than before and after a while she slept too.

He was awake when she stirred, so in the dawn she discovered a man who was again different, but this time because of her. The edges of his face had eased, the sense of strain softened. He shifted slightly and kissed her. 'My sweet. Do you know the exact moment I began to love you?'

Jean shook her head, feeling absurdly disappointed. She did not want pretence about love to spoil what they had gained. Once the slimy, sinuous tentacles of obligation wrapped around them, she would never know where — or if — truth had been taken by the scruff, and died. But perhaps he thought that because she had been virgin, she must be a romantic innocent who expected hackneyed phrases. She was, of course, which did not help.

His fingers drifted across her face and came to rest on her lips. ' ... When you stood on a footplate wondering how the hell we would ever shift a damned great locomotive. Your lips laughing and your eyes not giving a damn for anyone.'

'Coal dust on my face,' Jean said helpfully.

He laughed, an uninhibited rocket of delight which finished the conversation until much later. Over breakfast, which was the same sparse mush brought by the same morose youth, he remained extravagantly cheerful, laughing easily, words leaping from one irrelevance to another as if he refused to look beyond each moment as it came. He also seemed much younger and not in the least like an ex-president of the Retz Corporation, as if a great deal about him had never been let off a very tight leash before.

135

Jean watched him covertly, wondering.

She did not believe such unthinking ease could last, even while she enjoyed it enormously, and it didn't. She was almost pleased this time when he changed, because it showed she had begun to understand a little of him, if only hesitantly as yet.

The moment they had eaten the last unpalatable blob of gruel, he sobered up. His head slanted as if his senses consciously took up a burden, his movements becoming more restless until he was pacing from the door to the single window and back again; answering her in monosyllables. Now he looked again a man who had been driven hard for a long time, and was well used to finding enemies behind his back.

Jean knew he felt her watching him, but this time he obstinately refused to respond and seemed almost relieved when the guards on the door came in and beckoned for him to follow them.

'I'm coming too,' she said, alarmed.

Stephen hesitated. 'If I'm to do business with guerrillas it could be better if I went alone. Whatever they may say about freedom fighting, you can bet they won't have gotten around to sex equality in the ranks.'

'I'm coming,' she repeated stubbornly; she was afraid of being left alone, afraid also that he might negotiate some deal which brought her safety at his expense.

'If they'll let you,' he agreed reluctantly, caught between a preference for facing risk alone and awareness that once they separated, then life in the Kosti Valley was sufficiently precarious for them to be kept apart, whether by accident or design, for ever.

The guards mumbled angrily among themselves when Jean tagged along, and stared as if by coming she declared herself a whore, but clearly did not care sufficiently about any woman to make a fuss when Stephen said that if they left her behind then they would have to take him by force.

The village straggled along intersecting unsurfaced tracks, among what Jean at first thought were outcroppings of rock but later realised were the ruins of the earlier settlement Stephen had described. There were children and some skinny pigs running about, emaciated women walking under burdens and quite a lot of young men being drilled haphazardly by guerrillas, who were marked out from the rest by the olive green denims or khaki shirts they wore. One group squatted around a stripped machine-gun, the rest carried an assortment of other weapons, from automatic rifles to bladed knobkerries. Inscrutable faces turned as Jean and Stephen passed, a skull-like patience making them look dismayingly alike. Jean sensed distrust, and guilt maybe for the burned clinic, and one or two of the guerrillas spat as they passed, until their guards, who had been indifferently polite, began to shout and jostle them, enmity an infection which was very easily caught.

They passed gangs of women digging to reach water below a dry stream bed, on the far side of which the guerrillas had set up camp in a grove of prickly bushes. Jean guessed there might be as many as three or four hundred men camouflaged from the air by the scrub. Beyond this camp the parched fields began, above them the hills and glorious, pitiless blue sky.

They stopped outside a hastily built hut, their guards relaxing to chat to others there, sharing cigarettes which crackled like bonfires. To Jean's surprise, Saul, her companion in the truck on the journey from Kosti, stood among the idlers there, proudly fingering a grenade hanging from his belt.

'How is your stomach?' she asked at once; he still looked very sick.

He shrugged. 'Not bad.'

'Be careful. Rest as much as you can and drink —' She caught herself. How could she tell him to drink as much clean water as he could hold? 'Sip any water you are allowed throughout the day.'

'I will try,' he answered quietly, and held out his hand, palm up, in the same instinctive gesture of friendship as the woman, Turka, had used.

'I thought when I first reached here that these people had survived centuries of oppression with quite extraordinary dignity,' Stephen observed. 'Really, only Westerners think death matters so goddamn much. People here might prefer to endure starvation, if, after taking their food the guerrillas also offered them a chance to show they could fight as well, or better than the other armed gangs running around.'

If he was right, that could be very bad news for us, Jean thought.

A guerrilla hung with weapons came out of the hut and jerked his head for Stephen to enter. He tried to block Jean when she followed, but Stephen shouldered him aside and he wasn't quick enough over thinking what to do about it, since a brawl in his leader's hut could land him in trouble too. By then she was inside, and the first things she saw were her precious six cases of medical supplies being used as chairs. It was a tremendous relief to discover them again and a possible starting point for negotiations on beginning work at last. Otherwise, the hut contained quite a lot of people, a roughly nailed table, and weapons piled wherever there was space.

Behind the table sat a man with dark ruffled hair, trimmed-stubble cheeks and a mouth like a pair of thin-bladed scissors. Mezak lounged easily beside him, idly whittling at a packing case.

'You sit down, Steve,' he said, and snapped his fingers. 'Another sit for Missis Jean.'

Jean and Stephen sat circumspectly, pretending not to notice the other faces crowded around.

'This Michaels, our commander,' Mezak added, after a pause.

'Michael ... ?' asked Stephen tentatively.

'Michaels,' said Mezak firmly, and prised a long splinter off the edge of the table.

'We drink to our campaign, eh?' Michaels interrupted, and produced a bottle. 'Then we get down to business.' He spoke good English with an American accent and did not sound unfriendly, as if education at some college in the United States predisposed him in their favour. These courtesies were so different from anything Jean expected that she felt ridiculous, and failed to respond when he greeted her in turn, which might be just as well, since it soon became clear that Michaels' American education stopped short of expecting her to take any part in the proceedings. He turned back at once to Stephen and lifted his glass, smiling. 'To Forla's guts on a bonfire while he still lives to watch them burn, eh? Now I explain what I want you to do.'

Stephen drank, no point cavilling over the manner of Forla's death. 'Our work here is finished now we have helped to bring in food. I am sorry only four trucks got through, but we would be grateful for a chance to leave. Much needs to be done if more supplies are to reach Mananga.'

'It is not often given that men are able to follow their own desires,' answered Michaels blandly.

'That is true, but your fight against Forla is not our fight, and I am not a soldier. The reverse, in fact. I was born to a belief which says men should not take life.'

'That is a belief for slaves!' exclaimed Michaels, astonished, in

Manangan, so everyone in the hut echoed surprise and agreement even though they had not understood the argument. 'Forla is vermin, every man who is a man should help to exterminate him.'

Stephen shrugged without answering and Michaels laughed, before reverting to college American. 'Your story sound like bullshit, man, but it don't matter. Mezak told me about your rockets in Hamada and I want the same, only fuck much bigger, when we attack Mananga City.'

'And if I make them you will let us go?'

'Sure, if rockets do what I want.'

Stephen swirled the spirit remaining in his glass. 'And what is that?'

Mezak leaned forward eagerly. 'Steve, this give us Forla. I tell Michaels what you make and he say, There is ammunition ... heap?'

'Store?'

' ... Ammunition store in Mananga City. If we explode it the pigmen of Forla explode in bits too. Then the rest run when we attack, like in Hamada.'

'Those rockets I made were toys. Many sparks and a bang, but no power. They wouldn't punch through a bean can.'

'We have better explosives here.' Michaels was smiling again; a different kind of smile which was nothing to do with humour or a welcome.

'But no proper firing mechanisms or you wouldn't be asking me about rockets. Nor have you said how near the city this ammunition store is.'

Michaels put out his hand and Mezak immediately gave him his knife; no doubt about who was boss of the Kosti Valley now. Michaels stabbed at the table top. 'Here is Forla's palace, this —' Another stab. ' — the railroad depot. You been there?'

Stephen nodded. 'There's an avenue between the palace and the station, all clogged up with a market near the tracks.'

'Here,' the knife stuck quivering near the gouge which marked the station. 'Here is the store. A factory once, flat concrete roof. Everything Forla needs for his troops kept here. Loot. Fuel. Ammunition. Shells. Trucks and guns parked in the barrack next door. All under his eye. Everything go up if we explode it.'

'Together with most of the slums of Mananga City,' said Stephen drily.

'We're building a movement here, not playing baseball! Our people die willingly for victory over Forla. If we lose, then we dead too.'

A muscle jerked under Stephen's eye. 'No rocket I could make would penetrate a concrete roof, and even Forla has to store ammunition in flashproof bunkers. For God's sake, he can't keep much in the middle of a city. Emergency stocks maybe for quick response, the rest will be somewhere safer.'

'He's an idle bastard with shitheads for an army,' Michaels said dispassionately. 'Deserters tell me this warehouse is loaded with everything. No flashproof bunkers.'

Stephen put down the remains of his drink. 'Then they also told you that to blow up fuel and ammunition near a city will kill hundreds of civilians as well as soldiers, maybe thousands. Jesus, you've just drawn this warehouse next to the market.'

'If people die, everyone blame Forla for being so fucking ignorant. Then our cause unite the living of Mananga City, the dead not around to worry.'

Mezak slammed his fist on the table. 'I tell you, Steve good!'

'He full of bullshit too.' Michaels' eyes had become flat, black pits.

'Trust Michaels, Steve,' urged Mezak. 'If he say when that store explode you and the woman go free, he mean it.'

'I haven't said it yet.' Michaels hesitated and then added, 'Okay. You do what I want and I let you go.'

Stephen's eyes dropped to those stab marks on the table, shifted to Mezak and then back to Michaels again. 'I'll think about it.'

'Bet your ass you will,' Michaels snapped.

'I need to think about it,' Stephen repeated. He drank the spirits left in his glass and stood.

Jean stood too, dread stuck like vomit in her throat.

Michaels reached below the table and brought up a machine-pistol. 'This is the thinking that counts in Mananga.'

'Oh sure, and when your finger came off the trigger I'd be chopped, but you would have lost any chance of getting those rockets.' Stephen managed to sound sarcastic, but the colour had drained from behind the weathering on his face.

Unexpectedly, Michaels hooted with laughter, seized the bottle and tipped a huge gulp of raw spirits down his throat. 'Okay, think hard, Steve. Then you do what I say.'

Jean followed Stephen out into the sun, where half the village and most of the guerrillas must have been trying to hear what was going on inside their leader's hut. They and their guards needed to force their way through the crowd, and muttered speculation followed them all the way to the dry stream bed.

Their guards mumbled together, too, trailing several paces behind so that by the time they reached the village Jean and Stephen might almost have been alone. The sun was warm on their backs and the sky was sparklingly clear, the hills soft behind blowing haze. To Jean, briefly light-headed with relief that they had come alive out of Michaels' hut, the earth had seldom seemed more beautiful than the Kosti Valley did that afternoon.

Then, involuntarily, she looked over her shoulder to where crowds of people still watched, silent now. Their guards were hurrying to catch up, the guns they held pointed directly at her and Stephen's backs, guns which were as likely to be fired by accident as intent, and no one to care much about the difference.

Instantly, that moment of relief was over and Jean heard her lungs start grabbing for great gulps of air, while all her bones felt loose.

12

THEY sat in their bare hut, waiting.

The window wouldn't open and stale air became more unpleasant as the day drew on. A heavy sultriness was beginning to brood over the valley as if the rains might break at last; a different tension, too, as people whispered about a duel of wills between the guerrilla leader and his prisoner.

When Stephen tried to go out guns were instantly shoved into his ribs and the guards unceremoniously kicked him back inside. No food came and by dusk they were hungry and very thirsty.

'How to win friends,' Jean said. Better to joke, however feebly, than think incessantly about thirst.

Stephen came over from where he had been prowling around the hut and bent to kiss her, hands on her shoulders. 'I'd settle for winning anything at this moment.'

You won me, she thought. This must be where my inexperience shows, because in this extremity I would not change where I am, if by changing you were no longer with me. Even though all Stephen thinks about is escape.

'We have to get out of this hut before we can begin to figure the next move,' he said slowly now. 'If you have worked out any way of doing it without stringing Michaels along as best we can, then please say so. I think we might be able to burrow out through the roof, but it would take most of the night and without anywhere to run would only make matters worse.'

'What would you do if you were alone?' Jean stared at his spread fingers on her arm.

They curled tight. 'I am not alone.'

'But if you were?' She did not even know him well enough to judge whether she was behaving like a clod to persist.

'For God's sake, leave it, will you?' He went over to stand by the window again.

'It's my life as well as yours and I don't see why I should,' she said sharply. 'You'd tell Michaels to go to hell, wouldn't you? It's because I am here that you've decided you have to lie and cheat, set out to kill several hundred people in Mananga City with explosive rockets. Risk finding that your bluff turns sour and, because of me again, you actually have to do it. Well, I don't want that. Not because I'm brave, but because you would hate and despise me if you did.'

'No! You're quite wrong,' he said violently.

'Am I?' She felt sadness like the storm in the air around them. 'I don't think so.'

'The way I felt when I came to Mananga ... I wouldn't have minded telling Michaels to go to hell. As deaths go, a bullet is quicker than rotgut by the quart. Now I want to live if I can. I want you to live. God, how I want you to live!'

'Of course, play Michaels along; who wants to die?' She smiled, aware that this was not a time for high emotional temperatures. 'Certainly not me, after only one night on a hard mud floor with you. But promise you won't string along with guerrillas a single step further than you want, because of me. You have to be free to judge ... I have to be free to judge ... otherwise, even if we should get out of Mananga, you'll be back among those red-eyed snakes and I'll — ' She would have lost the man she loved, and the rest of her life could be spent in solitude worse than this stuffy, stinking hut.

Stephen did not deny it, but came back from the distance where he had stood, and this time offered something more than comfort. The roughness of his cheek against hers, his hands on her body a violent pleasure made more insistent by the ever-present undertow of terror.

'Promise?' Jean whispered, much later when it was dark.

'Oh Christ,' he said wearily, and moved almost with revulsion in her arms. 'It's years since I handled chemicals without a factory full of other guys doing the hard grind. I'm way out of my depth in Mananga, just kidding myself and you that maybe I can figure an angle to take us clear. I guess I've spent my life figuring angles, but not in a godforsaken valley where the nearest help is a bastard called Forla.'

She lay in his arms thinking, If I don't ask, I shall never hear any answers. 'You'll have to tell me why.'

'Why what?'

'Why you won't promise.'

'What the hell kid's stuff is that? I promised myself I'd save the Retz Corporation from being taken over, but it didn't make any difference and neither would anything I said now. I failed then and I shall probably fail again here, but I surely am not fighting Michaels, Mezak and Forla while carrying your conscience as baggage.'

'Yours, too.'

' ... Yes.' He was no longer holding her.

If, during the past two nights, Jean had started to discover how splendid love could be, she was also learning how much it hurt when the man she loved remained beyond her reach. Neither the dangers they faced nor physical desire had anything to do with it: the essence of Stephen Retz was no closer to her now than when they met in Hamada, a failure which left her own love desolate.

Ever since that first meeting she had sensed an unexpectedness in him, but put it down to her ignorance of men who ran large corporations. Only in passing had she thought it strange he should be wandering, solitary, in a place like Mananga, since what she responded to was his drive and apparent certainty, which made any explanation he chose to give sound reasonable. The most extravagant risk made scarcely to seem like a risk at all if he was there to judge the odds. Now, quite suddenly, she wasn't sure about him; nor which of them might in the end prove to be the stronger. God knew, she felt afraid; even more vulnerable than he was as a captive in the Kosti Hills. But the empty, unlucky years before she came to Mananga had seemed so long that she couldn't now regret the chance which had brought her here; the only trouble was, if Stephen cared for her at all then they ought by now to have felt less separate than before. Instead they lay apart, each thinking their secret and lonely thoughts.

'My dear, you're crying,' he said, much later.

'What the devil do you expect?' she answered fiercely. 'Go to sleep and leave me alone. I'll be all right in the morning.'

'This isn't any good, is it?' He rolled over and stood up, and a moment later Jean heard him angrily jerking on his clothes.

Jean dressed too, since it seemed absurd to stay lying on nobbled twigs while he ranged around the hut longing to get a whole lot further away from her. But, once unhappy introspection was replaced by the reality of a cramped and unlit hut with guards outside the door, she was immediately aware again of thirst and her stomach growled with hunger. 'How long do you think Michaels will leave us here?' She had not meant to speak.

'As long as it takes. All he's interested in is getting what he wants.'

'He hasn't got unlimited time, though, has he? He plans to march on Mananga City and wants you as an ally, but he has to leave soon, without you if he must, in case the rains come.'

'Maybe. But we only stay alive while we might come in useful. The day I say no and mean it, or he thinks I'm double-crossing him, we're dead.' His detached, expressionless voice came out of the dark, not detailing what else might happen to them, to her in particular, before they died.

'All right, so we make up some good lies as we go along. I'm pretty good at lying after all those years Phil lay in hospital, and I don't suppose you fought too many financial battles telling God's truth all the time,' Jean said.

'Yeah,' his voice sounded very soft and deadly out of the dark. 'And this time it's your life or those of a couple of thousand Manangans laid on the line for me to lose, not dollars and a corporation. I'm sorry, but I seem quite suddenly to have reached the end of making choices which leave me as a murderer.'

'But—' Jean's mind was shuttering on comprehension, lack of comprehension, admitting disjointed streaks of light. 'We string along like you said. With luck, a few lies will take us a little nearer home than this valley. If that luck runs out we shall at least be able to try and run, a shot in the back a cleaner death than being butchered here. We have the right to try and lie, make a few gambles first and see if by some miracle one pays off.'

'I'm not sure I can. That's what I have to tell you, which I guess sounds pretty spineless. I came to Mananga to get away from those choices I always lost, then chose again like the criminal I am. That splendid guy Retz, bringing food up to Kosti like the Seventh Cavalry on a charge. Bringing you, too. I'm not sure how many that particular idea has killed so far, but it includes all the valley people unable to follow Michaels as guerrillas, as well as those Austrian missionaries.'

'You didn't kill them!'

'They would be alive if I had stayed in the States.'

'And how many others dead from hunger and extortion?' If Jean had wondered before at his almost fanatical determination to succeed once things began to go wrong, she was learning some answers now. 'So you've decided to stand aside and let Michaels shoot or rape me, without even trying to prevent him?' she added brutally. She hated herself for staying across the room from him, for trying to make him face the meaning of his words, but didn't think softness was what he needed. A criminal, he called himself, which she found impossible to believe. Yet the truth was here, somewhere, if only she could recognise it, and must not be scuffled out of sight again.

'No. Of course ... no. I'd have to ... ' His voice trailed away.

'Take a knife to him?' she said sarcastically. 'Try to punch him on the jaw in a room so full of his followers a rat couldn't breathe? What's wrong with using the brain you've got, instead of muscle you haven't, when faced by a lump of tallow twice your weight and a lifetime quicker on a knife?'

'I'll try, of course I shall try. It was when I started to think how to try, that I couldn't see past that need to kill again. But as you said earlier: Leave me alone and in the morning I guess I'll be okay.' He sounded utterly defeated.

Jean took a deep breath, chasing her splintered thoughts into some kind of order. She wanted to yell at him to stop dithering

145

like a fool when his strength was what she needed: some things are more important than hobgoblins in the dark. Her life, for instance. And yet ... and yet ... there must be good reasons why, at this most disastrous of moments, a tough and resourceful man had become so hamstrung by uncertainty.

She groped across to that disembodied voice and held his arms tightly. 'I couldn't start choosing, either, between other people's lives.'

'You often have done as a nurse, and thought nothing of it. It's what you were trained for, and most often you would have chosen right.' He was as taut as wire under her hands. 'Judging chances came easy to me, too, decide what to do and on to the next problem. As a kid I rubbed everyone up. Then Vietnam came along. My family was Quaker but me, I didn't want to dodge the draft, lied about my age to make sure the war wasn't over before I reached it. To show my folks, I guess, God knows what or why. All I wanted was not to be different any longer and of course I wouldn't get shot. When I got there I realised fast enough that I very easily could be, but killing ... it seemed like knocking over rabbits, not personal at all. Then, one day — you can guess there weren't Quaker preachers in the army, so I used to stand guard while the rest of the platoon took mass. They were mostly Irish from back east, I don't know why. Well, that day the priest had just finished when I saw something move in a tree and if you wanted to live, you shot first in a war like that. And boy, did I want to live! I had an eye for sharp-shooting and a dead Viet Cong fell out of the branches; everyone slapped me on the back and chalked up another dead slant to our score. Only, he wasn't holding a gun on us, he'd had his hand on a crucifix under his shirt. He must have been raised on some French mission and risked his life to join in our mass and wear such a symbol of his faith in a Communist army. I didn't like shooting anyone too much after that, began thinking a few things which hadn't worried me before, was ready to make some apologies when I got home. Lucky for me the war was nearly over. Less lucky I didn't write how I felt, because Father was dead before we could talk. I was kind of crazy, I guess, a lot of us were after Vietnam, but when I quit the army I set out to build up his fertiliser company into a corporation everyone would notice. My idea of reparation maybe, which he would have thought deserved the godless end it got.'

146

'Thank you for telling me,' Jean said quietly. Whole blocks of his personality, which previously had baffled her, began to slide into place. Vietnam might have been the cruel dislocation in his life, but only successive shocks could have brought a naturally decisive man to the point where he hesitated over making any decision at all.

No kids, she remembered.

No Retz Corporation; probably no return to any faith.

No food for the Kosti Hills, when, against the odds, a few truck-loads had been brought up safely from Hamada. A highly complex, risky operation planned and carried through because of anger over the plight of people needlessly left to starve; yet Stephen Retz had come to Mananga to escape responsibility, failure, even a reality he could no longer bear. Another defeat the price for trying to use his own capacities again. She also remembered how, the night they met in Hamada, he had almost immediately been forced to kill a soldier: and what she saw afterwards was another failure, because it had been a serious mistake to strike down Lewis so harshly that he became a lasting enemy, especially while they faced a situation where unity was vital. A mistake to make so few allowances for the many compromises anyone dealing with Forla had to make. Yet, looking back and recalling his agitated fingers drumming on a table, Jean was sure, now, that from the moment Stephen killed that soldier he had been struggling to think coherently at all.

Now here they were, trapped in the Kosti Valley; and the life which this time depended on a whole series of impossible choices laid before him was her own.

The silence lengthened while Jean hesitated over what to say, any mistake now difficult to forgive.

Then the door behind her back crashed open, letting in a blast of dusty wind and Michaels was there, beating his hands together and bellowing for their guards to bring a lamp. 'Ah, Steve, how a woman helps a long night to pass!' He was clearly disappointed not to find them in bed together. 'Now you would like to take breakfast with me, eh?'

13

THAT dawn breakfast with Michaels was the best meal they had eaten since Pierre's cooking on Hamada dockside: hot instead of cold, dried spicy strips of meat and flat discs of bread instead of mush, pints of steaming brown liquid. At first Michaels' arrival took them both so much by surprise, and the effort needed to switch their minds from their own affairs was so great, that they simply sat down with him at the table, drank thirstily and ate whatever was put before them. Not that they could have done anything else. He had a knife in his belt, a holstered gun under one arm and held a machine-pistol across his knees.

'That is better, eh?' he said, wiping his mouth as they finished the last of the bread.

'Sure,' said Stephen. 'How many in the valley will eat like us today?'

Michaels winked. 'My men eat or they don't fight good. The rest are used to waiting until harvest.'

Stephen stood up and went to stand by the hearth, his face in shadow. 'Why did you come?'

'You are too direct, my friend.'

'I find it sometimes pays.'

Michaels clicked a catch on the machine-pistol several times, then hefted it left-handed and pointed it straight at Stephen. 'Maybe I came to shoot you.'

Jean's throat dried as she realised that Stephen had moved to give himself more space away from her when Michaels, inevitably, became aggressive. But somehow she must keep her nerve, and by staying still reassure him that she believed he was capable of making a deal with Michaels. Because at this moment there was no trace, no trace at all of that anguished self-doubt the guerrilla captain had interrupted. Those fissures of weakness were hidden by a façade of confidence, its brittleness something only she could know and owe him her equally false confidence in return.

'You didn't waste good rations if you meant to fill us afterwards with bullets,' he said flatly now.

Michaels shouted with laughter, like a man who hadn't enjoyed himself so harmlessly for years. 'I would not kill you, Steve. See, the catch is safe all the time.' He threw the gun at Stephen. Fortunately, he caught it and with the muzzle pointing upwards; the jerk sprayed bullets through the roof in a shattering roar.

Michaels laughed again. 'I forget sometimes which way to put so small a catch. Sit down, Steve. We do not need guns between us.' The sound of firing brought scared guards bursting in; he rapped an order at them and, bug-eyed, reluctantly, they withdrew.

Stephen leaned the gun carefully against the hearth and came over. 'My answer is still no.'

Michaels raised his hands in exaggerated surprise. 'I have not asked any question.'

'Not yet.'

'Steve, I came this time alone so no one hear their captain ask a favour. Mezak says you hate Forla, curse him for beating, looting and shooting us. Why should you refuse to help?'

Stephen shook his head. In slowly strengthening dawn light he looked sick, the façade as thin as paper now. 'Because I can't believe the winner wins in this kind of war. Only that men die and their families weep for them. If you succeed in taking Mananga City you will kill every Forla man you catch, burn alive his police, steal whatever you want. As they will kill and burn you, if they afterwards recapture it.'

'Should we let Forla stew us in our own lard for ever, so you may enjoy peace and profits in America? You do not smell rotting corpses if you are far away, eh? So that is the way you prefer it.'

'Yes,' said Stephen quietly. 'That is how I prefer it.'

Michaels slammed his hand down on the table. 'You are the one who should be burned on a bonfire!'

'Perhaps. Then I would be dead and, if I was fortunate, a woman would weep for me, but your cause not be helped at all.'

'How is it helped if I leave you alive?'

'You are about to tell me,' Stephen answered. He was sitting very still, every muscle strung tight.

Michaels spat full in his face, drawing the knife out of his belt in the same instant. 'Do not move, except to put your hands on the table. Slowly.'

Stephen wiped the gob of spittle off his cheek first, then put his hands on the table. He appeared calmer than before, as if his mind was cleared by crisis, although decision was still lacking. But what decision? Jean thought apprehensively. Surely he had left decision far too late and this was where weakness showed. If he intended to deceive Michaels then he should already have offered some glimmer of concession.

'You.' Michaels jerked his head contemptuously at Jean, and silently she put her hands on the table, too.

'Good,' he added, watching Stephen like a vulture. 'I speak and you jump, eh?'

'I am listening, as I was before,' Stephen answered.

'Forla feasts in Mananga City after finishing rebellion in rivers of blood. So he thinks. Everywhere guys fighting him are stomped into garbage and he think we are too few for him to worry about any more.' He flicked a thumbnail on his knife, the ting of metal, soft though it was, separate from the sounds of a village rousing to another day. 'Sure, we are too few unless we attack him where he don't expect it. That dump of ammunition and fuel, Steve. We have to blow it.'

Stephen's eyes lifted from his hands. 'That's your business.'

'Nope. Yours. Only an American could move openly around Mananga City without being clubbed to death, and even he would need to be lucky. You say you can't blow this dump with your rockets, and I question Mezak afterwards. Okay, maybe you're right and we have to blow it some other way.'

'You're asking us to walk in there —'

'You. The woman stays with me. How else can I trust you to do what I want? Yeah, I tell you to go to Mananga City, it's a ghost town like your Wild West. Everyone murdered or running into the country with Forla after them. You know explosives —'

'No. I'm a chemical engineer who used to sell fertiliser.'

'You know better than my men how to blow that dump. I give your woman back when you succeed.' He sighed. 'Holding a hostage is an old trick but it still works, I think.'

'I could very easily try, and fail.' Stephen spoke with soft and frightening venom, as if in his own mind he had already tried and failed.

'It is sad, but possible,' conceded Michaels amiably. 'Then you would not need your woman back.'

'That's no kind of bargain and no odds.'

'I keep her safe for you if you are good, where's the bad odds in that?' He flicked his knife carelessly where Jean's hand lay on the table, the sting of it oddly dry, the steel too sharp for instant pain as blood slid from her knuckles on to timber.

Both she and Michaels were instinctively staring at her blood so neither saw Stephen move; the edge of his hand chopping down at the tendons of Michaels' wrist. At the very last moment Michaels tried to snatch back, the blow landing on his fingers instead of the wrist, but it was too late and the knife clattered loose on the table top. Yet instead of snatching it up Stephen slapped his hand flat on the blade.

'You quite sure you want your men to see how you lost your gun and your knife to a prisoner?' he said, as Michaels' mouth opened to shout for help.

One second. Two. Tension snagging tight and tighter, Jean's heart like a drum against her ribs. Slowly that scissor mouth snapped shut again, a tight line of fury. 'What you want? You can't get no place.'

'A deal worth winning. A bet, double or quits, just between you and me.'

Another long, long silence before Michaels' scowl lifted. 'You understand us too well, Steve. Sure, a bet. I have to use you if I want to win.'

His eyes impersonal and glittering, no honour there for any bet won or lost.

'You say the city is deserted except for Forla's men?'

'Nearly. Everyone off the streets who can.'

'Then we have to break in and blow the dump in series. You say there's fuel as well, but even Forla must store that apart. You send in what men you like to watch and help, but the woman and I go together. And you give orders first that as soon as the dump explodes we can take our lives and go. At once.'

Michaels hesitated, the hand which had held the knife twitching as if he longed to grab at the gun still in his shoulder holster. But he could not afford to kill Stephen yet, it wasn't only fear of humiliation at having his knife taken which prevented him from shouting out for help. Later, he could change any deal. 'If you fail I have plenty time afterwards to watch you die,' he said malevolently, and stared at Stephen with such a blaze of hatred that trusting him while he drew another single breath seemed suicidal.

Stephen himself was hesitating, hesitating — that brutal need to choose again, while murderous memory tore loose. Kill Michaels now and take his gun, and there might be the faintest of chances they could escape across the waterless hills. Or trust their lives to a monstrous risk and a given word a child could see was unworthy of a moment's trust. You could scarcely call it choice.

Then slowly his hand relaxed. 'I'll keep your knife as a pledge,' he said, and thrust the bare blade into his belt.

Michaels' face cracked into genuine mirth. 'Castrate yourself while I laugh, Yankee. Save me from doing it for you.'

'Not if I win the bet.'

Michaels stood. 'Tell me what explosives you want and I say if we have them. You are free to leave this hut, but you wear only sandals until we march. Carry nothing and do not leave the village.' He picked up his machine-pistol from beside the hearth and stamped outside, bawling out the guards for some misdemeanour before the door was shut.

Inside, a silence fell which Jean was the first to break, astonished to discover she no longer felt particularly frightened. 'Do you really think he might hold to a bet easier than to a deal?'

'No.'

'But he might for a while, if you can make it look as if he's winning all the advantages?'

'Something like that,' he said after a pause. 'I was sure that if I disarmed him he wouldn't want to call the guard, have everyone know he'd behaved like a fool. Throwing machine-pistols around and losing his knife to a Yankee punk. And he does very much want me to help him blow that dump. Said Mananga City was deserted so I would think not too many would be killed. All I did was offer a different trade, which took both of us off a hook. Sure, Manangans have a macho sense of honour, but that's one bet neither of us will keep a minute longer than it suits us. Now let's get the hell out of here and reach some air.' Short clipped sentences about as loving as a boardroom brief, he could not have expressed more clearly his longing to be let alone.

Outside, it was full daylight. Their guards followed but did not stop them when they walked down to the place where water was laboriously wound up from diggings in the river bed, and when Turka came forward to welcome Jean again, she was glad to go with her to the women's latrine. Afterwards she was given thin skin sandals to wear. These had a single thong around the toe and were worn by most women and children, some old men; though comfortable in the heat, such footwear effectively prevented any travel over rough hills tussocked with thorns.

Afterwards Jean loitered through the village, partly to allow Stephen the privacy he craved; sat on a wall to watch some skinny children playing lackadaisically in the dust; exchanged smiles with curious passers-by, who, more often than not, hastily looked aside. Yet they did not seem an inhospitable people. A child brought her his only toy, a pair of smooth round stones, and was offended when she tried to give them back. A guard silently offered her one of his few crackling cigarettes, and Turka had apologised because there were only a few drops of water for them both to wash in.

Impossible to guess whether this contradiction came from guilt over the violent end of the clinic, from the harsh essentials of near-starvation, or simple fear of punishment by the guerrillas swarming in their village. It was also too pleasant, sunning herself on a wall after a day and night of confinement, to worry overmuch. Strange how quickly one learnt to live as if threat was just a game, and be grateful for whatever glimmer of pleasure came along.

Michaels, she thought. Michaels in this peaceful, settled, but desperate valley, followed by his posse of hating men; he would be as strange to peasant farmers as to herself. But as long as he continued to fuel their few remaining hopes, and also to seize their pathetically sparse supplies, they would keep their thoughts and hospitality to themselves.

As if to add further to her speculations, she saw Mezak sauntering towards her, who would scorn to guard his thoughts. 'You are well?' He stood with his hands on his hips, weight delicately poised.

'Yes, thank you. Your valley is so beautiful, I would love to have seen it in happier times,' Jean answered sincerely. 'Nor do I like eating food your people need so badly.'

'Eat,' he answered grandly, but she saw that he was pleased. 'If the rains come, then you see.'

'I think we have to leave soon for Mananga City.'

'You come back. Welcome, everybody welcome after Forla dead.' He drew his hand across his throat, grinning.

'You remember the six crates we brought from Hamada? I saw them in ... in ... ' She wasn't sure how to refer to Michaels without offence, a rival who must have put Mezak's pride out of joint.

153

'In the guerrilla hut where we went yesterday. There are medicines and surgical supplies inside. If you could get them for me I could help your people while we are waiting to leave.'

'Ah.' He winked, tipped his head on one side. 'Those cases belong to Michaels.'

'They belong to the sick people of the valley. Sent from a long way away to save them from suffering.'

'Michaels save our people. He also have good friends who send him gifts.'

Jean stiffened, remembering what Stephen had said about a black market in medical drugs. 'Michaels can't trade medicines from here, however badly he needs guns.'

Mezak laughed, delighted. 'He use all shiny guns sent to Forla in your cases.'

'It couldn't ... I saw those cases off the ship myself.'

'You saw 'em packed?'

She shook her head, feeling angry and uncertain. If Mezak wasn't lying then Michaels must have been delighted when he broke open those crates and found guns inside, the only possible conclusion that Forla's tentacles had spread corruption far beyond Mananga.

'I saw 'em when Michaels break open. Good guns, very good guns.' Mezak aimed an imaginary weapon and pulled the trigger, enjoying himself hugely. 'Hey, Steve!'

Jean had seen Stephen coming out of the corner of her eye, but had not turned, since Mezak would certainly expect her full attention. Now she was glad to see he looked calm and alert again.

He smiled at her but spoke to Mezak. 'Thanks for convincing Michaels that a rocket made out of pipe wouldn't penetrate six inches of concrete.'

'He no-good guerrilla, but we need him to help kill Forla. After, I kick him out of my valley.'

'The really difficult bits always do come after,' answered Stephen drily. 'When are we leaving?'

'When you fix explosive ready.' He blew out his cheeks and slapped his hands in a mock detonation.

'The guerrillas can carry what I want to Mananga City. I am surely not fixing any blasting charges here.'

Mezak looked at him speculatively. 'You right, Steve. Don't trust Michaels with nothing.'

154

'I'm not blowing my ass off on the march, either.'

'That a good pretence to say,' agreed Mezak generously. 'But your ass safer with explosive than with Michaels after you done what he want.'

'Yes,' said Stephen. 'I know. Thanks, Mezak.'

'If I owe, I pay. Michaels, no.' He touched the knife in Stephen's belt. 'He give, but it a trick.'

'If he had, I'm sure it would be.'

'You took?' Mezak whistled, slapped his thigh. 'Wow. I told Michaels you look no good, Steve, but really you hot stuff. Now he believe me! You watch that ass you like to keep not blown in bits.'

He went off laughing.

'Was that wise?' Jean asked soberly.

Stephen shrugged. 'We need someone around who isn't shit-scared of Michaels.'

She let it go but remained unconvinced. Mezak would never resist the temptation to tease Michaels about losing his knife to a prisoner, and the guerrilla captain felt quite vengeful enough towards them as it was.

Stephen was watching her expression. 'Michaels can't kill Mezak. Yet. He needs the valley as a base, the valley men to tote supplies and act as auxiliaries. Same as he prefers not to kill us until we've done what he wants. Mezak was making sure we knew that the moment we have, we're dead. I don't think he realises that the same goes for him, too, a leader Michaels sees as a rival. But offer an idea he can understand and Mezak's very quick; he'll read that rattlesnake look on Michaels' face five seconds after Michaels forgets to keep it out of sight.'

'Tell me, honestly, what do you think is going to happen?' Jean said into the silence of high hills all around. 'I'd really rather know.'

He gave the ghost of a laugh. 'Wouldn't we all? We should be safe for the march to Mananga City, and putting Michaels' knife in my belt means he has to go along with the idea of it being some kind of pledge. You, too. He has to let you come along while you're officially part of the deal.'

'And that's one hell of a victory,' Jean said gratefully. 'I don't think I would have lasted too well, left alone. Instead of that we're both on our way out of the valley.'

'We're still most probably dead,' he answered grimly.

'We've had one victory,' she insisted. That confidence of his was a fragile, precious thing, when for lack of it his mind seized up.

He looked at her directly, his voice level. 'I'm all right. You don't have to glue back pieces all the time. Once we reach Mananga City I'm not sure what will happen next, except our lives will depend on reacting faster than Michaels to whatever we find. We stick tight together and remember that the instant Michaels knows we refuse to blow that dump, he'll shoot us in the back.'

'Or order us to be kept for his amusement, later.'

His eyes flickered. 'Yes.'

'So we take the craziest risk rather than be brought back. I wanted you to know.'

He put his hands either side of her on the wall. 'And I want you to know I love you. I don't think you believed me before, and who should blame you? I'd been so goddamn lonely I mostly just wanted you. And two of us holed in a hut with Michaels holding a gun outside, love needs some imagination.'

'I love you too,' Jean said, smiling. 'To hell with Michaels. We can't do another thing about him until we reach Mananga City. Until we leave is ours. Holiday, honeymoon and celebration all rolled into one, I want to enjoy what I've got.'

He laughed, one of those uninhibited shouts of laughter which showed what he might have been like as a boy, but they walked decorously back to their hut without touching. The valley people would be scandalised by public displays of emotion, but once the door closed behind them, everything beyond themselves was miraculously shut out too: their lives before this time, hatred and murderous choices, threat and hunger, all were out of their control. This short time belonged to them alone.

They slept fitfully after loving, the knowledge of an imminent end to love impossible to ignore for ever. Tomorrow or the next day they would wake to hear the guerrilla camp stirring, and be compelled to leave this brief haven for the Mananga City road, the unimaginable hazards which waited at its end.

And yet, because nothing could safely be left for a better time, they loved as if loving had no end, talked, laughed and discovered more about each other than would have been possible in a more ordinary span of time.

In the event, they had two days of peace and forgetful happiness. Only when they woke on the last morning to grey light seeping across a veiled pink sky, did Stephen discover that Jean's cheek beside his was wet, her body trembling.

She felt his stir. 'Don't move. Not yet. Please.'

'My sweet, you mustn't cry.'

' ... I was sure I wouldn't, but I can't help it.'

He held her, warm remembering body against warm body, trying to conjure up past magic while all around an evil wilderness crept closer.

'Forgive me,' Jean whispered much later, her breast against the roughness of his jaw, her lips against his ear. 'It is tomorrow and I did not want yesterday to end.'

Both of them craving the other again as the only way to hold back the frightening, growing knowledge that this was the last loving they would know.

'I don't want you killed,' Jean also said, and by then the sun was promising another clear, hot day. 'I try to care about Forla and people living beside a fuel dump in Mananga City, but really I just care about you. I don't want you knifed, or shot or roasted on a fire. It's that simple.'

'I know, because it's the same with me,' he answered. 'But it isn't that simple, as you also know. We wouldn't love each other afterwards if it was.'

Her eyes closed, long lashes hiding wetness, soft cheeks above lips made for laughter; edged, determined jawbone. She sighed. 'Women are strange creatures. I think I could love you anywhere, on any terms.' Her eyes opened, her lips smiled. 'If we should get out of Mananga, will you remind me that simplicity was what I wanted?'

'My dear, yes. The rest of my life in bed with you. What could be simpler?'

They both laughed, and in laughter briefly forgot again.

Recognition; knowing; certainty. Their stay might be short, but this was a harbour most people never reached.

14

URING those days before Michaels set out with his guerrillas along the Mananga City road, the weather remained hot and settled. Many of the villagers wailed with despair as the distant thunderheads vanished, while Michaels rubbed his hands. If an early storm had come then floods could have held him up; the clear sky was an omen of success.

The first day of their march was easy: guerrillas, village men and stores piled haphazard into trucks and a single jeep while a tractor followed, pulling trailers, anything that would move. The women and children stood in the village street to watch them go, and Jean found it impossible to imagine what those inexpressive faces hoped for. The immemorial prayers of women watching their men go off to fight would be in their hearts, but hope? What could they hope for, since their men safely returned would not, in itself, save them or their families. They needed to return laden with looted food and freed from the fear of any revenge from Forla; from oppression by voracious guerrillas, too. You had only to consider such an unlikely gathering of circumstance to realise those blank faces were not a mask; they hoped for very little.

The men were different.

Once the convoy of vehicles left the straggle of huts behind, bowled through several more hamlets as like each other as knots on string, and began to climb the long dirt inclines which ultimately would lead to Mananga City, the men sat straighter, shouted boastful words, and looked around with quick, possessive glances. Their eager bearing arrogantly mixed hope and noisy babble, proclaiming they were not passive victims any more.

'Surely they have to rule better than Forla if they win,' Jean said to Stephen, sitting beside her in the jeep. Illogically, she had begun to want her gaolers to win, these sons of many generations who had never won before.

'I would like to think so,' he answered, but his tone said that Michaels was as likely to be capriciously cruel, improvidently selfish, as Forla; his followers, whether he won or lost, to remain victims as before.

The track was thick with dust but not rutted; in good seasons most of the produce of the Kosti Valley travelled this way to the capital, but for the past two years of drought it had been scarcely used. The hills either side of them became steeper as they travelled south, the area of cultivation forced into strips and terraces. Their pace was slow, the tractor lagging far behind on the flat, catching up on soft dust slopes, but nothing untoward happened that first day and Michaels was sufficiently delighted by their progress to allow an extra handful of beans in each pot for dinner.

Towards the end of the following morning an unexpected wind began blowing in their faces and the village men shouted between themselves that perhaps the rains would come soon after all. To them, the hope of success in Mananga City immediately became much less significant than this closer hope of fresh life for their valley after two years of death. Slowly the sun vanished behind wild-looking clouds and one by one everyone in their jeep fell silent as they realised that on this road, a storm, a real drought-breaking storm, could mean disaster.

'Why?' Mezak shouted, when his truck hauled alongside on a bend. 'In two days, yes. Yesterday, yes. Tonight, fuckit, no.'

The first fat blob of rain slapped on Jean's knee towards the end of the afternoon. The wind by then had dropped again, the air become enormously oppressive. Their column of trucks stopped briefly for instructions to be shouted back and then went on faster than before, leaping from rough surfaces, choking on each other's dust. Without warning an almost continuous roll of thunder began to echo around the higher hills and a flash of lightning leapt clean across the valley perhaps half a mile behind, a black screen of rain splitting sunlight into fragments. There were shouts of joy all down the column as water began to pour off the cliffs either side when rain hit the heights above, swirling down to form instant lakes on the iron-hard ground. Cheers turned to alarm as the storm moved faster than they could travel, filling the air with unearthly fire, their ears with crashes like split rock. Torrents formed where the dry husks of dead crops had been, their jeep slithering and whining on skidpan mud. Soon, the whole convoy was stalled and in great peril as a continuous deluge followed those first cataracts.

Fortunately they had reached a point where the road meandered part-way up a hillside, in a groove worn by centuries of men and beasts avoiding valuable cultivated ground below. Jean watched fascinated as they swiftly became marooned by a broken swirling flood bobbing with bushes, the occasional animal carcass, even rocks.

After quite a long while Michaels came sloshing back down the line of trucks, a man no longer to be hated but admired, not flustered, not weakened but strengthened by near-disaster.

'Your explosives okay,' he bawled at Stephen as he passed. 'I seal the case myself. We wait and water go down tomorrow.'

'What if it rains tomorrow, now it's begun?'

'We walk and you carry explosives.' He grinned, his lips curled back over his teeth. 'You pray it stops, eh?'

Her own teeth chattering from damp chills, Jean did pray during the night that the rain would stop. Huddled in Stephen's arms on a scrap of cloth under the jeep, it was the most miserable night of her life. It had been impossible to light fires for cooking, the parched grain scarcely worth the effort needed to choke it down, so that her stomach shuddered as much from hunger as the cold.

That endless night she began to think she might not survive.

The eventual dirty stain of dawn revealed a scene of utter devastation, also rain which had eased to a drizzle. It might have been Scotland, she thought; sunshine changed to blowing mist, steep valley sides noisy with falling water. But the men around her were literally dancing with delight because their drought was finished and they cared about nothing else.

'How nice someone's pleased,' she said, trying not to think how awful she must look.

'It's a knucklebuster in Michaels' plans, though. Something he didn't expect so early in the season, and any upset has to offer us a better chance,' Stephen answered.

'Not here.'

'God, no. If we didn't drown, we would certainly starve alone.' He went to help get the jeep started again.

All day they inched through mud thick enough to suck the hoofs off a bullock — the Gloucestershire saying from her childhood leapt vividly to Jean's mind — their only comfort that Forla was unlikely to hear of their approach in such weather. The unmade surface of the road was often washed out, the only answer to manhandle rocks until they filled the gap. It would have been easier to abandon their vehicles and march the remaining fifty miles or so to Mananga City, but the trucks were needed to haul the ammunition and stores they had to have for an assault. Stephen's trained eye was occasionally useful at the more sinister washouts, but mostly their progress was a case of endurance and brute muscle. In this situation only guerrilla virtues showed, their devotion admirable, their fortitude near-heroic. Even Stephen was impressed by their uncomplaining courage, which made it seem almost irrelevant that tomorrow they could as easily kill or torture their prisoners as toil monotonously to clear a road.

In fifteen hours their column had covered less than eight miles; the tractor with its precious trailers was lost when a section of road gave way and spilled screaming men and irreplaceable sacks of grain into the torrent below.

'Tomorrow will be better!' Michaels shouted as, swaying with exhaustion, they gathered to eat at dusk. The rain had stopped but more clouds boiled over the hills behind them. Their gruel was wonderfully hot because Michaels had agreed to a fire kindled out of disel and ruined tyres. A column of black smoke would announce their presence to anyone who looked, but the value of hot food outweighed the risk on a day when aircraft would be grounded: only one example of Michaels' swift clear thinking throughout the journey.

Even so, the villagers were becoming restless, their thoughts back with their families in danger from flash floods. 'There will be another great storm tomorrow!' one shouted as they finished eating. 'It is always thus in the rains.'

Stephen understood better than Jean, having been in Mananga longer, but she grasped the gist of shouted protest well enough.

'It is too late for doubt,' yelled back Michaels. 'Forla will learn that you helped us and kill you more surely than any flood if you leave him alive. We must go forward together.'

At that there were a great many shuffled feet, each man looking at his neighbour for support while Michaels' personal squad of élite guerrillas drifted closer to their leader. If there had been anywhere to run, this was a moment when Jean and Stephen might have vanished into the dark, but between dripping cliffs and washed out road lay only a treacherous quagmire that had been cultivated ground, divided by bawling torrents.

'Hey, boys, of course we go forward!' Mezak shouted, and moved to stand beside Michaels.

But his men remained uncertain and eventually Saul, who still suffered miseries from his burned stomach, dared to call back, 'We have fields, we have sons. Early rains last only a few days and our crops must be planted before the ground dries out again. Then the later wetness will fatten them. I say, call off this attack which has become a madness. Forla may take fright from what has already happened and treat us with less injustice.'

'Forla treat you fairly?' mocked Michaels. 'Now I know I am hearing a fool babble.'

'Saul is good! One of mine and all mine are good,' interrupted Mezak. 'We are also faithful. We say we come to Mananga City and we come. Is it not so, Saul?'

Saul hesitated, a hand to his stomach. Then, suddenly, he nodded, and the revolt was over as quickly as it had begun.

'You!' shouted Michaels to Stephen. 'You, come here!'

Beside her, Jean heard Stephen mutter something under his breath before he deliberately turned and walked away. The next thing she knew several shots were driving into the roadway beside her leg, splattering mud everywhere, men scattering in panic, one yelping in startled pain.

'I said, come here.' Michaels had not moved. His gun fired one-handed, those shots could have gone anywhere.

Lowering sky, battered trucks, filthy and dangerously exasperated men, all petrified in time while Stephen and Michaels stared at each other across suddenly emptied space. Michaels was grasping at this unexpected opportunity to reassert his authority; Stephen angered and humiliated by his inability to exercise any control at all over this witches' brew of disaster, a quite different nervous anxiety over past failures perhaps edging him towards a futile show of strength.

Jean's own instincts were torn between reluctant understanding and the knowledge that unless this pointless confrontation was defused fast, then Michaels was beyond the point where consideration of tomorrow's strategy would prevent him from firing now.

Her brain swatted feverishly at words, any words surely better than none. 'Do you suppose shooting at a guest could be his way of offering us a dry bed in his truck tonight? If so, I vote we accept.' She listened to her own voice, amazed by such inanity.

But it worked. Not without damage, since Stephen was too intelligent not to realise that by switching his mind she had saved him from a lethal mistake, and to resent it; but slowly his muscles relaxed, tension ebbed, and after a further moment of hesitation he walked to where Michaels waited with a derisive grin on his face.

'Yes?' he said curtly.

Michaels gestured with his gun. 'It's time we spoke about explosives and the attack on Mananga City.'

'Until I see that arms dump for myself, preferably from the inside, I can't begin to think of a safe way to destroy it.'

Michaels rubbed his chin with the stock of his gun. 'If we could get inside we explode it for ourselves.'

'Along with most of your men, the railroad terminal and several blocks of a capital city you hope to rule.'

Michaels grinned. 'You know that once I decide I can destroy it myself, I kill you early, eh? Okay, Steve. We wait and see who is right.'

'No offer of a dry bed,' Stephen observed dispassionately as Michaels shouldered his way off through the crowd, kicking men back to work. 'Well, let's see what we can fix for ourselves.'

He went over to the nearest truck and, ignoring a shout from their guard, began heaving sacks aside. The guard shouted again and ran over, waving his gun. 'For God's sake, we're not escaping.' Stephen turned his back, and hauled out another sack.

Jean climbed up to join him. 'After last night this would seem like the Ritz.'

'Hey, Steve, you playing up very bad,' Mezak called from the road.

'We aren't as tough as you. If we lie out another night I shan't be able to set fuses, or calculate a goddamn thing. I would also be grateful if you'd tell that bastard Michaels not to push me again, or he can pull his trigger and to hell with it.'

'Shooting always okay to Michaels.'

'Sure, and I'll watch my back in Mananga City. Tonight, you tell him he'd be a damned fool to try.' Hesitation was replaced by sureness of touch the moment rage shoved hesitation aside.

And afterwards, both of them were jammed together in the space he had cleared so that they could scarcely move, yet never had acute discomfort seemed more enviable. Michaels did not reappear to turn them out and no guerrilla dared to, so long as their chief appeared to accept the unusual situation of prisoners being more comfortable than their captors. Perhaps everyone left Mezak to tell him where they were, and he kept quiet. Whatever the reason, they slept intermittently from sheer exhaustion, and woke feeling agreeably warm even though their limbs were set like concrete.

By then the guerrillas were already cooking breakfast over smouldering fires, a few still lying where they had died of exposure in the night. Almost mechanically, Jean went to see if any of them could be roused, but when she found a man still alive no one was interested in roping him precariously to a load. Already feverish, he would only die in misery on these rough tracks, instead of slipping softly out of life.

It seemed dreadful to leave him all the same, when animals or vultures might come before he died. He was a young beardless guerrilla perhaps eighteen years old, and though she did what she could to rouse him only weak coughs rewarded all her efforts.

'We're moving off.' Stephen came up behind her.

'We can take him,' she said fiercely. 'Chuck off one of those damned boxes of ammunition. It's inhuman to drive away and leave him.'

'We are inhuman,' he answered harshly. 'There is no one here who would say he was worth a box of ammunition.'

'Not even you?'

Without answering, he bent and picked up the boy, grunting from the weight, walked over to the jeep, piled high with drums of fuel from a stranded truck. The driver shouted, punched the air: no room, no room. The jeep's engine sounded like rusty cans, straining under its load. Without taking any notice, Stephen placed the dying boy on the flat bonnet, the only unencumbered space. 'No!' shouted the driver. 'No! NO!' The jeep slithered sideways under this extra weight, so the boy would have fallen off if Stephen had not grabbed him.

'No,' said Mezak, running up from behind. 'Leave him, Steve. We leaving food. We can't take dead.'

'He isn't dead.'

'He dead soon.'

A small patch of sunlight was growing across the sky, and in its pale distance a speck was hovering: a vulture or a hawk which would swoop to peck out eyes. Stephen picked up the boy again.

164

'A truck wouldn't notice one body more or less.'

'Michaels say everyone walk. Trucks carry only stores.'

Head down, not answering, Stephen set out up the track with the boy in his arms. I started this, Jean thought desperately, and ran after him. Raw anxiety was overlying mercy now; even she knew the boy could not survive for long, wedged among shifting crates in a truck. 'Let me help carry him.'

Stephen shook his head, his breath coming in hard gasps. The guerrilla's head lolled against his arm, eyes rolling.

The next truck ahead was reloading freight spilled from another that had foundered, Michaels supervising operations. He turned. 'You gone crazy, man? Bust your heart for a corpse?'

'He's alive.' One-handed, Stephen jerked open the cab door, and turned sideways to hoist the boy on top of crammed equipment.

'Look,' said Michaels, not roughly. 'I care for my guys or they don't follow me. Today they need food and bullets, not corpses, in the trucks we got left. I don't wanna fight over a dying kid. You put him down and we forget it.'

'Take out a crate of guns and there's room for him.'

'Jesus Christ, put him down, will you! There'll be men dropping out of the march all day, but they'll last better if they know dropping out won't get them a ride. We also need those guns.' Michaels strode over, gripped the boy's face in his fingers, studied it. 'What you think he got, two hours to live?'

'I don't know.'

'Sure you know. You're playing fuckers with me now.' Michaels slammed the cab door shut again and looked at Jean. 'You're a nurse. You tell me. One hour or two?'

She stared at that speck in the sky, definitely a vulture and hovering now, then back at the boy's fever-bright eyes. 'I can't. No one could while he's still alive.'

Michaels shrugged, and turned back to Stephen. 'I'll tell your guard you can hold that kid as long as you want. When you drop him, he'll bring you to catch the convoy.'

His voice was sad rather than angry, but implacable. Stephen's eyes met his in some kind of acknowledgement both recognised, before lifting to study that circling vulture, others already appearing in the distance, attracted by the several dead of the night.

We are inhuman, Stephen had said.

In his arms the dying guerrilla kicked out, once, quite strongly,

and arched his spine as if terror was reaching through the mists of
fever. Stephen was sweating badly from his weight; there was only
one thing left for Jean to do.

She touched his arm. 'Put him over here.'

There was a small bank beside the track where the grass had not
been trampled into mud, and as Stephen laid him down the boy's
eyes seemed to tighten, the skin of his face to pucker; sense
remained closer than they thought.

Jean looked across at Michaels. 'Give me your gun.'

He stared back at her, wary, calculating, then slowly unholstered
his automatic and held it out, butt foremost.

Stephen reached for it ahead of her and shot the boy cleanly
through the head, the sound echoing like an ambush from the hills
around.

'He was a good guerrilla,' said Michaels, taking back his gun.

15

THEY lost another truck towards midday, when a section of
crudely repaired surface collapsed and tumbled it down a
landslide slope into brown water. Slowly it spun in the current, hit
a rock, and spun in the other direction before grounding on an
earthbank a mile from where it had gone over the edge. Only a
driver was on board and they never found his body; most of the
stores they were able to pull out of the flood were spoiled.

'That fucking truck carried our explosives,' shouted Michaels.
'Howja blow a dump without explosives, eh?'

'Have you any grenades, or mortar bombs maybe?' Stephen
asked.

'Grenades, yeah, sort of. You come and look. They seemed
kinda crap to me.'

Stephen sloshed with him to the leading truck. Only two and the
jeep left now. On the other hand they had made better progress
until this latest, disastrous landslide, for as the hills gradually began to flatten out on each side, the spate of water became less. It
had been cruel luck to lose another truck, which besides explosives
carried half their remaining food, when easier conditions were so

close. Jean had shared the guerrillas' dismay as it tumbled out of sight, felt her spirits plummet and not only for the driver, as if this attack on Mananga City had become her own. She watched with unmixed admiration as the guerrillas clambered slowly back to the track and started to repair that fatal weakness in the road.

While Stephen was away with Michaels she sat on the jeep's spare tyre feeling as if a pit had closed above her head, not so much physically exhausted, although without her dry night's rest she would have dropped out of the march before this, as mentally wrung out. Though that boy's death had not been due to any fault of hers, the shock of it lay like silt on her spirit.

'I surely would not like to be the guy who pulls the pin on those grenades,' Stephen said when he returned. 'I think they're Czech but so sticky and corroded it's hard to tell. The only date I possibly made out looked like 1961.'

'What did you tell Michaels?'

'I agreed they were crap, but they haven't anything else. He knows, now, that he needs to get inside the perimeter of that dump if he wants to destroy it. I also suggested to him that since he has to get inside, it might be a good idea to try and save some of Forla's stockpile for himself, instead of acting like a kid enjoying fire-crackers on the fourth of July.'

'Not quite in those words, I hope.' Jean was just thankful that a practical problem had cropped up to divert his mind from brooding on the boy he had shot that morning.

'He got the message. I think he realises, too, that we are now less expendable than we were. God knows what a dump where lunatics have piled up fuel and ammunition together will look like, but blowing only part of it isn't going to be easy. And if I don't know how the hell to set about it with leaking grenades, then a bunch of hick guerrillas ought to have a few doubts too.'

Jean looked around at rocky scrub taking over from hills and valley floor. 'Soon, we'd have a good chance of surviving if only we could get away.'

'Michaels knows that as well.'

'And?'

Stephen looked at her, and smiled. He had shaved in muddy cold water and looked surprisingly spruce, one of that tiny minority of the human race who can fall in a pond and emerge looking as if they chose duckweed as a buttonhole. 'He said to remember that

Forla's troops are scavenging out there, crazed with drink and blood.'

Jean shivered. 'Is it true, do you think?'

'I guess we'll soon find out.'

They finally left the Kosti Hills early that afternoon. Almost at once the land flattened into a burnt-grass plain punctuated by rock outcroppings, where their remaining trucks could at last have increased speed if they hadn't needed to keep pace with tired men marching stubbornly behind. An advance and flank guard now flung out in an attempt to avoid being surprised, although to Jean attack seemed most likely to come from the air.

'We will camp over there and tomorrow you see Mananga City!' Michaels waved at a conical hill on the horizon as he went past in a flurry of grit, using the jeep as sheepdog up and down the flagging column.

This open land held strange uncertain colours in the aftermath of rain — grey from blowing clouds, gold from gleams of sun, silver from wetness underfoot. In the hills behind them another storm was raging, but here the great parched plain seemed effortlessly to absorb any quantity of water. A few bright green blades of grass were already appearing; a smell of hot triumphant earth, too, as if to warn that even with rain no crops would grow here. As yet there were only scattered and mostly abandoned buildings to be seen, very little to suggest a capital city some twenty miles distant, the single variation in limitless flatness ahead that isolated cone-shaped hill.

Jean watched the plain around her turn from grey to yellow, begin to quiver below steam rising in the heat. This quite different landscape stirred fresh interest, until, without her noticing it, her depression began to lift and then rolled back like these same banks of blowing steam. The first signs of habitation rose above that mystical horizon soon afterwards: thin wisps of smoke curving delicately where they met cooler upper air, and for the first time Jean felt regret that almost from the day she arrived she should have been driven to think only about escape from this cruel and mighty continent. Escape from Hamada, from Kosti, then the valley; a growing dream of escape with Stephen, should his mind happen to work that way, a matter about which, after today, she was more unsure than before. Though he said he loved her and probably meant it, he had spoken only once of permanence and then as a joke. No permanence at all as she understood it; romantic, callow fool that she was.

Now she began to wonder, Where will I, too, find permanence again after so much has happened to change my life? Cosy Gloucestershire seemed an infinity distant as she watched, fascinated, the vast battle between rain and sun against a backdrop of African hills, the extraordinary shades of light between her and shadowy distance as far as sight could reach.

I don't know, she thought. I don't know.

Some time after that they saw the first strangers since leaving the many hamlets of the valley: huddled distant figures fleeing in terror at their approach. The smoke they had seen from a distance came from the smouldering ashes of a burned out roadside store, its owners incinerated and two dead soldiers lying in the roadway with their arms flung in rejoicing around each other's necks, but half-eaten by animals.

A charnel house stench was thick in the humid air, even the guerrillas holding their noses as they plodded past. The sudden clattering interruption of a helicopter was viciously unexpected.

'Stay where you are!' yelled Michaels, when everyone else would have scattered mindlessly into the scrub. 'Remember what I told you! There isn't any cover here.' He seized Jean and fairly flung her under a halted truck, and kicked at Stephen to follow. 'Stay out of sight!'

Bemused, Jean watched the guerrillas waver, staring up at the sky, before their movements abruptly settled into a different pattern. A few trotted up and down the track, one fired his submachine-gun. But the bullets whipped into the ground and not the helicopter, now rapidly coming closer.

'You have to hand it to Michaels,' Stephen said, crouched beside her under the truck. 'There's nowhere to hide out here, but those trucks were army vehicles once, and so he told everyone to act like they were soldiers too.'

The helicopter swept overhead in a blast of grit and Jean saw that the guerrillas were indeed acting like Forla's soldiers, flailing out at the valley men as if they were helpless civilians rather than allies, herding them into groups, beating some with their gun butts until they screamed, make-believe escalating on adrenalin. As for Michaels, he stood up in the jeep and saluted, any deficiency in his uniform hidden by the storms of dirt kicked up by the helicopter.

Once, twice it swept overhead, everyone choking and cursing, fright turning to jubilation as no one in the helicopter opened fire. Then it backed up and away, and flew swiftly towards the hills.

Jean wiped her lips on her arm, and wiped them again. Her eyes were streaming from whirled up dirt, the beat of her heart louder than the helicopter's receding clatter in her ears. 'Michaels must be insane to keep on the move out here in daylight.'

Stephen crawled from under the truck, and reached to help her on to her feet. 'He hasn't any choice. Move by night and it adds forty-eight hours to the time before he can attack. He's only visited Mananga City once, as a railroad trackman years ago, and needs all the time he can win to study the layout. But he only has enough rations for two days. He knows men have to be well fed and in good heart or they won't press home an attack. So he decided to travel straight through and thought out how to bluff observation if it came. Since his greatest strengths are nerve and guts, he's got away with it. This time.'

The number of refugees seen skulking at a distance increased after that, terrified demoralised people scuttling for safety at their approach. No one came close, and roadside signs for Coca-Cola and motor oil were mostly pocked by bullets.

'Surely we have to trip over some of Forla's men soon, and then they'll radio we're here,' Jean said, instinctively lowering her voice as if she might be overheard.

'If they have a radio, and the sense to think of anything except killing and loot. Michaels reckons they are so far out of control they've become hyena-packs.'

'Someone, somewhere, will have a radio in any army, however undisciplined it is.'

'I think so too.' Stephen was as tensed up as she, waiting for shots which might at any moment be fired from ambush, the leaping roar of engines which would destroy this illusory calm. There was no safety anywhere in this ravaged no man's land of shacks, smallholdings and straggle of concrete reaching out from the skirts of Mananga City.

It remained a land of wide horizons, even so, a semi-rural sprawl interspersed by stretches of infertile grass, stunted bushes, haphazard heaps of stones. A ragged child sucked its thumb on a shattered doorstep, and became the first human being not to run away at the sight of armed strangers: after that the signs of occupation

170

increased quite fast, the sense of frightened eyes watching from behind shutters, a hopeless abandonment to despair sifting underfoot with the dust.

But still no challenge. An occasional crackle of firing sounded in the distance, or a body in the gutter hummed with flies, but Michaels was having the luck his audacity deserved and had reached within ten miles of the capital without his column apparently being noticed in the chaos left by Forla's rampant, ravaging troops. As for Michaels himself, he stood hour after hour in the back of the jeep, Forla's Manangan flag clenched in one hand and the other mockingly saluting such wretched, abject people as dared to glance in his direction. Except that his men were ordered not to kill for the fun of it, they did in fact look little different from those soldiers Jean had seen in Hamada; only the valley men lacked uniforms and carried weapons which might have raised comment among onlookers who were not already crushed by losing everything they possessed. As it was, Michaels' guerrillas were accepted as another accursed Forla gang, and he even forced anyone his men could catch to kneel and salute the flag, which helped to eradicate any doubts.

As the hours passed Jean felt her brain becoming numb, anything beyond this nightmare march unreal. Never had she imagined such decimation of the human spirit, where even the urge to hate had vanished.

'How long?' she said once to Stephen, walking beside her and as much wrapped in silence as she herself. 'How long does it take to reduce a country I was told used to be moderately prosperous to this?'

'Three years of Forla. God knows how long since Mananga was handed over with all those pious hopes of democracy to someone who failed to make a democracy stick.'

'Was it as bad as this when you came through Mananga City last? I mean ... in London they said Forla was a brute, but I'm sure they wouldn't have let me come if they'd thought he was homicidal. He must be, though. As bad or worse than Idi Amin or Papa Doc Duvalier.'

'The State Department said he was corrupt as hell but kept Mananga quiet. Which may not be so different from London's view: safe for foreigners while they pay the bills. No, it wasn't so bad when I came through before. I didn't know what to expect and wasn't looking too far beneath any surface, but it felt okay in day-light on the streets. Sure, Forla's troops were everywhere and usu-ally drunk, people stepped in the gutter rather than go close, but they weren't running wild as must have happened since the uprising was put down.'

'Have you begun to feel any differently about blowing that dump? It's the only way Michaels might possibly win with so few men, isn't it?'

'Does that mean you do?'

'I want him to win, yes! I can't help it after what we've seen. You say Mananga wouldn't be any better off if he did, but you can't possibly know. One thing's certain, it's only ever going to be worse under Forla.'

'Forla came to power in a coup and was hailed as a liberator. Like Amin.'

'And now we're talking about a tough and nasty guerrilla who probably intends to kill us when we're no more use. I still say he has to be better than Forla.'

'Why? Sure, he's going to kill us when it suits him. No Third World ruler wants to admit he might have been helped to power by wicked Westerners, most especially when one of them is American.'

'You ask why?' said Jean angrily. 'Because he just might be better than Forla, that's all. Look around you and dare to tell me any different.'

'What does looking around me prove, except that war rots every-thing it touches? Maybe you forgot but I wanted never to be at war again, then the next thing is there's this boy I have to shoot. No one, including Michaels, thought he was worth a single box of bullets, I seem to recall.'

Both of them were suddenly railing at each other as the pent-up fear, uncertainty and self-disgust which had gathered like an abscess through a day of unspeakable sights burst out of control.

The boy I shot ... I shot ... I shot. The only reason Stephen had taken the gun from Michaels was to prevent her having to face the pitiless price of mercy, and yes, she had forgotten. Earlier, a life-time earlier on this unending day, she had remembered and sor-rowed for what she had forced him to do, yet felt no guilt for mercy. Then she had forgotten. There had been too many other horrors to remember, for the single life which made Stephen into a murderer again to remain fresh in her mind. As she would never

172

have forgotten if she had pulled the trigger. Justification, or the lack of it, was not the point. Somewhere in Vietnam he had returned to his Quaker roots, in gut-feeling if not in fact, this fresh violation an unimaginable burden for him to bear.

'I'm sorry,' she said helplessly, and all at once felt so tired she nearly wept. 'I can't help reacting to what I see, but who the hell am I to say what you or anyone should think?'

A nerve twitched at the side of his mouth. 'The trouble is, one always has to come back from thought. It isn't your fault you fetched up in a bloodstained place like Mananga with no one except a screwed-up nut for company.'

'My only happiness since I came here has been with you,' she answered.

'My dear, and mine with you.' He laughed, a bad hiccup of a laugh, but strain was eased again. 'How trite, but more than true. Don't worry, I've got so many ideas about how not to detonate that dump that Michaels ought to promote me from prisoner to favourite guerrilla.'

Jean was still trying to decide what he might have in mind when their column finally turned off the cracked tarmac highway and jolted across a mile or more of dry plain, climbed into and out of a gully and pulled up in the shadow of the conical hill she had seen all those hours before, when they first emerged from the hills.

16

JEAN supposed that Michaels must have instructed sentries to stay on guard while everyone else dropped into exhausted sleep, but if so it wasn't obvious. Perhaps he just trusted his luck would hold, his men so worn out by days of gruelling labour that one more risk which allowed his whole force to sleep was worth while. Even the energy to eat was lacking, although hunger was the sensation Jean remembered as she plunged into oblivion.

She stirred to the smell of food, ate in a daze and slept again, deeply this time. Cold woke her in a yellow clouded dawn and she lay looking at Stephen curled beside her, not minding much about the cold.

He woke, shivering, quite soon and laughed when he saw she was content to lie and freeze so long as she could watch him sleep beside her. They made love quickly and strongly then, aware of reprieve because secretly each had thought they might never make love again, the niche where they had slept a small and secret place surrounded by guerrillas. Beneath them was veined rock and above a smudged, unsettled sky; both of them knew that this was certainly their last respite.

The camp roused soon afterwards and Michaels came round, issuing rations, shouting orders for guns to be stripped and cleaned, and encouraging the valley men in particular, who ever since they left the hills had shown an inclination to huddle into groups, muttering disconsolately.

'They are chicken here away from their henhouse,' he said scornfully to Stephen. 'They better shift ass when we attack.'

'Any sign of Forla's army in the night?'

Michaels grinned and slapped the binoculars slung around his neck. 'They drink and shit at night, hunt like jackals in the day. We won't see no Forla bandits here, I tell you.'

'What about in Mananga City?'

'His personal guard there,' he conceded. 'Others too, I think. We go look, eh? From this hill there's a fucking good view.' He snapped his fingers for a pair of guards to follow them, this time two from his élite fifty, who wore machine-gun ammunition as a decoration, moved with self-conscious grace and were armed with modern weapons. These Jean had already mentally classed as future rulers of Mananga if Michaels should win. It was disagreeable to find them the least attractive among the guerrillas, the most deadpan, possessed by arrogant certainties which spilled over into contempt of everyone else.

The hill they now set out to climb reminded Jean of an overgrown molehill: almost conical, its surface granular and inadequately fissured for easy climbing. The effort of hauling from one toehold to the next up such smooth surfaces was out of all proportion to its height, but when they reached some eroded shelves near the top, the view was stupendous. Michaels nodded for his two men to wait on one of the lower ledges and himself climbed to the narrow summit, beckoning for Stephen to follow. He shrugged acceptance when Jean followed.

'You cheat my boys of their fun, eh?' He slapped her bottom

playfully, grunting a laugh. All of them were out of breath after that awkward climb, needing to rest before their eyes would focus on the city laid out for their inspection.

'There it is,' said Michaels softly. He was lying flat and staring through his binoculars, this final thrust of rock just wide enough for the three of them. 'Mananga City. Plenty of soldiers waiting for us there. That plop of pink shit is the president's palace.' He spat, and the gob flashed in the sun. 'There. That warehouse is Forla's stores, like I was told.'

'Could I look?' Stephen put on his glasses and held out a hand for the binoculars, Michaels passing them over as if they really were allies. Jean just stared at the distant web of buildings cast haphazard across the plain and wondered about the next extraordinary twist her life would take, as if it had become quite commonplace to be perched on a rock discussing with a guerrilla how to storm a munition store. Yesterday's mists had vanished and the city stood out clearly to the naked eye: an unimaginative grid of streets flanked by concrete boxes. Perhaps half a dozen buildings might be called high-rise, elsewhere construction was limited to basic rectangles. Away from the centre the streets soon became alleys, the outskirts of the city encrusted with shacks made of anything which came to hand.

There was quite a lot of traffic between the railway terminus and the airport, distantly in view on the far side of the city. Civilian movement looked very slight, the occasional vehicle sneaking unostentatiously through the sidestreets, some flashes of light off windscreens at downtown intersections. A single airliner climbed steeply from the airport runway, banked and passed close overhead. How extraordinary to think of passengers up there beginning to relax at leaving the perils of Mananga behind, looking forward to a drink, thinking already of reunions at journey's end.

'I'm surprised the airport is open,' Stephen commented, still studying the city through the binoculars.

'Why not? Forla use it for his air force and smuggling goods. The airlines pay him fees. There's only three, maybe four, flights a day but he make everyone disembark, spend good dollars on airport taxes and eating shit in the buffet. You see the barracks by the railroad terminal?'

'The square block near the freight yards?'

'Yeah, a finger right is the ammunition dump.'

175

'Jesus Christ,' said Stephen quietly.

'Good, eh?'

'They must be crazy.'

'Nope. They lazy, is all. Minds on good things, like loot. If ammunition and fuel come up by rail everyone think the freight yard an easy place to stack it. Barracks next door, it's an even better deal. The guards don't have so far to walk.'

'Even Forla couldn't be that stupid.'

'Where else better? On the plain someplace? You have plenty trouble keeping fucked-up troops out there to guard it. Or maybe someone you don't trust command the guard, and if you're Forla you don't trust no one, man. Then you think it could be safest in your own palace —' Michaels grinned. 'Forla like to keep it close, but not that close, I guess. By the airport? Yeah, I think he keeps bombs and stuff out there, but he's not too sure about his air force either. They make too much money smuggling for themselves. The army need him more, and he like to keep their stores where they're kinda handy if things go wrong in a hurry.'

Without answering, Stephen passed the binoculars over to Jean, and after a moment of fumbling with the focus, buildings and even individual vehicles jumped into view. Anonymous cubes became stained slums hung with washing, and what Michaels had described as pink shit resolved itself into a child's fantasy castle, complete with battlements, a drawbridge and turrets, all jumbled together and painted bright pink. A large extension was being built on the back, complete with a gold dome, a pair of battle tanks was parked by the gate, and several bunkers of guns dug into a traffic-free space beyond, which looked as if it had once been the hub of downtown Mananga City.

'Over a bit and to the right,' said Stephen. 'Follow the railroad track along.'

The single track crossed the plain in a wide curve after its ascent from Kosti and Hamada, and from about two miles outside the city the line was guarded by a barbed-wire fence on either side. As Jean followed the track along with the binoculars she saw that the closer it came to its terminus in the freight yards, the thicker this barrier of wire became. In places slum shacks must have been demolished to free the necessary space. The station building looked identical to the one in Hamada, the sidings considerably larger and stacked with carelessly piled sacks, drums and cases. Across a narrow road from the station was a three-storey concrete block surrounded by more wire and with military vehicles parked outside: the barracks, Jean supposed. To its right, about a hundred yards away and close to the sidings, stood a large warehouse; as she watched, a truck drove out of open double doors and another entered. What looked like a detail of soldiers lackadaisically unloaded drums from a freight train, but with little attempt at stacking anything tidily. 'They look as if they resent not enjoying themselves with their pals, robbing civilians,' she said aloud.

'What the motherfuckers don't know is, they only got today to live,' said Michaels, and turned to stare unblinkingly at Stephen.

There was a long silence, broken by the croak of a vulture as it flew almost level with where they lay, eyeing debris in the guerrilla camp below. This, quite suddenly, the moment in which Michaels finally assessed their worth to him, not by bluff or words but by the highly sensitive and developed instinct of a predator, surviving by his wits.

'Let me have another look.' Silently Jean gave back the binoculars, and watched while Stephen seemed to look long enough to map the place from memory.

Those two guerrillas left on the ledge below, she thought. If either of us says a single thing which makes Michaels believe we're not wholeheartedly trying to do what he wants, they'll push us off the hill as we climb down. An accident away from Mezak, who might otherwise protect them, a trouble-free way of getting rid of unwanted clutter on the eve of an assault.

'The easiest route in I can see is up the railroad track.' When Stephen spoke he might have been discussing an audit of accounts, the assumption made that their help was there for the asking, the sympathies forged during a difficult journey now overriding other considerations. 'The fence either side simply vanishes once it reaches open country. It's difficult to see so far, but it looks as if there's a watch tower where trains enter between those open ends of wire. Of course there'll be guards, but I'd be surprised if we couldn't slip past at night.'

Michaels rasped at his stubble with his thumbs. 'I thought the same, but I don't like all that walking. Half the night be gone by the time we hiked across that plain and then on our bellies up six kilometres of track. There'll be more guards inside the wire, we can't count on nothing once we pass that tower.'

'A train, then.'

'Now you're talking, but how we get on, man? You don't catch me jumping no train while it stops for a search and Forla bastards are crawling everywhere holding guns.'

'We'd have to board well out on the plain. No ... where trains pull out of the hills to reach the plain. I did that journey once, oh, months ago, and that last climb is steep. The locomotives are getting short of water and crawl up real slow. Not more than half a dozen of us could get on, of course, because there has to be a search at that watch tower. But we could use the jeep to reach that line by dusk; I'm tired of marching, too. Once we get inside the freight yard, so far as I can see there's only one place to start a fire where it won't blow us sky high as well as everyone else.'

'Where?'

Stephen smiled. 'You tell me.'

'I throw a mealie worm like you off this hill with one hand! You tell me what you see or I do it!'

Very slowly and carefully, offering as little excuse as possible for an instant assault, Stephen eased Michaels' knife from out of his belt and laid it on the rock. 'We had a bet, but after yesterday's march maybe I see things a little differently. I'm willing to help get rid of Forla, but if we're to succeed there won't be time to watch our backs as well. No bet this time, and no conditions, but allies in a cause. You take the guard off both of us and I give your knife back in token of that trust.'

'Okay. Forla dead a whole lot more important than a shithead like you.' Michaels' hand fastened hungrily on his knife. 'Now you tell me your plan.'

Jean looked at that open-scissor smile and saw what Stephen had meant earlier: Michaels wanted Forla dead, but foreign, particularly American, help in achieving it was a liability he intended quietly to bury. Success was as fatal to them as failure. Yet Michaels wanted to believe them gullible, and a play with bets and honour, when added to their quite genuine horror over the atrocities they had marched through yesterday, was something he might accept. And chuckle over; damn Yankees treating him like a hick peasant, who might indeed feel bound by pledges taken and offered over a knife.

'... there,' Stephen was saying, and Jean hurriedly pulled her wits together. 'Just blowing the dump wouldn't achieve what you want. But a fire ought to bring half the army in, to stop it happening. Forla himself, probably. While they're falling over hoses and diving for cover each time a box of ammunition explodes, Mananga City will be open for the taking.'

'You light anything there and they all be shitting in their pants. Forla never come near no dump of ammunition if he think it's going to blow.'

Stephen stared at the buildings, factories and homes of Mananga City. A tight line cut between his eyes, the sun reflected from his glasses hiding their expression, that same nerve jumping on his cheek; even Jean was quite uncertain what he was thinking. 'Look at it this way. You're Forla in that damned pink palace and someone telephones to say a train loaded with diesel has caught fire in the sidings. What would you answer?'

'Tell them to shift ass and shove it down the track away from my warehouse full of ammunition,' said Michaels tersely. 'No shit, Steve. That not bad, I think. Forla can't trust any motherfucker in that no-good army of his to do anything right, he have to come and shoot at their feet himself before he's sure they push out a burning train.' He rubbed his hands as a further range of possibilities crowded in. 'He feel Mr Big if he go and save Mananga City. Forla an animal, but unless he kinda rotted up, he not a coward.'

'One or two small explosions,' said Stephen thoughtfully. 'Enough to make sure no one wants to come too near, not so much we blow the dump. Above all, we mustn't make shoving out that train look impossible from the start.'

'You asking helluva lot.'

'But if we get it right and draw Forla himself to the freight yard —'

'Yeah, that worth a whole lotta trouble, but fuck it up and we fucked too. You set out to blow a warehouse full of explosive and all you gotta do is run like hell and listen to it rip. Fuck around lighting bonfires and we could get caught, or the fire don't burn or burn too bright ... Whaddaya going to do then?'

Stephen grinned. 'Knit up a few stitches in a hurry and try something else.'

Michaels stared at him. Muscled cheeks, outthrust jaw and secretive eyes all turned like a radar screen to detecting doubt or doublecross; Stephen apparently unaware of scrutiny, his fingers absently drumming on rock and his thoughts turned inward behind those damned deceiving glasses.

'Okay,' said Michaels at last, and seemed to sigh. 'You know we have to go in tonight?'

Stephen nodded. 'Give me an hour to think about some of the places we could go wrong, then I'd like to test those Czech grenades.'

'You mean, make an explosion?'

'I have to. They're so corroded I'm not even sure the pin will pull out.'

'How many explosions?'

'Two ... perhaps three.'

'Jesus, you want Forla hot shit out here?' He was bristling suspicion again.

'We heard firing several times yesterday and everyone accepted it as part of the scenery. If we're to have any chance at all of pulling this off, you must see I have to test those grenades. I can bury them so the sound oughtn't to carry far.'

Michaels shrugged and began to edge backwards off the ledge. 'You think you know it all, but I say you know fuck nothing,' he said venomously, as his head disappeared over the edge.

Jean and Stephen were left to find their own way down the hill. The lower ledge where their two guards had been waiting was empty when they reached it, Michaels himself already skidding down the lower slopes, partly on his rump and partly by jamming elbows and knees into such fissures as existed.

'Anyone else would slip and break his neck,' Jean observed.

'No such luck, when any other guerrilla must be easier to fool.'

'I think you did, though. He really does think you are some kind of an ally, until Forla is dead.'

'He also knows that if we see a chance to run, we will. Those guards may be pulled back a little, but they'll still have orders to shoot the moment we step out of line.' He gingerly began climbing down, a toehold at a time.

Jean waited until he reached the next crumbling ledge. 'You know what I think?'

He grunted, wedged a boot to take his weight and wiped the sweat off his face. 'I always did hate heights.'

'I think if I was Michaels I wouldn't bother about attacking Mananga City once Forla is lured to the railway sidings. I would

180

blow up that ammunition dump and wipe out him and his body-guard while I had the chance. To hell with all the other people getting killed.'

Stephen was silent for a moment, and then shrugged. 'I think so, too.'

'You knew that was the chance he must see, once you showed how Forla might be brought there?'

'Yes!' he said with sudden anger. 'Michaels was going to blow that dump anyway, wasn't he? Now, some other chances may grow along the way. For instance, he can't explode it until he gets himself and his men out, dug safely away from the blast. And stoking a limited blaze on a railroad wagon could keep him around helping longer than he realises. Sure, the whole thing is full of hellish risks, but after three days' hard thinking I haven't come up with anything else which might offer us the faintest of chances to get clear afterward.'

They went down the rest of the way in silence, because of the other things she also thought, and which he would know she thought. Because, if Michaels had to be kept too close to the dump safely to explode it, then perhaps the only chance they would have of preventing a disaster was somehow to kill Forla immediately he showed up. Once he was dead, even his personal guard would run and Michaels no longer wish to destroy a warehouse full of fuel and ammunition, but to preserve it for his own use.

A split-second death which only someone of ruthless, un-divided mind might possibly achieve, when surrounded by a chaos of burning oil drums and guerrillas poised for their own attack — Stephen Retz was the last man who should attempt it. Because, however subtle his plans, another killing, even of a brute like Forla, must surely come close to destroying him, bring fatal hesitation, castrate decision when instant judgement, alone, might mean the difference between life and death, not just for themselves but for a great many inhabitants of Mananga City.

Whereas I might not have to force myself too much at all, mused Jean. Her emotions were still so shaken by their desolate march yesterday and the many miseries she had witnessed since coming to Mananga, that she couldn't help reacting with a fierce desire to cut out the root of so much evil. Killing a monster like Forla scarcely seemed a crime; more like a mercy, when she really did believe that almost any other ruler must be better. The trouble was, she had never handled a gun in her life and Michaels would certainly keep both of them disarmed; Forla would be surrounded by a bodyguard wherever he went.

She sat a little apart, her chin on her knees, and brooded on their dilemma while Stephen went to test grenades. She heard a muffled double crack, a pause and then one more. The guerrillas around her fingered their weapons uneasily and muttered among themselves, but nothing happened which might suggest anyone official wondered what the explosions were. A fighter flew over, very low, early in the afternoon and sent everyone scattering into cover, the rip of sound shattering in its impact. The pilot didn't seem to be looking for anything particular and, watching his dangerously tight bank around their conical hill, Jean decided he was simply enjoying his own speed and power.

As maybe she was enjoying her own moral certainties, coolly judging between lesser evils while Stephen twisted this way and that to avoid the absolutes of decision?

Honestly, she did not think so.

She hated the idea of killing anyone, every feeling as well as her training revolted by killing even Forla, but driven into a corner as they were, if his life should be the price of saving several hundred slum-dwellers of Mananga City, then she refused to get too upset about it. And if, in a crunch, Stephen had actually become incapable of pulling a trigger, she wanted to save him the humiliation of discovering that the most ingenious, brilliantly thought-out plans could be brought to catastrophe by his own human failing, which in other circumstances would be thought admirable.

She had come to Mananga to heal, but here and now everything was different. Jean looked up unhappily and saw Stephen coming back, shoulders hunched, also lost in thought. The way he walked, the set of his head instantly recognisable from all others in the world, yet during the time she had known him there had only ever been the odd flash of expression, an occasional laugh, when he had been free from strain.

Strain tightening on them both, making them infinitely familiar, also infinitely unfamiliar to each other. Forced choices, hate and guilt everywhere she looked. How little, really, anyone managed to do just because they wanted to. In her case, everything had been tied up tight with duty and what-was-expected-of-you before she was twenty-one, and everything since she came to Mananga driven by the logic of violence. In all of her life she could only remember reading a few books, cherishing a few ideas, laughing with a few friends, simply for pleasure.

Anything else?

She had fallen in love with Stephen Retz.

'Hallo.' She smiled as he came close. 'Everything fixed?'

'If by everything you mean a great many blank spaces loosely linked by rusty grenades then yes, I guess so. We start in an hour.'

'I thought we would have to wait until dusk.'

'Saul seems the only one who knows the railroad well, he used to drive freight out of the yard. He says the last train comes up from Kosti about seven, and at night everything shuts down. We've quite a big detour to make if we hope to reach where the line comes up the last gradient to the plain without being spotted.' He was looking around him with quick suspicious glances, finding it impossible to relax even for an instant.

Jean stood up, dusting herself down. Another thing she mustn't think about was how filthy she felt. 'You know what Mezak said when he came past?'

Stephen shook his head.

' "Steve magic. He drive locomotive boom through station, wham all the way to Forla's palace, see if he don't." '

Even without looking, she felt his tension ease, heard a sound which was not too far from a laugh. 'I wish to God I could. A really powerful spell is exactly what we need.'

17

THREE guerrillas from the inner élite were chosen to jump the train with Michaels, Stephen, Jean and Saul, the only one out of all of them who knew the station layout personally. They piled somehow into the jeep, leaving the two trucks to help ferry the main force closer to the outside wire defending the station, barracks and warehouse area. They had to wait until dark to move, and Jean could see that Michaels was unhappy about the need to divide his force from his last-minute hesitation about separating himself from the bulk of his men during the early, most crucial phase of the operation: in this case an attack on the capital city of his enemy which he must have dreamed about for years, and which before tomorrow's dawn would have destroyed him or made him master of Mananga.

But he had seized on the value of Stephen's plan and now accepted the consequences that followed. Michaels was an eminently dislikeable man, but Jean respected him as she watched him turn away from his second-in-command and Mezak without last-minute fuss, swing himself into the jeep and slap at metal in an undramatic signal to drive away. The assault on Mananga City was under way.

Once embarked on their journey in the jeep, the discomfort of being piled on top of each other on metal seats soon prevented connected thought and worry alike. The ground was rough and often rocky, split by deep gullies as they detoured back into the Kosti Hills again, and the two guerrillas forced to cling to the spare wheel often fell off into the dust.

Probably their detour was no more than thirty miles, but when each mile needed caution because Forla's troops had to be scavenging somewhere close by, it seemed endless.

At last Michaels stirred and grunted; he sat in front and, with the driver, was the only person enjoying the luxury of a seat to himself. Jean still couldn't see anything except rock, but a few minutes later the jeep slithered down some scree and there was the railway line at the end of a miniature ravine, glinting in the sun. They all climbed out stiffly, thankful beyond words to stretch bruised limbs while Michaels and Saul went into a huddle which pointedly excluded Stephen.

'He's making sure everyone remembers the plan was his,' Jean remarked.

'He's welcome to it,' Stephen answered and they walked together to where the line passed the end of their ravine, but there was little to see. In the direction of Kosti the track almost immediately curled out of sight around some rock; to their right there was another very sharp bend as the rails reached flatter ground, Mananga City perhaps twenty miles away. 'I've never jumped a train before, but this looks a good place to me.' Stephen looked around carefully. 'I shouldn't think we would get much notice of it coming, though.'

After a few minutes Saul followed them; he still retched up

most food he tried to eat, but had leapt at the chance of joining guerrillas in the most dangerous part of the assault. 'I think a train come,' he said in Manangan, head tilted.

Stephen laid his hand on the rail. 'Are you sure?'

'No, but the air quivers.' He signalled urgently to Michaels.

Stephen had suggested that they ought to aim to board a train at dusk, but though the sun was low it would be some time yet before it set. 'Will there be another train tonight?' demanded Michaels, arriving at a run.

Saul shrugged. 'After so much fighting and terror there could be a train any time, or no train at all.'

No one answered and they stood willing him to be wrong, but within minutes they could all hear it: the gasping beat of an engine toiling up the gradient towards them.

Michaels spat orders at his men and they scattered along the track; Stephen, Jean and Saul crouched together under cover of some rocks. The train's noise deepened swiftly to a roar, and as it passed the last masking fold of hill it seemed to hurtle down on where they waited, screeching against badly set rails. As they had hoped, after such a climb it wasn't travelling fast, but the impression of noise and weight was enormous, its sudden appearance round that last corner unnerving.

Michaels stood the instant the driver's cab disappeared around the right-hand curve leading to the plain, and immediately they were all running together alongside the track, leaping ankle-trapping boulders. Jean just didn't seem able to run fast enough as wagons continued to overhaul her at a dismaying rate, tearing handholds past her outstretched fingers. She missed the first two freight wagons altogether, glimpsed Michaels' peeled-back smirk as he swung up in front of her. Their guard was still running just behind her, ready to kill if she failed to board with the rest. Flapping canvas, rusty metal, tearing past her; her breath stiffening in her lungs, heart hammering, as much with panic as exhaustion. Saul was up, all the guerrillas except that guard up, Michaels' expression changing to fury as he realised Stephen wouldn't jump without her. The whole enterprise destroyed by female inability to haul herself up by sheer muscle power as those freight cars gathered speed. She set her teeth and ran on, thinking now about a railwayman in the brake van which must appear around masking rock at any moment, even though Mananga's trains were as long as suffering locomotives could haul; she jumped desperately for the next flatcar to begin overtaking her, all or nothing now. For a terrifying instant her feet seemed sucked towards metal rail and maiming wheels, her arm nearly jerked out of its socket, then she was up and sprawled on dirty timber planking.

Stephen fell anyhow behind her, both of them feeling the train increase speed as this last uphill curve was negotiated and the plain gave an easy run into Mananga City's freight yards. 'I'm too old for Wild West stunts,' said Stephen ruefully, at the same time sounding as if he relished some action after too much thinking. Between them they untied some canvas, and crawled into cover beside stacked cases. 'Forla certainly ought to come running if he hears this lot is burning,' he added, pointing to stencil marks on a case.

WEAPONS TO THE PEOPLE! FREE GIFT FROM THE SOCIALIST
LIBYAN ARAB JAMAHARIYA!

'There might be safer explosives inside than corroded grenades,' Jean suggested.

He shook his head. 'Guns, I should think. God knows what is on the other freight cars; shells maybe, which could go all over the place. Starting a fire near a load like this is beginning not to appeal to me at all.'

The train was slowing again, brakes grabbing; already they must be approaching the most dangerous place on this part of the journey, where they had to pass the guards in their watch tower at the entry to the wire.

The train does not stop, Saul had insisted. There is a slope up to the freight yard and drivers prefer to keep moving. All that happens is, two or three guards swing up and travel with it to the station. They are meant to stay on board and watch all the time until it is unloaded, to prevent pilfering. But they drink and talk with friends and unloading takes so long they cannot watch all the time. The afternoon trains are not unloaded until the following day, anyway.

The train slowing, slowing. Whatever Saul had said, this one was going to stop. It stopped and stood panting while voices called and boots crunched on the track. Jean lay with her face pressed against Stephen's arm and felt waves of fright wash over her; her mood of earlier that same day seemed uncommonly foolish now. If they were caught on one of Forla's trains then they would be beaten into bloody shreds of flesh, she raped to death and no questions asked.

Outside, someone must have told a good joke because shouts of laughter drifted back to them from the direction of the locomotive, while from nearer at hand came the ominous click of a single boot sole on metal.

Both of them were holding their breath as a guard hoisted himself up a thickness of canvas from their faces, shuffled and spat. He had only to glance down and he would see that untied edge of canvas Stephen was holding flat against timber. Then he would guess at once that stowaways were aboard.

The train shuddered, creaked slowly forward, and clicked over a rail joint; that soldier was still as close as ever, cursing as he lurched to the motion of the train. When they rattled and swayed into the freight yard he lost his balance altogether and sprawled against the hard edge of a packing case, kicking Jean in the ribs as he did so, only a glancing blow, but it hurt like hell and for a moment she was winded, lay hearing her own breath whine. He had to hear her. He must be deaf not to hear her. She choked trying to stifle the whine, dug her face hard into Stephen's arm and nearly suffocated on a red-hot burning retch.

When she came up again for air the train had stopped and the soldier's boots were dancing angrily near her face while he yelled obscenities, presumably aimed at indifferent driving on Manangan State Railways.

After that they lay where they were for what seemed another endless length of time, while shouts and orders clashed ill-temperedly backwards and forwards between guards and officials on the platform. While stuffy heat became evening chill, their cramped position on hard timber intolerably uncomfortable. Voices and footsteps came and went, and there seemed to be far more people around than they had hoped. As evening faded into night everyone ought to be snug in their barracks, except for a few sentries whom Saul swore played crap games and drank for most of their spell of duty.

'When?' Jean breathed, some time after it became completely dark.

She felt Stephen's shoulder lift and fall. Only Michaels could decide when they could not afford to waste more time on caution. They waited ... waited ... waited, Michaels more cautious than

Jean had expected. When a hand silently lifted their flap of canvas at last there was only the occasional distant voice to be heard.

'Come now. All is well.' Saul's whisper.

She was stiffer than she anticipated, her legs as awkward as fencing posts, an ache in her ribs where that soldier's boot had caught her. But she was eager, very eager again now that action had begun at last. After complete darkness under that canvas cover, the scene which met her eyes looked like a large illuminated postage stamp, surcharged with gleaming drums and stacks of equipment, overprinted by shadow.

The train they had seen from the hill that morning was still only part-unloaded on a parallel siding; crates and hardware carelessly piled all around. Some trucks and at least one armoured car were parked outside the warehouse about a hundred yards away, and behind her was the darkened station building, protected by more wire and floodlit at the corners. A huddle of troops stood on guard at its entry, more at double gates through which in daytime any traffic from the warehouse joined the main road outside the station. Where they were standing between wagons in the sidings, there was less direct illumination. Even so, Jean could pick out movement where Michaels and his guerrillas stood waiting for them, the fullest of moons dangerously touching detail into life: here a pile of drums, there the outline of a locomotive. Also a machine-gun post they hadn't known about, in an angle of wall near the passenger platforms.

Jean glanced over her shoulder, and silhouetted against the night sky she could just see the conical hill where they had lain and looked at this scene, scheming how to reach where they now stood. She tipped her watch to the moon: eleven-thirty. It was later than she had thought.

'Wait here,' said Stephen softly. 'I mean it, Jean. I have grenades to fix, freight to move if necessary. I shall be safer alone.'

She waited a long time. Not worrying precisely, since the torpid routine of Mananga City railway terminal continued undisturbed, but feeling very tense. Also very much alone. A guerrilla hunkered nearby to keep watch on her, perhaps to give covering fire if anything went dramatically wrong: the only other people in sight those distant sentries. Michaels, Stephen and the other guerrillas had all vanished from sight and were covertly heaving freight to give Stephen the kind of fire he wanted.

Quite how much the ex-president of the Retz Corporation knew about arson Jean wasn't sure, but if he set out to burn a train — no, only partly to burn a train — then she expected him to do it efficiently. It was the other, more lethal things he might also have to do she was less sure about.

Her heart accelerated as time stretched on and on; this endless waiting was what flaked at courage and brought visions of disaster crowding in. Twice she thought she heard sounds which might have been a drum of diesel grating on timber, and the guerrilla beside her grunted in alarm, but no one else seemed to notice. As midnight came and went, Forla's military became noticeably less active. A single patrol now moved between the floodlights, elsewhere the only sign of guards was when the occasional figure stood up to urinate or smoke a cigarette.

And as Jean watched those lighted cigarette butts carelessly flicked into corners, she was amazed there hadn't been a major conflagration before in Mananga City base. If General Forla had ever visited his troops, then he ought not to feel too surprised by a report that a train had caught fire in the freight yard.

A drift of smoke from further over to the left than she expected was the first indication that Stephen was satisfied at last with his preparations. When her companion guerrilla smelt it too, he slapped the stock of his gun with excitement. Both of them were excited rather than frightened now. But, astonishingly, none of the guards seemed to notice: the base slumbered on and the patrol lolling under floodlights did not stir.

'I started with smoke so they wouldn't think it was sabotage, more like a cigarette starting something smouldering.' Stephen reappeared out of the dark to crouch beside her. 'I might as well have saved myself the bother, they're such a slovenly bunch.'

'They have to notice soon.' She gripped his hand, hard, where it rested on her arm and felt warmth right through to her ribs.

'Sure, once the rubbish we've piled up catches, even Forla's army couldn't miss the flames. But I didn't want them to be panicked into imagining anything except an accident.'

The smell of smoke was strengthening all the time, the slightest of crackles detectable to a listening ear. At last a tinny shout came from over by the warehouse and the patrol grabbed at its guns, leapt up in alarm, and shouted back. One man detached himself from the rest and began walking towards the sidings holding his weapon at the ready, hesitated and ran back, waving his arms.

'About time, too,' said Stephen with satisfaction.

'I never met a man yet who didn't enjoy lighting bonfires,' Jean whispered, and chuckled at his expression.

They watched while the base turned into an anthill of activity. Whistles blew and NCOs yelled orders; soldiers came and went and tripped over each other while unravelling leaking hoses until even Michaels, who had come to crouch beside them, slapped his thigh with delight. An officer appeared holding a long weighted cane and began lashing out at anyone in reach, making confusion worse. The water pressure was poor and the few braver men who had ventured near the fire turned in fury on those more cowardly souls who hung back, piddling pools of water which reached nowhere near the blaze. Blows were exchanged and in the middle of it all the first grenade exploded, followed swiftly by an empty, fume-filled drum. A spurt of brilliant yellow flame followed, bursting sparks through a pile of rubbish, which until then had been the only thing alight, and igniting a pool of oil.

'I thought you set fire to a freight wagon,' Jean kept her voice low, for Stephen alone, although the crackle of flames was now loud enough to absorb most other sounds.

'I changed my mind after I saw the cargo on the train we jumped. Our wagon may have only carried guns, but Michaels' flatbed had phosphorus and fragmentation shells. God knows what genocide that bastard Forla plans next, bringing in stuff like that. I couldn't chance those going up by lighting a fire too close, even at a distance it's one hell of a risk.' He shifted restlessly, his arm like wire encircling hers. 'I knew these were demoralised troops, but I didn't guess how deep the rot had gone. I thought they could stamp out a few burning planks, which would force Michaels into stirring things up. Then he couldn't possibly blow the dump, there'd never be time to get clear. And we might have a chance to slip away before he shot us too.'

Because nothing, really, was being done. The scale of activity was almost total, the impact of the fire less than zero. A small pool of fuel flared across concrete to ignite a stack of bagged flour, and from the bags a mist of dust rose like flickering fireflies to the station roof. This was some distance from the warehouse, but Stephen now was incapable of staying still. He stood up and rubbed his hands nervously on his trousers, his knucklebones cracking like shot; the next explosion was loud enough to snap Jean's eardrums and, as the firefighters led a rush into cover, she knew beyond doubt that he had taken risks with this fire which, but for her, he would never have dreamed of taking.

'Five grenades packed together into a drum half-filled with cinders.' Stephen's quiet voice contradicted worry. But hysteria was beginning to bite wherever they looked, as instead of realising that this fire as yet only licked at rubbish and fume-filled empty drums, everyone stared over their shoulder in understandable terror at a warehouse stocked with ammunition, the drums of fuel still loaded on yesterday's train in the siding.

'Holy shit, them bastards so scared they pee in their pants,' Michaels hissed. 'I pull out now, let everything blow, and Forla's army is bits stuck to walls.'

'It's still safe to wait, try and get Forla too!' Stephen's face was touched red by the fire, pouring sweat which gleamed as if it was blood. 'Otherwise you still have to face an enemy in command of tanks and aircraft and pampered personal troops, who will fight for their own skins as well as Forla's.'

'How much longer it safe?' Michaels was fiddling with a catch on his gun as if he, too, could scarcely bear to wait in this trap another moment in case something that mattered should explode. Both Jean and Stephen realised that he also debated with himself whether he had finished with them now, or whether Stephen's skills were worth retaining a little longer for unforeseen emergencies.

'As much as another half-hour.' Stephen's voice sounded steady but unreal. 'There's most of that case of grenades in the next pile of rubbish and a stack of timber behind. If no one has dared phone Forla so far, he has to hear those grenades explode for himself.'

'He hear bad explosion, he shit in his pants too and not come.' Michaels' eyes were roaming from the flames to his uncertain, scared men and back again to them, decision nearly formed.

'You said he was a brute, but not a coward.'

'Yeah, but I'm still here because you lit this fucking fire and tell me it is safe. If I was Forla and see this bomb-pile burn, I burrow in the cellar. Put my hands over my ears.'

'Would you? Would you really? When you knew that if you lost this lot, you lost half your treasury and most of your stores?' Stephen's arm on hers was beginning to tremble, surely this must

191

be his last bluff. A last truth, too, because he alone might possibly judge how much longer Michaels could afford to wait and expect to live. But how easily and fatally even his judgement could be wrong.

Michaels was hesitating, hesitating, very suspicious now; his men beginning to murmur. Brave they certainly were, but everyone knew a chance spark could set off some unstoppable disaster which would blow them into oblivion.

'You fucking me —' began Michaels.

A single loud report cut across his words, followed by a deep shuddering boom. The flames wavered and for an instant seemed almost to go out, a collective wail was wrenched from both Forla's and Michaels' men as they expected this breath to be their last. One second, two, of near darkness while everyone stood paralysed, then the flames leapt back and the whole garrison ran at once. To their credit the guerrillas stayed where they were, but one dropped on his knees and began to pray, another to curse aloud.

Michaels himself never moved, except to whip round and study the flames, which for a short space of time were definitely less, and smoke which was definitely more: eyes narrowed, stubbled chin reflecting redness, he might have been a poster of a revolutionary. He swung back to Stephen. 'Was that hustler's cough the fucking grenades?'

Stephen nodded, that tremble in his arm deeper now.

'They shitted on the flames. I told you to blow them across into that train.'

'It's too dangerous. There's shells and God knows what in those freight cars.'

'So you doublecross me, eh?' said Michaels softly. 'I say burn that train and you fuck off different how you damn well please.' His mouth twisted into a rictus of fury. 'You screw me, right? You think I do not kill you while only a godalmighty Yank can light pretty fires. I tell you, if Captain Michaels light a fire he throw your bones on top and no one put it out.' The muzzle of his machine-pistol jerked up to point at Stephen's belly, his lips drawn back, tongue flicking between them.

Jean's mouth was open too in a silent scream as only a few final seconds of enjoyment prevented Michaels from pulling that trigger. Not mercy, when violent jealousy was all he felt for anyone else's skill. Certainly not caution, which should have reminded him

192

that shots would announce an attack on the depot even to panic-stricken troops, all their efforts to make this seem an accident be wasted. Perhaps he thought that now Forla's men were utterly demoralised, it didn't matter.

Stephen stood absolutely still, suicidal so much as to twitch a muscle, his face mask-like in the strange light, his eyes lifting, staring. 'There's Forla now. I told you he would come if only you waited.' And, as Michaels instinctively turned, Stephen jerked Jean violently aside, both of them ducking, jinking, scrambling anyhow under couplings and across the track beyond. Tripping over roughness underfoot; God, they mustn't fall! Jean felt her feet hit a slope and instantly her back cringed from the shots Michaels must surely fire if they slowed, Stephen's hand still gripped on her arm and shoving her left, left, where they had to climb some kind of obstacle to reach life-saving shadow. Terror changing into a fever of excitement because they had broken free at last, one moment Michaels' black muzzle thrust into Stephen's stomach and the next this crazy race for safety in a burning freight yard filled with guerrillas and soldiers and tons of explosive. Soldiers who did not know they were there and guerrillas who did, but perhaps had regained enough sense to remember that random, wide-sprayed shots might easily set off fuel or explosives.

'It wasn't really Forla, was it?' breathed Jean, as they stood in an angle of wall watching to see if any of the guerrillas had followed to search for them.

'No. But unless he's dead drunk, he has to have heard those exploding grenades.'

'He could be, easily.'

Jean felt him shrug; there was nothing more they could do. Their own escape was the only thing that mattered now. From here, the nearest frontier must be three hundred miles away, Jean thought, and all at once was swept by a sense of the bizarre unbelievableness of everything that had happened, was still happening. This didn't even feel like her, Jean Gregory, watching dulled flame leap higher again, hearing a fresh and much sharper explosion as drums some way distant from the original fire began to burn.

'Damn Michaels to hell,' said Stephen furiously. 'The bastard has set fire to that train. He's decided to pull out and let Mananga City blow sky high, so long as the base goes too.'

'Can we shift those wagons ourselves? The ground slopes down.'
As soon as she spoke Jean realised the enormity of what she had
said, a humdrum offering of both their lives, and yet it didn't seem
to matter.

He turned, and in this much brighter light she could see his
expression clearly: incredulous, a flicker of amusement, followed
by more familiar swift deliberation. Then he smiled. 'We could
try.'

Both of them realised that to try would be very difficult, and
pinch out the remaining hope of their own escape. And yet ... perhaps fifty thousand people lived within half a mile of this train
whose rearmost freight car was now blazing, its cargo largely made
up of fuel drums, whose precise contents they did not know. On a
parallel siding stood the train on which they had hidden to ride in
here, which Stephen said carried phosphorus shells and small arms
ammunition. Once that began to explode and hurl missiles everywhere then the warehouse would certainly burn too. The teeming,
fragile slums of Mananga City would be ripped apart, showered
with blazing debris. This Stephen had deliberately risked, yet at
the same time taken infinite precautions to avoid. He could never
live with it if it happened, and nor could she.

An immense pall of smoke already towered above the heart of
this new fire, itself only occasionally visible as a small but growing
heart of flame. 'Diesel, thank God,' said Stephen. 'If it had been
gas or aviation fuel we wouldn't have had a chance.'

All the same, there was too little time to worry about concealment as they ran as hard as they could back to the siding. No time
to remember that only minutes before the guerrillas would have
killed them on sight. But, from the moment he fired the train,
Michaels must have started retreating as fast as possible, to wait at
a safe distance until the base exploded. Then he and his guerrillas
would come back shooting.

Perhaps because she and Stephen had deliberately chosen to set
aside their own best chance of survival, Jean felt terror draw back
a little. But everything around her was so shocking, so pointless
and happening so fast that this sense of coolness couldn't be
considered courage.

'As close to the fire as we can,' panted Stephen. 'We'll never
shift more than a couple of wagons.'

They would be lucky to shift one without the strength of madness, Jean thought. But a kind of madness was inspiring them, so they no longer heard the crackle of flames or felt the blast of heat.

The heavy metal couplings were bar-tight and hot to the touch. 'It's no good, I'll have to slam it up.' Stephen was wedged between Jean and the two wagons, struggling to lift rusted chain out of a curved hook. Taking the clip off had been easy, now they could not force even a fraction of slack into that coupling chain to allow it to disengage. Brake pipes, tubing, Jean managed somehow to release all the other greasy fastenings while Stephen crawled out to find something with which to force that chain up.

He came back with a pointsman's lever but still they could not do it. Grunting, sweating, frantic with haste, they seemed unable to shift it even by a millimetre, the roar of the fire becoming louder, a violent explosion streaking flame overhead. Soon the wagon's wheels might seize solid with the heat. Links and hook were held immovable by the slight slope out of the sidings which would help them if only they could get it off, get the accursed, fucking, FUCK-ING thing off ... It would not move. It would not.

No time left. They could not last many more seconds in this heat, had only lasted so far because the wagon shielded them. Deliberately, Stephen stood back and wiped his face on his arm as if forcing calculation back into frenzied effort. Then he shoved that lever through the links instead of using it to try to force them up, braced its end against the back of the wagon and threw his weight on the fulcrum of bar and coupling, and that anchored, twisting point. His own slight body used as a fulcrum too.

The coupling came off with a shock which hurled him back-wards on the track and rattled the wagon forward nearly a yard.

He picked himself up, half dazed. Jean was already shoving at that wagon and feeling it begin to move, which meant neither its wheels nor those of the blazing wagon in front had seized up yet. Shove now, with bursting heart and lungs because that incline instead of being cursed for holding the coupling tight was suddenly transformed into a marvellous, beckoning slope. Not really a slope until ... somewhere beyond the station yard, Jean thought, but she no longer remembered anything very clearly. Alone, surely they could not shove laden wagons down this slightest of inclines until it became a slope. What they needed now was half a dozen hefty soldiers.

As if in a dream she realised there were no longer two of them, but three. Perhaps they had been three for some time, toiling like figures in a painting of hell. The wagons were beginning to roll by their own weight, chunking solidly over hot rail joints, gliding between shoves, until they were pushing at a retching walk. Jean fell first, every shred of her strength expended, and when she roused only a moment later all she could see was some rubbish burning, but dully. Which must be Stephen's original fire, his placing of grenades exquisitely correct in a pile of cinders, so that when they exploded non-inflammable dust had doused much of the remaining flame. Waveringly, she climbed back on her feet and trudged down the track where a brilliant fire was steadily coasting out to the main line, past huts, hesitating over some points but ghosting on again, light dimming not because this fire got less but because the two wagons were picking up speed down the slope and out into open country. She was so delighted her exhaustion fell away and, not looking where she was going, tripped over Stephen. His face turned up to hers, their fingers groping and gripping, wordless in the dark.

The next thing she remembered was seeing him crouched beside another figure, that third man who had materialised out of smoke when, without him, they could not have moved those burning wagons far enough to start them coasting down the slope to safety. In the distance, the crackle of explosions and a flare of phosphorus showed where that burning cargo was at last beginning to explode. Stephen and the third man were dodging back towards her now, what still seemed like a miraculous deliverance arousing fresh hopes of escape and reminding them of the need for concealment.

The third man was Saul.

18

'My mother and sisters,' Saul had whispered, and stabbed a finger towards the slums of Mananga City. Whether he had stayed behind when Michaels withdrew because he wished to be with his family in death, or because he, too, had frantically tried to avert disaster and joined them when he saw someone else doing the same, they never discovered. Enough that he had been there when, without him, they would have failed; this was no time for unnecessary explanations.

His presence offered another instant gain, as with supple stealth he led them back down the length of the sidings, a jerked head indicating danger they could not hear, a shaken finger a lighted space he considered too exposed to cross. Shouts and vehicle noises indicated that some soldiers were already returning now the burning wagons were safely away on the plain and Stephen's original fire guttering out. A couple of shots snapped sharply, too, freezing them in their tracks, but they came from the direction of the station building rather than the wire. Beyond that wire Michaels must be in an agony of indecision, wondering whether he dared attack now the base had not exploded.

A blaring voice followed those shots, another single report initiating a furious burst of activity as soldiers raced like slovenly khaki sacks from one side of the compound to the other. 'Forla,' hissed Saul, and mimed firing a revolver to show how Forla habitually drove unwilling followers back to work.

Jean stared at the lighted station. The legendary brute who ruled Mananga by caprice and terror had finally arrived to make sure his power did not suffer a calamitous loss; if they had not succeeded against all odds in pushing those wagons out, he would probably have been among the many dead when his depot exploded.

Stephen touched her shoulder and she sensed rather than saw him smile in the same wry acknowledgement as herself, that Forla lived because of them. A touch, a flicker of expression and each knew what the other thought, as if a lifetime of understanding had been compressed into a few short weeks in Mananga. But as Jean stared at his back, just ahead of her as they picked their way between the sidings and some sheds, she did still try to make herself face the truth. This isn't real. Life in a hut and between railway sidings isn't ordinary life. Jean Gregory and Stephen Retz have only three extraordinary weeks in common.

The floodlights around the warehouse shone directly in front of them as they emerged from between some buffers; a tap from Saul's fingers: move now. They followed his wraithlike figure as closely as they could, weariness receding as hope returned. Saul had said he had family here as well as in the valley, friends too, perhaps, who might help them if only they could get out of here: Mananga City no longer a hostile wilderness but potentially a sanctuary. And with Saul as their guide, getting out of here no longer seemed quite so impossibly difficult.

All three of them crouched, petrified, as some soldiers ran past almost close enough to touch. God. Where could they have sprung from, so that even Saul was taken by surprise? Softly they moved forward again, each foot separately placed. When they reached the next shadow only an open space remained between them and the outer wire, partially lit by an overspill of light from the warehouse. They were also able to see a sandbagged bunker which until now had been hidden by stacked drums: normally a permanent guard would be kept there to watch that stretch of wire, and to man a cluster of anti-aircraft missile launchers they could also see. But now, while General Forla spat insults and fired shots at laggards in the distance, the post appeared deserted. Maybe. Those soldiers had come from somewhere.

'Do we have to get across here?' Jean breathed, and saw Stephen nod. Elsewhere the light was stronger or else there were guards nearby, so yes, they did. The only other choice was to retrace their steps the way they had come and find where Michaels had burrowed out. And there, most likely, the guerrillas would be waiting for them.

Whereas, if they could reach the wire from here, Saul appeared confident he could take them through it, using a route perhaps where slum dwellers came pilfering in the dump. That barrier of wire fifty, sixty paces away at most.

They waited, had to wait, not daring so much as to shift weight, while using eyes and ears to detect the slightest suggestion of a watcher in that space. Hope drummed insistently that it was crazy not to go at once when they were so nearly out.

Another beat of feet, still distant but coming closer, and trailed by an echo of bad-tempered commands, as if a pattern of regular patrols was being re-established. Wait any longer and they might never get across that space at all. Saul hissed between his teeth and then was running, head down and as sleekly as a fox across that open space; Stephen's hand on Jean's arm and both of them were running too. No cover, nothing, just space and patchy light, and speed the only way to cross it.

Saul had reached the wire when a guard stood up blearily from behind the sandbagged emplacement, one hand to his flies as if all he intended was to urinate. He appeared to be so stale drunk he had probably snored through fires, explosions, everything, and then chosen this moment to wake up, his head thick, his eyes squinted against a hangover so that he missed Saul altogether, by then no more than a flicker on the edge of vision. He could not possibly miss an unmistakably foreign man and girl running where only soldiers had ever been seen before, the range between them fifteen feet. Quite slowly, because he was still fuddled enough scarcely to believe his eyes, he reached for one of several guns left leaning against the side of the emplacement, loosed a stream of shots, and began yelling in alarm.

If that soldier's sight had not been swimming in nausea, Jean and Stephen must have been punched full of bullets as shots howled, ricocheted off the ground, the warehouse wall, everywhere. As it was, Jean heard Stephen exclaim, felt him lurch, his hand on her arm snatch away as he fell. 'Go on!' he said, quite quietly. 'Run, for Christ's sake.'

Jean grabbed at him, her mind squeezed by agonising fear. 'Where are you ... ?'

Stephen was half down on his side, his hand clamped to a dark stain spreading on his leg and shouting at her now, 'Get out! Get out!'

Shouts, too, from the patrol they had heard coming, the guard who had shot at them lunging out from his bunker. A clatter of boots as Jean tried mindlessly to haul Stephen back on his feet, and then confusion tore them apart, kicking feet, slashing weapons. One of the soldiers must have fired again, sparks from a gun barrel like firecrackers in the dark, but the others, fearful of being hit, rounded on him in fury and by the time they returned to beating up their prisoners an officer had come pelting over, screaming orders.

By then none of it made sense to Jean, although she grasped that the alternative to being beaten into bloody rags was death by interrogation. Live prisoners caught inside Forla's base were beginning to put a different complexion on a fire which previously had been accepted as an accident.

Her body was ringing with pain but seemingly whole; even fear for Stephen became irrelevant as life itself spun further and further out of reach. This then was the final end of their rough road, and the only memory that mattered was how good they had felt together.

The fantasy of escape their minds had woven was now revealed as absurd, indifference wavering back to very abject fear as consciousness rolled closer again; shading in soldiers on either side whose hands had fastened like shackles on her arm, light reaching out towards her, dazzling after so much dimness. Voices, a jeering laugh. Someone seized a handful of her hair and twisted, her head forced so far back that some of the hair tore loose, tears pouring down her face from pain and light.

A grunted command and the hand moved from her head to the small of her back, and thrust her into a room she couldn't see. Those same hands snatched off the satchel she had kept slung and safe even while heaving at freight wagons, a voice disgustedly cursing when all it contained was medical supplies. She stayed unsteadily upright while her eyes slowly cleared and dried, the scene around her streaked into focus.

A table. Two chairs. Concrete walls, an inaccessibly high window. Behind the table sat a man negligently tilting his chair, dressed in lavishly braided uniform. A swagger-stick rested across his knees and an old-fashioned, pearl-handled revolver lay on the table, beside it a Royal Worcester porcelain dish of a pattern Jean remembered admiring in Harrods the previous Christmas. The dish was piled high with what looked like the remains of half a sheep on gravy-soaked bread. Her stomach stirred, instinctively and ravenously, then died again: she was far too frightened for hunger now, because this man had to be General Forla, that baneful presence tainting every corner of Mananga. The servile atmosphere in itself was a kind of confirmation, that revolver another, when several times she had heard that Forla was known to galvanise his followers by firing shots at them in fun or deadly earnest, as he chose.

Once her mind began to clear, Jean immediately became more aware of pain: in her scalp, ribs, one hip. No bones broken, though. A lynching stopped before it was properly begun when someone smarter than the rest realised these prisoners should be made to squeal before they died. To Forla. She stared at that figure behind the table, conscious of surprise. She had imagined a brute and saw a handsome, elaborately-tailored soldier slightly run to fat; smiling lips, and eyes like flattened rivets.

He said something and Jean shook her head, her halting Manangan wouldn't help in this extremity.

Stephen answered instead, his voice sounding rough but clear, and relief swept over her. His face was colourless and he was favouring one leg, held upright by two soldiers while she was left to stand alone as best she might.

Forla rapped out another question, his accent baffling to someone who had only learned a smattering of the language, most recently from hillmen who spoke a different dialect to people from the plains, his fingers flicking the swagger-stick impatiently against his knee.

'Let me translate,' said a voice from the doorway behind them. 'The All Powerful, Supreme General of the Armed Forces Forla, would like to know what the hell you are doing in his base.'

It was Lewis Anderson. He smiled at Stephen, and came forward to stand to one side of Forla's table. 'Well, Mr Retz? We surely do meet in some unexpected corners of Mananga.'

Their guards jumped nervily as Forla snapped the legs of his chair down on the floor and uttered a long soft deadly sentence.

Lewis bowed respectfully, and turned back to them again. 'You will answer. What were you doing here?'

'We were taken prisoner by guerrillas after we trucked that load of food over the Kosti pass. They had killed the Austrian brothers who kept a clinic in the valley and burned their hospital. They would have killed us, too, except they discovered that I knew something about explosives.'

Lewis grinned. 'Those rockets at Hamada. I can see why you ducked mentioning those in front of the ruler of this state.' He spoke in Manangan to General Forla, and Jean thought he didn't mention rockets.

Forla jerked his head at Jean in an unspoken question and Lewis answered, smiling still, then added to her in English, 'You keep quiet and look admiring, okay? He isn't used to women staring him in the face. Dictators make people dance to their will by extravagant gifts as well as by cracking the whip, and I'll get you off if I can.'

'I wouldn't want to be his gift, or yours,' Jean answered contemptuously, but all the while that abject core of fear grew inside her like a cancer, only the desolate certainty that Stephen was unlikely ever to be offered mercy helping to stiffen pride.

'You completely out of your mind? Get in the All Mighty General's cellars and me getting you out wouldn't be worth a shit afterwards. And if your embassy should hear you were screaming someplace, a charge of carrying drugs would keep them quiet.' He jerked a thumb at her satchel and turned back to Stephen. 'You had reached where you helped a bunch of Marxist guerrillas, Mr Retz.'

'They didn't seem too Marxist, but would have killed us all the same. We were kept alive only because they thought I might help blow up this base the way they wanted it.'

'The way they wanted it? What way was that?'

'Slow. Bring General Forla here and make sure he got blown up too.'

Lewis whistled. 'You don't say. Hey, you haven't left any fancy booby traps around, now he does happen to be here?'

'No.'

'Then why were you left inside the wire and not dragged along wherever those guerrillas went?'

Stephen hesitated. More, Jean thought, from the impossibility of explaining complicated detail than any secret he ought to hide. His brain must be fogging up, concentration draining with his blood on to the floor.

She licked dry lips. 'We were scared any explosion here would kill people in the slums outside the wire. The fire Stephen lit was meant to satisfy guerrillas he was being cooperative, not spread to anything important. We hoped we might get lucky and escape in the confusion. Then Michaels —'

'Who the hell is he?'

'The guerrilla leader. It was him who set fire to that train in the sidings. When the guerrillas withdrew to watch it burn we could have escaped, but stayed to push it clear.'

'For Christ's sake, why?'

Jean shrugged, feeling very much as Stephen looked, too far gone for pointless explanation. When no explanation they gave would be believed it ceased to be important. Her head was spinning, spinning, if a soldier came to hold her arms he would be welcome. And because she was almost beyond stringing coherent thought together, she simply did the most natural thing: stepped to that vacant chair by the desk and sat down, her head on her knees.

Forla moved first, everyone else slack-jawed with astonishment that a woman — the fact she was a prisoner almost less important — had dared to sit uninvited in the All Mighty's presence. The stick from his knees slashed down across the desk, the tip catching Jean across the shoulder.

She jerked back and cried out, consciousness violently restored. 'I warned you,' said Lewis urgently. 'Look, I want to save you if I can.' He turned back to Forla and began on a long recitation of his titles, followed by compliments on the restored order at this base, his manner a skilful blend of valued supplier and admiring sidekick.

But Forla's scowl didn't lift as he listened, his earlier smile replaced by petulant fury. The two soldiers holding Stephen were petrified by fear, Stephen himself jerked tight by their grip, taut muscles forming sharp angles from cheekbone to jaw. Forla hissed a sentence back at Lewis, that stick flicking, flicking against the pale fine cloth of his breeches.

Jean still sat in her chair, leaning back, one hand to the flare of pain across her shoulder, her brain shocked into use and her eyes fixed on Forla's revolver on the table, less than three feet from where she sat. If Lewis's attention should waver for an instant ... in this situation, even though he might really want to help her, he could be more dangerous than Forla. The All Mighty General Forla was so used to everyone around him being eviscerated by fear that conceit prevented him from imagining any threat from prisoners; whereas profit and survival were Lewis's chief concern and he would do whatever was necessary to make sure he achieved both. The one mistake he could not afford was to offend his patron, General Forla, who, having captured two Western prisoners, might now harbour some doubts about Lewis Anderson's loyalty too.

Lewis had already turned back to Stephen, whether to divert Forla's attention from Jean or not, she couldn't tell and did not care. Guiltily, she tore her gaze away from that revolver, she mustn't offer even the flicker of a suggestion she might try to reach it. Probably it wouldn't help them to escape, but a quick shot through Stephen's head and her own was infinitely preferable to the other future which awaited them. She only wished she felt more alert. A chance, if it came, would last the fraction of a second.

'... the guerrillas?' She had missed most of what Lewis was saying.

'I don't think so,' Stephen answered. Clipped words, consciousness fiercely held. Not a glance in her direction, could he, too, have seen what she had seen?

'Why not?'

'The base hasn't exploded. The fire is under control —'

'It's out.'

'So, how could Michaels attack now? He hoped to take advantage of disaster. Kill Forla if he could.'

'Yeah,' said Lewis slowly. 'General Forla to you, buddy.' He drove his fist, hard, into Stephen's stomach; turned back to Forla, unconcerned.

Instinctively, Jean had blundered to her feet, but Lewis was too quick for her, grabbed and held her arm. 'Jesus, don't you ever listen? Retz is dead meat and nothing I did would save him, but women are either screwed into mush or ignored. You want to live, you stay ignored.' He signalled to one of the soldiers holding Stephen and he came over to shove his rifle in her back hard enough to hurt.

Which left Lewis himself to join the man holding Stephen, to force him back savagely against the wall. 'The Supreme General, Forla, asks where you put your booby traps.'

'There aren't any.'

'Who are you kidding? You wanted to kill our Almighty Ruler, didn't you? You were here in his depot, weren't you? Not run off with the guerrillas. I don't want to get blown apart, he doesn't want to get blown apart, so you tell me what I want to know, and fast, okay?' His hand slapped Stephen's face with each question, a knee driven into his groin; those booby traps seized on as a mechanism of interrogation, but above all a means of humiliating a man he hated.

Stephen did not, could not, answer, his face grey, only cruel hands holding him upright.

'No booby traps.' Jean's voice no more than a croak. 'Why would we push out a train? Forla ... General Forla would have been killed if it exploded.' Words unshaped and falling, she could scarcely control them any more.

Stephen was saying something now, but the words blurred. His eyes definitely flickered to that revolver, three shaped words for her alone.

'Bring her over here,' Lewis said to the soldier guarding Jean, and they practically fell together in his panic to obey.

Forla relaxed again behind his desk, his stick beating a joyful rhythm instead of menace on his knee. Lewis reached for Jean, his hands like hooks.

Perhaps Lewis Anderson needed to take some personal part in interrogating a fellow-American if he was ever to re-establish himself in the eyes of General Forla. And if he was to save Jean, then he had to be in a position to ask and be granted an exceptional favour. Perhaps. The bright sharp smile on his face also remembered that Stephen Retz had beaten him to this woman both had wanted. That altogether sexual smile grew while she fought his grip, scraping strength out of nowhere to fling against effortless muscle. And Jean watched, hypnotised by horror, as, slowly and taking pleasure in making it slow, Lewis forced her hand forward, his grip shifting to crush the sinews at her wrist, which involuntarily spread her fingers wide. Then he drove them, hard, into the blood on Stephen's thigh, tearing a sound from his throat she would never forget.

Then Lewis let her go, and laughed.

Forla was laughing too.

'Now tell me where those booby traps are,' Lewis said, as if nothing particular had happened.

Jean shot him as he turned.

In the chest because she had never shot anyone before and wasn't certain of her aim; shot him again as he hit the floor. Lewis had thrust her aside the moment he finished using her, neither he nor Forla remembering the revolver left lying on the table while they enjoyed an exotic twist of difference to inflicted pain.

Stephen sent the soldier beside him staggering across to cannon into the other, standing somewhere behind Jean's back. She could not imagine how he had patched sufficient nerve and sinew out of such great shock even to move; except he had become little more than an object to enjoy, which maybe helped.

Neither of those soldiers, nor Forla himself, reacted fast enough as Lewis Anderson died. If Jean had not been far, far beyond the reaches of normality, she, too, would have stood gaping at that killing which was hers. Instead, her senses were so stripped by anguish that purpose alone was left.

And so she stepped back from Lewis's body, and swung round to cover Forla, just in time to prevent him from flinging himself, bodily, on top of her. *Hold Forla after.* Those were the words Stephen had shaped, his eyes on that revolver on the table. The split-second opportunity she had prayed for, offered while their tormentors gloated.

The two soldiers were stupefied by such an unimaginable reversal of fortune, by the single sliver of restraint which separated their Almighty Leader from death. Jean groped for the Manangan words she needed. 'Stand where I see you. Drop guns ... kick them here.'

They did as she said, pop-eyed with justifiable fear; so damned lucky she didn't kill them too they melted where they stood.

When Forla began to shout at them she pulled that trigger without a second thought, recoil from such an old gun jolting all the way from her finger to her ear. The bullet punched through the table and kicked a chunk out of concrete floor between his feet. 'I don't care if I hit you,' she said flatly, in English, and he understood the tone if not the words, his expression murderous, his body fuelled by rage. Even a bullet might not stop him at this short range. Jean knew she couldn't, physically, hold him for much longer, but only the threat of death to their leader might keep his two soldiers cowed.

'Stephen!' she said urgently. 'Stephen — '

He had fallen after shoving those soldiers off balance and she did not think he could stand again unaided, yet she mustn't look aside for an instant, far less help him. But he stood and dragged himself to where the two soldiers were, their eyes dilating as he came. 'Find something for my leg.'

One of them scuttled across the room and came back with a dirty cloth, and all the time Stephen stood holding on to Forla's table and dripping blood on the floor. He looked quite dreadful, his face fallen in like a corpse and more blood smeared where Lewis had split his lip.

Forla shifted from one foot to the other, eyes darting from his men to the gun she held, a man of brawn and cunning who would decide very soon how best to crush their pitiful attempts at escape. Only his habit of firing a revolver whenever the fancy took him, at the feet of laggards or pot-shotting chance civilians, prevented more soldiers from bursting in on them from outside.

'Stephen,' she said again. 'Oh, God, are you all right?' Shock was beginning to make her crumble. And what an abysmal question; he was so far from all right that the realisation they were still inside a Manangan base and three hundred miles from the nearest frontier made this moment a death more dead than death itself.

'Tight,' said Stephen to the soldier who brought the cloth.

'Undo my trousers and wind it tight as hell.' He gestured, spoke words dredged anyhow out of English and Manangan. 'Then see if the American has a flask.'

Lewis did have a flask, and of Scotch instead of the local fire-water; Stephen took the gun from Jean and handed the flask over after he had drunk. The Scottish Highlands were hideously far away as she soared there on a mist of longing, but at least the whisky spread puff-ball warmth from throat to stomach and staved off collapse a little longer.

Stephen steadied himself on the edge of the table, and motioned Forla to stand against the wall.

'No!' Forla said, and for the first time changed colour. 'No! You cannot. I have a thousand men within call. You would be flayed alive, gutted, scream for mercy while your own guts fry.' At least, that was approximately what he said, while cunning nerved closer to resolution as he tried to judge whether Stephen was capable of hitting anything, even at a couple of paces.

'Do what he says.' Jean heard her own voice rise. 'Do what he says!' She picked up his swagger-stick, unsurprised by the loaded weight which had already split skin across her shoulder.

And this time he ignored her, rounded on his men and began spitting orders.

All Jean's hate boiled over; for brutishness and the obscenities witnessed on this and other days, for this man personally, who laughed at suffering and corrupted others to serve his power, in-cluding herself, who today had killed and felt no blame. Hate like black pus bursting as she slashed his own stick at his head, again and again with all the force she possessed. Hate was a convulsion, and when it was over she was looking down at the All Mighty, Supreme General Forla, sprawled on the concrete floor in a pool of blood, his eyes rolled up into his skull.

She turned, trembling. The room, Stephen, the two soldiers, swimming with the beat of her heart, the taste of vomit in her mouth.

'Jean?' said Stephen sharply.

She looked at him stupidly. If she lived, the memory of this room would never leave her.

'Don't think, and do exactly as I say. You hear? Don't think about anything beyond what you must do. Strip Anderson of coat, pants, and search him. I want his billfold and passport, any money and papers he is carrying. Your passport. It's on the floor someplace. If Forla has a shirt on under that fancy tunic, and if it hasn't too much blood on it, strip off that, too. And Jean ... be quick.' He turned to the soldiers. 'Face the wall.'

They exchanged terrified glances and fell on their knees, gabbling. They would, they said, be pegged out for the vultures if left behind to explain why they hadn't stopped a murderous attack on the Supreme Being, be tortured terribly for complicity with guerrillas. As they would have tortured Forla's prisoners, and probably had done in the past ... they weren't owed a shred of mercy. Except that they, like Jean when she killed Lewis, had been caught in a trap not of their own making, and mercy remained the only way back to sanity.

Stephen wiped his face muzzily. 'What do you suggest?'

The most intelligent, a sergeant perhaps from a great many fancy chevrons on his sleeve, gestured. 'We walk home.'

'No.'

'I have family, sons ... I swear — '

'Where is General Forla's car?'

Both hesitated and then the sergeant pointed over his shoulder. 'Outside.'

'The American? Did he come alone or with General Forla?'

He took a moment to grasp Stephen's meaning. 'No one, ever, travel with our Almighty Ruler.' His eyes slid back to that unstirring heap on the floor.

'The American came in another car?' Both soldiers nodded. 'Is that outside too? How close to the door?'

The sergeant held up three fingers. Paces? Yards? Miles? God, they were getting nowhere.

How could they get anywhere, past Forla's soldiers and then all those hundreds of miles to a frontier? Getting out of that door was probably more than Stephen could manage.

'Then you both come with us,' he was saying. 'We'll let you go if we pass the outer gate.'

'But — '

'That's the deal. You want to desert to save your skins, it'll be easier from outside. But first you do what you're told. Otherwise we tie you up, and you get pegged out for those vultures when General Forla recovers consciousness.'

They accepted.

Jean had thought Forla must be dead, and was surprised to discover she was glad that he wasn't. His snuffling body was scarcely worth thinking about any longer, except to curse his bulk which made stripping off his shirt a nightmare task. Lewis Anderson, on the other hand, seemed filled with rancour even in death, as if he could still reach out whenever he chose and destroy their futile efforts, then laugh as he had before.

Jean could see Stephen's thoughts congealing. He had decided on some plan she couldn't grasp but needed to fumble for each move, search for the place where plans are made. He could not possibly last to those impossibly distant frontiers.

Under his direction the two soldiers bundled up the clothes Jean brought, but even the sergeant refused to touch Forla, his breath now moaning in his nostrils, and she had to tie and gag him herself. Possibly she had fractured his skull: for which she felt no regrets at all. Really, she was most aware of the way time was slipping past. She could not begin to estimate how many hours had passed since they jumped a freight train out in the foothills and rode into Mananga sidings. Eternity. Eight or nine hours at least, surely.

As if in answer to her worry, someone tapped on the door. 'Excellency?'

They all jumped, then froze, Jean's eyes instantly drawn to the revolver in Stephen's hand. From the moment she seized it she had resolved to shoot both herself and him rather than fall into Forla's hands again.

Stephen's hand lifting ... now. 'Ask what they want,' he said softly to the sergeant.

The man licked his lips, but called out a question. He understood very well that he died or lived with them. 'They say they have another prisoner.'

Jean and Stephen stared at each other, the same speculation leaping into their minds: Saul.

'Tell them to shove him inside. Don't let them see past the pair of you holding guns.' Stephen dragged himself off the table edge, physically forced the two soldiers to stand with levelled weapons facing the door and himself opened it, keeping back out of sight.

Silence. The soldiers outside did not dare to enter into the presence of the All Highest uninvited, their own two guards struck dumb by a situation even harder to grasp than the trap which had already caught them in its jaws.

That silence tightened into a dreadful, homicidal farce as still no one moved or spoke. Then the soldier Jean thought of as a sergeant reached out and unceremoniously yanked the prisoner inside before slamming the door shut again with his boot. Saul fell on the floor, and outside the door Jean could hear his escort muttering apprehensively between themselves, wondering what they should do next. No one inside the room moved, all of them straining their ears, Saul staring disbelievingly from the floor at a scene which had no point of contact with his imaginings. Boots continued to shuffle uncertainly outside the door, before eventually dawdling away down the passage.

How far?

Not far, Jean decided. But in a base teeming with soldiers a few more in a passage hardly mattered.

The sergeant and his companion were grinning incredulously at each other, they had never realised deception could be so easy.

'Can you walk?' Stephen said to Saul.

He nodded, dazed. There was blood on his singlet but he looked more roughed up than injured. Another titbit brought in to divert Forla.

'Then listen.' Stephen cleared his throat and for a moment stared at Saul as if the effort of slotting him into his plans was a final, unendurable burden. 'We're getting out of here. Now. As prisoners. It's the only way we might have a chance. You too.'

Saul goggled at Forla, bloody, tied and gagged, and nodded, dumbstruck.

'Good. We look beat up enough so only two guards don't seem too crazy.' Stephen fumbled inside his trousers, and brought out his hand smeared bright with blood. 'Come here.' No time, no breath for more than the minimum of words, no meaning beyond driving necessity now. He slapped Saul's face, splattering blood, and wiped more blood on his singlet, across Jean's mouth and jaw. Then he tucked Forla's revolver out of sight inside his shirt, and turned to hammer instructions into their guards with slurring voice and signs and desperate urgency.

My satchel, Jean thought thankfully, it's here all the time and I forgot. If ever a man needed painkiller, stimulant, antibiotics, it was Stephen now.

The satchel had been thrown on the floor when nothing of interest was discovered inside, its contents scattered, syringes flattened, needles broken.

'Hurry,' Stephen said. 'We can't wait.'

'It's worth a few seconds or you'll black out.' Her fingers were steadied by a known professional job, but never in her life had she needed to crush a flattened plastic syringe into some kind of shape, fill it with a mixed and massive dose because she would never get all of it into him, a needle with the tip broken off the best that she could find. 'This is going to hurt.'

He shook his head giddily and somewhere there was the flicker of a smile. Under some circumstance pain had a very relative quality. He winced all the same when she fairly had to force the broken needle in, gagged on food she tore from the remains of Forla's meal.

Disgusting to eat his rejected leftovers, although the moment she tasted meat Jean's own hunger revived like a sword in her guts.

'Give me the guns.' Stephen was grinding sense into dislocated sentences by sheer effort of will. Jean had occasionally seen particularly tough-minded patients set out to prove that for them shock did not exist, she had never before watched anyone attempt to ignore its onset so completely.

When she brought the soldiers' automatic rifles over, he ejected the bullets before giving them back to their two guards. 'Sure what to do?'

Behind them, Forla unexpectedly moaned, making everyone jump. 'We go,' the sergeant said decidedly, and shoved a gun into his terrified companion's hand, hissing threats. They had been incredibly fortunate to find an ally who was so swiftly aware of his own best interests.

'Can you walk?' said Jean quietly to Stephen. 'Put your arm round my shoulders.'

His weight, slight as it was, bowed her like Atlas under the burden of the earth before he straightened carefully, using her only for balance. The drugs she had shot anyhow into him might soon begin to help a little. 'I can walk.'

If that sergeant made a run for it, shouted for help, there would be nothing they could do about it. But at a sign from Stephen he flung open the door, beginning perhaps to enjoy his own daring as he yelled threateningly at skulkers in the passage, bawled out his companion for not kicking their prisoners forward fast enough. As for that second soldier, he was so near being out of his wits with fear that he moved like a zombie. The gun he held when it touched Jean's back, his footsteps on concrete, everything about him shivered in spasms of distintegrating fright. She and Stephen were concentrating on staying on their feet, not needing to feign unsteady lurches.

God, don't let Saul give everything away, when they hadn't had time to give him more than the cloudiest notion that they might not be going out to execution. As, quite probably, they were. To get out of this base would be a miracle, yet, once out, with Stephen in his present state they would not be much nearer freedom. But out of here. Out in fresh soft wind, instead of breathing the stink of suffering. That in itself was worth any risk.

A wall jerked past Jean's lowered eyes, some mocking faces, torn posters on a board. Stephen staggered and nearly fell when they turned at the end of a passage, where a guard opened an outside door and kicked him while they waited. But there the breeze of Jean's imaginings reached out to revive them, rich with all the scents of life, full of strength and hope.

It was early dawn, a pale and lovely yellow light spreading across the eastern sky.

Directly outside the door stood an immense Rolls-Royce, its radiator gold-plated and with a gold-fringed Manangan flag flapping from each wing. General Forla's personal guard smirked as they lurched past, his chauffeur lazily climbing out from behind the wheel to admire his master's handiwork.

A guard of honour stood at ease across some tarmac, their officer making some exquisitely crude joke so that everyone fell about laughing at three prisoners blinking and swaying in air which acted like alcohol on their senses. Jean breathed as deeply as she could, keeping her head bowed and her body slack so that misery was all the onlookers saw.

The officer commanding the guard strolled over, his braid and lanyards winking in the first shaft of sunlight, and immediately doubtful when their sergeant called for Lewis Anderson's car to be brought over.

'If our Supreme Ruler says he don't care if prisoners bleed all over an American's car, who presumes to argue?' The sergeant sounded as if for two straws he would have said straight out that even an officer risked his life to argue with third-hand orders from General Forla.

And the guard commander got the point immediately, retreated in a flurry of delight that Almighty Forla should thumb his nose at American pigs who enriched themselves at Mananga's expense.

Lewis Anderson had certainly done himself well for transport, his sports Jaguar just one step back from Forla's Rolls. A sleek pale blue, its numberplates showed only the blazon of Forla's state, a crouching gold puma, so almost certainly he had been lent it out of the All Mighty's million-dollar garage as a particular sign of favour.

Lewis apparently had no driver, which wasn't surprising with several litres of glorious machinery which he could race along nearly deserted highways, but caused considerable consternation. Their sergeant hesitated over taking the wheel himself and consulted Forla's personal chauffeur, while everyone disclaimed any desire to return to the Supreme Being to ask who he wanted to drive one of his own cars if Anderson wasn't there. Finally their sergeant accepted the responsibility of driving, everyone grinning with relief that they had not by accident become implicated in an act of *lèse-majesté*; there was more than one commiserating glance, too, since a sergeant who dared to drive one of All Mighty Forla's favourite cars without permission was clearly doomed. It was the kind of Catch-22 situation which struck out of nowhere in Mananga, where anyone who returned to their ruler's presence to imply that his original order had been insufficiently explicit could only expect a bullet through the skull.

Jean, Saul and finally Stephen were shoved anyhow in the back, their other guard hysterically waving his rifle at them, his boots in their faces, by now more than half wild with his own terrors. Such open terror ought, surely, to alert someone among the many watchers that there was something wrong, except that terror in those who served Forla could be accepted as a natural state of mind. Their sergeant was running round to the Jaguar's front seat, racing the engine and missing a gear shift while everyone sniggered; a dozen toadies would already be planning to tell Forla how his car had been abused.

Then the Jaguar accelerated past the guard of honour, past some charred and reeking drums, past the warehouse, a tractor towing loaded trailers swerving to avoid them. From where she was lying,

Jean glimpsed rows of racks inside the warehouse, which might have contained anything from beans to bombs.

Could it have exploded and razed half Mananga City?

Now no one would ever know.

The main gate to the base was coming up now, the barracks to their right seething with jittery soldiers swapping stories about the excitements of the night; on their left the station building besieged by early passengers wanting to know why the trains weren't running. They would be lucky if they ran in a week, since the track must be torn in fragments where that burning wagon had eventually exploded.

'Prisoners for the All Highest's personal attention,' their sergeant bawled at the gate guard, and, tense as she was, Jean felt a quite different shiver in her spine. It could so easily have been true; would still be true if they allowed themselves to be recaptured alive.

The splendid numberplate, the size of car, which could only belong to an intimate of their Supreme Being and had arrived in his company earlier, was nearly enough for the guard. Their glance inside was awestruck rather than searching, the thick bundle of papers Lewis Anderson had carried fingered rather than read, the stamps and encrusted seals bearing Forla's likeness a matter for fear not critical examination. Boots stamped in salute and a soldier tripped in his haste to open the gate. Then they were through. Past a length of track and between run-down buildings, where the few early workers kept their eyes to themselves as an official car went past. Gaudy advertising signs and a tangle of overhead wires were rushing past; glimpses of ordinary life which were as alien as a dream. The official and shopping sections of the city, together with Forla's palace, still lay some way ahead.

But not very far ahead. The sergeant was taking them across intersections at horrific speed and blaring his horn if anyone dared get in the way. Unless they turned aside soon, they would reach Forla's palace and streets where every building would be guarded, checkpoints only to be expected.

Quite soon, very soon, someone must summon sufficient courage to knock again at General Forla's door, at the base they had just left. How long after that before they also dared to look inside uninvited, once they received no answer?

Possibly only a few more minutes from now. With luck, perhaps as much as another hour. But long before then they must have vanished, in a city where everyone was too terrified not to be hostile, where most intersections boasted a truckful of troops. This conspicuous car was a monstrous liability now, which must be abandoned fast. Yet Stephen could not walk more than a few yards unaided, none of them pass a single gun-toting guard unquestioned once they left the cover of Forla's insignia and car.

19

THE first check to their headlong progress came when a tank clattered over a crossing just ahead. Even their sergeant, drunk as he was on his own daring, decided not to tangle with that and braked with a screech, swearing furiously.

'Turn right,' said Stephen, on his knees, one hand grasping the seat in front.

'Right?' The sergeant sounded surprised, as if he had actually expected to drive them all the way to Forla's pink front door, and swerved so sharply they nearly collided with the tank after all.

'Right again,' said Stephen at the next intersection and immediately they were back in the narrow streets, passers-by staring curiously now. Such a glittering vehicle as this might occasionally be seen elsewhere in the city, but never in their lives had these ragged, undernourished people seen a pale blue Jaguar roadster in their dirty alleys, the gold insignia of General Forla glinting malignantly as it passed.

Soon, they reached an area of run-down or shuttered small factories and workshops, the economic life of Mananga long since spilled in ruins; dumps, tin shanties, potholes which made even a Jaguar leap. No soldiers here, although those waiting squads in trucks were only minutes away.

'See if there's cover to pull up somewhere behind a wall,' said Stephen. He had Forla's revolver in his hand; he, Jean and Saul were on the back seat now, the soldier squeezed into their place on the floor, where he seemed to be praying.

A crowd of children stared up from where they played in the dust as the Jaguar passed. Not too many adults here, but someone would report whichever way they went: what they needed now was an inconspicuous vehicle and darkness, instead they had a pale blue Jaguar and the sun lifting higher in a cloudless sky.

Jean's own mind had become disconcertingly incapable of holding more than one thought at a time, and the moment strain eased by a fraction it filled with the memory of how, less than an hour before, she had killed a man. Not Forla, but Lewis Anderson, a man she had known and for whom she had wanted to find excuses. Even now, she was able to imagine that he had started setting up deals with Forla for the same reason Stephen stole food and trains: to get results. But then he caught the infection of violence and hate raging through Mananga; ultimately needed to fight to keep himself safe. Until, in the end, she happened to be the one who killed him. A tremble spread outward from her spine until the earth itself seemed to shake, an earth where the same sun rose as yesterday, the same scents drifted on the wind; only she was so different that she didn't belong there any more.

Stephen glanced at her. 'Don't think about it, only what comes next.'

'Is that what someone said to you, all those years ago after Vietnam?' she asked bitterly.

'Yes, and it's still what I have to try and do. So long as you're not alone the worst can eventually be forgotten, the best remembered.'

Jean swallowed and nodded; some things can never be forgotten, she thought but did not say. He knew, and had lived much longer with the knowledge.

He had already turned back to the sergeant. An exactly judged minimum of time spared for comfort; not even a hand free to touch her, while he held a gun and needed the other to brace himself against rough jolts over potholes.

They stopped soon afterwards, the clock on the Jaguar's dashboard showing twenty-two minutes since they passed the guard on the main base gates. By Jean's calculation, there couldn't possibly be many more left before someone summoned sufficient daring to enter Forla's presence.

'How long after that before the alarm goes out?' she said aloud.

'After they find Forla? I hope no one will get further than knocking on his door for maybe another half-hour. Then they'll be like rats in a pit until he makes sense, and you gave him one hell of a beating.' They had pulled in behind some corrugated shacks perhaps two hundred yards from the nearest inhabited dwelling. There would still be eyes watching and wondering from a distance but, briefly, there was no one close. Stephen had already half-fallen out of the car. 'Help me change into the clothes we brought.'

Of course the chaos when the Supreme Being was discovered tied up and concussed on the floor would be indescribable, but surely they would need to be more than just lucky to win much more time out of mere chaos? Meanwhile they were wasting it changing clothes, Saul crawling under the Jaguar to drain water out of the radiator in which to wash, their two guards shaking hands before vanishing into scrub which here encroached on the edges of the city, a handful of Lewis's dollars each and congratulations to the sergeant, who deserved to go far in anyone's Mananga. Rumour and counter-rumour must be blowing like a storm through the alleys they had used to reach here, and as soon as they pulled away again curious people would come to stare where they had been, to jabber among themselves and by doing so set pursuit back on their scent.

Stephen was swaying as she and Saul stripped off his bloodied clothes; giddily shaved in rusty water, insisted that she washed too and brushed her hair with the Jaguar's carpet brush. Jean stared at the dirty bandaging around his thigh, probably there was a bullet in him somewhere, but when she tried to protest he told her brusquely to pad and cover where the blood was seeping through and leave everything else alone. Her memory cringed afresh as she remembered how his torn flesh had felt under her stabbing fingers, the beginnings of abject apology confusing everything.

'Jesus,' he said roughly, 'don't start apologising for other men's dirt. You've done so much ... I can't believe how much you've done. Saul — '

'I am here,' Saul was using his shirt to wad that wound tighter, so that blood wouldn't seep through Lewis's trousers.

'You have ... somewhere to go?'

He nodded. 'My mother.'

'You could have reached her ... if you had gone when we were caught.' Stephen was beginning to have difficulty with his voice.

'I do not run,' he answered stiffly.

Stephen nodded. 'You waited to see if you could help us.'

He flipped a hand. 'It was not a good hope.'

'It was a very brave hope ... but please go now. Quickly. Man-anga needs its courageous sons.'

Saul bit his lips in embarrassment, shook hands and accepted some of Lewis's dollars, although he would have been insulted if Stephen had offered his own. He lagged away a few steps, then came back. 'I do not wish to leave you for Forla to find.'

Stephen straightened unsteadily and gave him a push. 'Forla isn't going to get us, okay?'

This time he went, looking over his shoulder all the way.

'Oh God, I hope he stays safe,' Jean said.

'I hope we make it, too.' He glanced at the clock on the Jaguar's dashboard. Surely, by now Forla must be found, troops be falling over themselves in panic before some order was restored. Stephen half fell into the car, leaned back, eyes closed; if he had not been speaking rationally a moment before she would have thought him unconscious. Without opening his eyes, he added thickly, 'You drive. Fast, for the airport. Keep to these slum lots, across scrub if you can. It's this side of town.'

Jean started the engine, feeling sick. 'For God's sake ... the airport?'

'You did pick your passport off the floor?'

She nodded, their tyres howling on hot surfaces as she cornered past some fighting dogs, jounced across ruts edged by shacks and derelict hardware.

'We have to risk the early morning flight we saw yesterday. Anderson had a return ticket. Money in his billfold to buy you one at the desk. We bribe whoever needs to be bribed to get on that plane before anyone thinks we might try anything so crazy.'

Jean glanced down at her dirty jeans and stained shirt. There was blood spattered there as well as dirt, and Stephen's hasty shave and change into Lewis's trousers and jacket, Forla's shirt, only emphasised the shocking contrast with his bruised, drained face. 'There are bound to be guards at the checkout, whether the alarm is out for us or not. We'll never get past looking how we do.'

'Then we have to clean up some more,' he answered grimly. 'There will be washrooms at the airport ... even if the drains don't work. People pestering passengers to buy local products, peasant skirts, things like that. You dress in those, they'll only think you screwy like other foreigners.'

'But —'

218

'We haven't any choice. You're a nurse, you know how quickly wounds get infected in a place like this. I shall have a fever by tonight, blood poisoning soon after. Neither of us can last much longer ... much less walk to a frontier across the hills. It has to be the airport.'

Jean could think of so many objections she didn't know where to begin, except of course he was right. When they broke out of the base she had known that even shot full of painkiller he couldn't last more than hours; both of them were exhausted beyond belief. All her experience agreed with his analysis, and if they didn't get out today then probably he would be too delirious to try tomorrow. By then, anyway, the airport would long since be closed against them.

Refuge in the US or British embassies was not worth thinking about, when both were situated in the middle of town where patrols must surely intercept them. Western diplomats might dislike dealing with dictators, but seldom stuck their necks out to oppose their methods. She was also guilty of murder and both of them of assaulting the Manangan head of state and associating with guerrillas; legal representation at a rigged trial was the best they could hope for if they should somehow reach inside the diplomatic compound.

The blue Jaguar had never felt more conspicuous as they left the city behind and scorched across open plain, jinking between spiky bushes for whatever cover they might offer, avoiding using a road until they were less than half a mile from the airport. But when they finally lurched up on to the grandiose four-lane highway which led from Mananga City to the air terminal, there was very little other traffic and Jean fancied she could hear sirens behind her in the distant streets.

The airport was certain to be guarded whatever the state of alert, her worst fears confirmed when an armoured gun-carrier swung across the road just as they reached its outer gate. But the soldiers were talking among themselves and only stared because a woman was driving such a splendid car. They came so close to stare that Jean was forced off the tarmac and into garbage lying beside the road, the soldiers drumming on armourplate in delight because a woman had been shoved in the ditch where she belonged. But at least any alert flashed into the streets of Mananga did not seem to have reached the airport yet. Those soldiers would not forget them, though.

'Anderson had some high-powered security clearances in his billfold,' Stephen was saying, and Jean wasn't sure he had even noticed that armoured carrier. 'They should help get us past the checkout ... I have to use his passport too.'

'You don't look in the least like him!' Using a false passport seemed a quite lunatic and unnecessary chance to take.

'Then I have to bluff. Even three months ago Mananga airport was full of bureaucratic bastards looking for trouble. Bags taken apart. Body searches at the slightest excuse. They see us ... really look ... we'd be stripped at once and I could never explain a bullet in the thigh. You must be badly bruised — ' Jean nodded. Her shoulder hurt fiercely, her whole body ached and a rib felt as if it might be cracked. 'They won't like that, and if you feel like me ... you couldn't face being stripped by Manangans anyhow.' She nodded again. Even the idea of more rough hands, more jeering humiliation made her want to vomit. 'So we have to stop them looking ... Anderson's papers are the only way we might.'

The airport carpark was half empty, Mananga was not on anyone's tourist route. Jean parked the Jaguar as unobtrusively as she could, between a shed and a fuel bowser, but dared not go too far from the terminal building, when Stephen must somehow walk to the entry. 'Wait here while I see if the early flight is on time,' she said.

He nodded. The effort of holding on to consciousness while he planned how to get them out might be nearly over, but the effort of standing, walking, bluffing, was still to come. Jean thought even he was beginning to wonder how he would ever manage it.

The terminal was unexpectedly seething with people, which was just as well. Jean was horribly conscious of her dirty and dishevelled state, which perfunctory washing and brushing during their hurried stop had only marginally improved. Looking around, she decided most of the crowd were touting pitiful scraps of goods or begging coins off the few departing passengers. Certainly there ought to be spare seats on any outgoing flight. Early-morning passengers already gathered morosely in line, most of them looking like Forla henchmen on their way to clinch some dubious deal, or foreign officials delighted to be leaving one of the world's least desirable postings. When she ventured to ask one of these about the flight, he stared astonished at her wild state, before saying it was late as usual but expected to start loading soon. Breathing a very preliminary sigh of relief, Jean began pushing through a throng which clutched at her arms, thrust cloth, carvings, heaven knew what, in her face, almost openly tried to pick her pockets. She didn't even try to bargain for an embroidered shirt and skirt, the crowd becoming almost mad with excitement when she handed over the first price she was asked.

She bolted for the washroom the instant she had bought them, and paid the attendant to keep the mob outside while she changed. There wasn't a mirror, which was probably just as well for her self-confidence, and none of the taps worked. Drowned beetles floated in the bucket of cold water the attendant brought her in exchange for five more of Lewis's dollars, so after she had washed she felt almost dirtier than before.

Outside, some of the crowd was waiting for her, a kind of camouflage perhaps but plucking and whining like a swarm of hornets. When she reached the airline desk at last the clerk tried to tell her there weren't any tickets left, but with Lewis's and Stephen's wad of dollars firmly held out of sight, that at least was one hurdle she did not intend to fall over. 'How much would it cost if there was a ticket?'

The clerk's eyes flickered. 'Where to?'

'Comato.' Apparently this flight went nowhere else, but Comato would do. How wonderfully it would do. A modern city with a hospital, hotels, and spectacularly bad relations with Mananga.

'Eight hundred dollars US. It is a luxury flight, you understand.'

Jean was certain it would be nothing of the sort, but had expected extortion. Money simply didn't matter any more, and Lewis had provided himself with enough cash to do business in a nation virtually stripped of any banking system. When, after only token argument, she produced the full eight hundred, the crowd around her gasped. 'I've got a hot date in Comato tonight.'

The clerk smiled, an uncomplicated grin of delight at his undreamed-of luck. 'If you want a reservation for today's flight, that will be another hundred dollars.'

This time she haggled, swallowing her impatience, fearful that otherwise he might decide to tip off a superior to take a share in such largesse. She also made a great play that this was her last hundred, since otherwise she would certainly be robbed, the police perhaps be called, during her fight back through the crowded terminal. Tears were easy to find when she felt so overwrought, and the clerk eventually compromised on eighty dollars in exchange for two boarding passes instead of one, grandly explaining that he did not wish to leave her penniless.

When she went to look there seemed an alarming number of guards on the checkout barrier, indiscriminately pointing guns and staring at the crowd from under arrogant steel helmets. More soldiers were drinking on the terrace, although there didn't seem any particular sign of panic security, and more again standing on the tarmac, where the crew of an Airavia Boeing was keeping its engines running as if they expected Manangan engineers to demand a bribe for starting them up again. Jean stared avidly at that Boeing's jaunty international colours before hurrying back to Stephen, a mob of pestering children still on her heels, although the adults seemed to have gone after more promising prey.

They withdrew slightly when they realised she wasn't alone after all, and further when Stephen swore at them. Even children could sense that this wasn't a moment to take chances with Stephen Retz.

'Don't you think you really ought to use your own passport?' Jean asked anxiously. The idea of using Lewis's had become even less attractive now she had seen all those guards on the checkout. Lewis David Anderson, six foot two, age twenty-eight, looked out of those pages. Even an illiterate could see that picture wasn't Stephen Retz, who must be ten years older and today looked sick enough to die.

'No,' he said, and fumbled upright, holding on to the car door. 'Getting past those guards won't be easy however we play it, and without some pull could take all day. We have to be on this flight, not held at gunpoint while they decide maybe to let us go tomorrow.'

Jean couldn't argue with that, but hated above all to leave Forla's revolver hidden in the Jaguar when they locked and left it. Not because they could shoot their way out of trouble, but for the ultimate escape it represented.

Now they could be taken alive again.

She had to help Stephen hobble to the terminal, climb sweating and one at a time up the steps. A mob of beggars might be a pest, but how much better to be surrounded by their importunity than try to pass, alone, the guards inside the door at the top of those steps while he was scarcely able to walk. As if by accident, Jean dropped some loose change down the steps and instantly was nearly knocked off her feet by the scramble; she needed to grab tight on to Stephen to prevent him from falling. The two of them shuffled past the menacing guards while almost submerged by an importunate rabble; it was so difficult to walk at all that a limp like a spavined horse went unnoticed in the crush.

Next he had to go to the washroom where she could not help him, the minutes ticking past while she stood outside imagining he must have lost consciousness or been caught swabbing blood. By then, the passengers for Airavia's morning flight out of Mananga had been shoved into an ill-natured queue in front of a kiosk bulging with officials. When he emerged at last, his appearance was smarter but everything else far worse; more fragile strength burned up, the effect of her injection also beginning to wear off. By then the check-in queue was beginning sluggishly to move towards that kiosk, where clerks wore red collar patches and gold leaves as if each was a field marshal, macho boots and patent-leather belts. Jean stood trying to shield Stephen from chance jostling and wondered how they could possibly pass such leisurely and malignant scrutiny. She again tried to calculate how long must have passed since Forla had been discovered, but could not concentrate long enough to guess an answer.

The streets of Mananga City had to be heaving with troops by now, the order to search all vehicles, block all roads have been given. There wasn't a telephone on the checkout kiosk, but a couple of tanks were parked on the runway apron. They ought to be in radio contact with their headquarters, the very same barracks perhaps from which they had escaped. God, how she loathed a country crawling with insolent troops.

Someone bumped into her so hard that she staggered and had to clutch an elderly diplomat to prevent herself from cannoning into Stephen. 'I'm sorry, I'm sorry,' she said distractedly, panic congealing in her lungs.

'N'importe, madame,' he answered, staring.

A woman selling plaited straw belts thrust past, shouting, and this time Jean heard Stephen grunt from the impact. He was as near finished as a man could be and still stay conscious, and there were still six people between them and that barrier.

The Manangan officials were taking several minutes to clear each passenger, leisurely scrutinising documents, demanding that pockets should be turned out, occasionally hauling someone off for a body search amid shouts of execration. Jean stared at them and at the guards fingering their weapons just behind and hated every one of them just for existing.

After a few more crawling minutes Stephen stirred, disengaged from her grip, and tucked her hand under his arm. 'My brother at the State Department told me a story before I came out here. A missionary, oh, a hundred years ago, was rebuked for not even attempting to treat the Manangan population as if their beliefs might matter, and he replied: "Sir, I did not come here to serve their beliefs, but mine." '

Jean licked her lips, wondering whether he was delirious already. Only the French diplomat stood between them and that guarded barrier now. 'The missionaries came out here wanting to do good, I suppose. Like us,' she added angrily, as recollection of Lewis's bloodstained body again swung sickly on the edge of memory.

'Sure, and it was an honest answer. Usually we prefer to kid ourselves about why we're hated in places like this.' He released her arm and smiled. 'My dear, try not to look too worried and I guess we'll be okay.'

Jean found herself facing a clerk with a wide mean mouth, narrow moustache, and pinched cheeks, another scowling by his side as if he had already succeeded in putting her behind bars. One of the armed soldiers said something, clearly about her, and all three snickered, enjoying watching her squirm. But as that first clerk slapped contemptuously at her passport she consciously forced herself to forget the courage of Mezak, the self-sacrifice of Saul, and try instead to imagine that it was past exploitations which had made Manangan officials and rulers what they were. Stephen had told her that story because he did not want her to face them while so filled with hate and fear that instinct alone must tell them that something was wrong.

'Your passport was not stamped by the Hamada police.' The clerk pointed to her visa. 'When you enter our country you must always check in with the police.'

'They came on board the ship when I arrived. Look, you can see their stamp. Afterwards we were kept behind wire on the quay.' Jean forced lips which felt like cardboard into a ghastly smile.

He gave her a long unfriendly stare. 'You reached here. You could have checked in somewhere on the journey.'

'I'm sorry,' she said, and felt her guts begin to shake. 'The police on the ship said to stay behind wire until the railway ran again. When it did, General Forla forbade foreigners to work in the hill country. So I thought I'd better leave Mananga while everything settled down.' The seconds stretched out and her nerves with them, until she didn't know how to stop those men from seeing how badly she was shaking, or hearing the falseness in her voice. Both the guards were watching her with open lust, undressing her with their eyes, the clerk about to snap her passport shut, unstamped, and yell that she couldn't pass without some different police stamp she hadn't a hope of getting.

Behind her, Stephen said something impatient and the clerk jerked round indignantly, prepared to blast insolence.

'Your great ruler, Supreme General Forla, has sent me on an urgent mission and I am worried the aircraft will leave if this woman takes up too much time.' Stephen took out Anderson's papers, to which was clipped a letter of personal welcome from Forla and a special police pass stamped all over in crimson and yellow, the national colours of Mananga. Absently, he put the pass back in his pocket while making sure the clerks and soldiers saw it first, smoothed out the letter to show Forla's scrawled signature and a personal seal the size of a teacup. That pass had included a large clear photograph of Lewis Anderson which the most over-awed clerk could not miss, but they had seen the colours and police stamps, and were staring reverently at the All Highest's signature on the letter. Even the guards stood straighter.

'Sir — ' stammered the clerk. 'You should not have waited with the rest.'

Stephen waved his hand. 'I am here now. But get this woman through and out of the way, I don't want to waste more time.'

They fairly flung Jean's stamped passport at her and turned back to Stephen. Lewis's linen suit was far too long in the leg for him, but only the jacket showed above the kiosk edge and it looked well cut and respectable; the shirt was Forla's own because Lewis's had been bloodstained. It was Stephen's face which should have made any security man start asking questions. Ashen. Bruised and puffy where Lewis had hit him, almost fleshless in cruelly bright morning light. From where she watched, agonised, on the other side of the barrier, Jean thought he looked as if he must collapse at any moment.

But they were close, so unbelievably close to getting out, and while breath and hope remained, Stephen was the kind of man who would somehow flog his body into responding to his will.

'Perhaps you could stamp this for me, as well as my passport,' he added, indicating Forla's letter. 'As a receipt for my passage, you understand. I am on a mission for your government and I expect afterwards to claim the cost of my ticket.'

'I cannot possibly deface our Supreme Ruler's signature!' exclaimed the clerk, aghast.

'Why not? All I want is evidence of my flight today, so that later I may be repaid the cost. Or would you prefer to stamp my ticket stub?'

The clerks agreed fervently that they would very much prefer it, caught between Stephen's confident manner and fear of defacing their leader's own letter with a stamp which could be traced back personally to them. 'A ticket stub, certainly, Mr Anderson. That is Airavia's property and not our concern at all.' It was stamped with a flourish. 'I am sorry to see you have injured your face in our country, sir.'

'I'm much obliged to you.' Stephen folded papers and ticket away and brought out Lewis's passport. No possible way of avoiding a photograph there. 'Life is a good deal tougher at the moment on other faces than mine among some bandits we were fighting in the Kosti Hills. I am happy to say the last of them should now be giving Mananga's vultures indigestion.'

Everyone laughed, as if at the best joke of the year.

But Jean was watching that clerk's hand. His fingers flipping through the passport pages, flattening the binding ready for inspection while he still talked to Stephen. He must not look down. Dear God, let him not look down for more than seconds of perfunctory routine. His face was losing its bureaucratic surliness as he eagerly agreed with Stephen about the bloody fate awaiting ignorant savages who dared oppose the mighty Forla. Between his hands, Lewis Anderson's photograph was plain for anyone to see, fair hair, ingenuous college smile fairly leaping to meet the eye.

The second clerk said something and they all, including Stephen and the guards, joined in an excited discussion about the achievements of Mananga under Forla which made rebellion particularly reprehensible, that passport still open between them on the desk. Jean tore her eyes away in case the million volts of tension held inside her should flash across the space between her and those clerks and focused instead on the restless queue, not one of whom ventured to complain about such unnecessary delay. Stephen drew attention to it in the end. 'I shall not dare fly back into Mananga tomorrow now, when some of these people will still be waiting if I take up much more of your time!' He nodded to the guards. 'I shall see you again if you are on duty.'

The two soldiers saluted and the clerk stamped Anderson's passport, both of them standing to hand it back. 'A good flight and a safe return to all friends of our great republic.'

They were through.

Jean stumbled on the steep steps leading up to the aircraft, turned in panic in case Stephen fell, but he was just behind her. 'It's too late to have second thoughts about leaving,' he said, smiling, and they entered the Boeing together. They sat and strapped themselves in while grit blown up by the idling engines whipped through the open door, bearing the stenches of Mananga with it.

Please shut that door, Jean thought. For the love of God, roll those steps back and shut it.

Her fingers were gripping Stephen's hand hard enough to hurt, his eyes shut and head back against the rest. More minutes crawled past, as passengers still straggled in ones and twos across the tarmac. The sound she dreaded most of all cut without warning through the roar of their aircraft's jets, the squeal of tracks as one of the tanks by the terminal building suddenly swivelled, its turret swinging too. At this very last of last seconds they were going to be stopped, kicked out on the tarmac and marched away.

The door closed with a thump as if the pilot, too, had seen that tank move and sensed a last-minute hitch after far too long spent waiting around already, wasting fuel by keeping his engines running. Quite probably Airavia had had aircraft impounded in Mananga before, and been forced to pay to get them released. Even the stewardess didn't bother about her patter, merely looked delighted they were on their way.

The Boeing was taxiing fast and dangerously, because both those tanks were quite definitely moving now.

Neither Jean nor Stephen spoke as they felt the aircraft's wheels leave the ground. The rest of their lives remained for all that needed to be said, for love and for remorseless memory. Now it was enough to watch the horizon slant as they banked above the

Manangan plain, to pick out the thread of a single track railway as they climbed to clear the Kosti Hills.

One day perhaps they would be back, and discover more of the good things about Mananga.